P9-ARX-010

Drawn by Walter Russell.

"*On his withers banged and bumped the kettledrums draped in crape, and on his back, very stiff and soldierly, sat a bareheaded skeleton.*"

The Rout of the White Hussars—Vol. ii., p. 390.

SELECTED WORKS

OF

RUDYARD KIPLING

THE LIGHT THAT FAILED

PLAIN TALES FROM THE HILLS

Volume Two

NEW YORK
PETER FENELON COLLIER, PUBLISHER

CONTENTS

VOLUME TWO

PLAIN TALES FROM THE HILLS

DEDICATION

IF I were hanged on the highest hill,
Mother o' mine, O mother o' mine!
I know whose love would follow me still,
Mother o' mine, O mother o' mine!

If I were drowned in the deepest sea,
Mother o' mine, O mother o' mine!
I know whose tears would come down to me,
Mother o' mine, O mother o' mine!

If I were damned of body and soul,
I know whose prayers would make me whole,
Mother o' mine, O mother o' mine!

PREFACE

THIS is the story of "The Light that Failed" as it was originally conceived by the Writer.

RUDYARD KIPLING

THE LIGHT THAT FAILED

CHAPTER ONE

So we settled it all when the storm was done
  As comf'y as comf'y could be;
And I was to wait in the barn, my dears,
  Because I was only three,
And Teddy would run to the rainbow's foot,
  Because he was five and a man;
And that's how it all began, my dears,
  And that's how it all began.—*Big Barn Stories*

"WHAT do you think she'd do if she caught us? We oughtn't to have it, you know," said Maisie.

"Beat me, and lock you up in your bedroom," Dick answered, without hesitation. "Have you got the cartridges?"

"Yes; they're in my pocket, but they are joggling horribly. Do pin-fire cartridges go off of their own accord?"

"Don't know. Take the revolver, if you are afraid, and let me carry them."

"I'm *not* afraid." Maisie strode forward swiftly, a hand in her pocket and her chin in the air. Dick followed with a small pin-fire revolver.

The children had discovered that their lives would be unendurable without pistol-practice. After much forethought and self-denial, Dick had saved seven shillings and sixpence, the price of a badly constructed Belgian revolver. Maisie could only contribute half a crown to the syndicate for the purchase of a hundred cartridges. "You can save better than I can, Dick," she explained; "I like nice things to eat, and it doesn't matter to you. Besides, boys ought to do these things."

Dick grumbled a little at the arrangement, but went out and made the purchases, which the children were then on their way to test. Revolvers did not lie in the scheme of their daily life as decreed for them by the guardian who was incorrectly supposed to stand in the place of a mother to these two orphans. Dick had been under her care for six years, during which time she had made her profit of the allowances supposed to be expended on his clothes, and, partly through thoughtlessness, partly through a natural desire to pain—she was a widow of some years anxious to marry again—had made his days burdensome on his young shoulders. Where he had looked for love, she gave him first aversion and then hate. Where he growing older had sought a little sympathy, she gave him ridicule. The many hours that she could spare from the ordering of her small house she devoted to what she called the home-training of Dick Heldar. Her religion, manufactured in the main by her own intelligence and a keen study of the Scriptures, was an aid to her in this matter. At such times as she herself was not personally displeased with Dick, she left him to understand that he had a heavy account to settle with his Creator; wherefore Dick learned to loathe his God as intensely as he loathed Mrs. Jennett; and this is not a wholesome frame of mind for the young. Since she chose to regard him as a hopeless liar, when dread of pain drove him to his first untruth he naturally developed into a liar, but an economical and self-contained one, never throwing away the least unnecessary fib, and never hesitating at the blackest, were it only plausible, that might make his life a little easier. The treatment taught him at least the power of living alone—a power that was of service to him when he went to a public school and the boys laughed at his clothes, which were poor in quality and much mended. In the holidays he returned to the teachings of Mrs. Jennett, and, that the chain of discipline might not be weakened by association with the world, was generally beaten, on one count or another, before he had been twelve hours under her roof.

The autumn of one year brought him a companion in bondage, a long-haired, gray-eyed little atom, as self-contained as himself, who moved about the house silently, and for the first few weeks spoke only to the goat that was her chiefest friend on earth and lived in the back-garden. Mrs. Jennett objected to the goat on the grounds that he was un-Christian — which he certainly was. "Then," said the atom, choosing her words very deliberately, "I shall write to my lawyer-peoples and tell them that you are a very bad woman. Amomma is mine, mine, mine!" Mrs. Jennett made a movement to the hall, where certain umbrellas and canes stood in a rack. The atom understood as clearly as Dick what this meant. "I have been beaten before," she said, still in the same passionless voice; "I have been beaten worse than you can ever beat me. If you beat me I shall write to my lawyer-peoples and tell them that you do not give me enough to eat. I am not afraid of you." Mrs. Jennett did not go into the hall, and the atom, after a pause to assure herself that all danger of war was past, went out, to weep bitterly on Amomma's neck.

Dick learned to know her as Maisie, and at first mistrusted her profoundly, for he feared that she might interfere with the small liberty of action left to him. She did not, however; and she volunteered no friendliness until Dick had taken the first steps. Long before the holidays were over, the stress of punishment shared in common drove the children together, if it were only to play into each other's hands as they prepared lies for Mrs. Jennett's use. When Dick returned to school, Maisie whispered, "Now I shall be all alone to take care of myself; but," and she nodded her head bravely, "I can do it. You promised to send Amomma a grass collar. Send it soon." A week later she asked for that collar by return of post, and was not pleased when she learned that it took time to make. When at last Dick forwarded the gift she forgot to thank him for it.

Many holidays had come and gone since that day, and Dick had grown into a lanky hobbledehoy more than ever conscious of his bad clothes. Not for a moment had Mrs. Jennett relaxed her tender care of him, but the average canings of a public school — Dick fell under punishment about three times a month—filled him with contempt for her powers. "She doesn't hurt," he explained to Maisie, who urged him to rebellion, "and she is kinder to you after she has whacked me." Dick shambled through the days unkempt in body and savage in soul, as the smaller boys of the school learned to know, for when the spirit moved him he would hit them, cunningly and with science. The same spirit made him more than once try to tease Maisie, but the girl refused to be made unhappy. "We are both miserable as it is," said she. "What is the use of trying to make things worse? Let's find things to do, and forget things."

The pistol was the outcome of that search. It could only be used on the muddiest foreshore of the beach, far away from bathing-machines and pierheads, below the grassy slopes of Fort Keeling. The tide ran out nearly two miles on that coast and the many-colored mud-banks, touched by the sun, sent up a lamentable smell of dead weed. It was late in the afternoon when Dick and Maisie arrived on their ground, Amomma trotting patiently behind them.

"Mf!" said Maisie, sniffing the air. "I wonder what makes the sea so smelly. I don't like it."

"You never like anything that isn't made just for you," said Dick bluntly. "Give me the cartridges, and I'll try first shot. How far does one of these little revolvers carry?"

"Oh, half a mile," said Maisie promptly. "At least it makes an awful noise. Be careful with the cartridges; I don't like those jagged stick-up things on the rim. Dick, do be careful."

"All right. I know how to load. I'll fire at the breakwater out there."

He fired, and Amomma ran away bleating. The bullet threw up a spurt of mud to the right of the weed-wreathed piles.

"Throws high and to the right. You try, Maisie. Mind, it's loaded all round."

Maisie took the pistol and stepped delicately to the verge of the mud, her hand firmly closed on the butt, her mouth and left eye screwed up. Dick sat down on a tuft of bank and laughed. Amomma returned very cautiously. He was accustomed to strange experiences in his afternoon walks, and, finding the cartridge-box unguarded, made investigations with his nose. Maisie fired, but could not see where the bullet went.

"I think it hit the post," she said, shading her eyes and looking out across the sailless sea.

"I know it has gone out to the Marazion Bell Buoy," said Dick, with a chuckle. "Fire low and to the left; then perhaps you'll get it. Oh, look at Amomma!—he's eating the cartridges!"

Maisie turned, the revolver in her hand, just in time to see Amomma scampering away from the pebbles Dick threw after him. Nothing is sacred to a billy goat. Being well fed and the adored of his mistress, Amomma had naturally swallowed two loaded pin-fire cartridges. Maisie hurried up to assure herself that Dick had not miscounted the tale.

"Yes, he's eaten two."

"Horrid little beast! Then they'll joggle about inside him and blow up, and serve him right . . . . Oh, Dick! have I killed you?"

Revolvers are tricky things for young hands to deal with. Maisie could not explain how it had happened, but a veil of reeking smoke separated her from Dick, and she was quite certain that the pistol had gone off in his face. Then she heard him sputter, and dropped on her knees beside him, crying, "Dick, you aren't hurt, are you? I didn't mean it."

"Of course you didn't," said Dick, coming out of the smoke and wiping his cheek. "But you nearly blinded me.

That powder stuff stings awfully." A neat little splash of gray lead on a stone showed where the bullet had gone. Maisie began to whimper.

"Don't," said Dick, jumping to his feet and shaking himself. "I'm not a bit hurt."

"No, but I might have killed you," protested Maisie, the corners of her mouth drooping. "What should I have done then?"

"Gone home and told Mrs. Jennett." Dick grinned at the thought; then, softening, "Please don't worry about it. Besides, we are wasting time. We've got to get back to tea. I'll take the revolver for a bit."

Maisie would have wept on the least encouragement, but Dick's indifference, albeit his hand was shaking as he picked up the pistol, restrained her. She lay panting on the beach while Dick methodically bombarded the breakwater. "Got it at last!" he exclaimed, as a lock of weed flew from the wood.

"Let me try," said Maisie imperiously. "I'm all right now."

They fired in turns till the rickety little revolver nearly shook itself to pieces, and Amomma the outcast—because he might blow up at any moment—browsed in the background and wondered why stones were thrown at him. Then they found a balk of timber floating in a pool which was commanded by the seaward slope of Fort Keeling, and they sat down together before this new target.

"Next holidays," said Dick, as the now thoroughly fouled revolver kicked wildly in his hand, "we'll get another pistol —central fire—that will carry further."

"There won't be any next holidays for me," said Maisie. "I'm going away."

"Where to?"

"I don't know. My lawyers have written to Mrs. Jennett, and I've got to be educated somewhere—in France, perhaps—I don't know where; but I shall be glad to go away."

"I shan't like it a bit. I suppose I shall be left. Look

here, Maisie, is it really true you're going? Then these holidays will be the last I shall see anything of you; and I go back to school next week. I wish—"

The young blood turned his cheeks scarlet. Maisie was picking grass-tufts and throwing them down the slope at a yellow sea-poppy nodding all by itself to the illimitable levels of the mud-flats and the milk-white sea beyond.

"I wish," she said, after a pause, "that I could see you again some time. You wish that too?"

"Yes, but it would have been better if—if—you had—shot straight over there—down by the breakwater."

Maisie looked with large eyes for a moment. And this was the boy who only ten days before had decorated Amomma's horns with cut-paper ham-frills and turned him out, a bearded derision, among the public ways! Then she dropped her eyes: this was not the boy.

"Don't be stupid," she said reprovingly, and with swift instinct attacked the side-issue. "How selfish you are! Just think what I should have felt if that horrid thing had killed you! I'm quite miserable enough already."

"Why? Because you're going away from Mrs. Jennett?"

"No."

"From me, then?"

No answer for a long time. Dick dared not look at her. He felt, though he did not know, all that the past four years had been to him, and this the more acutely since he had no knowledge to put his feelings in words.

"I don't know," she said. "I suppose it is."

"Maisie, you must know. *I'm* not supposing."

"Let's go home," said Maisie weakly.

But Dick was not minded to retreat.

"I can't say things," he pleaded, "and I'm awfully sorry for teasing you about Amomma the other day. It's all different now, Maisie, can't you see? And you might have told me that you were going, instead of leaving me to find out."

"You didn't. I did tell. Oh, Dick, what's the use of worrying?"

"There isn't any; but we've been together years and years, and I didn't know how much I cared."

"I don't believe you ever did care."

"No, I didn't; but I do—I care awfully now. Maisie," he gulped—"Maisie, darling, say you care too, please."

"I do; indeed I do; but it won't be any use."

"Why?"

"Because I am going away."

"Yes, but if you promise before you go. Only say—will you?" A second "darling" came to his lips more easily than the first. There were few endearments in Dick's home or school life; he had to find them by instinct. Dick caught the little hand blackened with the escaped gas of the revolver.

"I promise," she said solemnly; "but if I care there is no need for promising."

"And you do care?" For the first time in the past few minutes their eyes met and spoke for them who had no skill in speech. . . .

"Oh, Dick, don't! please don't! It was all right when we said good-morning; but now it's all different!" Amomma looked on from afar. He had seen his property quarrel frequently, but he had never seen kisses exchanged before. The yellow sea-poppy was wiser, and nodded its head approvingly. Considered as a kiss, that was a failure, but since it was the first, other than those demanded by duty, in all the world that either had ever given or taken, it opened to them new worlds, and every one of them glorious, so that they were lifted above the consideration of any worlds at all, especially those in which tea is necessary, and sat still, holding each other's hands and saying not a word.

"You can't forget now," said Dick at last. There was that on his cheek that stung more than gunpowder.

"I shouldn't have forgotten anyhow," said Maisie, and they looked at each other and saw that each was changed from the companion of an hour ago to a wonder and a mystery they could not understand. The sun began to set, and a night-wind thrashed along the bents of the foreshore.

"We shall be awfully late for tea," said Maisie. "Let's go home."

"Let's use the rest of the cartridges first," said Dick; and he helped Maisie down the slope of the fort to the sea—a descent that she was quite capable of covering at full speed. Equally gravely Maisie took the grimy hand. Dick bent forward clumsily; Maisie drew the hand away, and Dick blushed.

"It's very pretty," he said.

"Pooh!" said Maisie, with a little laugh of gratified vanity. She stood close to Dick as he loaded the revolver for the last time and fired over the sea with a vague notion at the back of his head that he was protecting Maisie from all the evils in the world. A puddle far across the mud caught the last rays of the sun and turned into a wrathful red disk. The light held Dick's attention for a moment, and as he raised his revolver there fell upon him a renewed sense of the miraculous, in that he was standing by Maisie who had promised to care for him for an indefinite length of time till such date as— A gust of the growing wind drove the girl's long black hair across his face as she stood with her hand on his shoulder calling Amomma "a little beast," and for a moment he was in the dark—a darkness that stung. The bullet went singing out to the empty sea.

"Spoiled my aim," said he, shaking his head. "There aren't any more cartridges; we shall have to run home." But they did not run. They walked very slowly, arm in arm. And it was a matter of indifference to them whether the neglected Amomma with two pin-fire cartridges in his inside blew up or trotted beside them; for they had come into a golden heritage and were disposing of it with all the wisdom of all their years.

"And I shall be—" quoth Dick valiantly. Then he checked himself: "I don't know what I shall be. I don't seem to be able to pass any exams., but I can make awful caricatures of the masters. Ho! ho!"

"Be an artist, then," said Maisie. "You're always laughing at my trying to draw; and it will do you good."

"I'll never laugh at anything you do," he answered. "I'll be an artist, and I'll do things."

"Artists always want money, don't they?"

"I've got a hundred and twenty pounds a year of my own. My guardians tell me I'm to have it when I come of age. That will be enough to begin with."

"Ah, I'm rich," said Maisie. "I've got three hundred a year all my own when I'm twenty-one. That's why Mrs. Jennett is kinder to me than she is to you. I wish, though, that I had somebody that belonged to me—just a father or a mother."

"You belong to me," said Dick, "for ever and ever."

"Yes, we belong—forever. It's very nice." She squeezed his arm. The kindly darkness hid them both, and, emboldened because he could only just see the profile of Maisie's cheek with the long lashes veiling the gray eyes, Dick at the front door delivered himself of the words he had been boggling over for the last two hours.

"And I—love you, Maisie," he said, in a whisper that seemed to him to ring across the world—the world that he would to-morrow or the next day set out to conquer.

There was a scene, not, for the sake of discipline, to be reported, when Mrs. Jennett would have fallen upon him, first for disgraceful unpunctuality, and secondly for nearly killing himself with a forbidden weapon.

"I was playing with it, and it went off by itself," said Dick, when the powder pocked cheek could no longer be hidden, "but if you think you're going to lick me you're wrong. You are never going to touch me again. Sit down and give me my tea. You can't cheat us out of that, anyhow."

Mrs. Jennett gasped and became livid. Maisie said nothing, but encouraged Dick with her eyes, and he behaved abominably all that evening. Mrs. Jennett prophesied an immediate judgment of Providence and a descent into Tophet later, but Dick walked in Paradise and would not hear. Only when he was going to bed Mrs. Jennett recovered and asserted herself. He had bidden Maisie good-night with down-dropped eyes and from a distance.

"If you aren't a gentleman you might try to behave like one," said Mrs. Jennett spitefully. "You've been quarreling with Maisie again."

This meant that the usual good-night kiss had been omitted. Maisie, white to the lips, thrust her cheek forward with a fine air of indifference, and was duly pecked by Dick, who tramped out of the room red as fire. That night he dreamed a wild dream. He had won all the world and brought it to Maisie in a cartridge-box, but she turned it over with her foot, and, instead of saying, "Thank you," cried—

"Where is the grass collar you promised for Amomma? Oh, how selfish you are!"

CHAPTER TWO

Then we brought the lances down, then the bugles blew,
When we went to Kandahar, ridin' two an' two,
Ridin', ridin', ridin', two an' two,
Ta-ra-ra-ra-ra-ra-ra,
All the way to Kandahar, ridin' two an' two.
—*Barrack-Room Ballad*

"I'm not angry with the British public, but I wish we had a few thousand of them scattered among these rocks. They wouldn't be in such a hurry to get at their morning papers then. Can't you imagine the regulation householder —Lover of Justice, Constant Reader, Paterfamilias, and all that lot—frizzling on hot gravel?"

"With a blue veil over his head, and his clothes in strips. Has any man here a needle? I've got a piece of sugar sack."

"I'll lend you a packing-needle for six square inches of it then. Both my knees are worn through."

"Why not six square acres, while you're about it? But lend me the needle, and I'll see what I can do with the selvage. I don't think there's enough to protect my royal body from the cold blast as it is. What are you doing with that everlasting sketch-book of yours, Dick?"

"Study of our Special Correspondent repairing his wardrobe," said Dick gravely, as the other man kicked off a pair of sorely-worn riding-breeches and began to fit a square of coarse canvas over the most obvious open space. He grunted disconsolately as the vastness of the void developed itself.

"Sugar-bags, indeed! Hi! you pilot-man there! lend me all the sails of that whale-boat."

A fez-crowned head bobbed up in the sternsheets, divided itself into exact halves with one flashing grin, and bobbed down again. The man of the tattered breeches, clad only in a Norfolk jacket and a gray flannel shirt, went on with his clumsy sewing, while Dick chuckled over the sketch.

Some twenty whale-boats were nuzzling a sand-bank which was dotted with English soldiery of half a dozen corps, bathing or washing their clothes. A heap of boat rollers, commissariat-boxes, sugar-bags, and flour- and small-arm-ammunition-cases showed where one of the whale-boats had been compelled to unload hastily; and a regimental carpenter was swearing aloud as he tried, on a wholly insufficient allowance of white lead, to plaster up the sun-parched gaping seams of the boat herself.

"First the bloomin' rudder snaps," said he to the world in general; "then the mast goes; an' then, s' 'elp me, when she can't do nothin' else, she opens 'erself out like a cock-eyed Chinese lotus."

"Exactly the case with my breeches, whoever you are," said the tailor, without looking up. "Dick, I wonder when I shall see a decent shop again."

There was no answer, save the incessant angry murmur of the Nile as it raced round a basalt-walled bend and foamed across a rock-ridge half a mile up-stream. It was as though the brown weight of the river would drive the white men back to their own country. The indescribable scent of Nile mud in the air told that the stream was falling and that the next few miles would be no light thing for the whale-boats to overpass. The desert ran down almost to the banks, where, among gray, red, and black hillocks, a camel-corps was encamped. No man dared even for a day lose touch of the slow-moving boats; there had been no fighting for weeks past, and throughout all that time the Nile had never spared them. Rapid had followed rapid, rock rock, and island-group island-group, till the rank and file had long since lost all count of direction and very nearly of time. They were moving somewhere, they did not know why, to do something, they did not know what. Before them lay the Nile, and at the other end of it was one Gordon, fighting for the dear life, in a town called Khartoum. There were columns of British troops in the desert, or in one of the many deserts; there were columns on the river; there were yet more columns waiting to embark on the river; there were fresh drafts waiting at Assioot and Assuan; there were lies and rumors running over the face of the hopeless land from Suakin to the Sixth Cataract, and men supposed generally that there must be some one in authority to direct the general scheme of the many movements. The duty of that particular river-column was to keep the whale-boats afloat in the water, to avoid trampling on the villagers' crops when the gangs "tracked" the boats with lines thrown from midstream, to get as much sleep and food as was possible, and, above all, to press on without delay in the teeth of the churning Nile.

With the soldiers sweated and toiled the correspondents of the newspapers, and they were almost as ignorant as their companions. But it was above all things necessary that England at breakfast should be amused and thrilled and interested, whether Gordon lived or died, or half the British army went to pieces in the sands. The Soudan campaign was a picturesque one, and lent itself to vivid word-painting. Now and again a "Special" managed to get slain—which was not altogether a disadvantage to the paper that employed him—and more often the hand-to-hand nature of the fighting allowed of miraculous escapes which were worth telegraphing home at eighteenpence the word. There were many correspondents with many corps and columns—from the veterans who had followed on the heels of the cavalry that occupied Cairo in '82, what time Arabi Pasha called himself king, who had seen the first miserable work round Suakin when the sentries were cut up nightly and the scrub swarmed with spears, to youngsters jerked into the business at the end of a telegraph-wire to take the place of their betters killed or invalided.

Among the seniors—those who knew every shift and change in the perplexing postal arrangements, the value of the seediest, weediest Egyptian garron offered for sale in Cairo or Alexandria, who could talk a telegraph clerk into amiability and soothe the ruffled vanity of a newly appointed staff-officer when press regulations became burdensome—was the man in the flannel shirt, the black-browed Torpenhow. He represented the Central Southern Syndicate in the campaign, as he had represented it in the Egyptian war, and elsewhere. The syndicate did not concern itself greatly with criticisms of attack and the like. It supplied the masses, and all it demanded was picturesqueness and abundance of detail; for there is more joy in England over a soldier who insubordinately steps out of square to rescue a comrade than over twenty generals slaving even to baldness at the gross details of transport and commissariat.

He had met at Suakin a young man, sitting on the edge of a recently abandoned redoubt about the size of a hatbox, sketching a clump of shell-torn bodies on the gravel plain.

"What are you for?" said Torpenhow. The greeting of the correspondent is that of the commercial traveler on the road.

"My own hand," said the young man, without looking up. "Have you any tobacco?"

Torpenhow waited till the sketch was finished, and when he had looked at it said, "What's your business here?"

"Nothing; there was a row, so I came. I'm supposed to be doing something down at the painting-slips among the boats, or else I'm in charge of the condenser on one of the water-ships. I've forgotten which."

"You've cheek enough to build a redoubt with," said Torpenhow, and took stock of the new acquaintance. "Do you always draw like that?"

The young man produced more sketches. "Row on a Chinese pig-boat," said he sententiously, showing them one after another.—"Chief mate dirked by a comprador.—Junk ashore off Hakodate.—Somali muleteer being flogged.—Star-shell bursting over camp at Berbera.—Slave-dhow being chased round Tajurrah Bay.—Soldier lying dead in the moonlight outside Suakin—throat cut by Fuzzies."

"H'm!" said Torpenhow, "can't say I care for Verestchagin-and-water myself, but there's no accounting for tastes. Doing anything now, are you?"

"No. I'm amusing myself here."

Torpenhow looked at the aching desolation of the place. "'Faith, you've queer notions of amusement. 'Got any money?"

"Enough to go on with. Look here: do you want me to do war-work?"

"*I* don't. My syndicate may, though. You can draw more than a little, and I don't suppose you care much what you get, do you?"

"Not this time. I want my chance first."

Torpenhow looked at the sketches again, and nodded. "Yes, you're right to take your first chance when you can get it."

He rode away swiftly through the Gate of the Two War-Ships, rattled across the causeway into the town, and wired to his syndicate, "Got man here, picture-work. Good and cheap. Shall I arrange? Will do letterpress with sketches."

The man on the redoubt sat swinging his legs and mur-

muring, "I knew the chance would come, sooner or later. By Gad, they'll have to sweat for it if I come through this business alive!"

In the evening Torpenhow was able to announce to his friend that the Central Southern Agency was willing to take him on trial, paying expenses for three months. "And, by the way, what's your name?" said Torpenhow.

"Heldar. Do they give me a free hand?"

"They've taken you on chance. You must justify the choice. You'd better stick to me. I'm going up-country with a column, and I'll do what I can for you. Give me some of your sketches taken here, and I'll send 'em along." To himself he said, "That's the best bargain the Central Southern has ever made; and they got me cheaply enough."

So it came to pass that, after some purchase of horseflesh and arrangements financial and political, Dick was made free of the New and Honorable Fraternity of war correspondents, who all possess the inalienable right of doing as much work as they can and getting as much for it as Providence and their owners shall please. To these things are added in time, if the brother be worthy, the power of glib speech that neither man nor woman can resist when a meal or a bed is in question, the eye of a horse-coper, the skill of a cook, the constitution of a bullock, the digestion of an ostrich, and an infinite adaptability to all circumstances. But many die before they attain to this degree, and the past-masters in the craft appear for the most part in dress-clothes when they are in England, and thus their glory is hidden from the multitude.

Dick followed Torpenhow wherever the latter's fancy chose to lead him, and between the two they managed to accomplish some work that almost satisfied themselves. It was not an easy life in any way, and under its influence the two were drawn very closely together, for they ate from the same dish, they shared the same water-bottle, and, most binding tie of all, their mails went off together. It was Dick who managed to make gloriously drunk a telegraph clerk in a palm hut far beyond the Second Cataract, and, while the man lay in bliss on the floor, possessed himself of some laboriously acquired exclusive information, forwarded by a confiding correspondent of an opposition syndicate, made a careful duplicate of the matter, and brought the result to Torpenhow, who said that all was fair in love or war correspondence, and built an excellent descriptive article from his rival's riotous waste of words. It was Torpenhow who—but the tale of their adventures, together and apart, from Philæ to the waste wilderness of Herawi and Muella, would fill many books. They had been penned into a square side by side, in deadly fear of being shot by overexcited soldiers; they had fought with baggage-camels in the chill dawn; they had jogged along in silence under blinding sun on indefatigable little Egyptian horses; and they had floundered on the shallows of the Nile when the whale-boat in which they had found a berth chose to hit a hidden rock and rip out half her bottom-planks.

Now they were sitting on the sand-bank, and the whale-boats were bringing up the remainder of the column.

"Yes," said Torpenhow, as he put the last rude stitches into his overlong-neglected gear, "it has been a beautiful business."

"The patch or the campaign?" said Dick. "Don't think much of either, myself."

"You want the 'Euryalus' brought up above the Third Cataract, don't you? and eighty-one-ton guns at Jakdul? Now, *I'm* quite satisfied with my breeches." He turned round gravely to exhibit himself, after the manner of a clown.

"It's very pretty. Specially the lettering on the sack. G.B.T. Government Bullock Train. That's a sack from India."

"It's my initials—Gilbert Belling Torpenhow. I stole the cloth on purpose. What the mischief are the camel-corps doing yonder?" Torpenhow shaded his eyes and looked across the scrub-strewn gravel.

A bugle blew furiously, and the men on the bank hurried to their arms and accouterments.

"'Pisan soldiery surprised while bathing,'" remarked Dick calmly. "D'you remember the picture? It's by Michelangelo; all beginners copy it. That scrub's alive with enemy."

The camel-corps on the bank yelled to the infantry to come to them, and a hoarse shouting down the river showed that the remainder of the column had wind of the trouble and was hastening to take share in it. As swiftly as a reach of still water is crisped by the wind, the rock-strewn ridges and scrub-topped hills were troubled and alive with armed men. Mercifully, it occurred to these to stand far off for a time, to shout and gesticulate joyously. One man even delivered himself of a long story. The camel-corps did not fire. They were only too glad of a little breathing-space, until some sort of square could be formed. The men on the sand-bank ran to their side; and the whale-boats, as they toiled up within shouting distance, were thrust into the nearest bank and emptied of all save the sick and a few men to guard them. The Arab orator ceased his outcries, and his friends howled.

"They look like the Mahdi's men," said Torpenhow, elbowing himself into the crush of the square; "but what thousands of 'em there are! The tribes hereabout aren't against us, I know."

"Then the Mahdi's taken another town," said Dick, "and set all these yelping devils free to chaw us up. Lend us your glass."

"Our scouts should have told us of this. We've been trapped," said a subaltern. "Aren't the camel-guns ever going to begin? Hurry up, you men!"

There was no need for any order. The men flung themselves panting against the sides of the square, for they had good reason to know that whoso was left outside when the fighting began would very probably die in an extremely unpleasant fashion. The little hundred-and-fifty-pound camel-guns posted at one corner of the square opened the ball as the square moved forward by its right to get possession of a knoll of rising ground. All had fought in this manner many times before, and there was no novelty in the entertainment: always the same hot and stifling formation, the smell of dust and leather, the same boltlike rush of the enemy, the same pressure on the weakest side of the square, the few minutes of desperate hand-to-hand scuffle, and then the silence of the desert, broken only by the yells of those whom the handful of cavalry attempted to pursue. They had grown careless. The camel-guns spoke at intervals, and the square slouched forward amid the protests of the camels. Then came the attack of three thousand men who had not learned from books that it is impossible for troops in close order to attack against breech-loading fire. A few dropping shots heralded their approach, and a few horsemen led, but the bulk of the force was naked humanity, mad with rage, and armed with the spear and the sword. The instinct of the desert, where there is always much war, told them that the right flank of the square was the weakest, for they swung clear of the front. The camel-guns shelled them as they passed, and opened for an instant lanes through their midst, most like those quick-closing vistas in a Kentish hop-garden seen when the train races by at full speed; and the infantry fire, held till the opportune moment, dropped them in close-packed hundreds. No civilized troops in the world could have endured the hell through which they came, the living leaping high to avoid the dying who clutched at their heels, the wounded cursing and staggering forward, till they fell—a torrent black as the sliding water above a mill-dam—full on the right flank of the square. Then the line of the dusty troops and the faint blue desert sky overhead went out in rolling smoke, and the little stones on the heated ground and the tinder-dry clumps of scrub became matters of surpassing interest, for men measured their agonized retreat and recovery by these things, counting mechanically and hewing their way back to chosen pebble and branch. There was no semblance of any concerted fighting. For aught the men knew, the enemy might be attempting all four sides of the square at once. Their business was to destroy what lay in front of them, to bayonet in the back those who passed over them, and, dying, to drag down the slayer till he could be knocked on the head by some avenging gun-butt. Dick waited quietly with Torpenhow and a young doctor till the stress became unendurable. There was no hope of attending to the wounded till the attack was repulsed, so the three moved forward gingerly toward the weakest side. There was a rush from without, the short *hough-hough* of the stabbing spears, and a man on a horse, followed by thirty or forty others, dashed through, yelling and hacking. The right flank of the square sucked in after them, and the other sides sent help. The wounded, who knew that they had but a few hours more to live, caught at the enemy's feet and brought them down, or, staggering to a discarded rifle, fired blindly into the scuffle that raged in the center of the square. Dick was conscious that somebody had cut him violently across his helmet, that he had fired his revolver into a black, foam-flecked face which forthwith ceased to bear any resemblance to a face, and that Torpenhow had gone down under an Arab whom he had tried to "collar low," and was turning over and over with his captive, feeling for the man's eyes. The doctor was jabbing at a venture with a bayonet, and a helmetless soldier was firing over Dick's shoulder: the flying grains of powder stung his cheek. It was to Torpenhow that Dick turned by instinct. The representative of the Central Southern Syndicate had shaken himself clear of his enemy, and rose, wiping his thumb on his trousers. The Arab, both hands to his forehead, screamed aloud, then snatched up his spear and rushed at Torpenhow, who was panting under shelter of Dick's revolver. Dick fired twice, and the man dropped limply. His upturned face lacked one eye. The musketry-fire redoubled, but cheers mingled with it. The rush had failed, and the enemy were flying. If the heart of the square were shambles, the ground beyond was a butcher's shop. Dick thrust his way forward between the maddened men. The remnant of the enemy were retiring, as the few—the very few—English cavalry rode down the laggards.

Beyond the lines of the dead, a broad blood-stained Arab spear cast aside in the retreat lay across a stump of scrub, and beyond this again the illimitable dark levels of the desert. The sun caught the steel and turned it into a savage red disk. Some one behind him was saying, "Ah, get away, you brute!" Dick raised his revolver and pointed toward the desert. His eye was held by the red splash in the distance, and the clamor about him seemed to die down to a very far-away whisper, like the whisper of a level sea. There was the revolver and the red light, . . . and the voice of some one scaring something away, exactly as had fallen somewhere before—probably in a past life. Dick waited for what should happen afterward. Something seemed to crack inside his head, and for an instant he stood in the dark—a darkness that stung. He fired at random, and the bullet went out across the desert as he muttered, "Spoiled my aim. There aren't any more cartridges. We shall have to run home." He put his hand to his head and brought it away covered with blood.

"Old man, you're cut rather badly," said Torpenhow. "I owe you something for this business. Thanks. Stand up! I say, you can't be ill here."

Dick had fallen stiffly on Torpenhow's shoulder, and was muttering something about aiming low and to the left. Then he sank to the ground and was silent. Torpenhow dragged him off to a doctor and sat down to work out an account of what he was pleased to call "a sanguinary battle, in which our arms had acquitted themselves," etc.

All that night, when the troops were encamped by the whale-boats, a black figure danced in the strong moonlight on the sand-bar and shouted that Khartoum the accursed one was dead—was dead—was dead—that two steamers were rock-staked on the Nile outside the city, and that of all their crews there remained not one; and Khartoum was dead—was dead—was dead!

But Torpenhow took no heed. He was watching Dick, who was calling aloud to the restless Nile for Maisie—and again Maisie!

"Behold a phenomenon," said Torpenhow, rearranging the blanket. "Here is a man, presumably human, who mentions the name of one woman only. And I've seen a good deal of delirium, too.—Dick, here's some fizzy drink."

"Thank you, Maisie," said Dick.

CHAPTER THREE

So he thinks he shall take to the sea again
For one more cruise with his buccaneers,
To singe the beard of the King of Spain,
And capture another Dean of Jaen
And sell him in Algiers.—*A Dutch Picture*

THE Soudan campaign and Dick's broken head had been some months ended and mended, and the Central Southern Syndicate had paid Dick a certain sum on account for work done, which work they were careful to assure him was not altogether up to their standard. Dick heaved the letter into the Nile at Cairo, cashed the draft in the same town, and bade a warm farewell to Torpenhow at the station.

"I am going to lie up for a while and rest," said Torpenhow. "I don't know where I shall live in London, but if God brings us to meet, we shall meet. Are you staying here on the off-chance of another row? There will be none till the Southern Soudan is reoccupied by our troops. Mark that. Good-by; bless you; come back when your money's spent; and give me your address."

Dick loitered in Cairo, Alexandria, Ismaïlia, and Port Said—especially Port Said. There is iniquity in many parts of the world, and vice in all, but the concentrated essence of all the iniquities and all the vices in all the continents finds itself at Port Said. And through the heart of that sand-bordered hell, where the mirage flickers day long above the Bitter Lakes, move, if you will only wait, most of the men and women you have known in this life. Dick established himself in quarters more riotous than respectable. He spent his evenings on the quay, and boarded many ships, and saw very many friends—gracious Englishwomen with whom he had talked not too wisely in the veranda of Shepheard's Hotel, hurrying war correspondents, skippers of the contract troopships employed in the campaign, army officers by the score, and others of less reputable trades. He had choice of all the races of the East and West for studies, and the advantage of seeing his subjects under the influence of strong excitement, at the gaming-tables, saloons, dancing-hells, and elsewhere. For recreation there was the straight vista of the Canal, the blazing sands, the procession of shipping, and the white hospitals where the English soldiers lay. He strove to set down in black and white and color all that Providence sent him, and when that supply was ended sought about for fresh material. It was a fascinating employment, but it ran away with his money, and he had drawn in advance the hundred and twenty pounds to which he was entitled yearly. "Now I shall have to work and starve!" thought he, and was addressing himself to this new fate when a mysterious telegram arrived from Torpenhow in England, which said, "Come back, quick: you have caught on. Come."

A large smile overspread his face. "So soon! that's good hearing," said he to himself. "There will be an orgie to-night. I'll stand or fall by my luck. 'Faith, it's time it came!" He deposited half of his funds in the hands of his well-known friends Monsieur and Madame Binat, and ordered himself a Zanzibar dance of the finest. Monsieur Binat was shaking with drink, but Madame smiled sympathetically—

"Monsieur needs a chair, of course, and of course Monsieur will sketch: Monsieur amuses himself strangely."

Binat raised a blue-white face from a cot in the inner room. "I understand," he quavered. "We all know Monsieur. Monsieur is an artist, as I have been." Dick nodded. "In the end," said Binat, with gravity, "Monsieur will descend alive into hell, as I have descended." And he laughed.

"You must come to the dance, too," said Dick; "I shall want you."

"For my face? I knew it would be so. For my face? My God! and for my degradation so tremendous! I will not. Take him away. He is a devil. Or at least do thou, Céleste, demand of him more." The excellent Binat began to kick and scream.

"All things are for sale in Port Said," said Madame. "If my husband comes it will be so much more. Eh, 'ow you call—'alf a sovereign."

The money was paid, and the mad dance was held at night in a walled courtyard at the back of Madame Binat's house. The lady herself, in faded mauve silk always about to slide from her yellow shoulders, played the piano, and to the tin-pot music of a Western waltz the naked Zanzibari girls danced furiously by the light of kerosene lamps. Binat sat upon a chair and stared with eyes that saw nothing, till the whirl of the dance and the clang of the rattling piano stole into the drink that took the place of blood in his veins, and his face glistened. Dick took him by the chin brutally and turned that face to the light. Madame Binat looked over her shoulder and smiled with many teeth. Dick leaned against the wall and sketched for an hour, till the kerosene lamps began to smell, and the girls threw themselves panting on the hard-beaten ground. Then he shut his book with a snap and moved away, Binat plucking feebly at his elbow. "Show me," he whimpered. "I too was once an artist, even I!" Dick showed him the rough sketch. "Am I that?" he screamed. "Will you take that away with you and show all the world that it is I—Binat?" He moaned and wept.

"Monsieur has paid for all," said Madame. "To the pleasure of seeing Monsieur again."

The courtyard gate shut, and Dick hurried up the sandy street to the nearest gambling-hell, where he was well known. "If the luck holds, it's an omen; if I lose, I must stay here." He placed his money picturesquely about the board, hardly daring to look at what he did. The luck held. Three turns of the wheel left him richer by twenty pounds, and he went down to the shipping to make friends with the captain of a decayed cargo-steamer, who landed him in London with fewer pounds in his pocket than he cared to think about.

A thin gray fog hung over the city, and the streets were very cold; for summer was in England.

"It's a cheerful wilderness, and it hasn't the knack of altering much," Dick thought, as he tramped from the Docks westward. "Now, what must I do?"

The packed houses gave no answer. Dick looked down the long lightless streets and at the appalling rush of traffic. "Oh, you rabbit-hutches!" said he, addressing a row of highly-respectable semi-detached residences. "Do you know what you've got to do later on? You have to supply me with men-servants and maid-servants"—here he smacked his lips—"and the peculiar treasure of kings. Meantime I'll get clothes and boots, and presently I will return and trample on you." He stepped forward energetically; he saw that one of his shoes was burst at the side. As he stooped to make investigations, a man jostled him into the gutter. "All right," he said. "That's another nick in the score. I'll jostle you later on."

Good clothes and boots are not cheap, and Dick left his last shop with the certainty that he would be respectably arrayed for a time, but with only fifty shillings in his pocket. He returned to streets by the Docks, and lodged himself in one room, where the sheets on the bed were almost audibly marked in case of theft, and where nobody seemed to go to bed at all. When his clothes arrived he sought the Central Southern Syndicate for Torpenhow's address, and got it, with the intimation that there was still some money owing to him.

"How much?" said Dick, as one who habitually dealt in millions.

"Between thirty and forty pounds. If it would be any convenience to you, of course we could let you have it at once; but we usually settle accounts monthly."

"If I show that I want anything now, I'm lost," he said to himself. "All I need I'll take later on." Then, aloud, "It's hardly worth while; and I'm going into the country for a month, too. Wait till I come back, and I'll see about it."

"But we trust, Mr. Heldar, that you do not intend to sever your connection with us?"

Dick's business in life was the study of faces, and he watched the speaker keenly. "That man means something," he said. "I'll do no business till I've seen Torpenhow. There's a big deal coming." So he departed, making no promises, to his one little room by the Docks. And that day was the seventh of the month, and that month, he reckoned with awful distinctness, had thirty-one days in it!

It is not easy for a man of catholic tastes and healthy appetites to exist for twenty-four days on fifty shillings. Nor is it cheering to begin the experiment alone in all the loneliness of London. Dick paid seven shillings a week for his lodging, which left him rather less than a shilling a day for food and drink. Naturally, his first purchase was of the materials of his craft; he had been without them too long. Half a day's investigation and comparison brought him to the conclusion that sausages and mashed potatoes, twopence a plate, were the best food. Now, sausages once or twice a week for breakfast are not unpleasant. As lunch, even, with mashed potatoes, they become monotonous. As dinner they are impertinent. At the end of three days Dick loathed sausages, and, going forth, pawned his watch to revel on sheep's head, which is not as cheap as it looks, owing to the bones and the gravy. Then he returned to sausages and mashed potatoes. Then he confined himself entirely to mashed potatoes for a day, and was unhappy because of pain in his inside. Then he pawned his waistcoat and his tie, and thought regretfully of money thrown away in times past. There are few things more edifying unto Art than the actual belly-pinch of hunger, and Dick in his few walks abroad—he did not care for exercise; it raised desires that could not be satisfied—found himself dividing mankind into two classes—those who looked as if they might give him something to eat, and those who looked otherwise. "I never knew what I had to learn about the human face before," he thought; and, as a reward for his humility, Providence caused a cab-driver at a sausage-shop where Dick fed that night to leave half eaten a great chunk of bread. Dick took it—would have fought all the world for its possession—and it cheered him.

The month dragged through at last, and, nearly prancing with impatience, he went to draw his money. Then he hastened to Torpenhow's address and smelt the smell of cooking meats all along the corridors of the chambers. Torpenhow was on the top floor, and Dick burst into his room, to be received with a hug which nearly cracked his ribs, as Torpenhow dragged him to the light and spoke of twenty different things in the same breath.

"But you're looking tucked up," he concluded.

"Got anything to eat?" said Dick, his eye roaming round the room.

"I shall be having breakfast in a minute. What do you say to sausages?"

"No, anything but sausages! Torp, I've been starving on that accursed horseflesh for thirty days and thirty nights."

"Now, what lunacy has been your latest?"

Dick spoke of the last few weeks with unbridled speech. Then he opened his coat; there was no waistcoat below. "I ran it fine, awfully fine, but I've just scraped through."

"You haven't much sense, but you've got a backbone, anyhow. Eat, and talk afterward." Dick fell upon eggs and bacon and gorged till he could gorge no more. Torpenhow handed him a filled pipe, and he smoked as men smoke who for three weeks have been deprived of good tobacco.

"Ouf!" said he. "That's heavenly! Well?"

"Why in the world didn't you come to me?"

"Couldn't; I owe you too much already, old man. Besides, I had a sort of superstition that this temporary starvation—that's what it was, and it hurt—would bring me more luck later. It's over and done with now, and none of the syndicate know how hard up I was. Fire away. What's the exact state of affairs as regards myself?"

"You had my wire? You've caught on here. People like your work immensely. I don't know why, but they do. They say you have a fresh touch and a new way of drawing things. And, because they're chiefly home-bred English, they say you have insight. You're wanted by half a dozen papers; you're wanted to illustrate books."

Dick grunted scornfully.

"You're wanted to work up your smaller sketches and sell them to the dealers. They seem to think the money sunk in you is a good investment. Good Lord! who can account for the fathomless folly of the public?"

"They're a remarkably sensible people."

"They are subject to fits, if that's what you mean; and you happen to be the object of the latest fit among those who are interested in what they call Art. Just now you're a fashion, a phenomenon, or whatever you please. I appeared to be the only person who knew anything about you here, and I have been showing the most useful men a few of the sketches you gave me from time to time. Those coming after your work on the Central Southern Syndicate appear to have done your business. You're in luck."

"Huh! call it luck! Do call it luck, when a man has been kicking about the world like a dog, waiting for it to come! I'll luck 'em later on. I want a place to work in first."

"Come here," said Torpenhow, crossing the landing. "This place is a big box room really, but it will do for you. There's your skylight, or your north light, or whatever window you call it, and plenty of room to thrash about in, and a bedroom beyond. What more do you need?"

"Good enough," said Dick, looking round the large room

that took up a third of a top story in the rickety chambers overlooking the Thames. A pale yellow sun shone through the skylight and showed the much dirt of the place. Three steps led from the door to the landing, and three more to Torpenhow's room. The well of the staircase disappeared into darkness, pricked by tiny gas-jets, and there were sounds of men talking and doors slamming seven flights below, in the warm gloom.

"Do they give you a free hand here?" said Dick cautiously. He was Ishmael enough to know the value of liberty.

"Anything you like: latch-keys and license unlimited. We are permanent tenants for the most part here. 'Tisn't a place I would recommend for a Young Men's Christian Association, but it will serve. I took these rooms for you when I wired."

"You're a great deal too kind, old man."

"You didn't suppose you were going away from me, did you?" Torpenhow put his hand on Dick's shoulder, and the two walked up and down the room, henceforward to be called the studio, in sweet and silent communion. They heard rapping at Torpenhow's door. "That's some ruffian come up for a drink," said Torpenhow; and he raised his voice cheerily. There entered no one more ruffianly than a portly middle aged gentleman in a satin-faced frockcoat. His lips were parted and pale, and there were deep pouches under the eyes.

"Weak heart," said Dick to himself, and, as he shook hands, "very weak heart. His pulse is shaking his fingers."

The man introduced himself as the head of the Central Southern Syndicate and "one of the most ardent admirers of your work, Mr. Heldar. I assure you, in the name of the syndicate, that we are immensely indebted to you; and I trust, Mr. Heldar, you won't forget that we were largely instrumental in bringing you before the public." He panted because of the seven flights of stairs.

Dick glanced at Torpenhow, whose left eyelid lay for a moment dead on his cheek.

"I shan't forget," said Dick, every instinct of defense roused in him. "You've paid me so well that I couldn't, you know. By the way, when I am settled in this place I should like to send and get my sketches. There must be nearly a hundred and fifty of them with you."

"That is er—is what I came to speak about. I fear we can't allow it exactly, Mr. Heldar. In the absence of any specified agreement, the sketches are our property, of course."

"Do you mean to say that you are going to keep them?"

"Yes; and we hope to have your help, on your own terms, Mr. Heldar, to assist us in arranging a little exhibition, which, backed by our name and the influence we naturally command among the press, should be of material service to you. Sketches such as yours—"

"Belong to me. You engaged me by wire, you paid me the lowest rates you dared. You can't mean to keep them! Good God alive, man, they're all I've got in the world!"

Torpenhow watched Dick's face and whistled.

Dick walked up and down, thinking. He saw the whole of his little stock in trade, the first weapon of his equipment, annexed at the outset of his campaign by an elderly gentleman whose name Dick had not caught aright, who said that he represented a syndicate, which was a thing for which Dick had not the least reverence. The injustice of the proceedings did not much move him; he had seen the strong hand prevail too often in other places to be squeamish over the moral aspects of right and wrong. But he ardently desired the blood of the gentleman in the frockcoat, and when he spoke again it was with a strained sweetness that Torpenhow knew well for the beginning of strife.

"Forgive me, sir, but you have no—no younger man who can arrange this business with me?"

"I speak for the syndicate. I see no reason for a third party to—"

"You will in a minute. Be good enough to give back my sketches."

The man stared blankly at Dick, and then at Torpenhow, who was leaning against the wall. He was not used to ex-employés who ordered him to be good enough to do things.

"Yes, it is rather a cold-blooded steal," said Torpenhow critically; "but I'm afraid, I am very much afraid, you've struck the wrong man. Be careful, Dick: remember, this isn't the Soudan."

"Considering what services the syndicate have done you in putting your name before the world—"

This was not a fortunate remark; it reminded Dick of certain vagrant years lived out in loneliness and strife and unsatisfied desires. The memory did not contrast well with the prosperous gentleman who proposed to enjoy the fruit of those years.

"I don't know quite what to do with you," began Dick meditatively. "Of course you're a thief, and you ought to be half killed, but in your case you'd probably die. I don't want you dead on this floor, and, besides, it's unlucky just as one's moving in. Don't hit, sir; you'll only excite yourself." He put one hand on the man's forearm and ran the other down the plump body beneath the coat. "My goodness!" said he to Torpenhow, "and this gray oaf dares to be a thief! I have seen an Esneh camel-driver have the black hide taken off his body in strips for stealing half a pound of wet dates, and *he* was as tough as whipcord. This thing's soft all over—like a woman."

There are few things more poignantly humiliating than being handled by a man who does not intend to strike. The head of the syndicate began to breathe heavily. Dick walked round him, pawing him, as a cat paws a soft hearthrug. Then he traced with his forefinger the leaden pouches underneath the eyes, and shook his head. "You were going to steal my things—mine, mine, mine!—you, who don't know when you may die. Write a note to your office—you say you're the head of it—and order them to give Torpenhow my sketches—every one of them. Wait a minute: your hand's shaking. Now!" He thrust a pocket-book before him. The note was written. Torpenhow took it and departed without a word, while Dick walked round and round the spellbound captive, giving him such advice as he conceived best for the welfare of his soul. When Torpenhow returned with a gigantic portfolio, he heard Dick say, almost soothingly, "Now, I hope this will be a lesson to you; and if you worry me when I have settled down to work with any nonsense about actions for assault, believe me, I'll catch you and manhandle you, and you'll die. You haven't very long to live, anyhow. Go! *Imshi*, *Vootsak*—get out!" The man departed, staggering and dazed. Dick drew a long breath: "Phew! what a lawless lot these people are! The first thing a poor orphan meets is gang robbery, organized burglary! Think of the hideous blackness of that man's mind! Are my sketches all right, Torp?"

"Yes, one hundred and forty-seven of them. Well, I *must* say, Dick, you've begun well."

"He was interfering with me. It only meant a few pounds to him, but it was everything to me. I don't think he'll bring an action. I gave him some medical advice gratis about the state of his body. It was cheap at the little flurry it cost him. Now, let's look at my things."

Two minutes later Dick had thrown himself down on the floor and was deep in the portfolio, chuckling lovingly as he turned the drawings over and thought of the price at which they had been bought.

The afternoon was well advanced when Torpenhow came to the door and saw Dick dancing a wild saraband under the skylight.

"I builded better than I knew, Torp," he said, without stopping the dance. "They're good! They're damned good! They'll go like flame! I shall have an exhibition of them on my own brazen hook. And that man would have cheated me out of it! Do you know that I'm sorry now that I didn't actually hit him?"

"Go out," said Torpenhow—"go out and pray to be delivered from the sin of arrogance, which you never will be. Bring your things up from whatever place you're staying in, and we'll try to make this barn a little more shipshape."

"And then—oh, then," said Dick, still capering, "we will spoil the Egyptians!"

CHAPTER FOUR

The wolf-cub at even lay hid in the corn,
  When the smoke of the cooking hung gray;
He knew where the doe made a couch for her fawn,
  And he looked to his strength for his prey.
  But the moon swept the smoke-wreaths away.
And he turned from his meal in the villager's close,
And he bayed to the moon as she rose.—*In Seonee*

"Well, and how does success taste?" said Torpenhow, some three months later. He had just returned to chambers, after a holiday in the country.

"Good," said Dick, as he sat licking his lips before the easel in the studio. "I want more—heaps more. The lean years have passed, and I approve of these fat ones."

"Be careful, old man. That way lies bad work."

Torpenhow was sprawling in a long chair with a small fox terrier asleep on his chest, while Dick was preparing a canvas. A dais, a background, and a lay-figure were the only fixed objects in the place. They rose from a wreck of oddments that began with felt-covered water-bottles, belts, and regimental badges, and ended with a small bale of second-hand uniforms and a stand of mixed arms. The mark of muddy feet on the dais showed that a military model had just gone away. The watery autumn sunlight was failing, and shadows sat in the corners of the studio.

"Yes," said Dick deliberately, "I like the power; I like the fun; I like the fuss; and above all I like the money. I almost like the people who make the fuss and pay the money. Almost. But they're a queer gang—an amazingly queer gang!"

"They have been good enough to you, at any rate. That tin-pot exhibition of your sketches must have paid. Did you see that the papers called it the 'Wild Work Show'?"

"Never mind. I sold every shred of canvas I wanted to; and, on my word, I believe it was because they believed I was a self-taught flagstone artist. I should have got better prices if I had worked my things on wool or scratched them on camel-bone instead of using mere black and white and color. Verily, they are a queer gang, these people. Limited isn't the word to describe 'em. I met a fellow the other day who told me that it was impossible that shadows on white sand should be blue—ultramarine—as they are. I found out, later, that that man had been as far as Brighton beach; but he knew all about Art, confound him. He gave me a lecture on it, and recommended me to go to school to learn technique. I wonder what old Kami would have said to that."

"When were you under Kami, man of extraordinary beginnings?"

"I studied with him for two years in Paris. He taught by personal magnetism. All he ever said was, '*Continuez, mes enfants*,' and you had to make the best you could of that. He had a divine touch, and he knew something about color. Kami used to dream color; I swear he could never have seen the genuine article; but he evolved it; and it was good."

"Recollect some of those views in the Soudan?" said Torpenhow, with a provoking drawl.

Dick squirmed in his place. "Don't! It makes me want to get out there again. What color that was! Opal and umber and amber and claret and brick-red and sulphur—cockatoo-crest sulphur—against brown, with a nigger-black rock sticking up in the middle of it all, and a decorative frieze of camels festooning in front of a pure pale turquoise sky." He began to walk up and down. "And yet you know, if you try to give these people the thing as God gave it, keyed down to their comprehension and according to the powers He has given you—"

"Modest man! Go on."

"Half a dozen epicene young pagans who haven't even been to Algiers will tell you, first, that your notion is borrowed, and, secondly, that it isn't Art."

"This comes of my leaving town for a month. Dickie, you've been promenading among the toy-shops and hearing people talk."

"I couldn't help it," said Dick penitently. "You weren't here, and it was lonely these long evenings. A man can't work forever."

"A man might have gone to a pub, and got decently drunk."

"I wish I had; but I foregathered with some men of sorts. They said they were artists, and I knew some of them could draw—but they wouldn't draw. They gave me tea—tea at five in the afternoon!—and talked about Art and the state of their souls. As if their souls mattered. I've heard more about Art and seen less of her in the last six months than in the whole of my life. Do you remember Cassavetti, who worked for some continental syndicate, out with the desert column? He was a regular Christmas-tree of contraptions when he took the field in full fig, with his water-bottle, lanyard, revolver, writing-case, housewife, gig-lamps, and the Lord knows what all. He used to fiddle about with 'em and show us how they worked; but he never seemed to do much except fudge his reports from the Nilghai. See?"

"Dear old Nilghai! He's in town, fatter than ever. He ought to be up here this evening. I see the comparison perfectly. You should have kept clear of all that man-millinery. Serves you right; and I hope it will unsettle your mind."

"It won't. It has taught me what Art—holy sacred Art—means."

"You've learned something while I've been away. What is Art?"

"Give 'em what they know, and when you've done it once do it again." Dick dragged forward a canvas laid face to the wall. "Here's a sample of real Art. It's going to be a facsimile reproduction for a weekly. I called it 'His Last Shot.' It's worked up from the little water-color I made outside El Maghrib. Well, I lured my model, a beautiful rifleman, up here with drink; I drored him, and I redrored him, and I tredrored him, and I made him a flushed, disheveled, bedeviled scallawag, with his helmet at the back of his head, and the living fear of death in his eye, and the blood oozing out of a cut over his ankle-bone. He wasn't pretty, but he was all soldier and very much man."

"Once more, modest child!"

Dick laughed. "Well, it's only to you I'm talking. I did him just as well as I knew how, making allowance for the slickness of oils. Then the art-manager of that abandoned paper said that his subscribers wouldn't like it. It was brutal and coarse and violent—man being naturally gentle when he's fighting for his life. They wanted something more restful, with a little more color. I could have said a good deal, but you might as well talk to a sheep as an art-manager. I took my 'Last Shot' back. Behold the result! I put him into a lovely red coat without a speck on it. That is Art. I polished his boots—observe the high light on the toe. That is Art. I cleaned his rifle—rifles are always clean on service—because that is Art. I pipeclayed his helmet—pipeclay is always used on active service, and is indispensable to Art. I shaved his chin, I washed his hands, and gave him an air of fatted peace. Result, military tailor's pattern-plate. Price, thank Heaven, twice as much as for the first sketch, which was moderately decent."

"And do you suppose you're going to give that thing out as your work?"

"Why not? I did it. Alone I did it, in the interests of sacred, home-bred Art and 'Dickenson's Weekly.'"

Torpenhow smoked in silence for a while. Then came the verdict, delivered from rolling clouds: "If you were only a mass of blathering vanity, Dick, I wouldn't mind—I'd let you go to the deuce on your own mahl-stick; but when I consider what you are to me, and when I find that to vanity you add the twopenny-halfpenny pique of a twelve-year-old girl, then I bestir myself in your behalf. Thus!"

The canvas ripped as Torpenhow's booted foot shot through it, and the terrier jumped down, thinking rats were about.

"If you have any bad language to use, use it. You have not. I continue. You are an idiot, because no man born of woman is strong enough to take liberties with his public, even though they be—which they ain't—all you say they are."

"But they don't know any better. What can you expect from creatures born and bred in this light?" Dick pointed to the yellow fog. "If they want furniture-polish, let them have furniture-polish, so long as they pay for it. They are only men and women. You talk as though they were gods."

"That sounds very fine, but it has nothing to do with the case. They are the people you have to work for, whether you like it or not. They are your masters. Don't be deceived, Dickie, you aren't strong enough to trifle with them —or with yourself, which is more important. Moreover— Come back, Binkie: that red daub isn't going anywhere —unless you take precious good care, you will fall under the damnation of the check-book, and that's worse than death. You will get drunk—you're half drunk already—on easily-acquired money. For that money and your own infernal vanity you are willing to deliberately turn out bad work. You'll do quite enough bad work without knowing it. And, Dickie, as I love you and as I know you love me, I am not going to let you cut off your nose to spite your face for all the gold in England. That's settled. Now swear."

"Don't know," said Dick. "I've been trying to make myself angry, but I can't, you're so abominably reasonable. There will be a row on 'Dickenson's Weekly,' I fancy."

"Why the Dickenson do you want to work on a weekly paper? It's slow bleeding of power."

"It brings in the very desirable dollars," said Dick, his hands in his pockets.

Torpenhow watched him with large contempt. "Why, I thought it was a man!" said he. "It's a child."

"No, it isn't," said Dick, wheeling quickly. "You've no notion what the certainty of cash means to a man who has always wanted it badly. Nothing will pay me for some of my life's joys; on that Chinese pig-boat, for instance, when we ate bread and jam for every meal, because Ho-Wang wouldn't allow us anything better, and it all tasted of pig—Chinese pig. I've worked for this, I've sweated and I've starved for this, line on line and month after month. And now I've got it I am going to make the most of it while it lasts. Let them pay—they've no knowledge."

"What does Your Majesty please to want? You can't smoke more than you do; you won't drink; you're a gross feeder; and you dress in the dark, by the look of you. You wouldn't keep a horse the other day when I suggested, because, you said, it might fall lame, and whenever you cross the street you take a hansom. Even you are not foolish enough to suppose that theaters and all the live things you can buy thereabout mean Life. What earthly need have you for money?"

"It's there, bless its golden heart," said Dick. "It's there all the time. Providence has sent me nuts while I have teeth to crack 'em with. I haven't yet found the nut I wish to crack, but I'm keeping my teeth filed. Perhaps some day you and I will go for a walk round the wide earth."

"With no work to do, nobody to worry us, and nobody to compete with? You would be unfit to speak to in a week. Besides, I shouldn't go. I don't care to profit by the price of a man's soul—for that's what it would mean. Dick, it's no use arguing. You're a fool."

"Don't see it. When I was on that Chinese pig-boat, our captain got enormous credit for saving about twenty-five thousand very seasick little pigs, when our old tramp of a steamer fell foul of a timber-junk. Now, taking those pigs as a parallel—"

"Oh, confound your parallels! Whenever I try to improve your soul, you always drag in some irrelevant anecdote from your very shady past. Pigs aren't the British public; credit on the high seas isn't credit here; and self-respect is self-respect all the world over. Go out for a walk and try to catch some self-respect. And, I say, if the Nilghai comes up this evening can I show him your diggings?"

"Surely. You'll be asking whether you must knock at my door, next." And Dick departed, to take counsel with himself in the rapidly-gathering London fog.

Half an hour after he had left, the Nilghai labored up the staircase. He was the chiefest, as he was the hugest, of the war correspondents, and his experiences dated from the birth of the needle-gun. Saving only his ally, Keneu the Great War Eagle, there was no man mightier in the craft than he, and he always opened his conversation with the news that there would be trouble in the Balkans in the spring. Torpenhow laughed as he entered.

"Never mind the trouble in the Balkans. Those little states are always screeching. You've heard about Dick's luck?"

"Yes; he has been called up to notoriety, hasn't he? I hope you keep him properly humble. He wants suppressing from time to time."

"He does. He's beginning to take liberties with what he thinks is his reputation."

"Already! By Jove, he has cheek! I don't know about his reputation, but he'll come a cropper if he tries that sort of thing."

"So I told him. I don't think he believes it."

"They never do when they first start off. What's that wreck on the ground there?"

"Specimen of his latest impertinence." Torpenhow thrust the torn edges of the canvas together and showed the well-groomed picture to the Nilghai, who looked at it for a moment and whistled.

"It's a chromo," said he—"a chromo-litholeomargarine fake! What possessed him to do it? And yet how thoroughly he has caught the note that catches a public who think with their boots and read with their elbows! The cold-blooded insolence of the work almost saves it; but he mustn't go on with this. Hasn't he been praised and cockered up too much? You know these people here have no sense of proportion. They'll call him a second Detaille and a third-hand Meissonier while his fashion lasts. It's windy diet for a colt."

"I don't think it affects Dick much. You might as well call a young wolf a lion and expect him to take the compliment in exchange for a shin-bone. Dick's soul is in the bank. He's working for cash."

"Now he has thrown up war work, I suppose he doesn't see that the obligations of the service are just the same, only the proprietors are changed."

"How should he know? He thinks he is his own master."

"Does he? I could undeceive him for his good, if there's any virtue in print. He wants the whip-lash."

"Lay it on with science, then. I'd flay him myself, but I like him too much."

"I've no scruples. He had the audacity to try to cut me out with a woman at Cairo once. I forgot that, but I remember now."

"Did he cut you out?"

"You'll see when I have dealt with him. But, after all, what's the good? Leave him alone and he'll come home, if he has any stuff in him, dragging or wagging his tail behind him. There's more in a week of life than in a lively weekly. None the less I'll slate him. I'll slate him ponderously in the 'Cataclysm.' "

"Good luck to you; but I fancy nothing short of a crowbar would make Dick wince. His soul seems to have been fired before we came across him. He's intensely suspicious and utterly lawless."

"Matter of temper," said the Nilghai. "It's the same with horses. Some you wallop and they work, some you wallop and they jib, and some you wallop and they go out for a walk with their hands in their pockets."

"That's exactly what Dick has done," said Torpenhow. "Wait till he comes back. In the meantime, you can begin your slating here. I'll show you some of his last and worst work in his studio."

Dick had instinctively sought running water for a comfort to his mood of mind. He was leaning over the Embankment wall, watching the rush of the Thames through the arches of Westminster Bridge. He began by thinking of Torpenhow's advice, but, as of custom, lost himself in the study of the faces flocking past. Some had death written on their features, and Dick marveled that they could laugh. Others, clumsy and coarse-built for the most part, were alight with love; others were merely drawn and lined with work; but there was something, Dick knew, to be made out of them all. The poor at least should suffer that he might learn, and the rich should pay for the output of his learning. Thus his credit in the world and his cash balance at the bank would be increased. So much the better for him. He had suffered. Now he would take toll of the ills of others.

The fog was driven apart for a moment, and the sun shone, a blood-red wafer, on the water. Dick watched the spot till he heard the voice of the tide between the piers die down like the wash of the sea at low tide. A girl hard pressed by her lover shouted shamelessly, "Ah, get away, you beast!" and a shift of the same wind that had opened the fog drove across Dick's face the black smoke of a river-steamer at her berth below the wall. He was blinded for the moment, then spun round and found himself face to face with—Maisie.

There was no mistaking. The years had turned the child to a woman, but they had not altered the dark-gray eyes, the thin scarlet lips, or the firmly modeled mouth and chin; and, that all should be as it was of old, she wore a closely-fitting gray dress.

Since the human soul is finite and not in the least under its own command, Dick, advancing, said, "Halloo!" after the manner of schoolboys, and Maisie answered, "Oh, Dick, is that you?" Then, against his will, and before the brain newly released from considerations of the cash balance had time to dictate to the nerves, every pulse of Dick's body throbbed furiously and his palate dried in his mouth. The fog shut down again, and Maisie's face was pearl-white through it. No word was spoken, but Dick fell into step at her side, and the two paced the Embankment together, keeping the step as perfectly as in their afternoon excursions to the mud-flats. Then Dick, a little hoarsely—

"What has happened to Amomma?"

"He died, Dick. Not cartridges; over-eating. He was always greedy. Isn't it funny?"

"Yes. No. Do you mean Amomma?"

"Ye—es. No. This. Where have you come from?"

"Over there." He pointed eastward through the fog. "And you?"

"Oh, I'm in the north—the black north, across all the Park. I am very busy."

"What do you do?"

"I paint a great deal. That's all I have to do."

"Why, what's happened? You had three hundred a year."

"I have that still. I am painting; that's all."

"Are you alone, then?"

"There's a girl living with me. Don't walk so fast, Dick; you're out of step."

"Then you noticed it too?"

"Of course I did. You're always out of step."

"So I am. I'm sorry. You went on with the painting?"

"Of course. I said I should. I was at the Slade, then at Merton's in St. John's Wood, the big studio, then I pepper-potted—I mean I went to the National—and now I'm working under Kami."

"But Kami is in Paris surely?"

"No; he has his teaching studio at Vitry-sur-Marne. I work with him in the summer and I live in London in the winter. I'm a householder."

"Do you sell much?"

"Now and again, but not often. There is my 'bus. I must take it or lose half an hour. Good-by, Dick."

"Good-by, Maisie. Won't you tell me where you live? I must see you again; and perhaps I could help you. I—I paint a little myself."

"I may be in the Park to-morrow, if there is no working light. I walk from the Marble Arch down and back again; that is my little excursion. But of course I shall see you again." She stepped into the omnibus and was swallowed up by the fog.

"Well—I—am—damned!" exclaimed Dick, and returned to the chambers.

Torpenhow and the Nilghai found him sitting on the steps to the studio door, repeating the phrase with an awful gravity.

"You'll be more damned when I've done with you," said the Nilghai, upheaving his bulk from behind Torpenhow's shoulder and waving a sheaf of half-dry manuscript. "Dick, it is of common report that you are suffering from swelled head."

"Hallo, Nilghai. Back again? How are the Balkans and all the little Balkans? One side of your face is out of drawing, as usual."

"Never mind that. I am commissioned to smite you in print. Torpenhow refuses from false delicacy. I've been overhauling the pot-boilers in your studio. They are simply disgraceful."

"Oho! that's it, is it? If you think you can slate me, you're wrong. You can only describe, and you need as much room to turn in, on paper, as a P. and O. cargo-boat. But continue, and be swift. I'm going to bed."

"H'm! h'm! h'm! The first part only deals with your pictures. Here's the peroration: 'For work done without conviction, for power wasted on trivialities, for labor expended with levity for the deliberate purpose of winning the easy applause of a fashion-driven public—' "

"That's 'His Last Shot,' second edition. Go on."

"—'Public, there remains but one end—the oblivion that is preceded by toleration and cenotaphed with contempt. From that fate Mr. Heldar has yet to prove himself out of danger.' "

"*Wow—wow—wow—wow—wow!*" said Dick profanely. "It's a clumsy ending and vile journalese, but it's quite true. And yet"—he sprang to his feet and snatched at the manuscript—"you scarred, deboshed, battered old gladiator! you're sent out when a war begins, to minister to the blind, brutal, British public's bestial thirst for blood. They have no arenas now, but they must have special correspondents. You're a fat gladiator who comes up through a trap-door and talks of what he's seen. You stand on precisely the same level as an energetic bishop, an affable actress, a devastating cyclone, or—mine own sweet self. And you presume to lecture me about my work! Nilghai, if it were worth while I'd caricature you in four papers!"

The Nilghai winced. He had not thought of this.

"As it is, I shall take this stuff and tear it small—so!" The manuscript fluttered in slips down the dark well of the staircase. "Go home, Nilghai," said Dick; "go home to your lonely little bed, and leave me in peace. I am about to turn in till to-morrow."

"Why, it isn't seven yet!" said Torpenhow, with amazement.

"It shall be two in the morning, if I choose," said Dick, backing to the studio door. "I go to grapple with a serious crisis, and I shan't want any dinner."

The door shut and was locked.

"What can you do with a man like that?" said the Nilghai.

"Leave him alone. He's as mad as a hatter."

At eleven there was kicking on the studio door. "Is the Nilghai with you still?" said a voice from within. "Then tell him he might have condensed the whole of his lumbering nonsense into an epigram: 'Only the free are bond, and only the bond are free.' Tell him he's an idiot, Torp, and tell him I'm another."

"All right. Come out and have supper. You're smoking on an empty stomach."

There was no answer.

CHAPTER FIVE

"I have a thousand men," said he,
"To wait upon my will,
And towers nine upon the Tyne,
And three upon the Till."

"And what care I for your men," said she,
"Or towers from Tyne to Till,
Sith you must go with me," she said,
"To wait upon my will?"

—*Sir Hoggie and the Fairies*

NEXT morning Torpenhow found Dick sunk in deepest repose of tobacco.

"Well, madman, how d'you feel?"

"I don't know. I'm trying to find out."

"You had much better do some work."

"Maybe; but I'm in no hurry. I've made a discovery. Torp, there's too much Ego in my Cosmos."

"Not really! Is this revelation due to my lectures, or the Nilghai's?"

"It came to me suddenly, all on my own account. Much too much Ego; and now I'm going to work."

He turned over a few half-finished sketches, drummed on a new canvas, cleaned three brushes, set Binkie to bite the toes of the lay figure, rattled through his collection of arms and accouterments, and then went out abruptly, declaring that he had done enough for the day.

"This is positively indecent," said Torpenhow, "and the first time that Dick has ever broken up a light morning. Perhaps he has found out that he has a soul, or an artistic temperament, or something equally valuable. That comes of leaving him alone for a month. Perhaps he has been going out of evenings. I must look to this." He rang for the bald-headed old housekeeper, whom nothing could astonish or annoy.

"Beeton, did Mr. Heldar dine out at all while I was out of town?"

"Never laid 'is dress-clothes out once, sir, all the time. Mostly 'e dined in; but 'e brought some most remarkable fancy young gentlemen up 'ere after theaters once or twice. Remarkable fancy they was. You gentlemen on the top floor does very much as you likes, but it do seem to me, sir, droppin' a walkin'-stick down five flights o' stairs an' then goin' down four abreast to pick it up again at half-past two in the mornin' singin', 'Bring back the whisky, Willie darlin' '—not once or twice, but scores o' times—isn't charity to the other tenants. What I say is, 'Do as you would be done by.' That's my motto."

"Of course! of course! I'm afraid the top floor isn't the quietest in the house."

"I make no complaints, sir. I have spoke to Mr. Heldar friendly, an' he laughed, an' did me a picture of the missis that is as good as a colored print. It 'asn't the 'igh shine of a photograph, but what I say is, 'Never look a gift-horse in the mouth.' Mr. Heldar's dress-clothes 'aven't been on him for weeks."

"Then it's all right," said Torpenhow to himself. "Orgies are healthy, and Dick has a head of his own, but when it comes to women making eyes I'm not so certain.—Binkie, never you be a man, little dorglums. They're contrary brutes, and they do things without any reason."

Dick had turned northward across the Park, but he was walking in the spirit on the mud-flats with Maisie. He laughed aloud as he remembered the day when he had decked Amomma's horns with the ham-frills, and Maisie, white with rage, had cuffed him. How long those four years seemed in review, and how closely Maisie was connected with every hour of them! Storm across the sea, and Maisie in a gray dress on the beach, sweeping her drenched hair out of her eyes and laughing at the homeward race of the fishing-smacks; hot sunshine on the mud-flats, and Maisie sniffing scornfully, with her chin in the air; Maisie flying before the wind that threshed the foreshore and drove the sand like small shot about her ears; Maisie, very composed and independent, telling lies to Mrs. Jennett while Dick supported her with coarser perjuries; Maisie picking her way delicately from stone to stone, a pistol in her hand and her teeth firm-set; and Maisie in a gray dress sitting on the grass between the mouth of a cannon and a nodding yellow sea-poppy. The pictures passed before him one by one, and the last stayed the longest. Dick was perfectly happy with a quiet peace that was as new to his mind as it was foreign to his experience. It never occurred to him that there might be other calls upon his time than loafing across the Park in the forenoon.

"There's a good working light now," he said, watching his shadow placidly. "Some poor devil ought to be grateful for this. And there's Maisie."

She was walking toward him from the Marble Arch, and he saw that no mannerism of her gait had been changed. It was good to find her still Maisie, and, so to speak, his next-door neighbor. No greeting passed between them, because there had been none in the old days.

"What are you doing out of your studio at this hour?" said Dick, as one who was entitled to ask.

"Idling. Just idling. I got angry with a chin and scraped it out. Then I left it in a little heap of paint-chips and came away."

"I know what palette-knifing means. What was the piccy?"

"A fancy head that wouldn't come right—horrid thing!"

"I don't like working over scraped paint when I'm doing flesh. The grain comes up woolly as the paint dries."

"Not if you scrape properly." Maisie waved her hand to illustrate her methods. There was a dab of paint on the white cuff. Dick laughed.

"You're as untidy as ever."

"That comes well from you. Look at your own cuff."

"By Jove, yes! It's worse than yours. I don't think we've much altered in anything. Let's see, though." He looked at Maisie critically. The pale blue haze of an autumn day crept between the tree-trunks of the Park and made a background for the gray dress, the black velvet toque above the black hair, and the resolute profile.

"No, there's nothing changed. How good it is! D'you remember when I fastened your hair into the snap of a hand-bag?"

Maisie nodded, with a twinkle in her eyes, and turned her full face to Dick.

"Wait a minute," said he. "That mouth is down at the corners a little. Who's been worrying you, Maisie?"

"No one but myself. I never seem to get on with my work, and yet I try hard enough, and Kami says—"

"'*Continuez, mesdemoiselles. Continuez, toujours, mes enfants.*' Kami is depressing. I beg your pardon."

"Yes, that's what he says. He told me last summer that I was doing better and he'd let me exhibit this year."

"Not in this place, surely?"

"Of course not. The Salon."

"You fly high."

"I've been beating my wings long enough. Where do you exhibit, Dick?"

"I don't exhibit. I sell."

"What is your line, then?"

"Haven't you heard?" Dick's eyes opened. Was this thing possible? He cast about for some means of conviction. They were not far from the Marble Arch. "Come up Oxford Street a little and I'll show you."

A small knot of people stood round a print-shop that Dick knew well. "Some reproduction of my work inside," he said, with suppressed triumph. Never before had success tasted so sweet upon the tongue. "You see the sort of things I paint. D'you like it?"

Maisie looked at the wild whirling rush of a field-battery going into action under fire. Two artillerymen stood behind her in the crowd.

"They've chucked the off lead-'orse," said one to the other. "'E's tore up awful, but they're makin' good time with the others. That lead-driver drives better nor you, Tom. See 'ow cunnin' 'e's nursin' 'is 'orse."

"Number Three'll be off the limber, next jolt," was the answer.

"No 'e won't. See 'ow 'is foot's braced against the iron? 'E's all right."

Dick watched Maisie's face and swelled with joy—fine, rank, vulgar triumph. She was more interested in the little crowd than in the picture. That was something that she could understand.

"And I wanted it so! Oh, I did want it so!" she said at last, under her breath.

"Me—all me!" said Dick placidly. "Look at their faces. It hits 'em. They don't know what makes their eyes and mouths open; but I know. And I know my work's right."

"Yes. I see. Oh, what a thing to have come to one!"

"Come to one, indeed! I had to go out and look for it. What do you think?"

"I call it success. Tell me how you got it."

They returned to the Park, and Dick delivered himself of the saga of his own doings, with all the arrogance of a young man speaking to a woman. From the beginning he told the tale, the I—I—I's flashing through the records as telegraph-poles fly past the traveler. Maisie listened and nodded her head. The histories of strife and privation did not move her a hair's-breadth. At the end of each canto he would conclude, "And *that* gave me some notion of handling color," or light, or whatever it might be that he had set out to pursue and understand. He led her breathless across half the world, speaking as he had never spoken in his life before. And in the flood-tide of his exaltation there came upon him a great desire to pick up this maiden who nodded her head and said, "I understand. Go on"—to pick her up and to carry her away with him, because she was Maisie, and because she understood, and because she was his right, and a woman to be desired above all women.

Then he checked himself abruptly. "And so I took all I wanted," he said, "and I had to fight for it. Now you tell."

Maisie's tale was almost as gray as her dress. It covered years of patient toil backed by savage pride that would not be broken, though dealers laughed, and fogs delayed work, and Kami was unkind and even sarcastic, and girls in other studios were painfully polite. It had a few bright spots, in pictures accepted at provincial exhibitions, but it wound up with the oft-repeated wail, "And so you see, Dick, I had no success, though I worked so hard."

Then pity filled Dick. Even thus had Maisie spoken when she could not hit the breakwater, half an hour before she had kissed him. And that had happened yesterday.

"Never mind," he said. "I'll tell you something, if you'll believe it." The words were shaping themselves of their own accord. "The whole thing, lock, stock, and barrel, isn't worth one big yellow sea-poppy below Fort Keeling."

Maisie flushed a little. "It's all very well for you to talk, but you've had the success and I haven't."

"Let me talk, then. I know you'll understand. Maisie, dear, it sounds a bit absurd, but those ten years never existed, and I've come back again. It really is just the same. Can't you see? You're alone now and I'm alone. What's the use of worrying? Come to me instead, darling."

Maisie poked the gravel with her parasol. They were sitting on a bench. "I understand," she said slowly. "But I've got my work to do, and I must do it."

"Do it with me, then, dear. I won't interrupt."

"No, I couldn't. It's my work — mine—mine—mine! I've been alone all my life in myself, and I'm not going to belong to anybody except myself. I remember things as well as you do, but that doesn't count. We were babies, then, and we didn't know what was before us. Dick, don't be selfish. I think I see my way to a little success next year. Don't take it away from me."

"I beg your pardon, darling. It's my fault for speaking stupidly. I can't expect you to throw up all your life just because I'm back. I'll go to my own place and wait a little."

"But, Dick, I don't want you to—go—out of—my life, now you've just come back."

"I'm at your orders; forgive me." Dick devoured the troubled little face with his eyes. There was triumph in them, because he could not conceive that Maisie should refuse sooner or later to love him, since he loved her.

"It's wrong of me," said Maisie, more slowly than before; "it's wrong and selfish; but, oh, I've been so lonely! No, you misunderstand. Now I've seen you again—it's absurd, but I want to keep you in my life."

"Naturally. We belong."

"We don't; but you always understood me, and there is so much in my work that you could help me in. You know things and the ways of doing things. You must."

"I do, I fancy, or else I don't know myself. Then I suppose you won't care to lose sight of me altogether, and you want me to help you in your work?"

"Yes; but remember, Dick, nothing will ever come of it. That's why I feel so selfish. Let things stay as they are. I do want your help."

"You shall have it. But let's consider. I must see your pics first, and overhaul your sketches, and find out about your tendencies. You should see what the papers say about my tendencies! Then I'll give you good advice, and you shall paint according. Isn't that it, Maisie?"

Again there was unholy triumph in Dick's eye.

"It's too good of you—much too good. Because you are consoling yourself with what will never happen, and I know that, and yet I wish to keep you. Don't blame me later, please."

"I'm going into the matter with my eyes open. Moreover, the queen can do no wrong. It isn't your selfishness that impresses me. It's your audacity in proposing to make use of me."

"Pooh! You're only Dick—and a print-shop."

"Very good: that's all I am. But, Maisie, you believe, don't you, that I love you? I don't want you to have any false notions about brothers and sisters."

Maisie looked up for a moment and dropped her eyes.

"It's absurd, but—I believe. I wish I could send you away before you get angry with me. But—but the girl that lives with me is red-haired, and an impressionist, and all our notions clash."

"So do ours, I think. Never mind. Three months from to-day we shall be laughing at this together."

Maisie shook her head mournfully. "I knew you wouldn't understand, and it will only hurt you more when you find out. Look at my face, Dick, and tell me what you see."

They stood up and faced each other for a moment. The fog was gathering, and it stifled the roar of the traffic of London beyond the railings. Dick brought all his painfully acquired knowledge of faces to bear on the eyes, mouth, and chin underneath the black velvet toque.

"It's the same Maisie, and it's the same me," he said. "We've both nice little wills of our own, and one or other of us has to be broken. Now about the future. I must come and see your pictures some day—I suppose when the red-haired girl is on the premises."

"Sundays are my best times. You must come on Sundays. There are such heaps of things I want to talk about and ask your advice about. Now I must get back to work."

"Try to find out before next Sunday what I am," said

Dick. "Don't take my word for anything I've told you. Good-by, darling, and bless you."

Maisie stole away like a little gray mouse. Dick watched her till she was out of sight, but he did not hear her say to herself, very soberly, "I'm a wretch—a horrid, selfish wretch. But it's Dick, and Dick will understand."

No one has yet explained what actually happens when an irresistible force meets the immovable post, though many have thought deeply, even as Dick thought. He tried to assure himself that Maisie would be led in a few weeks by his mere presence and discourse to a better way of thinking. Then he remembered much too distinctly her face and all that was written on it.

"If I know anything of heads," he said, "there's everything in that face but love. I shall have to put that in myself; and that chin and mouth won't be won for nothing. But she's right. She knows what she wants, and she's going to get it. What insolence! Me! Of all the people in the wide world, to use me! But then she's Maisie. There's no getting over that fact; and it's good to see her again. This business must have been simmering at the back of my head for years. . . . She'll use me as I used Binat at Port Said. She's quite right. It will hurt a little. I shall have to see her every Sunday—like a young man courting a housemaid. She's sure to come round; and yet—that mouth isn't a yielding mouth. I shall be wanting to kiss her all the time, and I shall have to look at her pictures—I don't even know what sort of work she does yet—and I shall have to talk about Art—Woman's Art! Therefore, particularly and perpetually, damn all varieties of Art. It did me a good turn once, and now it's in my way. I'll go home and do some Art."

Half-way to the studio, Dick was smitten with a terrible thought. The figure of a solitary woman in the fog suggested it.

"She's all alone in London, with a red-haired impressionist girl, who probably has the digestion of an ostrich.

Most red-haired people have. Maisie's a bilious little body. They'll eat like lone women—meals at all hours, and tea with all meals. I remember how the students in Paris used to pig along. She may fall ill at any minute, and I shan't be able to help. Whew! this is ten times worse than owning a wife."

Torpenhow came into the studio at dusk, and looked at Dick with his eyes full of the austere love that springs up between men who have tugged at the same oar together and are yoked by custom and use and the intimacies of toil. This is a good love, and, since it allows, and even encourages, strife, recrimination, and the most brutal sincerity, does not die, but increases, and is proof against any absence and evil conduct.

Dick was silent after he handed Torpenhow the filled pipe of council. He thought of Maisie and her possible needs. It was a new thing to think of anybody but Torpenhow, who could think for himself. Here at last was an outlet for that cash balance. He could adorn Maisie barbarically with jewelry—a thick gold necklace round that little neck, bracelets upon the rounded arms, and rings of price upon her hands—the cool, temperate, ringless hands that he had taken between his own. It was an absurd thought, for Maisie would not even allow him to put one ring on one finger, and she would laugh at golden trappings. It would be better to sit with her quietly in the dusk, his arm round her neck and her face on his shoulder, as befitted husband and wife. Torpenhow's boots creaked that night and his strong voice jarred. Dick's brows contracted and he murmured an evil word because he had taken all his success as a right and part payment for past discomfort, and now he was checked in his stride by a woman who admitted all the success and did not instantly care for him.

"I say, old man," said Torpenhow, who had made one or two vain attempts at conversation, "I haven't put your back up by anything I've said lately, have I?"

"You! No. How could you?"

"Liver out of order?"

"The truly healthy man doesn't know he has a liver. I'm only a bit worried about things in general. I suppose it's my soul."

"The truly healthy man doesn't know he has a soul. What business have you with luxuries of that kind?"

"It came of itself. Who's the man that says that we're all islands shouting lies to each other across seas of misunderstanding?"

"He's right, whoever he is—except about the misunderstanding. I don't think we could misunderstand each other."

The blue smoke curled back from the ceiling in clouds. Then Torpenhow, insinuatingly—

"Dick, is it a woman?"

"Be hanged if it's anything remotely resembling a woman; and if you begin to talk like that, I'll hire a red-brick studio with white paint trimmings, and begonias and petunias and blue Hungarias to play among three-and-sixpenny pot-palms, and I'll mount all my pics in aniline-dye plush plasters, and I'll invite every woman who yelps and maunders and moans over what her guide-books tell her is Art, and you shall receive 'em, Torp—in a snuff-brown velvet coat with yellow trousers and an orange tie. You'll like that."

"Too thin, Dick. A better man than you denied with cursing and swearing on a memorable occasion. You've overdone it, just as he did. It's no business of mine, of course, but it's comforting to think that somewhere under the stars there's saving up for you a tremendous thrashing. Whether it'll come from heaven or earth, I don't know, but it's bound to come and break you up a little. You want hammering."

Dick shivered. "All right," said he. "When this island is disintegrated it will call for you."

"I shall come round the corner and help to disintegrate it some more. We're talking nonsense. Come along to a theater."

CHAPTER SIX

"And you may lead a thousand men,
  Nor ever draw the rein,
But ere ye lead the Faery Queen
  'Twill burst your heart in twain."

He has slipped his foot from the stirrup-bar,
  The bridle from his hand,
And he is bound by hand and foot
  To the Queen o' Faeryland.

—*Sir Hoggie and the Fairies*

SOME weeks later, on a very foggy Sunday, Dick was returning across the Park to his studio. "This," he said, "is evidently the thrashing that Torp meant. It hurts more than I expected; but the queen can do no wrong; and she certainly has some notion of drawing."

He had just finished a Sunday visit to Maisie—always under the green eyes of the red-haired impressionist girl, whom he learned to hate at sight—and was tingling with a keen sense of shame. Sunday after Sunday, putting on his best clothes, he had walked over to the untidy house north of the Park, first to see Maisie's pictures, and then to criticise and advise upon them as he realized that they were productions on which advice would not be wasted. Sunday after Sunday, and his love grew with each visit, he had been compelled to cram his heart back from between his lips when it prompted him to kiss Maisie several times and very much indeed. Sunday after Sunday, the head above the heart had warned him that Maisie was not yet attainable, and that it would be better to talk as connectedly as possible upon the mysteries of the craft that was all in all to her. Therefore it was his fate to endure weekly torture in the studio built out over the clammy back garden of a frail stuffy little villa where nothing was ever in its right place and nobody ever called—to endure and to watch Maisie moving to and fro with the teacups. He abhorred tea, but, since it gave him a little longer time in her presence, he drank it devoutly, and the red-haired girl sat in an untidy heap and eyed him without speaking. She was always watching him. Once, and only once, when she had left the studio, Maisie showed him an album that held a few poor cuttings from provincial papers—the briefest of hurried notes on some of her pictures sent to outlying exhibitions. Dick stooped and kissed the paint-smudged thumb on the open page. "Oh, my love, my love," he muttered, "do you value these things? Chuck 'em into the waste-paper basket!"

"Not till I get something better," said Maisie, shutting the book.

Then Dick, moved by no respect for his public and a very deep regard for the maiden, did deliberately propose, in order to secure more of these coveted cuttings, that he should paint a picture which Maisie should sign.

"That's childish," said Maisie, "and I didn't think it of you. It must be my work. Mine—mine—mine!"

"Go and design decorative medallions for rich brewers' houses. You are thoroughly good at that." Dick was sick and savage.

"Better things than medallions, Dick," was the answer, in tones that recalled a gray-eyed atom's fearless speech to Mrs. Jennett. Dick would have abased himself utterly but that the other girl trailed in.

Next Sunday he laid at Maisie's feet small gifts of pencils that could almost draw of themselves and colors in whose permanence he believed, and he was ostentatiously attentive to the work in hand. It demanded, among other things, an exposition of the faith that was in him. Torpenhow's hair would have stood on end had he heard the fluency with which Dick preached his own gospel of Art.

A month before, Dick would have been equally astonished; but it was Maisie's will and pleasure, and he dragged his words together to make plain to her comprehension all that had been hidden to himself of the whys and wherefores of work. There is not the least difficulty in doing a thing if you only know how to do it; the trouble is to explain your method.

"I could put this right if I had a brush in my hand," said Dick despairingly, over the modeling of a chin that Maisie complained would not "look flesh"—it was the same chin that she had scraped out with the palette-knife—"but I find it almost impossible to teach you. There's a queer grim Dutch touch about your painting that I like; but I've a notion that you're weak in drawing. You foreshorten as though you never used the model, and you've caught Kami's pasty way of dealing with flesh in shadow. Then, again, though you don't know it yourself, you shirk hard work. Suppose you spend some of your time on line alone. Line doesn't allow of shirking. Oils do, and three square inches of flashy, tricky stuff in the corner of a pic sometimes carry a bad thing off—as I know. That's immoral. Do line-work for a little while, and then I can tell more about your powers, as old Kami used to say."

Maisie protested: she did not care for the pure line.

"I know," said Dick. "You want to do your fancy heads with a bunch of flowers at the base of the neck to hide bad modeling." The red-haired girl laughed a little. "You want to do landscapes with cattle knee-deep in grass to hide bad drawing. You want to do a great deal more than you can do. You have sense of color, but you want form. Color's a gift—put it aside and think no more about it—but form you can be drilled into. Now, all your fancy heads—and some of them are very good—will keep you exactly where you are. With line you must go forward or backward, and it will show up all your weaknesses."

"But other people—" began Maisie.

"You mustn't mind what other people do. If their souls were your soul, it would be different. You stand and fall by your own work, remember, and it's waste of time to think of any one else in this battle."

Dick paused, and the longing that had been so resolutely put away came back into his eyes. He looked at Maisie, and the look asked as plainly as words, Was it not time to leave all this barren wilderness of canvas and counsel and join hands with Life and Love?

Maisie assented to the new programme of schooling so adorably that Dick could hardly restrain himself from picking her up then and there and carrying her off to the nearest registrar's office. It was the implicit obedience to the spoken word and the blank indifference to the unspoken desire that baffled and buffeted his soul. He held authority in that house—authority limited, indeed, to one-half of one afternoon in seven, but very real while it lasted. Maisie had learned to appeal to him on many subjects, from the proper packing of pictures to the condition of a smoky chimney. The red-haired girl never consulted him about anything. On the other hand, she accepted his appearances without protest, and watched him always. He discovered that the meals of the establishment were irregular and fragmentary. They depended chiefly on tea, pickles, and biscuit, as he had suspected from the beginning. The girls were supposed to market week and week about, but they lived, with the help of a charwoman, as casually as the young ravens. Maisie spent most of her income on models, and the other girl reveled in apparatus as refined as her work was rough. Armed with knowledge dear-bought from the Docks, Dick warned Maisie that the end of semi-starvation meant the crippling of power to work, which was considerably worse than death. Maisie took the warning, and gave more thought to what she ate and drank. When his trouble returned upon him, as it generally did in the long winter twilights, the remembrance of that little act of domestic authority and his coercion with a hearth-brush of the smoky drawing-room chimney stung Dick like a whip lash.

He conceived that this memory would be the extreme of his sufferings, till, one Sunday, the red-haired girl announced that she would make a study of Dick's head, and that he would be good enough to sit still, and—quite as an afterthought—look at Maisie. He sat, because he could not well refuse, and for the space of half an hour he reflected on all the people in the past whom he had laid open for the purposes of his own craft. He remembered Binat most distinctly—that Binat who had once been an artist and talked about degradation.

It was the merest monochrome roughing in of a head, but it presented the dumb waiting, the longing, and, above all, the hopeless enslavement of the man, in a spirit of bitter mockery.

"I'll buy it," said Dick promptly, "at your own price."

"My price is too high, but I daresay you'll be as grateful if—" The wet sketch fluttered from the girl's hand and fell into the ashes of the studio stove. When she picked it up it was hopelessly smudged.

"Oh, it's all spoiled!" said Maisie. "And I never saw it. Was it like?"

"Thank you," said Dick under his breath to the red-haired girl, and he removed himself swiftly.

"How that man hates me!" said the girl. "And how he loves you, Maisie!"

"What nonsense! I know Dick's very fond of me, but he has his work to do, and I have mine."

"Yes, he is fond of you, and I think he knows there is something in impressionism, after all. Maisie, can't you see?"

"See? See what?"

"Nothing; only, I know that if I could get any man to look at me as that man looks at you, I'd—I don't know what I'd do. But he hates me. Oh, how he hates me!"

She was not altogether correct. Dick's hatred was tempered with gratitude for a few moments, and then he forgot the girl entirely. Only the sense of shame remained, and he was nursing it across the Park in the fog. "There'll be an explosion one of these days," he said wrathfully. "But it isn't Maisie's fault; she's right, quite right, as far as she knows, and I can't blame her. This business has been going on for three months nearly. Three months!—and it cost me ten years' knocking about to get at the notion, the merest raw notion, of my work. That's true; but then I didn't have pins, drawing-pins and palette-knives, stuck into me every Sunday. Oh, my little darling, if ever I break you, somebody will have a very bad time of it. No, she won't. I'd be as big a fool about her as I am now. I'll poison that red-haired girl on my wedding-day—she's unwholesome—and now I'll pass on these present bad times to Torp."

Torpenhow had been moved to lecture Dick more than once lately on the sin of levity, and Dick had listened and replied not a word. In the weeks between the first few Sundays of his discipline he had flung himself savagely into his work, resolved that Maisie should at least know the full stretch of his powers. Then he had taught Maisie that she must not pay the least attention to any work outside her own, and Maisie had obeyed him all too well. She took his counsels, but was not interested in his pictures.

"Your things smell of tobacco and blood," she said once. "Can't you do anything except soldiers?"

"I could do a head of you that would startle you," thought Dick—this was before the red-haired girl had brought him under the guillotine—but he only said, "I am very sorry," and harrowed Torpenhow's soul that evening with blasphemies against Art. Later, insensibly and to a large extent against his own will, he ceased to interest himself in his own work. For Maisie's sake, and to soothe the self-respect that it seemed to him he lost each Sunday, he would not consciously turn out bad stuff, but, since Maisie did not care even for his best, it were better not to do anything at all save wait and mark time between Sunday and Sunday. Torpenhow was disgusted as the weeks went by fruitless, and then attacked him one Sunday evening when Dick felt utterly exhausted after three hours' biting self-restraint in Maisie's presence. There was Language, and Torpenhow withdrew to consult the Nilghai, who had come in to talk continental politics.

"Bone-idle, is he? Careless, and touched in the temper?" said the Nilghai. "It isn't worth worrying over. Dick is probably playing the fool with a woman."

"Isn't that bad enough?"

"No. She may throw him out of gear and knock his work to pieces for a while. She may even turn up here some day and make a scene on the staircase: one never knows. But until Dick speaks of his own accord you had better not touch him. He is no easy-tempered man to handle."

"No; I wish he were. He is such an aggressive, cock-sure, you-be-damned fellow."

"He'll get that knocked out of him in time. He must learn that he can't storm up and down the world with a box of moist tubes and a slick brush. You're fond of him?"

"I'd take any punishment that's in store for him if I could; but the worst of it is, no man can save his brother."

"No, and the worser of it is, there is no discharge in this war. Dick must learn his lesson like the rest of us. Talking of war, there'll be trouble in the Balkans in the spring."

"That trouble is long coming. I wonder if we could drag Dick out there when it comes off?"

Dick entered the room soon afterward, and the question was put to him. "Not good enough," he said shortly. "I'm too comf'y where I am."

"Surely you aren't taking all the stuff in the papers seriously?" said the Nilghai. "Your vogue will be ended in less than six months—the public will know your touch and go on to something new—and where will you be then?"

"Here, in England."

"When you might be doing decent work among us out there? Nonsense! I shall go, the Keneu will be there, Torp will be there, Cassavetti will be there, and the whole lot of us will be there, and we shall have as much as ever we can do, with unlimited fighting and the chance for you of seeing things that would make the reputation of three Verestchagins."

"Um!" said Dick, pulling at his pipe.

"You prefer to stay here and imagine that all the world is gaping at your pictures? Just think how full an average man's life is of his own pursuits and pleasures. When twenty thousand of him find time to look up between mouthfuls and grunt something about something they aren't the least interested in, the net result is called fame, reputation, or notoriety, according to the taste and fancy of the speller, my lord."

"I know that as well as you do. Give me credit for a little gumption."

"Be hanged if I do!"

"*Be* hanged, then; you probably will be—for a spy, by excited Turks. Heigh-ho! I'm weary, dead weary, and virtue has gone out of me." Dick dropped into a chair, and was fast asleep in a minute.

"That's a bad sign," said the Nilghai, in an undertone.

Torpenhow picked the pipe from the waistcoat where it was beginning to burn, and put a pillow behind the head. "We can't help; we can't help," he said. "It's a good ugly sort of old cocoanut, and I'm fond of it. There's the scar of the wipe he got when he was cut over in the square."

"Shouldn't wonder if that has made him a trifle mad."

"I should. He's a most businesslike madman."

Then Dick began to snore furiously.

"Oh, here, no affection can stand this sort of thing. Wake up, Dick, and go and sleep somewhere else, if you intend to make a noise about it."

"When a cat has been out on the tiles all night," said the Nilghai in his beard, "I notice that she usually sleeps all day. This is natural history."

Dick staggered away rubbing his eyes and yawning. In the night-watches he was overtaken with an idea, so simple and so luminous that he wondered he had never conceived it before. It was full of craft. He would seek Maisie on a week-day—would suggest an excursion, and would take her by train to Fort Keeling, over the very ground that they two had trodden together ten years ago.

"As a general rule," he explained to his chin-lathered reflection in the morning, "it isn't safe to cross an old trail twice. Things remind one of things, and a cold wind gets up, and you feel sad; but this is an exception to every rule that ever was. I'll go to Maisie at once."

Fortunately, the red-haired girl was out shopping when he arrived, and Maisie in a paint-spattered blouse was warring with her canvas. She was not pleased to see him; for week-day visits were a stretch of the bond; and it needed all his courage to explain his errand.

"I know you've been working too hard," he concluded, with an air of authority. "If you do that, you'll break down. You had much better come."

"Where?" said Maisie wearily. She had been standing before her easel too long, and was very tired.

"Anywhere you please. We'll take a train to-morrow and see where it stops. We'll have lunch somewhere, and I'll bring you back in the evening."

"If there's a good working light to-morrow I lose a day." Maisie balanced the heavy white chestnut palette irresolutely.

Dick bit back an oath that was hurrying to his lips. He had not yet learned patience with the maiden to whom her work was all in all.

"You'll lose ever so many more, dear, if you use every hour of working light. Overwork's only murderous idleness. Don't be unreasonable. I'll call for you to-morrow after breakfast early."

"But surely you are going to ask—"

"No, I am not. I want you and nobody else. Besides, she hates me as much as I hate her. She won't care to come. To-morrow, then; and pray that we get sunshine."

Dick went away delighted, and by consequence did no work whatever. He strangled a wild desire to order a special train, but bought a great gray kangaroo cloak lined with glossy black marten, and then retired into himself to consider things.

"I'm going out for the day to-morrow with Dick," said Maisie to the red-haired girl when the latter returned, tired, from marketing in the Edgware Road.

"He deserves it. I shall have the studio floor thoroughly scrubbed while you're away. It's very dirty."

Maisie had enjoyed no sort of holiday for months, and looked forward to the little excitement, but not without misgivings.

"There's nobody nicer than Dick when he talks sensibly," she thought, "but I'm sure he'll be silly and worry me, and I'm sure I can't tell him anything he'd like to hear. If he'd only be sensible I should like him so much better."

Dick's eyes were full of joy when he made his appearance next morning and saw Maisie, gray-ulstered and black-velvet-hatted, standing in the hallway. Palaces of marble, and not sordid imitations of grained wood, were surely the fittest background for such a divinity. The red-haired girl drew her into the studio for a moment and kissed her hurriedly. Maisie's eyebrows climbed to the top of her forehead; she was altogether unused to these demonstrations. "Mind my hat," she said, hurrying away, and ran down the steps to Dick waiting by the hansom.

"Are you quite warm enough? Are you sure you wouldn't like some more breakfast? Put this cloak over your knees."

"I'm quite comf'y, thanks. Where are we going, Dick? Oh, do stop singing like that. People will think we're mad."

"Let 'em think—if the exertion doesn't kill them. They don't know who we are, and I'm sure I don't care who they are. My faith, Maisie, you're looking lovely!"

Maisie stared directly in front of her and did not reply. The wind of a keen clear winter morning had put color into her cheeks. Overhead, the creamy-yellow smoke-clouds were thinning away one by one against a pale-blue sky, and the improvident sparrows broke off from water-spout committees and cab-rank cabals to clamor of the coming of spring.

"It will be lovely weather in the country," said Dick.

"But where are we going?"

"Wait and see."

They stopped at Victoria, and Dick sought tickets. For less than half the fraction of an instant it occurred to Maisie, comfortably settled by the waiting-room fire, that it was much more pleasant to send a man to the booking-office than to elbow one's own way through the crowd. Dick put her into a Pullman—solely on account of the warmth there; and she regarded the extravagance with grave scandalized eyes as the train moved out into the country.

"I wish I knew where we are going," she repeated for the twentieth time. The name of a well-remembered station flashed by, toward the end of the run, and Maisie was enlightened.

"Oh, Dick, you villain!"

"Well, I thought you might like to see the place again. You haven't been here since old times, have you?"

"No. I never cared to see Mrs. Jennett again; and she was all that was ever there."

"Not quite. Look out a minute. There's the windmill above the potato-fields; they haven't built villas there yet; d'you remember when I shut you up in it?"

"Yes. How she beat you for it! I never told it was you."

"She guessed. I jammed a stick under the door and told you that I was burying Amomma alive in the potatoes, and you believed me. You had a trusting nature in those days."

They laughed and leaned to look out, identifying ancient landmarks with many reminiscences. Dick fixed his weather eye on the curve of Maisie's cheek, very near his own, and watched the blood rise under the clear skin. He congratulated himself upon his cunning, and looked that the evening would bring him a great reward.

When the train stopped they went out to look at an old town with new eyes. First, but from a distance, they regarded the house of Mrs. Jennett.

"Suppose she should come out now, what would you do?" said Dick, with mock terror.

"I should make a face."

"Show, then," said Dick, dropping into the speech of childhood.

Maisie made that face in the direction of the mean little villa, and Dick laughed aloud.

" 'This is disgraceful,' " said Masie, mimicking Mrs. Jennett's tone. " 'Maisie, you run in at once, and learn the collect, gospel, and epistle for the next three Sundays. After all I've taught you, too, and three helps every Sunday at dinner! Dick's always leading you into mischief. If you aren't a gentleman, Dick, you might at least—"

The sentence ended abruptly. Maisie remembered when it had last been used.

" 'Try to behave like one,' " said Dick promptly. "Quite right. Now we'll get some lunch and go on to Fort Keeling —unless you'd rather drive there?"

"We must walk, out of respect to the place. How little changed it all is!"

They turned in the direction of the sea through unaltered streets, and the influence of old things lay upon them. Presently they passed a confectioner's shop much considered in the days when their joint pocket-money amounted to a shilling a week.

"Dick, have you any pennies?" said Maisie, half to herself.

"Only three; and if you think you're going to have two of 'em to buy peppermints with, you're wrong. She says peppermints aren't ladylike."

Again they laughed, and again the color came into Maisie's cheeks as the blood boiled through Dick's heart. After a large lunch they went down to the beach and to Fort Keeling across the waste, wind-bitten land that no builder had thought it worth his while to defile. The winter breeze came in from the sea and sang about their ears.

"Maisie," said Dick, "your nose is getting a crude Prussian blue at the tip. I'll race you as far as you please for as much as you please."

She looked round cautiously, and with a laugh set off, swiftly as the ulster allowed, till she was out of breath.

"We used to run miles," she panted. "It's absurd that we can't run now."

"Old age, dear. This it is to get fat and sleek in town. When I wished to pull your hair you generally ran for three miles, shrieking at the top of your voice. I ought to know, because those shrieks were meant to call up Mrs. Jennett with a cane and—"

"Dick, I never got you a beating on purpose in my life."

"No, of course you never did. Good heavens! look at the sea."

"Why, it's the same as ever!" said Maisie.

Torpenhow had gathered from Mr. Beeton that Dick, properly dressed and shaved, had left the house at half-past eight in the morning with a traveling-rug over his arm. The Nilghai rolled in at midday for chess and polite conversation.

"It's worse than anything I imagined," said Torpenhow.

"Oh, the everlasting Dick, I suppose! You fuss over him like a hen with one chick. Let him run riot if he thinks it'll amuse him. You can whip a young pup off feather, but you can't whip a young man."

"It isn't a woman. It's one woman; and it's a girl."

"Where's your proof?"

"He got up and went out at eight this morning—got up in the middle of the night, by Jove! a thing he never does except when he's on service. Even then, remember, we had to kick him out of his blankets before the fight began at El-Maghrib. It's disgusting."

"It looks odd; but maybe he's decided to buy a horse at last. He might get up for that, mightn't he?"

"Buy a blazing wheelbarrow! He'd have told us if there was a horse in the wind. It's a girl."

"Don't be certain. Perhaps it's only a married woman."

"Dick has some sense of humor, if you haven't. Who gets up in the gray dawn to call on another man's wife? It's a girl."

"Let it be a girl, then. She may teach him that there's somebody else in the world besides himself."

"She'll spoil his hand. She'll waste his time, and she'll marry him, and ruin his work forever. He'll be a respectable married man before we can stop him, and—he'll never go on the long trail again."

"All quite possible, but the earth won't spin the other way when it happens. . . . Ho! ho! I'd give something to see Dick 'go wooing with the boys.' Don't worry about it. These things be with Allah, and we can only look on. Get the chessmen."

The red-haired girl was lying down in her own room, staring at the ceiling. The footsteps of people on the pavement sounded, as they grew indistinct in the distance, like a many-times-repeated kiss that was all one long kiss. Her hands were by her side, and they opened and shut savagely from time to time.

The charwoman in charge of the scrubbing of the studio knocked at her door: "Beg y' pardon, miss, but in cleanin' of a floor there's two, not to say three, kind of soap, which is yaller, an' mottled, an' disinfectink. Now, jist before I took my pail into the passage I thought it would be pre'aps jest as well if I was to come up 'ere an' ask you what sort of soap you was wishful that I should use on them boards. The yaller soap, miss—"

There was nothing in the speech to have caused the paroxysm of fury that drove the red-haired girl into the middle of the room, almost shouting—

"Do you suppose *I* care what you use? Any kind will do! —*any* kind!"

The woman fled, and the red-haired girl looked at her own reflection in the glass for an instant and covered her face with her hands. It was as though she had shouted some shameless secret aloud.

CHAPTER SEVEN

Roses red and roses white
Plucked I for my love's delight.
She would none of all my posies—
Bade me gather her blue roses.

Half the world I wandered through,
Seeking where such flowers grew;
Half the world unto my quest
Answered but with laugh and jest.

It may be beyond the grave
She shall find what she would have.
Oh, 'twas but an idle quest—
Roses white and red are best!

—*Blue Roses*

INDEED the sea had not changed. Its waters were low on the mud-banks, and the Marazion bell-buoy clanked and swung in the tideway. On the white beach-sand dried stumps of sea-poppy shivered and chattered together.

"I don't see the old breakwater," said Maisie under her breath.

"Let's be thankful that we have as much as we have. I don't believe they've mounted a single new gun on the fort since we were here. Come and look."

They came to the glacis of Fort Keeling, and sat down in a nook sheltered from the wind under the tarred throat of a forty-pounder cannon.

"Now, if Amomma were only here!" said Maisie.

For a long time both were silent. Then Dick took Maisie's hand and called her by her name.

She shook her head and looked out to sea.

"Maisie, darling, doesn't it make any difference?"

"No!" between clinched teeth. "I'd—I'd tell you if it did; but it doesn't. Oh, Dick, please be sensible."

"Don't you think that it ever will?"

"No, I'm sure it won't."

"Why?"

Maisie rested her chin on her hand, and, still regarding the sea, spoke hurriedly:

"I know what you want perfectly well, but I can't give it you, Dick. It isn't my fault; indeed it isn't. If I felt that I could care for any one— But I don't feel that I care. I simply don't understand what the feeling means."

"Is that true, dear?"

"You've been very good to me, Dickie; and the only way I can pay you back is by speaking the truth. I daren't tell a fib. I despise myself quite enough as it is."

"What in the world for?"

"Because—because I take everything that you give me and I give you nothing in return. It's mean and selfish of me, and whenever I think of it it worries me."

"Understand once for all, then, that I can manage my own affairs, and if I choose to do anything you aren't to blame. You haven't a single thing to reproach yourself with, darling."

"Yes, I have, and talking only makes it worse."

"Then don't talk about it."

"How can I help myself? If you find me alone for a minute you are always talking about it; and when you aren't you look it. You don't know how I despise myself sometimes."

"Great goodness!" said Dick, nearly jumping to his feet. "Speak the truth now, Maisie, if you never speak it again! Do I—does this worrying bore you?"

"No. It does not."

"You'd tell me if it did?"

"I should let you know, I think."

"Thank you. The other thing is fatal. But you must learn to forgive a man when he's in love. He's always a nuisance. You must have known that?"

Maisie did not consider the last question worth answering, and Dick was forced to repeat it.

"There were other men, of course. They always worried just when I was in the middle of my work, and wanted me to listen to them."

"Did you listen?"

"At first; and they couldn't understand why I didn't care. And they used to praise my pictures; and I thought they meant it. I used to be proud of the praise, and tell Kami, and—I shall never forget—once Kami laughed at me."

"You don't like being laughed at, Maisie, do you?"

"I hate it. I never laugh at other people unless—unless they do bad work. Dick, tell me honestly what you think of my pictures generally—of everything of mine that you've seen."

"'Honest, honest, and honest over!'" quoted Dick from a catchword of long ago. "Tell me what Kami always says."

Maisie hesitated. "He—he says that there is feeling in them."

"How dare you tell me a fib like that? Remember, I was under Kami for two years. I know exactly what he says."

"It isn't a fib."

"It's worse; it's a half-truth. Kami says, when he puts his head on one side—so—'*Il y a du sentiment, mais il n'y a pas de parti pris.*'" He rolled the *r* threateningly, as Kami used to do.

"Yes, that is what he says; and I'm beginning to think that he is right."

"Certainly he is." Dick admitted that two people in the world could do and say no wrong. Kami was the man.

"And now you say the same thing. It's so disheartening."

"I'm sorry, but you asked me to speak the truth. Besides, I love you too much to pretend about your work. It's strong, it's patient sometimes—not always—and sometimes there's power in it, but there's no special reason why it should be done at all. At least, that's how it strikes me."

"There's no special reason why anything in the world

should ever be done. You know that as well as I do. I only want success."

"You're going the wrong way to get it, then. Hasn't Kami ever told you so?"

"Don't quote Kami to me. I want to know what you think. My work's bad, to begin with."

"I didn't say that, and I don't think it."

"It's amateurish, then."

"That it most certainly is not. You're a work-woman, darling, to your boot-heels, and I respect you for that."

"You don't laugh at me behind my back?"

"No, dear. You see, you are more to me than any one else. Put this cloak thing round you, or you'll get chilled."

Maisie wrapped herself in the soft marten skins, turning the gray kangaroo fur to the outside.

"This is delicious," she said, rubbing her chin thoughtfully along the fur. "Well? Why am I wrong in trying to get a little success?"

"Just because you try. Don't you understand, darling? Good work has nothing to do with—doesn't belong to—the person who does it. It's put into him or her from outside."

"But how does that affect—"

"Wait a minute. All we can do is to learn how to do our work, to be masters of our materials instead of servants, and never to be afraid of anything."

"I understand that."

"Everything else comes from outside ourselves. Very good. If we sit down quietly to work out notions that are sent to us, we may or we may not do something that isn't bad. A great deal depends on being master of the bricks and mortar of the trade. But the instant we begin to think about success and the effect of our work—to play with one eye on the gallery—we lose power and touch and everything else. At least that's how I have found it. Instead of being quiet and giving every power you possess to your work, you're fretting over something which you can neither help nor hinder by a minute. See?"

"It's so easy for you to talk in that way. People like what you do. Don't you ever think about the gallery?"

"Much too often; but I'm always punished for it by loss of power. It's as simple as the Rule of Three. If we make light of our work by using it for our own ends, our work will make light of us, and, as we're the weaker, we shall suffer."

"I don't treat my work lightly. You know that it's everything to me."

"Of course; but, whether you realize it or not, you give two strokes for yourself to one for your work. It isn't your fault, darling. I do exactly the same thing, and know that I'm doing it. Most of the French schools, and all the schools here, drive the students to work for their own credit, and for the sake of their pride. I was told that all the world was interested in my work, and everybody at Kami's talked turpentine, and I honestly believed that the world needed elevating and influencing, and all manner of impertinences, by my brushes. By Jove, I actually believed that! When my little head was bursting with a notion that I couldn't handle because I hadn't sufficient knowledge of my craft, I used to run about wondering at my own magnificence and getting ready to astonish the world."

"But surely one can do that sometimes?"

"Very seldom with malice aforethought, darling. And when it's done it's such a tiny thing, and the world's so big, and all but a millionth part of it doesn't care. Maisie, come with me and I'll show you something of the size of the world. One can no more avoid working than eating—that goes on by itself—but try to see what you are working for. I know such little heavens that I could take you to—islands tucked away under the Line. You sight them after weeks of crashing through water as black as black marble because it's so deep, and you sit in the forechains day after day and see the sun rise almost afraid because the sea's so lonely."

"Who is afraid?—you, or the sun?"

"The sun, of course. And there are noises under the sea, and sounds overhead in a clear sky. Then you find your island alive with hot moist orchids that make mouths at you and can do everything except talk. There's a waterfall in it three hundred feet high, just like a silver of green jade laced with silver; and millions of wild bees live up in the rocks; and you can hear the fat cocoanuts falling from the palms; and you order an ivory-white servant to sling you a long yellow hammock with tassels on it like ripe maize, and you put up your feet and hear the bees hum and the water fall till you go to sleep."

"Can one work there?"

"Certainly. One must do something always. You hang your canvas up in a palm-tree and let the parrots criticise. When they scuffle you heave a ripe custard apple at them, and it bursts in a lather of cream. There are hundreds of places. Come and see them."

"I don't quite like that place. It sounds lazy. Tell me another."

"What do you think of a big, red, dead city built of red sandstone, with raw green aloes growing between the stones, lying out neglected on honey-colored sands? There are forty dead kings there, Maisie, each in a gorgeous tomb finer than all the others. You look at the palaces and streets and shops and tanks, and think that men must live there, till you find a wee gray squirrel rubbing its nose all alone in the market-place, and a jeweled peacock struts out of a carved doorway and spreads its tail against a marble screen as fine pierced as point-lace. Then a monkey—a little black monkey—walks through the main square to get a drink from a tank forty feet deep. He slides down the creepers to the water's edge, and a friend holds him by the tail, in case he should fall in."

"Is all that true?"

"I have been there and seen. Then evening comes, and the lights change till it's just as though you stood in the heart of a king-opal. A little before sundown, as punctually as clockwork, a big bristly wild boar, with all his family following, trots through the city gate, churning the foam on his tusks. You climb on the shoulder of a blind black stone god and watch that pig choose himself a palace for the night and stump in wagging his tail. Then the night-wind gets up, and the sands move, and you hear the desert outside the city singing, 'Now I lay me down to sleep,' and everything is dark till the moon rises. Maisie darling, come with me and see what the world is really like. It's very lovely, and it's very horrible—but I won't let you see anything horrid—and it doesn't care your life or mine for pictures or anything else except doing its own work and making love. Come, and I'll show you how to brew sangaree, and sling a hammock, and—oh, thousands of things, and you'll see for yourself what color means, and we'll find out together what love means, and then, maybe, we shall be allowed to do some good work. Come away!"

"Why?" said Maisie.

"How can you do anything until you have seen everything, or as much as you can? And besides, darling, I love you. Come along with me. You have no business here; you don't belong to this place; you're half a gypsy—your face tells that; and I—even the smell of open water makes me restless. Come across the sea and be happy!"

He had risen to his feet, and stood in the shadow of the gun, looking down at the girl. The very short winter afternoon had worn away, and, before they knew, the winter moon was walking the untroubled sea. Long ruled lines of silver showed where a ripple of the rising tide was turning over the mud-banks. The wind had dropped, and in the intense stillness they could hear a donkey cropping the frosty grass many yards away. A faint beating, like that of a muffled drum, came out of the moon-haze.

"What's that?" said Maisie quickly. "It sounds like a heart beating. Where is it?"

Dick was so angry at this sudden wrench to his pleadings that he could not trust himself to speak, and in this silence caught the sound. Maisie from her seat under the gun watched him with a certain amount of fear. She wished so much that he would be sensible and cease to worry her with over-sea emotion that she both could and could not understand. She was not prepared, however, for the change in his face as he listened.

"It's a steamer," he said—"a twin-screw steamer, by the beat. I can't make her out, but she must be standing very close inshore. Ah!" as the red of a rocket streaked the haze, "she's standing in to signal before she clears the Channel."

"Is it a wreck?" said Maisie, to whom these words were as Greek.

Dick's eyes were turned to the sea. "Wreck! What nonsense! She's only reporting herself. Red rocket forward—there's a green light aft now, and two red rockets from the bridge."

"What does that mean?"

"It's the signal of the Cross Keys Line running to Australia. I wonder which steamer it is." The note of his voice had changed; he seemed to be talking to himself, and Maisie did not approve of it. The moonlight broke the haze for a moment, touching the black sides of a long steamer working down Channel. "Four masts and three funnels—she's in deep draught, too. That must be the 'Barralong,' or the 'Bhutia.' No, the 'Bhutia' has a clipper bow. It's the 'Barralong,' to Australia. She'll lift the Southern Cross in a week—lucky old tub!—oh, lucky old tub!"

He stared intently, and moved up the slope of the fort to get a better view, but the mist on the sea thickened again, and the beating of the screws grew fainter. Maisie called to him a little angrily, and he returned, still keeping his eyes to seaward. "Have you ever seen the Southern Cross blazing right over your head?" he asked. "It's superb!"

"No," she said shortly, "and I don't want to. If you think it's so lovely, why don't you go and see it yourself?"

She raised her face from the soft blackness of the marten skins about her throat, and her eyes shone like diamonds. The moonlight on the gray kangaroo fur turned it to frosted silver of the coldest.

"By Jove, Maisie, you look like a little heathen idol tucked up there." The eyes showed that they did not appreciate the compliment. "I'm sorry," he continued. "The Southern Cross isn't worth looking at unless some one helps you to see. That steamer's out of hearing."

"Dick," she said quietly, "suppose I were to come to you now—be quiet a minute—just as I am, and caring for you just as much as I do."

"Not as a brother, though? You said you didn't—in the Park."

"I never had a brother. Suppose I said, 'Take me to those places, and in time, perhaps, I might really care for you,' what would you do?"

"Send you straight back to where you came from, in a cab. No, I wouldn't; I'd let you walk. But you couldn't do it, dear. And I wouldn't run the risk. You're worth waiting for till you can come without reservation."

"Do you honestly believe that?"

"I have a hazy sort of idea that I do. Has it never struck you in that light?"

"Ye—es. I feel so wicked about it."

"Wickeder than usual?"

"You don't know all I think. It's almost too awful to tell."

"Never mind. You promised to tell me the truth—at least."

"It's so ungrateful of me, but—but, though I know you care for me, and I like to have you with me, I'd—I'd even sacrifice you, if that would bring me what I want."

"My poor little darling! I know that state of mind. It doesn't lead to good work."

"You aren't angry? Remember, I do despise myself."

"I'm not exactly flattered—I had guessed as much before—but I'm not angry. I'm sorry for you. Surely you ought to have left a littleness like that behind you, years ago."

"You've no right to patronize me! I only want what I

have worked for so long. It came to *you* without any trouble, and—and I don't think it's fair."

"What can I do? I'd give ten years of my life to get you what you want. But I can't help you; even I can't help."

A murmur of dissent from Maisie. He went on—

"And I know by what you have just said that you're on the wrong road to success. It isn't got at by sacrificing other people—I've had that much knocked into me; you must sacrifice yourself, and live under orders, and never think for yourself, and never have real satisfaction in your work except just at the beginning, when you're reaching out after a notion."

"How can you believe all that?"

"There's no question of belief or disbelief. That's the law, and you take it or refuse it as you please. I try to obey, but I can't, and then my work turns bad on my hands. Under any circumstances, remember, four-fifths of everybody's work must be bad. But the remnant is worth the trouble for its own sake."

"Isn't it nice to get credit even for bad work?"

"It's much too nice. But— May I tell you something? It isn't a pretty tale, but you're so like a man that I forget when I'm talking to you."

"Tell me."

"Once when I was out in the Soudan I went over some ground that we had been fighting on for three days. There were twelve hundred dead; and we hadn't time to bury them."

"How ghastly!"

"I had been at work on a big double-sheet sketch, and I was wondering what people would think of it at home. The sight of that field taught me a good deal. It looked just like a bed of horrible toadstools in all colors, and—I'd never seen men in bulk go back to their beginnings before. So I began to understand that men and women were only material to work with, and that what they said or did was of no consequence. See? Strictly speaking, you might just as well put your ear down to the palette to catch what your colors are saying."

"Dick, that's disgraceful!"

"Wait a minute. I said, strictly speaking. Unfortunately, everybody must be either a man or a woman."

"I'm glad you allow that much."

"In your case I don't. You aren't a woman. But ordinary people, Maisie, must behave and work as such. That's what makes me so savage." He hurled a pebble toward the sea as he spoke. "I know that it is outside my business to care what people say; I can see that it spoils my output if I listen to 'em; and yet, confound it all"—another pebble flew seaward—"I can't help purring when I'm rubbed the right way. Even when I can see on a man's forehead that he is lying his way through a clump of pretty speeches, those lies make me happy and play the mischief with my hand."

"And when he doesn't say pretty things?"

"Then, belovedest"—Dick grinned—"I forget that I am the steward of these gifts, and I want to make that man love and appreciate my work with a thick stick. It's too humiliating altogether; but I suppose even if one were an angel and painted humans altogether from outside, one would lose in touch what one gained in grip."

Maisie laughed at the idea of Dick as an angel.

"But you seem to think," she said, "that everything nice spoils your hand."

"I don't think. It's the law—just the same as it was at Mrs. Jennett's. Everything that is nice does spoil your hand. I'm glad you see so clearly."

"I don't like the view."

"Nor I. But—have got orders: what can do? Are you strong enough to face it alone?"

"I suppose I must."

"Let me help, darling. We can hold each other very tight and try to walk straight. We shall blunder horribly, but it will be better than stumbling apart. Maisie, can't you see reason?"

"I don't think we should get on together. We should be two of a trade, so we should never agree."

"How I should like to meet the man who made that proverb! He lived in a cave and ate raw bear, I fancy. I'd make him chew his own arrow-heads. Well?"

"I should be only half married to you. I should worry and fuss about my work, as I do now. Four days out of the seven I'm not fit to speak to."

"You talk as if no one else in the world had ever used a brush. D'you suppose that I don't know the feeling of worry and bother and can't-get-at-ness? You're lucky if you only have it four days out of the seven. What difference would that make?"

"A great deal—if you had it too."

"Yes, but I could respect it. Another man might not. He might laugh at you. But there's no use talking about it. If you can think in that way you can't care for me—yet."

The tide had nearly covered the mud-banks, and twenty little ripples broke on the beach before Maisie chose to speak.

"Dick," she said slowly, "I believe very much that you are better than I am."

"This doesn't seem to bear on the argument—but in what way?"

"I don't quite know, but in what you said about work and things; and then you're so patient. Yes, you're better than I am."

Dick considered rapidly the murkiness of an average man's life. There was nothing in the review to fill him with a sense of virtue. He lifted the hem of the cloak to his lips.

"Why," said Maisie, making as though she had not noticed, "can you see things that I can't? I don't believe what you believe; but you're right, I believe."

"If I've seen anything, God knows I couldn't have seen it but for you, and I know that I couldn't have said it except to you. You seemed to make everything clear for a minute;

but I don't practice what I preach. You would help me. . . . There are only us two in the world for all purposes, and—and you like to have me with you?"

"Of course I do. I wonder if you can realize how utterly lonely I am!"

"Darling, I think I can."

"Two years ago, when I first took the little house, I used to walk up and down the back-garden trying to cry. I never can cry. Can you?"

"It's some time since I tried. What was the trouble? Overwork?"

"I don't know; but I used to dream that I had broken down, and had no money, and was starving in London. I thought about it all day, and it frightened me—oh, how it frightened me!"

"I know that fear. It's the most terrible of all. It wakes me up in the night sometimes. You oughtn't to know anything about it."

"How do *you* know?"

"Never mind. Is your three hundred a year safe?"

"It's in Consols."

"Very well. If any one comes to you and recommends a better investment—even if I should come to you—don't you listen. Never shift the money for a minute, and never lend a penny of it—even to the red-haired girl."

"Don't scold me so! I'm not likely to be foolish."

"The earth is full of men who'd sell their souls for three hundred a year; and women come and talk, and borrow a five-pound note here and a ten-pound note there; and a woman has no conscience in a money debt. Stick to your money, Maisie; for there's nothing more ghastly in the world than poverty in London. It's scared me. By Jove, it put the fear into *me!* And one oughtn't to be afraid of anything."

To each man is appointed his particular dread—the terror that, if he does not fight against it, must cow him even to the loss of his manhood. Dick's experience of the sordid misery of want had entered into the deeps of him, and, lest he might find virtue too easy, that memory stood behind him, tempting to shame, when dealers came to buy his wares. As the Nilghai quaked against his will at the still green water of a lake or a mill-dam, as Torpenhow flinched before any white arm that could cut or stab and loathed himself for flinching, Dick feared the poverty he had once tasted half in jest. His burden was heavier than the burdens of his companions.

Maisie watched the face working in the moonlight.

"You've plenty of pennies now," she said soothingly.

"I shall never get enough," he began, with vicious emphasis. Then, laughing, "I shall always be threepence short in my accounts."

"Why threepence?"

"I carried a man's bag once from Liverpool Street Station to Blackfriars Bridge. It was a sixpenny job—you needn't laugh; indeed it was—and I wanted the money desperately. He only gave me threepence; and he hadn't even the decency to pay in silver. Whatever money I make, I shall never get that odd threepence out of the world."

This was not language befitting the man who had preached of the sanctity of work. It jarred on Maisie, who preferred her payment in applause, which, since all men desire it, must be of the right. She hunted for her little purse and gravely took out a threepenny bit.

"There it is," she said. "I'll pay you, Dickie; and don't worry any more; it isn't worth while. Are you paid?"

"I am," said the very human apostle of fair craft, taking the coin. "I'm paid a thousand times, and we'll close that account. It shall live on my watch-chain; and you're an angel, Maisie."

"I'm very cramped, and I'm feeling a little cold. Good gracious! the cloak is all white, and so is your mustache! I never knew it was so chilly."

A light frost lay white on the shoulder of Dick's ulster. He, too, had forgotten the state of the weather. They laughed together, and with that laugh ended all serious discourse.

They ran inland across the waste to warm themselves, then turned to look at the glory of the full tide under the moonlight and the intense black shadows of the furze-bushes. It was an additional joy to Dick that Maisie could see color even as he saw it—could see the blue in the white of the mist, the violet that is in gray palings, and all things else as they are—not of one hue, but a thousand. And the moonlight came into Maisie's soul, so that she, usually reserved, chattered of herself and of the things she took interest in—of Kami, wisest of teachers, and of the girls in the studio—of the Poles, who will kill themselves with overwork if they are not checked; of the French, who talk at great length of much more than they will ever accomplish; of the slovenly English, who toil hopelessly and cannot understand that inclination does not imply power; of the Americans, whose rasping voices in the hush of a hot afternoon strain tense-drawn nerves to breaking-point, and whose suppers lead to indigestion; of tempestuous Russians, neither to hold nor to bind, who tell the girls ghost-stories till the girls shriek; of stolid Germans, who come to learn one thing, and, having mastered that much, stolidly go away and copy pictures for evermore. Dick listened enraptured because it was Maisie who spoke. He knew the old life.

"It hasn't changed much," he said. "Do they still steal colors at lunch-time?"

"Not steal. Attract is the word. Of course they do. I'm good—I only attract ultramarine; but there are students who'd attract flake-white."

"I've done it myself. You can't help it when the palettes are hung up. Every color is common property once it runs down—even though you do start it with a drop of oil. It teaches people not to waste their tubes."

"I should like to attract some of your colors, Dick. Perhaps I might catch your success with them."

"I mustn't say a bad word, but I should like to. What

in the world, which you've just missed a lovely chance of seeing, does success or want of success, or a three-storied success, matter compared with— No, I won't open that question again. It's time to go back to town."

"I'm sorry, Dick, but—"

"You're much more interested in that than you are in me."

"I don't know. I don't think I am."

"What will you give me if I tell you a sure short-cut to everything you want—the trouble and the fuss and the tangle and all the rest? Will you promise to obey me?"

"Of course."

"In the first place, you must never forget a meal because you happen to be at work. You forgot your lunch twice last week," said Dick, at a venture, for he knew with whom he was dealing.

"No, no—only once, really."

"That's bad enough. And you mustn't take a cup of tea and a biscuit in place of a regular dinner, because dinner happens to be a trouble."

"You're making fun of me!"

"I never was more in earnest in my life. Oh, my love, my love, hasn't it dawned on you yet what you are to me? Here's the whole earth in a conspiracy to give you a chill, or run over you, or drench you to the skin, or cheat you out of your money, or let you die of overwork and underfeeding, and I haven't the mere right to look after you. Why, I don't even know if you have sense enough to put on warm things when the weather's cold."

"Dick, you're the most awful boy to talk to—really! How do you suppose I managed when you were away?"

"I wasn't here, and I didn't know. But now I'm back I'd give everything I have for the right of telling you to come in out of the rain."

"Your success too?"

This time it cost Dick a severe struggle to refrain from bad words.

"As Mrs. Jennett used to say, you're a trial, Maisie!

You've been cooped up in the schools too long, and you think every one is looking at you. There aren't twelve hundred people in the world who understand pictures. The others pretend and don't care. Remember, I've seen twelve hundred men dead in toadstool-beds. It's only the voice of the tiniest little fraction of people that makes success. The real world doesn't care a tinker's—doesn't care a bit. For aught you or I know, every man in the world may be arguing with a Maisie of his own."

"Poor Maisie!"

"Poor Dick, I think. Do you believe while he's fighting for what's dearer than his life he wants to look at a picture? And even if he did, and if all the world did, and a thousand million people rose up and shouted hymns to my honor and glory, would that make up to me for the knowledge that you were out shopping in the Edgware Road on a rainy day without an umbrella? Now we'll go to the station."

"But you said on the beach—" persisted Maisie with a certain fear.

Dick groaned aloud: "Yes, I know what I said. My work is everything I have, or am, or hope to be, to me, and I believe I've learned the law that governs it; but I've some lingering sense of fun left—though you've nearly knocked it out of me. I can just see that it isn't everything to all the world. Do what I say, and not what I do."

Maisie was careful not to reopen debatable matters, and they returned to London joyously. The terminus stopped Dick in the midst of an eloquent harangue on the beauties of exercise. He would buy Maisie a horse—such a horse as never yet bowed head to bit—would stable it, with a companion, some twenty miles from London, and Maisie, solely for her health's sake, should ride with him twice or thrice a week.

"That's absurd," said she. "It wouldn't be proper."

"Now, who in all London to-night would have sufficient interest or audacity to call us two to account for anything we chose to do?"

Maisie looked at the lamps, the fog, and the hideous turmoil. Dick was right; but horseflesh did not make for Art as she understood it.

"You're very nice sometimes, but you're very foolish more times. I'm not going to let you give me horses, or take you out of your way to-night. I'll go home by myself. Only I want you to promise me something. You won't think any more about that extra threepence, will you? Remember, you've been paid; and I won't allow you to be spiteful and do bad work for a little thing like that. You can be so big that you mustn't be tiny."

This was turning the tables with a vengeance. There remained only to put Maisie into her hansom.

"Good-by," she said simply. "You'll come on Sunday. It has been a beautiful day, Dick. Why can't it be like this always?"

"Because love's like line-work: you must go forward or backward; you can't stand still. By the way, go on with your line-work. Good-night, and, for my—for any sake, take care of yourself."

He turned to walk home, meditating. The day had brought him nothing that he hoped for, but—surely this was worth many days—it had brought him nearer to Maisie. The end was only a question of time now, and the prize well worth the waiting. By instinct, once more, he turned to the river.

"And she understood at once," he said, looking at the water. "She found out my pet besetting sin on the spot, and paid it off. My God, how she understood! And she said I was better than she was! Better than she was!" He laughed at the absurdity of the notion. "I wonder if girls guess at one-half a man's life. They can't, or—they wouldn't marry us." He took her gift out of his pocket, and considered it in the light of a miracle and a pledge of the comprehension that, one day, would lead to perfect happiness. Meantime, Maisie was alone in London, with none to save her from danger. And the packed wilderness was very full of danger.

Dick made his prayer to Fate disjointedly after the manner of the heathen as he threw the piece of silver into the river. If any evil were to befall, let him bear the burden and let Maisie go unscathed, since the threepenny piece was dearest to him of all his possessions. It was a small coin in itself, but Maisie had given it, and the Thames held it, and surely the Fates would be bribed for this once.

The drowning of the coin seemed to cut him free from thought of Maisie for the moment. He took himself off the bridge and went whistling to his chambers with a strong yearning for some man-talk and tobacco after his first experience of an entire day spent in the society of a woman. There was a stronger desire at his heart when there rose before him an unsolicited vision of the "Barralong" dipping deep and sailing free for the Southern Cross.

CHAPTER EIGHT

> And these two, as I have told you,
> Were the friends of Hiawatha,
> Chibiabos, the musician,
> And the very strong man, Kwasind.
>
> —*Hiawatha*

Torpenhow was paging the last sheets of some manuscript, while the Nilghai, who had come for chess and remained to talk tactics, was reading through the first part, commenting scornfully the while.

"It's picturesque enough and it's sketchy," said he; "but as a serious consideration of affairs in Eastern Europe, it's not worth much."

"It's off my hands at any rate. . . . Thirty-seven, thirty-eight, thirty-nine slips altogether, aren't there? That should make between eleven and twelve pages of valuable misinformation. Heigho!" Torpenhow shuffled the writing together and hummed:

"Young lambs to sell, young lambs to sell,
If I'd as much money as I could tell,
I never would cry, Young lambs to sell!"

Dick entered, self-conscious and a little defiant, but in the best of tempers with all the world.

"Back at last?" said Torpenhow.

"More or less. What have you been doing?"

"Work. Dickie, you behave as though the Bank of England were behind you. Here's Sunday, Monday, and Tuesday gone and you haven't done a line. It's scandalous."

"The notions come and go, my children—they come and go like our 'baccy," he answered, filling his pipe. "Moreover," he stooped to thrust a spill into the grate, "Apollo does not always stretch his— Oh, confound your clumsy jests, Nilghai!"

"This is not the place to preach the theory of direct inspiration," said the Nilghai, returning Torpenhow's large and workmanlike bellows to their nail on the wall. "We believe in cobblers' wax. *La!*—where you sit down."

"If you weren't so big and fat," said Dick, looking round for a weapon, "I'd—"

"No skylarking in my rooms. You two smashed half my furniture last time you threw the cushions about. You might have the decency to say How d' you do? to Binkie. Look at him."

Binkie had jumped down from the sofa and was fawning round Dick's knee, and scratching at his boots.

"Dear man!" said Dickie, snatching him up, and kissing him on the black patch above his right eye. "Did ums was, Binks? Did that ugly Nilghai turn you off the sofa? Bite him, Mr. Binkle." He pitched him on the Nilghai's stomach, as the big man lay at ease, and Binkie pretended to destroy the Nilghai inch by inch, till a sofa cushion extinguished him, and panting he stuck out his tongue at the company.

"The Binkie-boy went for a walk this morning before you were up, Torp. I saw him making love to the butcher at the corner when the shutters were being taken down—just as if he hadn't enough to eat in his own proper house," said Dick.

"Binks, is that a true bill?" said Torpenhow severely. The little dog retreated under the sofa-cushion, and showed by the fat white back of him that he really had no further interest in the discussion.

"'Strikes me that another disreputable dog went for a walk, too," said the Nilghai. "What made you get up so early? Torp said you might be buying a horse?"

"He knows it would need three of us for a serious business like that. No, I felt lonesome and unhappy, so I went out to look at the sea, and watch the pretty ships go by."

"Where did you go?"

"Somewhere on the Channel. Progly or Snigly, or some one-horse watering-place was its name; I've forgotten; but it was only two hours' run from London and the ships went by."

"Did you see anything you knew?"

"Only the 'Barralong' outward to Australia, and an Odessa grain-boat loaded down by the head. It was a thick day, but the sea smelled good."

"Wherefore put on one's best trousers to see the 'Barralong'?" said Torpenhow, pointing.

"Because I've nothing except these things and my painting duds. Besides, I wanted to do honor to the sea."

"Did she make you feel restless?" asked the Nilghai keenly.

"Crazy. Don't speak of it. I'm sorry I went."

Torpenhow and the Nilghai exchanged a look as Dick, stooping, busied himself among the former's boots and trees.

"These will do," he said at last; "I can't say I think much of your taste in slippers, but the fit's the thing." He slipped his feet into a pair of sock-like sambhur-skin foot coverings, found a long chair, and lay at length.

"They're my own pet pair," Torpenhow said. "I was just going to put them on myself."

"All your reprehensible selfishness. Just because you see me happy for a minute you want to worry me and stir me up. Find another pair."

"Good for you that Dick can't wear your clothes, Torp. You two live communistically," said the Nilghai.

"Dick never has anything that I can wear. He's only useful to sponge upon."

"Confound you, have you been rummaging round among my caches, then?" said Dick. "I put a sovereign in the tobacco-jar yesterday. How do you expect a man to keep his accounts properly if you—"

Here the Nilghai began to laugh, and Torpenhow joined him.

"Hid a sovereign yesterday! You're no sort of a financier. You lent me a fiver about a month back. Do you remember?" Torpenhow said.

"Yes, of course."

"Do you remember that I paid it you ten days later, and you put it at the bottom of the tobacco?"

"By Jove, did I? I thought it was in one of my color-boxes."

"You thought! About a week ago I went into your studio to get some 'baccy and found it."

"What did you do with it?"

"Took the Nilghai to a theater and fed him."

"You couldn't feed the Nilghai under twice the money—not though you gave him Army beef. Well, I suppose I should have found it out sooner or later. What is there to laugh at?"

"You're a most amazing cuckoo in many directions," said the Nilghai, still chuckling over the thought of the dinner. "Never mind. We had both been working very hard, and it was your unearned increment we spent, and as you're only a loafer it didn't matter."

"That's pleasant—from the man who is bursting with my meat, too. I'll get that dinner back one of these days. Suppose we go to a theater now."

"Put our boots on--and dress—*and* wash?" The Nilghai spoke very lazily.

"I withdraw the motion."

"Suppose, just for a change—as a startling variety, you know—we, that is to say *we*, get our charcoal and our canvas and go on with our work." Torpenhow spoke pointedly, but Dick only wriggled his toes inside the soft leather moccasins.

"What a one-idea'd clucker it is! If I had any unfinished figures on hand, I haven't any model; if I had my model, I haven't any spray, and I never leave charcoal unfixed overnight; and if I had my spray and twenty photographs of backgrounds, I couldn't do anything to-night. I don't feel that way."

"Binkie-dog, he's a lazy hog, isn't he?" said the Nilghai.

"Very good, I *will* do some work," said Dick, rising swiftly. "I'll fetch the Nungapunga Book, and we'll add another picture to the Nilghai Saga."

"Aren't you worrying him a little too much?" asked the Nilghai, when Dick had left the room.

"Perhaps, but I know what he can turn out if he likes. It makes me savage to hear him praised for past work when I know what he ought to do. You and I are arranged for—"

"By Kismet and our own powers, more's the pity. I have dreamed of a good deal."

"So have I, but we know our limitations now. I'm dashed if I know what Dick's may be when he gives himself to his work. That's what makes me so keen about him."

"And when all's said and done, you will be put aside—quite rightly—for a female girl."

"I wonder . . . . Where do you think he has been today?"

"To the sea. Didn't you see the look in his eyes when he talked about her? He's as restless as a swallow in autumn."

"Yes; but did he go alone?"

"I don't know, and I don't care, but he has the beginnings of the go-fever upon him. He wants to up-stakes and move out. There's no mistaking the signs. Whatever he may have said before, he has the call upon him now."

"It might be his salvation," Torpenhow said.

"Perhaps—if you care to take the responsibility of being a savior: I'm averse to tampering with souls myself."

Dick returned with a great clasped sketch-book that the Nilghai knew well and did not love too much. In it Dick had drawn in his playtime all manner of moving incidents, experienced by himself or related to him by the others, of all the four corners of the earth. But the wider range of the Nilghai's body and life attracted him most. When truth failed here he fell back on fiction of the wildest, and represented incidents in the Nilghai's career that were unseemly—his marriages with many African princesses, his shameless betrayal, for Arab wives, of army corps to the Mahdi, his tattooment by skilled operators in Burmah, his interview (and his fears) with the yellow headsman in the blood-stained execution-ground of Canton, and finally, the passings of his spirit into the bodies of whales, elephants, and toucans. Torpenhow from time to time had added rhymed descriptions, and the whole was a curious piece of art, because Dick decided, having regard to the name of the book which being interpreted means "naked," that it would be wrong to draw the Nilghai with any clothes on, under any circumstances. Consequently the last sketch, representing that much-enduring man calling on the War Office to press his claims to the Egyptian medal, was hardly delicate. He settled himself comfortably at Torpenhow's table and turned over the pages.

"What a fortune you would have been to Blake, Nilghai!" he said. "There's a succulent pinkness about some of these sketches that's more than life-like. 'The Nilghai surrounded while bathing by the Madieh'—that was founded on fact, eh?"

"It was very nearly my last bath, you irreverent dauber. Has Binkie come into the Saga yet?"

"No; the Binkie-boy hasn't done anything except eat and kill cats. Let's see. Here you are as a stained-glass saint in a church. 'Deuced decorative lines about your anatomy;

you ought to be grateful for being handed down to posterity in this way. Fifty years hence you'll exist in rare and curious facsimiles at ten guineas each. What shall I try this time? The domestic life of the Nilghai?"

"'Hasn't got any."

"The undomestic life of the Nilghai, then. Of course! Mass-meeting of his wives in Trafalgar Square. That's it. They came from the ends of the earth to attend Nilghai's wedding to an English bride. This shall be in sepia. It's a sweet material to work with."

"It's a scandalous waste of time," said Torpenhow.

"Don't worry; it keeps one's hand in—specially when you begin without the pencil." He set to work rapidly. "That's Nelson's Column. Presently the Nilghai will appear shinning up it."

"Give him some clothes this time."

"Certainly—a veil and an orange-wreath, because he's been married."

"Gad, that's clever enough!" said Torpenhow over his shoulder, as Dick brought out of the paper with three twirls of the brush a very fat back and laboring shoulder pressed against the stone.

"Just imagine," Dick continued, "if we could publish a few of these dear little things every time the Nilghai subsidizes a man who can write, to give the public an honest opinion of my pictures."

"Well, you'll admit I always tell you when I have done anything of that kind. I know I can't hammer you as you ought to be hammered, so I give the job to another. Young Maclagan, for instance—"

"No-o—one half-minute, old man; stick your hand out against the dark of the wall-paper—you only burble and call me names. That left shoulder's out of drawing. I must literally throw a veil over that. Where's my pen-knife? Well, what about Maclagan?"

"I only gave him his riding-orders to—to lambast you on general principles for not producing work that will last."

"Whereupon that young fool"—Dick threw back his head and shut one eye as he shifted the page under his hand—"being left alone with an ink-pot and what he conceived were his own notions, went and spilled them both over me in the papers. You might have engaged a grown man for the business, Nilghai. How do you think the bridal veil looks now, Torp?"

"How the deuce do three dabs and two scratches make the stuff stand away from the body as it does?" said Torpenhow, to whom Dick's methods were always new.

"It just depends on where you put 'em. If Maclagan had known that much about his business he might have done better."

"Why don't you put the damned dabs into something that will stay, then?" insisted the Nilghai, who had really taken considerable trouble in hiring for Dick's benefit the pen of a young gentleman who devoted most of his waking hours to an anxious consideration of the aims and ends of Art, which, he wrote, was one and indivisible.

"Wait a minute till I see how I am going to manage my procession of wives. You seem to have married extensively, and I must rough 'em in with the pencil—Medes, Parthians, Edomites. . . . Now, setting aside the weakness and the wickedness and—and the fat-headedness of deliberately trying to do work that will live, as they call it, I'm content with the knowledge that I've done my best up to date, and I shan't do anything like it again for some hours at least—probably years. Most probably never."

"What! any stuff you have in stock your best work?" said Torpenhow.

"Anything you've sold?" said the Nilghai.

"Oh, no. It isn't here and it isn't sold. Better than that, it can't be sold, and I don't think any one knows where it is. I'm sure I don't. . . . And yet more and more wives, on the north side of the square. Observe the virtuous horror of the lions!"

"You may as well explain," said Torpenhow, and Dick lifted his head from the paper.

"The sea reminded me of it," he said slowly. "I wish it hadn't. It weighs some few thousand tons—unless you cut it out with a cold chisel."

"Don't be an idiot. You can't pose with us here," said the Nilghai.

"There's no pose in the matter at all. It's a fact. I was loafing from Lima to Auckland in a big, old, condemned passenger-ship turned into a cargo-boat and owned by a second-hand Italian firm. She was a crazy basket. We were cut down to fifteen ton of coal a day, and we thought ourselves lucky when we kicked seven knots an hour out of her. Then we used to stop and let the bearings cool down, and wonder whether the crack in the shaft was spreading."

"Were you a steward or a stoker in those days?"

"I was flush for the time being, so I was a passenger, or else I should have been a steward, I think," said Dick with perfect gravity, returning to the procession of angry wives. "I was the only other passenger from Lima, and the ship was half empty, and full of rats and cockroaches and scorpions."

"But what has this to do with the picture?"

"Wait a minute. She had been in the China passenger trade and her lower deck had bunks for two thousand pigtails. Those were all taken down, and she was empty up to her nose, and the lights came through the port-holes—most annoying lights to work in till you got used to them. I hadn't anything to do for weeks. The ship's charts were in pieces and our skipper daren't run south for fear of catching a storm. So he did his best to knock all the Society Islands out of the water one by one, and I went into the lower deck, and did my picture on the portside as far forward in her as I could go. There was some brown paint and some green paint that they used for the boats, and some black paint for ironwork, and that was all I had."

"The passengers must have thought you mad."

"There was only one, and it was a woman; but it gave me the notion of my picture."

"What was she like?" said Torpenhow.

"She was a sort of Negroid-Jewess-Cuban; with morals to match. She couldn't read or write, and she didn't want to, but she used to come down and watch me paint, and the skipper didn't like it, because he was paying her passage and had to be on the bridge occasionally."

"I see. That must have been cheerful."

"It was the best time I ever had. To begin with, we didn't know whether we should go up or go down any minute when there was a sea on; and when it was calm it was paradise; and the woman used to mix the paints and talk broken English, and the skipper used to steal down every few minutes to the lower deck, because he said he was afraid of fire. So, you see, we could never tell when we might be caught, and I had a splendid notion to work out in only three keys of color."

"What was the notion?"

"Two lines in Poe—

" 'Neither the angels in Heaven above nor the demons down
under the sea,
Can ever dissever my soul from the soul of the beautiful
Annabel Lee.'

It came out of the sea—all by itself. I drew that fight, fought out in green water over the naked, choking soul, and the woman served as the model for the devils and the angels both—sea-devils and sea-angels, and the soul half drowned between them. It doesn't sound much, but when there was a good light on the lower deck it looked very fine and creepy. It was seven by fourteen feet, all done in shifting light for shifting light."

"Did the woman inspire you much?" said Torpenhow.

"She and the sea between them—immensely. There was a heap of bad drawing in that picture. I remember I went out of my way to foreshorten for sheer delight of doing it, and I foreshortened damnably, but for all that it's the best thing I've ever done; and now I suppose the ship's broken up or gone down. Whew! What a time that was!"

"What happened after all?"

"It all ended. They were loading her with wool when I left the ship, but even the stevedores kept the picture clear to the last. The eyes of the demons scared them, I honestly believe."

"And the woman?"

"She was scared too when it was finished. She used to cross herself before she went down to look at it. Just three colors and no chance of getting any more, and the sea outside and unlimited love-making inside, and the fear of death atop of everything else, O Lord!" He had ceased to look at the sketch, but was staring straight in front of him across the room.

"Why don't you try something of the same kind now?" said the Nilghai.

"Because those things come not by fasting and prayer. When I find a cargo-boat and a Jewess-Cuban and another notion and the same old life, I may."

"You won't find them here," said the Nilghai.

"No, I shall not." Dick shut the sketch-book with a bang. "This room's as hot as an oven. Open the window, some one."

He leaned into the darkness, watching the greater darkness of London below him. The chambers stood much higher than the other houses, commanding a hundred chimneys—crooked cowls that looked like sitting cats as they swung round, and other uncouth brick and zinc mysteries supported by iron stanchions and clamped by S-pieces. Northward the lights of Piccadilly Circus and Leicester Square threw a copper-colored glare above the black roofs, and southward lay all the orderly lights of the Thames. A train rolled out across one of the railway bridges, and its thunder drowned for a minute the dull roar of the streets. The Nilghai looked at his watch and said shortly, "That's the Paris night-mail. You can book from here to St. Petersburg if you choose."

Dick crammed head and shoulders out of the window and looked across the river. Torpenhow came to his side, while the Nilghai passed over quietly to the piano and opened it. Binkie, making himself as large as possible, spread out upon the sofa with the air of one who is not to be lightly disturbed.

"Well," said the Nilghai to the two pairs of shoulders, "have you never seen this place before?"

A steam-tug on the river hooted as she towed her barges to wharf. Then the boom of the traffic came into the room. Torpenhow nudged Dick. "Good place to bank in—bad place to bunk in, Dickie, isn't it?"

Dick's chin was in his hand as he answered, in the words of a general not without fame, still looking out on the darkness—" 'My God, what a city to loot'!"

Binkie found the night air tickling his whiskers and sneezed plaintively.

"We shall give the Binkie-dog a cold," said Torpenhow. "Come in," and they withdrew their heads. "You'll be buried in Kensal Green, Dick, one of these days, if it isn't closed by the time you want to go there—buried within two feet of some one else, his wife and his family."

"Allah forbid! I shall get away before that time comes. Give a man room to stretch his legs, Mr. Binkle." Dick flung himself down on the sofa and tweaked Binkie's velvet ears, yawning heavily the while.

"You'll find that wardrobe-case very much out of tune," Torpenhow said to the Nilghai. "It's never touched except by you."

"A piece of gross extravagance," Dick grunted. "The Nilghai only comes when I'm out."

"That's because you're always out. Howl, Nilghai, and let him hear."

"The life of the Nilghai is fraud and slaughter,
His writings are watered Dickens and water;
But the voice of the Nilghai raised on high
Makes even the Mahdieh glad to die!"

Dick quoted from Torpenhow's letter-press in the Nunga-punga Book. "How do they call moose in Canada, Nilghai?"

The man laughed. Singing was his one polite accomplishment, as many Press-tents in far-off lands had known.

"What shall I sing?" said he, turning in the chair.

"'Moll Roe in the Morning,'" said Torpenhow at a venture.

"No," said Dick sharply, and the Nilghai opened his eyes. The old chanty whereof he, among a very few, possessed all the words was not a pretty one, but Dick had heard it many times before without wincing. Without prelude he launched into that stately tune that calls together and troubles the hearts of the gypsies of the sea—

> "Farewell and adieu to you, Spanish ladies,
> Farewell and adieu to you, ladies of Spain."

Dick turned uneasily on the sofa, for he could hear the bows of the "Barralong" crashing into the green seas on her way to the Southern Cross. Then came the chorus—

> "We'll rant and we'll roar like true British sailors,
> We'll rant and we'll roar across the salt seas,
> Until we take soundings in the Channel of Old
> England
> From Ushant to Scilly 'tis forty-five leagues."

"Thirty-five—thirty-five," said Dick petulantly. "Don't tamper with Holy Writ. Go on, Nilghai."

> "The first land we made it was called the Deadman,"

and they sang to the end very vigorously.

"That would be a better song if her head were turned the other way—to the Ushant light, for instance," said the Nilghai.

"Flinging its arms about like a mad windmill," said Torpenhow. "Give us something else, Nilghai. You're in fine fog-horn form to-night."

"Give us the 'Ganges Pilot': you sang that in the square the night before El-Maghrib. By the way, I wonder how many of the chorus are alive to-night," said Dick.

Torpenhow considered for a minute. "By Jove! I believe only you and I. Raynor, Vickery, and Deenes—all dead; Vincent caught small-pox in Cairo, carried it here and died of it. Yes, only you and I and the Nilghai."

"Umph! And yet the men here who've done their work in a well-warmed studio all their lives, with a policeman at each corner, say that I charge too much for my pictures."

"They are buying your work, not your insurance policies, dear child," said the Nilghai.

"I gambled with one to get at the other. Don't preach. Go on with the 'Pilot.' Where in the world did you get that song?"

"On a tombstone," said the Nilghai. "On a tombstone in a distant land. I made it an accompaniment with heaps of bass chords."

"Oh, Vanity! Begin." And the Nilghai began:

"I have slipped my cable, messmates, I'm drifting down with the tide,
I have my sailing orders, while ye at anchor ride.
And never on fair June morning have I put out to sea
With clearer conscience or better hope, or a heart more light and free.

"Shoulder to shoulder, Joe, my boy, into the crowd like a wedge,
Strike with the hangers, messmates, but do not cut with the edge.
Cries Charnock, 'Scatter the fagots, double that Brahmin in two,
The tall pale widow for me, Joe, the little brown girl for you!'

"Young Joe (you're nearing sixty), why is your hide so dark?
Katie has soft fair blue eyes, who blackened yours?—Why, hark!"

They were all singing now, Dick with the roar of the wind of the open sea about his ears as the deep bass voice let itself go.

" The morning gun—Ho, steady!—the arquebuses to me!
I ha' sounded the Dutch High Admiral's heart as my lead doth sound the sea.

" Sounding, sounding the Ganges, floating down with the tide,
Moor me close to Charnock, next to my nut-brown bride.
My blessing to Kate at Fairlight—Holwell, my thanks to you;
Steady! We steer for Heaven, through sand-drifts cold and blue."

"Now what is there in that nonsense to make a man restless?" said Dick, hauling Binkie from his feet to his chest.

"It depends on the man," said Torpenhow.

"The man who has been down to look at the sea," said the Nilghai.

"I didn't know she was going to upset me in this fashion."

"That's what men say when they go to say good-by to a woman. It's more easy though to get rid of three women than a piece of one's life and surroundings."

"But a woman can be—" began Dick unguardedly.

"A piece of one's life," continued Torpenhow. "No, she can't." His face darkened for a moment. "She says she wants to sympathize with you and help you in your work, and everything else that clearly a man must do for himself. Then she sends round five notes a day to ask why the dickens you haven't been wasting your time with her."

"Don't generalize," said the Nilghai. "By the time you arrive at five notes a day you must have gone through a good deal and behaved accordingly. 'Shouldn't begin these things, my son."

"I shouldn't have gone down to the sea," said Dick, just a little anxious to change the conversation. "And you shouldn't have sung."

"The sea isn't sending you five notes a day," said the Nilghai.

"No, but I'm fatally compromised. She's an enduring

old hag, and I'm sorry I ever met her. Why wasn't I born and bred and dead in a three-pair back?"

"Hear him blaspheming his first love! Why in the world shouldn't you listen to her?" said Torpenhow.

Before Dick could reply the Nilghai lifted up his voice with a shout that shook the windows, in "The Men of the Sea," that begins, as all know, "The sea is a wicked old woman," and after racing through eight lines whose imagery is truthful, ends in a refrain, slow as the clacking of a capstan when the boat comes unwillingly up to the bars where the men sweat and tramp in the shingle.

"'Ye that bore us, O restore us!
She is kinder than ye;
For the call is on our heart-strings!'
Said The Men of the Sea."

The Nilghai sang that verse twice, with simple craft, intending that Dick should hear. But Dick was waiting for the farewell of the men to their wives.

"'Ye that love us, can ye move us?
She is dearer than ye;
And your sleep will be the sweeter,'
Said The Men of the Sea."

The rough words beat like the blows of the waves on the bows of the rickety boat from Lima in the days when Dick was mixing paints, making love, drawing devils and angels in the half dark, and wondering whether the next minute would place the Italian captain's knife between his shoulder-blades. And the go-fever, which is more real than many doctors' diseases, waked and raged, urging him who loved Maisie beyond anything in the world, to go away and taste the old hot, unregenerate life again—to scuffle, swear, gamble, and love light loves with his fellows; to take ship and know the sea once more, and by her beget pictures; to talk to Binat among the sands of Port Said while Yellow 'Tina mixed the drinks; to hear the crackle of musketry, and see the smoke roll outward, thin and thicken again till the shining black faces came through, and in that hell every man was strictly responsible for his own head, and his alone, and struck with an unfettered arm. It was impossible, utterly impossible, but—

"'Oh, our fathers, in the churchyard,
She is older than ye,
And our graves will be the greener,'
Said The Men of the Sea."

"What *is* there to hinder?" said Torpenhow, in the long hush that followed the song.

"You said a little time since that you wouldn't come for a walk round the world, Torp."

"That was months ago, and I only objected to your making money for traveling expenses. You've shot your bolt here and it has gone home. Go away and do some work, and see some things."

"Get some of the fat off you; you're disgracefully out of condition," said the Nilghai, making a plunge from the chair and grasping a handful of Dick generally over the right ribs. "Soft as putty—pure tallow born of overfeeding. Train it off, Dickie."

"We're all equally gross, Nilghai. Next time you have to take the field you'll sit down, wink your eyes, gasp, and die in a fit."

"Never mind. You go away on a ship. Go to Lima again, or to Brazil. There's always trouble in South America."

"Do you suppose I want to be told where to go? Great Heavens, the only difficulty is to know where I'm to stop. But I shall stay here, as I told you before."

"Then you'll be buried in Kensal Green and turn into adipocere with the others," said Torpenhow. "Are you thinking of commissions in hand? Pay forfeit and go. You've money enough to travel as a king if you please."

"You've the grisliest notions of amusement, Torp. I

think I see myself shipping first-class on a six-thousand-ton hotel, and asking the third engineer what makes the engines go round, and whether it isn't very warm in the stokehold. Ho! ho! I should ship as a loafer if ever I shipped at all, which I'm not going to do. I shall compromise, and go for a small trip to begin with."

"That's something at any rate. Where will you go?" said Torpenhow. "It would do you all the good in the world, old man."

The Nilghai saw the twinkle in Dick's eye and refrained from speech.

"I shall go in the first place to Rathray's stable, where I shall hire one horse, and take him very carefully as far as Richmond Hill. Then I shall walk him back again, in case he should accidentally burst into a lather and make Rathray angry. I shall do that to-morrow, for the sake of air and exercise."

"Bah!" Dick had barely time to throw up his arm and ward off the cushion that the disgusted Torpenhow heaved at his head.

"Air and exercise indeed," said the Nilghai, sitting down heavily on Dick. "Let's give him a little of both. Get the bellows, Torp."

At this point the conference broke up in disorder, because Dick would not open his mouth till the Nilghai held his nose fast, and there was some trouble in forcing the nozzle of the bellows between his teeth; and even when it was there he weakly tried to puff against the force of the blast, and his cheeks blew up with a great explosion; and the enemy becoming helpless with laughter he so beat them over the head with a soft sofa-cushion that that became unsewn and distributed its feathers, and Binkie, interfering in Torpenhow's interests, was bundled into the half-empty bag and advised to scratch his way out, which he did after a while, traveling rapidly up and down the floor in the shape of an agitated green haggis, and when he came out looking for satisfaction, the three pillars of his world were picking feathers out of their hair.

"A prophet has no honor in his own country," said Dick ruefully, dusting his knees. "This filthy fluff will never brush off my bags."

"It was all for your good," said the Nilghai. "'Nothing like air and exercise."

"All for your good," said Torpenhow, not in the least with reference to past clowning. "It would let you focus things at their proper worth and prevent your becoming slack in this hothouse of a town. Indeed it would, old man. I shouldn't have spoken if I hadn't thought so. Only, you make a joke of everything."

"Before God I do no such thing," said Dick quickly and earnestly. "You don't know me if you think that."

"*I* don't think it," said the Nilghai.

"How can fellows like ourselves, who know what life and death really mean, dare to make a joke of anything? I know we pretend it, to save ourselves from breaking down or going to the other extreme. Can't I see, old man, how you're always anxious about me, and try to advise me to make my work better? Do you suppose I don't think about that myself? But you can't help me—you can't help me—not even you. I must play my own hand alone in my own way."

"Hear, hear," from the Nilghai.

"What's the one thing in the Nilghai Saga that I've never drawn in the Nungapunga Book?" Dick continued to Torpenhow, who was a little astonished at the outburst.

Now there was one blank page in the book given over to the sketch that Dick had not drawn of the crowning exploit in the Nilghai's life; when that man, being young and forgetting that his body and bones belonged to the paper that employed him, had ridden over sunburned slippery grass in the rear of Bredow's brigade on the day that the troopers flung themselves at Canrobert's artillery, and for aught they knew twenty battalions in front, to save the battered 24th German Infantry, to give time to decide the fate of Vionville, and to learn ere their remnant came back to Flavigay that cavalry can attack and crumple and break unshaken infantry. Whenever he was inclined to think over a life that might have been better, an income that might have been larger, and a soul that might have been considerably cleaner, the Nilghai would comfort himself with the thought, "I rode with Bredow's brigade at Vionville," and take heart for any lesser battle the next day might bring.

"I know," he said very gravely. "I was always glad that you left it out."

"I left it out because Nilghai taught me what the German army learned then, and what Schmidt taught their cavalry. I don't know German. What is it? 'Take care of the time and the dressing will take care of itself.' I must ride my own line to my own beat, old man."

"*Tempo ist richtung.* You've learned your lesson well," said the Nilghai. "He must go alone. He speaks truth, Torp."

"Maybe I'm as wrong as I can be—hideously wrong. I must find that out for myself, as I have to think things out for myself, but I daren't turn my head to dress by the next man. It hurts me a great deal more than you know not to be able to go, but I cannot, that's all. I must do my own work and live my own life in my own way, because I'm responsible for both. Only don't think I frivol about it, Torp. I have my own matches and sulphur, and I'll make my own hell, thanks."

There was an uncomfortable pause. Then Torpenhow said blandly, "What did the Governor of North Carolina say to the Governor of South Carolina?"

"Excellent notion. It *is* a long time between drinks. There are the makings of a very fine prig in you, Dick," said the Nilghai.

"I've liberated my mind, estimable Binkie, with the feathers in his mouth." Dick picked up the still indignant one and shook him tenderly. "You're tied up in a sack and made to run about blind, Binkie-wee, without any reason, and it has hurt your little feelings. Never mind. *Sic volo, sic jubeo, stet pro ratione voluntas*, and don't sneeze in my eye because I talk Latin. Good-night."

He went out of the room.

"That's distinctly one for you," said the Nilghai. "I told you it was hopeless to meddle with him. He's not pleased."

"He'd swear at me if he weren't. I can't make it out. He has the go-fever upon him and he won't go. I only hope that he mayn't have to go some day when he doesn't want to," said Torpenhow.

. . . .

In his own room Dick was settling a question with himself—and the question was whether all the world, and all that was therein, and a burning desire to exploit both, was worth one threepenny piece thrown into the Thames.

"It came of seeing the sea, and I'm a cur to think about it," he decided. "After all the honeymoon will be that tour—with reservations; only . . . only I didn't realize that the sea was so strong. I didn't feel it so much when I was with Maisie. These damnable songs did it. He's beginning again."

But it was only Herrick's Nightpiece to Julia that the Nilghai sang, and before it was ended Dick reappeared on the threshold, not altogether clothed indeed, but in his right mind, thirsty and at peace.

The mood had come and gone with the rising and the falling of the tide by Fort Keeling.

CHAPTER NINE

"If I have taken the common clay
  And wrought it cunningly
In the shape of a god that was digged a clod,
  The greater honor to me."

"If thou hast taken the common clay,
  And thy hands be not free
From the taint of the soil, thou hast made thy spoil
  The greater shame to thee."—*The Two Potters*

HE did no work of any kind for the rest of the week. Then came another Sunday. He dreaded and longed for the day always, but since the red-haired girl had sketched him there was rather more dread than desire in his mind.

He found that Maisie had entirely neglected his suggestions about line-work. She had gone off at score filled with some absurd notion for a "fancy head." It cost Dick something to command his temper.

"What's the good of suggesting anything?" he said pointedly.

"Ah, but this will be a picture—a real picture; and I know that Kami will let me send it to the Salon. You don't mind, do you?"

"I suppose not. But you won't have time for the Salon."

Maisie hesitated a little. She even felt uncomfortable.

"We're going over to France a month sooner because of it. I shall get the idea sketched out here and work it up at Kami's."

Dick's heart stood still, and he came very near to being disgusted with his queen who could do no wrong. "Just when I thought I had made some headway, she goes off chasing butterflies. It's too maddening!"

There was no possibility of arguing, for the red-haired

girl was in the studio. Dick could only look unutterable reproach.

"I'm sorry," he said, "and I think you make a mistake. But what's the idea of your new picture?"

"I took it from a book."

"That's bad, to begin with. Books aren't the places for pictures. And—"

"It's this," said the red-haired girl behind him. "I was reading it to Maisie the other day from 'The City of Dreadful Night.' D'you know the book?"

"A little. I am sorry I spoke. There are pictures in it. What has taken her fancy?"

"The description of the Melancolia—

" 'Her folded wings as of a mighty eagle,
But all too impotent to lift the regal
Robustness of her earth-born strength and pride.'

And here again. (Maisie, get the tea, dear.)

" 'The forehead charged with baleful thoughts and dreams,
The household bunch of keys, the housewife's gown,
Voluminous indented, and yet rigid
As though a shell of burnished metal frigid,
Her feet thick-shod to tread all weakness down.' "

There was no attempt to conceal the scorn of the lazy voice. Dick winced.

"But that has been done already by an obscure artist of the name of Dürer," said he. "How does the poem run?—

" 'Three centuries and threescore years ago,
With phantasies of his peculiar thought.'

You might as well try to rewrite 'Hamlet.' It will be waste of time."

"No, it won't," said Maisie, putting down the teacups with clatter to reassure herself. "And I mean to do it. Can't you see what a beautiful thing it would make?"

"How in perdition can one do work when one hasn't had

the proper training? Any fool can get a notion. It needs training to drive the thing through—training and conviction; not rushing after the first fancy." Dick spoke between his teeth.

"You don't understand," said Maisie. "I think I can do it."

Again the voice of the girl behind him—

" 'Baffled and beaten back, she works on still;
    Weary and sick of soul, she works the more.
Sustained by her indomitable will,
    The hands shall fashion, and the brain shall pore,
And all her sorrow shall be turned to labor—'

I fancy Maisie means to embody herself in the picture."

"Sitting on a throne of rejected pictures? No, I shan't, dear. The notion in itself has fascinated me.—Of course you don't care for fancy heads, Dick. I don't think you could do them. You like blood and bones."

"That's a direct challenge. If you can do a Melancolia that isn't merely a sorrowful female head, I can do a better one; and I will, too. What d'you know about Melancolias?" Dick firmly believed that he was even then tasting three-quarters of all the sorrow in the world.

"She was a woman," said Maisie, "and she suffered a great deal—till she could suffer no more. Then she began to laugh at it all, and then I painted her and sent her to the Salon."

The red-haired girl rose up and left the room, laughing.

Dick looked at Maisie humbly and hopelessly.

"Never mind about the picture," he said. "Are you really going back to Kami's a month before your time?"

"I must, if I want to get the picture done."

"And that's all you want?"

"Of course. Don't be stupid, Dick."

"You haven't the power. You have only the ideas—the ideas and the little cheap impulses. How you could have kept at your work for ten years steadily is a mystery to me. So you are really going—a month before you need?"

"I must do my work."

"Your work—bah! . . . No, I didn't mean that. It's all right, dear. Of course you must do your work, and—I think I'll say good-by for this week."

"Won't you even stay for tea?"

"No, thank you. Have I your leave to go, dear? There's nothing more you particularly want me to do, and the line-work doesn't matter."

"I wish you could stay, and then we could talk over my picture. If only one single picture's a success it draws attention to all the others. I know some of my work is good, if only people could see. And you needn't have been so rude about it."

"I'm sorry. We'll talk the Melancolia over some one of the other Sundays. There are four more—yes, one, two, three, four—before you go. Good-by, Maisie."

Maisie stood by the studio window, thinking, till the red-haired girl returned, a little white at the corners of her lips.

"Dick's gone off," said Maisie. "Just when I wanted to talk about the picture. Isn't it selfish of him?"

Her companion opened her lips as if to speak, shut them again, and went on reading "The City of Dreadful Night."

Dick was in the Park, walking round and round a tree that he had chosen as his confidant for many Sundays past. He was swearing audibly, and when he found that the infirmities of the English tongue hemmed in his rage, he sought consolation in Arabic, which is expressly designed for the use of the afflicted. He was not pleased with the reward of his patient service; nor was he pleased with himself; and it was long before he arrived at the proposition that the queen could do no wrong.

"It's a losing game," he said. "I'm worth nothing when a whim of hers is in question. But in a losing game at Port Said we used to double the stakes and go on. She do a Melancolia! She hasn't the power, or the insight, or the training. Only the desire. She's cursed with the curse of Reuben. She won't do line-work, because it means real work; and yet she's stronger than I am. I'll make her understand that I can beat her on her own Melancolia. Even then she wouldn't care. She says I can only do blood and bones. I don't believe she has blood in her veins. All the same I love her; and I must go on loving her; and if I can humble her inordinate vanity I will. I'll do a Melancolia that shall be something like a Melancolia—'the Melancolia that transcends all wit.' I'll do it at once, con—bless her."

He discovered that the notion would not come to order, and that he could not free his mind for an hour from the thought of Maisie's departure. He took very small interest in her rough studies for the Melancolia when she showed them next week. The Sundays were racing past, and the time was at hand when all the church bells in London could not ring Maisie back to him. Once or twice he said something to Binkie about "hermaphroditic futilities," but the little dog received so many confidences both from Torpenhow and Dick that he did not trouble his tulip-ears to listen.

Dick was permitted to see the girls off. They were going by the Dover night-boat; and they hoped to return in August. It was then February, and Dick felt that he was being hardly used. Maisie was so busy stripping the small house across the Park, and packing her canvases, that she had no time for thought. Dick went down to Dover and wasted a day there fretting over a wonderful possibility. Would Maisie at the very last allow him one small kiss? He reflected that he might capture her by the strong arm, as he had seen women captured in the Southern Soudan, and lead her away; but Maisie would never be led. She would turn her gray eyes upon him and say, "Dick, how selfish you are!" Then his courage would fail him. It would be better, after all, to beg for that kiss.

Maisie looked more than usually kissable as she stepped from the night-mail on to the windy pier, in a gray waterproof and a little gray cloth traveling-cap. The red-haired girl was not so lovely. Her green eyes were hollow and her lips were dry. Dick saw the trunks aboard, and went to Maisie's side in the darkness under the bridge. The mail-bags were thundering into the forehold, and the red-haired girl was watching them.

"You'll have a rough passage to-night," said Dick. "It's blowing outside. I suppose I may come over and see you if I'm good?"

"You mustn't. I shall be busy. At least, if I want you I'll send for you. But I shall write from Vitry-sur-Marne. I shall have heaps of things to consult you about. Oh, Dick, you have been so good to me!—so good to me!"

"Thank you for that, dear. It hasn't made any difference, has it?"

"I can't tell a fib. It hasn't—in that way. But don't think I'm not grateful."

"Damn the gratitude!" said Dick huskily to the paddle-box.

"What's the use of worrying? You know I should ruin your life, and you'd ruin mine, as things are now. You remember what you said when you were so angry that day in the Park? One of us has to be broken. Can't you wait till that day comes?"

"No, love. I want you unbroken—all to myself."

Maisie shook her head. "My poor Dick, what can I say?"

"Don't say anything. Give me a kiss? Only one kiss, Maisie. I'll swear I won't take any more. You might as well, and then I can be sure you're grateful."

Maisie put her cheek forward, and Dick took his reward in the darkness. It was only one kiss, but, since there was no time-limit specified, it was a long one. Maisie wrenched herself free angrily, and Dick stood abashed and tingling from head to heel.

"Good-by, darling. I didn't mean to scare you. I'm sorry. Only—keep well and do good work—specially the Melancolia. I'm going to do one, too. Remember me to Kami, and be careful what you drink. Country drinking-water is bad everywhere, but it's worse in France. Write to me if you want anything, and good-by. Say good-by to the what-you-call-um girl, and—can't I have another kiss? No. You're quite right. Good-by."

A shout told him that it was not seemly to charge up the mail-bag incline. He reached the pier as the steamer began to move off, and he followed her with his heart.

"And there's nothing—nothing in the wide world—to keep us apart except her obstinacy. These Calais night-boats are much too small. I'll get Torp to write to the papers about it. She's beginning to pitch already."

Maisie stood where Dick had left her till she heard a little gasping cough at her elbow. The red-haired girl's eyes were alight with cold flame.

"He kissed you!" she said. "How could you let him, when he wasn't anything to you? How dared you take a kiss from him? Oh, Maisie, let's go to the ladies' cabin. I'm sick—deadly sick."

"We aren't into open water yet. Go down, dear, and I'll stay here. I don't like the smell of the engines. . . . Poor Dick! He deserved one—only one. But I didn't think he'd frighten me so."

Dick returned to town next day just in time for lunch, for which he had telegraphed. To his disgust, there were only empty plates in the studio. He lifted up his voice like the bears in the fairy-tale, and Torpenhow entered, looking very guilty.

"H'sh!" said he. "Don't make such a noise. I took it. Come into my rooms, and I'll show you why."

Dick paused amazed at the threshold, for on Torpenhow's sofa lay a girl asleep and breathing heavily. The little cheap sailor-hat, the blue-and-white dress, fitter for June than for February, dabbled with mud at the skirts, the jacket trimmed with imitation Astrakhan and ripped at the shoulder-seams, the one-and-elevenpenny umbrella, and, above all, the disgraceful condition of the kid-topped boots, declared all things.

"Oh, I say, old man, this is too bad! You mustn't bring this sort up here. They steal things from the rooms."

"It looks bad, I admit, but I was coming in after lunch, and she staggered into the hall. I thought she was drunk at first, but it was collapse. I couldn't leave her as she was, so I brought her up here and gave her your lunch. She was fainting from want of food. She went fast asleep the minute she had finished."

"I know something of that complaint. She's been living on sausages, I suppose. Torp, you should have handed her over to a policeman for presuming to faint in a respectable house. Poor little wretch! Look at that face! There isn't an ounce of immorality in it. Only folly—slack, fatuous, feeble, futile folly. It's a typical head. D'you notice how the skull begins to show through the flesh padding on the face and cheek-bone?"

"What a cold-blooded barbarian it is! Don't hit a woman when she's down. Can't we do anything? She was simply dropping with starvation. She almost fell into my arms, and when she got to the food she ate like a wild beast. It was horrible."

"I can give her money, which she would probably spend in drinks. Is she going to sleep forever?"

The girl opened her eyes and glared at the men between terror and effrontery.

"Feeling better?" said Torpenhow.

"Yes. Thank you. There aren't many gentlemen that are as kind as you are. Thank you."

"When did you leave service?" said Dick, who had been watching the scarred and chapped hands.

"How did you know I was in service? I was. General servant. I didn't like it."

"And how do you like being your own mistress?"

"Do I look as if I liked it?"

"I suppose not. One moment. Would you be good enough to turn your face to the window?"

The girl obeyed, and Dick watched her face keenly

—so keenly that she made as if to hide behind Torpenhow.

"The eyes have it," said Dick, walking up and down. "They are superb eyes for my business. And, after all, every head depends on the eyes. This has been sent from heaven to make up for—what was taken away. Now the weekly strain's off my shoulders, I can get to work in earnest. Evidently sent from heaven. Yes. Raise your chin a little, please."

"Gently, old man, gently. You're scaring somebody out of her wits," said Torpenhow, who could see the girl trembling.

"Don't let him hit me! Oh, please don't let him hit me! I've been hit cruel to-day because I spoke to a man. Don't let him look at me like that! He's reg'lar wicked, that one. Don't let him look at me like that, neither! Oh, I feel as if I hadn't nothing on when he looks at me like that!"

The overstrained nerves in the frail body gave way, and the girl wept like a little child and began to scream. Dick threw open the window, and Torpenhow flung the door back.

"There you are," said Dick soothingly. "My friend here can call for a policeman, and you can run through that door. Nobody is going to hurt you."

The girl sobbed convulsively for a few minutes, and then tried to laugh.

"Nothing in the world to hurt you. Now listen to me for a minute. I'm what they call an artist by profession. You know what artists do?"

"They draw the things in red and black ink on the pop-shop labels."

"I daresay. I haven't risen to pop-shop labels yet. Those are done by the Academicians. I want to draw your head."

"What for?"

"Because it's pretty. That is why you will come to the room across the landing three times a week at eleven in the morning, and I'll give you three quid a week just for sitting still and being drawn. And there's a quid on account."

"For nothing? Oh, my!" The girl turned the sovereign in her hand, and with more foolish tears: "Ain't neither o' you two gentlemen afraid of my bilking you?"

"No. Only ugly girls do that. Try and remember this place. And, by the way, what's your name?"

"I'm Bessie—Bessie— It's no use giving the rest. Bessie Broke—Stone-broke if you like. What's your names? But there—no one ever gives the real ones."

Dick consulted Torpenhow with his eyes.

"My name's Heldar, and my friend's called Torpenhow; and you must be sure to come here. Where do you live?"

"South-the-water—one room—five and sixpence a week. Aren't you making fun of me about that three quid?"

"You'll see later on. And, Bessie, next time you come, remember, you needn't wear that paint. It's bad for the skin, and I have all the colors you'll be likely to need."

Bessie withdrew, scrubbing her cheek with a ragged pocket-handkerchief. The two men looked at each other.

"You're a man," said Torpenhow.

"I'm afraid I've been a fool. It isn't our business to run about the earth reforming Bessie Brokes. And a woman of any kind has no right on this landing."

"Perhaps she won't come back."

"She will if she thinks she can get food and warmth here. I know she will, worse luck. But remember, old man, she isn't a woman: she's my model; and be careful."

"The idea! She's a dissolute little scarecrow—a gutter snippet and nothing more."

"So you think. Wait till she has been fed a little and freed from fear. That fair type recovers itself very quickly. You won't know her in a week or two, when that abject fear has died out of her eyes. She'll be too happy and smiling for my purposes."

"But surely you're taking her out of charity?—to please me?"

"I am not in the habit of playing with hot coals to please

anybody. She has been sent from heaven, as I may have remarked before, to help me with my Melancolia."

"Never heard a word about the lady before."

"What's the use of having a friend, if you must sling your notions at him in words? You ought to know what I'm thinking about. You've heard me grunt lately?"

"Even so; but grunts mean anything in your language, from bad 'baccy to wicked dealers. And I don't think I've been much in your confidence for some time."

"It was a high and soulful grunt. You ought to have understood that it meant the Melancolia." Dick walked Torpenhow up and down the room, keeping silence. Then he smote him in the ribs. "*Now* don't you see it? Bessie's abject futility, and the terror in her eyes, welded on to one or two details in the way of sorrow that have come under my experience lately. Likewise some orange and black—two keys of each. But I can't explain on an empty stomach."

"It sounds mad enough. You'd better stick to your soldiers, Dick, instead of maundering about heads and eyes and experiences."

"Think so?" Dick began to dance on his heels, singing—

" 'They're as proud as a turkey when they hold the ready cash,
You ought to 'ear the way they laugh an' joke;
They are tricky an' they're funny when they've got the ready money—
Ow! but see 'em when they're all stone-broke.' "

Then he sat down to pour out his heart to Maisie in a four-sheet letter of counsel and encouragement, and registered an oath that he would get to work with an undivided heart as soon as Bessie should reappear.

The girl kept her appointment unpainted and unadorned, afraid and overbold by turns. When she found that she was merely expected to sit still, she grew calmer, and criticised the appointments of the studio with freedom and some point. She liked the warmth and the comfort and the release from fear of physical pain. Dick made two or three studies of her head in monochrome, but the actual notion of the Melancolia would not arrive.

"What a mess you keep your things in!" said Bessie, some days later, when she felt herself thoroughly at home. "I s'pose your clothes are just as bad. Gentlemen never think what buttons and tape are made for."

"I buy things to wear, and wear 'em till they go to pieces. I don't know what Torpenhow does."

Bessie made diligent inquiry in the latter's room, and unearthed a bale of disreputabe socks. "Some of these I'll mend now," she said, "and some I'll take home. D'you know, I sit all day long at home doing nothing, just like a lady, and no more noticing them other girls in the house than if they was so many flies? I don't have any unnecessary words, but I put 'em down quick, I can tell you, when they talk to me. No; it's quite nice these days. I lock my door, and they can only call me names through the keyhole, and I sit inside, just like a lady, mending socks. Mr. Torpenhow wears his socks out both ends at once."

"Three quid a week from me, and the delights of my society. No socks mended. Nothing from Torp except a nod on the landing now and again, and all his socks mended. Bessie is very much a woman," thought Dick; and he looked at her between half-shut eyes. Food and rest had transformed the girl, as Dick knew they would.

"What are you looking at me like that for?" she said quickly. "Don't. You look reg'lar bad when you look that way. You don't think much o' me, do you?"

"That depends on how you behave."

Bessie behaved beautifully. Only it was difficult at the end of a sitting to bid her go out into the gray streets. She very much preferred the studio and a big chair by the stove, with some socks in her lap as an excuse for delay. Then Torpenhow would come in, and Bessie would be moved to tell strange and wonderful stories of her past, and still stranger ones of her present improved circumstances. She would make them tea as though she had a right to make it; and once or twice on these occasions Dick caught Torpenhow's eyes fixed on the trim little figure, and because Bessie's flittings about the room made Dick ardently long for Maisie, he realized whither Torpenhow's thoughts were tending. And Bessie was exceedingly careful of the condition of Torpenhow's linen. She spoke very little to him, but sometimes they talked together on the landing.

"I was a great fool," Dick said to himself. "I know what red firelight looks like when a man's trampling through a strange town; and ours is a lonely, selfish sort of life at the best. I wonder Maisie doesn't feel that sometimes. But I can't order Bessie away. That's the worst of beginning things. One never knows where they stop."

One evening, after a sitting prolonged to the last limit of the light, Dick was roused from a nap by a broken voice in Torpenhow's room. He jumped to his feet. "Now what ought I to do? It looks foolish to go in.—Oh, bless you, Binkie!" The little terrier thrust Torpenhow's door open with his nose and came out to take possession of Dick's chair. The door swung wide unheeded, and Dick across the landing could see Bessie in the half-light making her little supplication to Torpenhow. She was kneeling by his side, and her hands were clasped across his knee.

"I know—I know," she said thickly. "'Tisn't right o' me to do this, but I can't help it; and you were so kind—so kind; and you never took any notice o' me. And I've mended all your things so carefully—I did. Oh, please, 'tisn't as if I was asking you to marry me. I wouldn't think of it. But cou—couldn't you take and live with me till Miss Right comes along? I'm only Miss Wrong, I know, but I'd work my hands to the bare bone for you. And I'm not ugly to look at. Say you will?"

Dick hardly recognized Torpenhow's voice in reply:

"But look here. It's no use. I'm liable to be ordered off anywhere at a minute's notice if a war breaks out. At a minute's notice—dear."

"What does that matter? Until you go, then. Until you go. 'Tisn't much I'm asking, and—you don't know how good I can cook." She had put an arm round his neck and was drawing his head down.

"Until—I—go, then."

"Torp," said Dick across the landing. He could hardly steady his voice. "Come here a minute, old man. I'm in trouble."—"Heaven send he'll listen to me!" There was something very like an oath from Bessie's lips. She was afraid of Dick, and disappeared down the staircase in panic, but it seemed an age before Torpenhow entered the studio. He went to the mantel-piece, buried his head on his arms, and groaned like a wounded bull.

"What the devil right have you to interfere?" he said, at last.

"Who's interfering with which? Your own sense told you long ago you couldn't be such a fool. It was a tough rack, St. Anthony, but you're all right now."

"I oughtn't to have seen her moving about these rooms as if they belonged to her. That's what upset me. It gives a lonely man a sort of hankering, doesn't it?" said Torpenhow piteously.

"Now you talk sense. It does. But, since you aren't in a condition to discuss the disadvantages of double housekeeping, do you know what you're going to do?"

"I don't. I wish I did."

"You're going away for a season on a brilliant tour to regain tone. You're going to Brighton, or Scarborough, or Prawle Point, to see the ships go by. And you're going at once. Isn't it odd? I'll take care of Binkie, but out you go immediately. Never resist the devil. He holds the bank. Fly from him. Pack your things and go."

"I believe you're right. Where shall I go?"

"And you call yourself a special correspondent! Pack first and inquire afterward."

An hour later Torpenhow was dispatched into the night in a hansom. "You'll probably think of some place to go to while you're moving," said Dick. "Go to Euston, to begin with, and—oh yes—get drunk to-night."

He returned to the studio, and lighted more candles, for he found the room very dark.

"Oh, you Jezebel! you futile little Jezebel! Won't you hate me to-morrow?—Binkie, come here."

Binkie turned over on his back on the hearth-rug, and Dick stirred him with a meditative foot.

"I said she was not immoral. I was wrong. She said she could cook. That showed premeditated sin. Oh, Binkie, if you are a man you will go to perdition; but if you are a woman, and say that you can cook, you will go to a much worse place."

CHAPTER TEN

What's yon that follows at my side?—
  The foe that ye must fight, my lord.—
That hirples swift as I can ride?—
  The shadow of the night, my lord.—
Then wheel my horse against the foe!—
  He's down and overpast, my lord.
Ye war against the sunset glow:
  The darkness gathers fast, my lord.

—*The Fight of Heriot's Ford*

"THIS is a cheerful life," said Dick, some days later. "Torp's away; Bessie hates me; I can't get at the notion of the Melancolia; Maisie's letters are scrappy; and I believe I have indigestion. What gives a man pains across his head and spots before his eyes, Binkie? Shall us take some liver pills?"

Dick had just gone through a lively scene with Bessie. She had for the fiftieth time reproached him for sending Torpenhow away. She explained her enduring hatred for Dick, and made it clear to him that she only sat for the sake of his money. "And Mr. Torpenhow's ten times a better man than you," she concluded.

"He is. That's why he went away. *I* should have stayed and made love to you."

The girl sat with her chin on her hand, scowling. "To me! I'd like to catch you! If I wasn't afraid o' being hung I'd kill you. That's what I'd do. D'you believe me?"

Dick smiled wearily. It is not pleasant to live in the company of a notion that will not work out, a fox-terrier that cannot talk, and a woman who talks too much. He would have answered, but at that moment there unrolled itself from one corner of the studio a veil, as it were, of the filmiest gauze. He rubbed his eyes, but the gray haze would not go.

"This is disgraceful indigestion. Binkie, we will go to a medicine-man. We can't have our eyes interfered with, for by these we get our bread; also mutton-chop bones for little dogs."

The doctor was an affable local practitioner with white hair, and he said nothing till Dick began to describe the gray film in the studio.

"We all want a little patching and repairing from time to time," he chirped. "Like a ship, my dear sir—exactly like a ship. Sometimes the hull is out of order, and we consult the surgeon; sometimes the rigging, and then I advise; sometimes the engines, and we go to the brain-specialist; sometimes the look-out on the bridge is tired, and then we see an oculist. I should recommend you to see an oculist. A little patching and repairing from time to time is all we want. An oculist, by all means."

Dick sought an oculist—the best in London. He was certain that the local practitioner did not know anything about his trade, and more certain that Maisie would laugh at him if he were forced to wear spectacles.

"I've neglected the warnings of my lord the stomach too long. Hence these spots before the eyes, Binkie. I can see as well as I ever could."

As he entered the dark hall that led to the consulting-room a man cannoned against him. Dick saw the face as it hurried out into the street.

"That's the writer-type. He has the same modeling of the forehead as Torp. He looks very sick. Probably heard something he didn't like."

Even as he thought, a great fear came upon Dick, a fear that made him hold his breath as he walked into the oculist's waiting-room, with the heavy carved furniture, the dark-green paper, and the sober-hued prints on the wall. He recognized a reproduction of one of his own sketches.

Many people were waiting their turn before him. His eye was caught by a flaming red-and-gold Christmas-carol book. Little children came to that eye-doctor, and they needed large-type amusement.

"That's idolatrous bad Art," he said, drawing the book toward himself. "From the anatomy of the angels, it has been made in Germany." He opened it mechanically, and there leaped to his eyes a verse printed in red ink:

"The next good joy that Mary had,
It was the joy of three,
To see her good Son Jesus Christ
Making the blind to see;
Making the blind to see, good Lord,
And happy may we be.
Praise Father, Son, and Holy Ghost
To all eternity!"

Dick read and re-read the verse till his turn came, and the doctor was bending above him seated in an armchair. The blaze of a gas-microscope in his eyes made him wince. The doctor's hand touched the scar of the sword-cut on Dick's head, and Dick explained briefly how he had come by it. When the flame was removed, Dick saw the doctor's face, and the fear came upon him again. The doctor wrapped himself in a mist of words. Dick caught allusions to "scar," "frontal bone," "optic nerve," "extreme caution," and the "avoidance of mental anxiety."

"Verdict?" he said faintly. "My business is painting, and I daren't waste time. What do you make of it?"

Again the whirl of words, but this time they conveyed a meaning.

"Can you give me anything to drink?"

Many sentences were pronounced in that darkened room, and the prisoners often needed cheering. Dick found a glass of liquor brandy in his hand.

"As far as I can gather," he said, coughing above the spirit, "you call it decay of the optic nerve, or something, and therefore hopeless. What is my time-limit, avoiding all strain and worry?"

"Perhaps one year."

"My God! And if I don't take care of myself?"

"I really could not say. One cannot ascertain the exact amount of injury inflicted by the sword-cut. The scar is an old one, and—exposure to the strong light of the desert, did you say?—with excessive application to fine work? I really could not say."

"I beg your pardon, but it has come without any warning. If you will let me, I'll sit here for a minute, and then I'll go. You have been very good in telling me the truth. Without any warning; without any warning. Thanks."

Dick went into the street, and was rapturously received by Binkie. "We've got it very badly, little dog! Just as badly as we can get it. We'll go to the Park to think it out."

They headed for a certain tree that Dick knew well, and they sat down to think, because his legs were trembling under him and there was cold fear at the pit of his stomach.

"How could it have come without any warning? It's as sudden as being shot. It's the living death, Binkie. We're to be shut up in the dark in one year if we're careful, and we shan't see anybody, and we shall never have anything we want, not though we live to be a hundred." Binkie wagged his tail joyously. "Binkie, we must think. Let's see how it feels to be blind." Dick shut his eyes, and flaming commas and Catherine-wheels floated inside the lids. Yet when he looked across the Park the scope of his vision was not contracted. He could see perfectly, until a procession of slow-wheeling fireworks defiled across his eyeballs.

"Little dorglums, we aren't at all well. Let's go home. If only Torp were back, now!"

But Torpenhow was in the south of England, inspecting dockyards in the company of the Nilghai. His letters were brief and full of mystery.

Dick had never asked anybody to help him in his joys or his sorrows. He argued, in the loneliness of the studio, henceforward to be decorated with a film of gray gauze in one corner, that, if his fate were blindness, all the Torpenhows in the world could not save him. "I can't call him off his trip to sit down and sympathize with me. I must pull through the business alone," he said. He was lying on the sofa, eating his mustache and wondering what the darkness of the night would be like. Then came to his mind the memory of a quaint scene in the Soudan. A soldier had been nearly hacked in two by a broad-bladed Arab spear. For one instant the man felt no pain. Looking down, he saw that his life-blood was going from him. The stupid bewilderment on his face was so intensely comic that both Dick and Torpenhow, still panting and unstrung from a fight for life, had roared with laughter, in which the man seemed as if he would join, but, as his lips parted in a sheepish grin, the agony of death came upon him, and he pitched grunting at their feet. Dick laughed again, remembering the horror. It seemed so exactly like his own case. "But I have a little more time allowed me," he said. He paced up and down the room, quietly at first, but afterward with the hurried feet of fear. It was as though a black shadow stood at his elbow and urged him to go forward; and there were only weaving circles and floating pin-dots before his eyes.

"We must be calm, Binkie; we must be calm." He talked aloud for the sake of distraction. "This isn't nice at all. What shall we do? We must do something. Our time is short. I shouldn't have believed that this morning; but now things are different. Binkie, where was Moses when the light went out?"

Binkie smiled from ear to ear, as a well-bred terrier should, but made no suggestion.

"'Were there but world enough and time, This coyness, Binkie, were no crime. . . . But at my back I always hear—'" He wiped his forehead, which was unpleasantly damp. "What can I do? What can I do? I haven't any notions left, and I can't think connectedly, but I must do something, or I shall go off my head."

The hurried walk recommenced, Dick stopping every now and again to drag forth long-neglected canvases and old note-books; for he turned to his work by instinct, as a thing that could not fail. "You won't do, and you won't do," he said, at each inspection. "No more soldiers. I couldn't paint 'em. Sudden death comes home too nearly, and this is battle and murder both for me."

The day was failing, and Dick thought for a moment that the twilight of the blind had come upon him unawares. "Allah Almighty!" he cried despairingly, "help me through the time of waiting, and I won't whine when my punishment comes. What can I do now, before the light goes?"

There was no answer. Dick waited till he could regain some sort of control over himself. His hands were shaking, and he prided himself on their steadiness; he could feel that his lips were quivering, and the sweat was running down his face. He was lashed by fear, driven forward by the desire to get to work at once and accomplish something, and maddened by the refusal of his brain to do more than repeat the news that he was about to go blind. "It's a humiliating exhibition," he thought, "and I'm glad Torp isn't here to see. The doctor said I was to avoid mental worry. Come here and let me pet you, Binkie."

The little dog yelped because Dick nearly squeezed the bark out of him. Then he heard the man speaking in the twilight, and, doglike, understood that his trouble stood off from him—

"Allah is good, Binkie. Not quite so gentle as we could wish, but we'll discuss that later. I think I see my way to it now. All those studies of Bessie's head were nonsense, and they nearly brought your master into a scrape. I hold the notion now as clear as crystal—'the Melancolia that transcends all wit.' There shall be Maisie in that head, because I shall never get Maisie; and Bess, of course, because she knows all about Melancolia, though she doesn't know she knows; and there shall be some drawing in it, and it shall all end up with a laugh. That's for myself. Shall she giggle or grin? No, she shall laugh right out of the canvas, and every man and woman that ever had a sorrow of their own shall—what is it the poem says?—

> " 'Understand the speech and feel a stir
> Of fellowship in all disastrous fight.'

'In all disastrous fight'? That's better than painting the thing merely to pique Maisie. I can do it now because I have it inside me. Binkie, I'm going to hold you up by your tail. You're an omen. Come here."

Binkie swung head downward for a moment without speaking.

" 'Rather like holding a guinea-pig; but you're a brave little dog, and you don't yelp when you're hung up. It is an omen."

Binkie went to his own chair, and as often as he looked saw Dick walking up and down, rubbing his hands and chuckling. That night Dick wrote a letter to Maisie full of the tenderest regard for her health, but saying very little about his own, and dreamed of the Melancolia to be born. Not till morning did he remember that something might happen to him in the future.

He fell to work, whistling softly, and was swallowed up in the clean, clear joy of creation, which does not come to man too often, lest he should consider himself the equal of his God, and so refuse to die at the appointed time. He forgot Maisie, Torpenhow, and Binkie at his feet, but remembered to stir Bessie, who needed very little stirring, into a tremendous rage, that he might watch the smoldering lights in her eyes. He threw himself without reservation into his work, and did not think of the doom that was to overtake him, for he was possessed with his notion, and the things of this world had no power upon him.

"You're pleased to-day," said Bessie.

Dick waved his mahl-stick in mystic circles and went to the sideboard for a drink. In the evening, when the exaltation of the day had died down, he went to the sideboard again, and after some visits became convinced that the eye-doctor was a liar, since he still could see everything very clearly. He was of opinion that he would even make a home for Maisie, and that whether she liked it or not she should be his wife. The mood passed next morning, but the sideboard and all upon it remained for his comfort. Again he set to work, and his eyes troubled him with spots and dashes and blurs till he had taken counsel with the sideboard, and the Melancolia both on the canvas and in his own mind appeared lovelier than ever. There was a delightful sense of irresponsibility upon him, such as they feel who walking among their fellowmen know that the death-sentence of disease is upon them, and, since fear is but waste of the little time left, are riotously happy. The days passed without event. Bessie arrived punctually always, and, though her voice seemed to Dick to come from a distance, her face was always very near, and the Melancolia began to flame on the canvas, in the likeness of a woman who had known all the sorrow in the world and was laughing at it. It was true that the corners of the studio draped themselves in gray film and retired into the darkness, that the spots in his eyes and the pains across his head were very troublesome, and that Maisie's letters were hard to read and harder still to answer. He could not tell her of his trouble, and he could not laugh at her accounts of her own Melancolia which was always going to be finished. But the furious days of toil and the nights of wild dreams made amends for all, and the sideboard was his best friend on earth. Bessie was singularly dull. She used to shriek with rage when Dick stared at her between half-closed eyes. Now she sulked, or watched him with disgust, saying very little.

Torpenhow had been absent for six weeks. An incoherent note heralded his return. "News! great news!" he wrote. "The Nilghai knows, and so does the Keneu. We're all back on Thursday. Get lunch and clean your accouterments."

Dick showed Bessie the letter, and she abused him for that he had ever sent Torpenhow away and ruined her life.

"Well," said Dick, "you're better as you are, instead of making love to some drunken beast in the street." He felt that he had rescued Torpenhow from great temptation.

"I don't know if that's any worse than sitting to a drunken beast in a studio. *You* haven't been sober for three weeks. You've been soaking the whole time; and yet you pretend you're better than me!"

"What d'you mean?" said Dick.

"Mean! You'll see when Mr. Torpenhow comes back."

It was not long to wait. Torpenhow met Bessie on the staircase without a sign of feeling. He had news that was more to him than many Bessies, and the Keneu and the Nilghai were trampling behind him, calling for Dick.

"Drinking like a fish," Bessie whispered. "He's been at it for nearly a month." She followed the men stealthily to hear judgment done.

They came into the studio, rejoicing, to be welcomed over-effusively by a drawn, lined, shrunken, haggard wreck—unshaven, blue-white about the nostrils, stooping in the shoulders, and peering under his eyebrows nervously. The drink had been at work as steadily as Dick.

"Is this you?" said Torpenhow.

"All that's left of me. Sit down. Binkie's quite well, and I've been doing some good work." He reeled where he stood.

"You've done some of the worst work you've ever done in your life. Man alive, you're—"

Torpenhow turned to his companions appealingly, and they left the room to find lunch elsewhere. Then he spoke; but, since the reproof of a friend is much too sacred and intimate a thing to be printed, and since Torpenhow used figures and metaphors which were unseemly, and contempt untranslatable, it will never be known what was actually said to Dick, who blinked and winked and picked at his hands. After a time the culprit began to feel the need of a little self-respect. He was quite sure that he had not in any way departed from virtue, and there were reasons, too, of which Torpenhow knew nothing. He would explain.

He rose, tried to straighten his shoulders, and spoke to the face he could hardly see.

"You are right," he said. "But I am right, too. After you went away I had some trouble with my eyes. So I went to an oculist, and he turned a gasogene—I mean a gas-engine—into my eye. That was very long ago. He said, 'Scar on the head—sword-cut and optic nerve.' Make a note of that. So I am going blind. I have some work to do before I go blind, and I suppose that I must do it. I cannot see much now, but I can see best when I am drunk. I did not know I was drunk till I was told, but I must go on with my work. If you want to see it, there it is." He pointed to the all but finished Melancolia and looked for applause.

Torpenhow said nothing, and Dick began to whimper feebly, for joy at seeing Torpenhow again, for grief at misdeeds—if indeed they were misdeeds—that made Torpenhow remote and unsympathetic, and for childish vanity hurt, since Torpenhow had not given a word of praise to his wonderful picture.

Bessie looked through the keyhole after a long pause, and saw the two walking up and down as usual, Torpenhow's hand on Dick's shoulder. Hereat she said something so improper that it shocked even Binkie, who was dribbling patiently on the landing with the hope of seeing his master again.

CHAPTER ELEVEN

The lark will make her hymn to God,
  The partridge call her brood,
While I forget the heath I trod,
  The fields wherein I stood.
'Tis dule to know not night from morn,
  But deeper dule to know
I can but hear the hunter's horn
  That once I used to blow.—*The Only Son*

It was the third day after Torpenhow's return, and his heart was heavy.

"Do you mean to tell me that you can't see to work without whisky? It's generally the other way about."

"Can a drunkard swear on his honor?" said Dick.

"Yes, if he has been as good a man as you."

"Then I give you my word of honor," said Dick, speaking hurriedly through parched lips. "Old man, I can hardly see your face now. You've kept me sober for two days—if I ever was drunk—and I've done no work. Don't keep me back any more. I don't know when my eyes may give out. The spots and dots and the pains and things are crowding worse than ever. I swear I can see all right when I'm—when I'm moderately screwed, as you say. Give me three more sittings from Bessie and all the—stuff I want, and the picture will be done. I can't kill myself in three days. It only means a touch of D. T. at the worst."

"If I give you three days more will you promise me to stop work and—the other thing, whether the picture's finished or not?"

"I can't. You don't know what that picture means to me. But surely you could get the Nilghai to help you, and knock me down and tie me up. I shouldn't fight for the whisky, but I should for the work."

"Go on, then. I give you three days; but you're nearly breaking my heart."

Dick returned to his work, toiling as one possessed; and the yellow devil of whisky stood by him and chased away the spots in his eyes. The Melancolia was nearly finished, and was all or nearly all that he had hoped she would be. Dick jested with Bessie, who reminded him that he was "a drunken beast"; but the reproof did not move him.

"You can't understand, Bess. We are in sight of land now, and soon we shall lie back and think about what we've done. I'll give you three months' pay when the picture's finished, and next time I have any more work in hand—but that doesn't matter. Won't three months' pay make you hate me less?"

"No, it won't! I hate you, and I'll go on hating you. Mr. Torpenhow won't speak to me any more. He's always looking at map-things and red-backed books."

Bessie did not say that she had again laid siege to Torpenhow, or that he had at the end of her passionate pleading picked her up, given her a kiss, and put her outside the door with a recommendation not to be a little fool. He spent most of his time in the company of the Nilghai, and their talk was of war in the near future, the hiring of transports, and secret preparations among the dockyards. He did not care to see Dick till the picture was finished.

"He's doing first-class work," he said to the Nilghai, "and it's quite out of his regular line. But, for the matter of that, so's his infernal drinking."

"Never mind. Leave him alone. When he has come to his senses again we'll carry him off from this place and let him breathe clean air. Poor Dick! I don't envy you, Torp, when his eyes fail."

"Yes, it will be a case of 'God help the man who's chained to our Davie.' The worst is that we don't know when it will happen; and I believe the uncertainty and the waiting have sent Dick to the whisky more than anything else."

"How the Arab who cut his head open would grin if he knew!"

"He's at perfect liberty to grin if he can. He's dead. That's poor consolation now."

In the afternoon of the third day Torpenhow heard Dick calling for him. "All finished!" he shouted. "I've done it! Come in! Isn't she a beauty? Isn't she a darling? I've been down to hell to get her; but isn't she worth it?"

Torpenhow looked at the head of a woman who laughed—a full-lipped, hollow-eyed woman who laughed from out of the canvas as Dick had intended she should.

"Who taught you how to do it?" said Torpenhow. "The touch and notion have nothing to do with your regular work. What a face it is! What eyes, and what insolence!" Unconsciously he threw back his head and laughed with her. "She's seen the game played out—I don't think she had a good time of it—and now she doesn't care. Isn't that the idea?"

"Exactly."

"Where did you get the mouth and chin from? They don't belong to Bess."

"They're—some one else's. But isn't it good? Isn't it thundering good? Wasn't it worth the whisky? I did it. Alone I did it, and it's the best I can do." He drew his breath sharply, and whispered, "Just God! what could I not do ten years hence, if I can do this now!—By the way, what do you think of it, Bess?"

The girl was biting her lips. She loathed Torpenhow because he had taken no notice of her.

"I think it's just the horridest, beastliest thing I ever saw," she answered, and turned away.

"More than you will be of that way of thinking, young woman.—Dick, there's a sort of murderous, viperine suggestion in the poise of the head that I don't understand," said Torpenhow.

"That's trick-work," said Dick, chuckling with delight of being completely understood. "I couldn't resist one little bit of sheer swagger. It's a French trick, and you wouldn't understand; but it's got at by slewing round the head a trifle, and a tiny, tiny foreshortening of one side of the face from the angle of the chin to the top of the left ear. That, and deepening the shadow under the lobe of the ear. It was flagrant trick-work; but, having the notion fixed, I felt entitled to play with it.—Oh, you beauty!"

"Amen! She is a beauty. I can feel it."

"So will every man who has any sorrow of his own," said Dick, slapping his thigh. "He shall see his trouble there, and, by the Lord Harry, just when he's feeling properly sorry for himself he shall throw back his head and laugh —as she is laughing. I've put the life of my heart and the light of my eyes into her, and I don't care what comes. . . . I'm tired—awfully tired. I think I'll get to sleep. Take away the whisky, it has served its turn, and give Bessie thirty-six quid, and three over for luck. Cover the picture."

He dropped asleep in the long chair, his face white and haggard, almost before he had finished the sentence. Bessie tried to take Torpenhow's hand. "Aren't you never going to speak to me any more?" she said; but Torpenhow was looking at Dick.

"What a stock of vanity the man has! I'll take him in hand to-morrow and make much of him. He deserves it.—Eh! what was that, Bess?"

"Nothing. I'll put things tidy here a little, and then I'll go. You couldn't give me that three months' pay now, could you? He said you were to."

Torpenhow gave her a check and went to his own rooms. Bessie faithfully tidied up the studio, set the door ajar for flight, emptied half a bottle of turpentine on a duster, and began to scrub the face of the Melancolia viciously. The paint did not smudge quickly enough. She took a palette-knife and scraped, following each stroke with the wet duster. In five minutes the picture was a formless, scarred muddle of colors. She threw the paint-stained duster into the studio stove, stuck out her tongue at the sleeper, and whispered,

"Bilked!" as she turned to run down the staircase. She would never see Torpenhow any more, but she had at least done harm to the man who had come between her and her desire and who used to make fun of her. Cashing the check was the very cream of the jest to Bessie. Then the little privateer sailed across the Thames, to be swallowed up in the gray wilderness of South-the-water.

Dick slept till late into the evening, when Torpenhow dragged him off to bed. His eyes were as bright as his voice was hoarse. "Let's have another look at the picture," he said, insistently as a child.

"You—go—to—bed," said Torpenhow. "You aren't at all well, though you mayn't know it. You're as jumpy as a cat."

"I reform to-morrow. Good-night."

As he repassed through the studio, Torpenhow lifted the cloth above the picture, and almost betrayed himself by outcries: "Wiped out!—scraped out and turped out! If Dick knows this to-night he'll go perfectly mad. He's on the verge of jumps as it is. That's Bess—the little fiend! Only a woman could have done that!—with the ink not dry on the check, too! Dick will be raving mad to-morrow. It was all my fault for trying to help gutter-devils. Oh, my poor Dick, the Lord is hitting you very hard!"

Dick could not sleep that night, partly for pure joy, and partly because the well-known Catherine-wheels inside his eyes had given place to crackling volcanoes of many-colored fire. "Spout away," he said aloud. "I've done my work, and now you can do what you please." He lay still, staring at the ceiling, the long-pent-up delirium of drink in his veins, his brain on fire with racing thoughts that would not stay to be considered, and his hands crisped and dry. He had just discovered that he was painting the face of the Melancolia on a revolving dome ribbed with millions of lights, and that all his wondrous thoughts stood embodied hundreds of feet below his tiny swinging plank, shouting together in his honor, when something cracked inside his temples like an overstrained bowstring, the glittering dome broke inward, and he was alone in the thick night.

"I'll go to sleep. The room's very dark. Let's light a lamp and see how the Melancolia looks. There ought to have been a moon."

It was then that Torpenhow heard his name called by a voice that he did not know—in the rattling accents of deadly fear.

"He's looked at the picture," was his first thought, as he hurried into the bedroom and found Dick sitting up and beating the air with his hands.

"Torp! Torp! Where are you? For pity's sake, come to me!"

"What's the matter?"

Dick clutched at his shoulder. "Matter! I've been lying here for hours in the dark, and you never heard me. Torp, old man, don't go away. I'm all in the dark. In the dark, I tell you!"

Torpenhow held the candle within a foot of Dick's eyes, but there was no light in those eyes. He lit the gas, and Dick heard the flame catch. The grip of his fingers on Torpenhow's shoulder made Torpenhow wince.

"Don't leave me. You wouldn't leave me alone now, would you? I can't see. D'you understand? It's black—quite black—and I feel as if I was falling through it all."

"Steady, does it." Torpenhow put his arm round Dick and began to rock him gently to and fro.

"That's good. Now don't talk. If I keep very quiet for a while, this darkness will lift. It seems just on the point of breaking. H'sh!" Dick knit his brows and stared desperately in front of him. The night air was chilling Torpenhow's toes.

"Can you stay like that a minute?" he said. "I'll get my dressing-gown and some slippers."

Dick clutched the bed-head with both hands and waited for the darkness to clear away. "What a time you've been!"

he cried, when Torpenhow returned. "It's as black as ever. What are you banging about in the doorway?"

"Long chair—horse-blanket—pillow. Going to sleep by you. Lie down now; you'll be better in the morning."

"I shan't!" The voice rose to a wail. "My God! I'm blind! I'm blind, and the darkness will never go away." He made as if to leap from the bed, but Torpenhow's arms were round him, and Torpenhow's chin was on his shoulder, and his breath was squeezed out of him. He could only gasp, "Blind!" and wriggle feebly.

"Steady, Dickie, steady!" said the deep voice in his ear, and the grip tightened. "Bite on the bullet, old man, and don't let them think you're afraid." The grip could draw no closer. Both men were breathing heavily. Dick threw his head from side to side and groaned.

"Let me go," he panted. "You're cracking my ribs. We—we mustn't let them think we're afraid, must we—all the powers of darkness and that lot?"

"Lie down. It's all over now."

"Yes," said Dick obediently. "But would you mind letting me hold your hand? I feel as if I wanted something to hold on to. One drops through the dark so."

Torpenhow thrust out a large and hairy paw from the long chair. Dick clutched it tightly, and in half an hour had fallen asleep. Torpenhow withdrew his hand, and, stooping over Dick, kissed him lightly on the forehead, as men do sometimes kiss a wounded comrade in the hour of death, to ease his departure.

In the gray dawn Torpenhow heard Dick talking to himself. He was adrift on the shoreless tides of delirium, speaking very quickly—

"It's a pity—a great pity; but it's helped, and it must be eaten, Master George. Sufficient unto the day is the blindness thereof, and, further, putting aside all Melancolias and false humors, it is of obvious notoriety—such as mine was—that the queen can do no wrong. Torp doesn't know that. I'll tell him when we're a little further into the desert. What a bungle those boatmen are making of the steamer-ropes! They'll have that four-inch hawser chafed through in a minute. I told you so—there she goes! White foam on green water, and the steamer slewing round. How good that looks! I'll sketch it. No, I can't. I'm afflicted with ophthalmia. That was one of the ten plagues of Egypt, and it extends up the Nile in the shape of cataract. Ha! that's a joke, Torp. Laugh, you graven image, and stand clear of the hawser. . . . It'll knock you into the water and make your dress all dirty, Maisie dear."

"Oh!" said Torpenhow. "This happened before. That night on the river."

"She'll be sure to say it's my fault if you get muddy, and you're quite near enough to the breakwater. Maisie, that's not fair. Ah! I knew you'd miss. Low and to the left, dear. But you've no conviction. Everything in the world except conviction. Don't be angry, darling. I'd cut my hand off if it would give you anything more than obstinacy. My right hand, if it would serve."

"Now we mustn't listen. Here's an island shouting across seas of misunderstanding with a vengeance. But it's shouting truth, I fancy," said Torpenhow.

The babble continued. It all bore upon Maisie. Sometimes Dick lectured at length on his craft, then he cursed himself for his folly in being enslaved. He pleaded to Maisie for a kiss—only one kiss—before she went away, and called to her to come back from Vitry-sur-Marne, if she would; but through all his ravings he bade heaven and earth witness that the queen could do no wrong.

Torpenhow listened attentively, and learned every detail of Dick's life that had been hidden from him. For three days Dick raved through his past, and then slept a natural sleep. "What a strain he has been running under, poor chap!" said Torpenhow. "Dick, of all men, handing himself over like a dog! And I was lecturing him on arrogance! I ought to have known that it was no use to judge a man. But I did it. What a demon that girl must be! Dick's

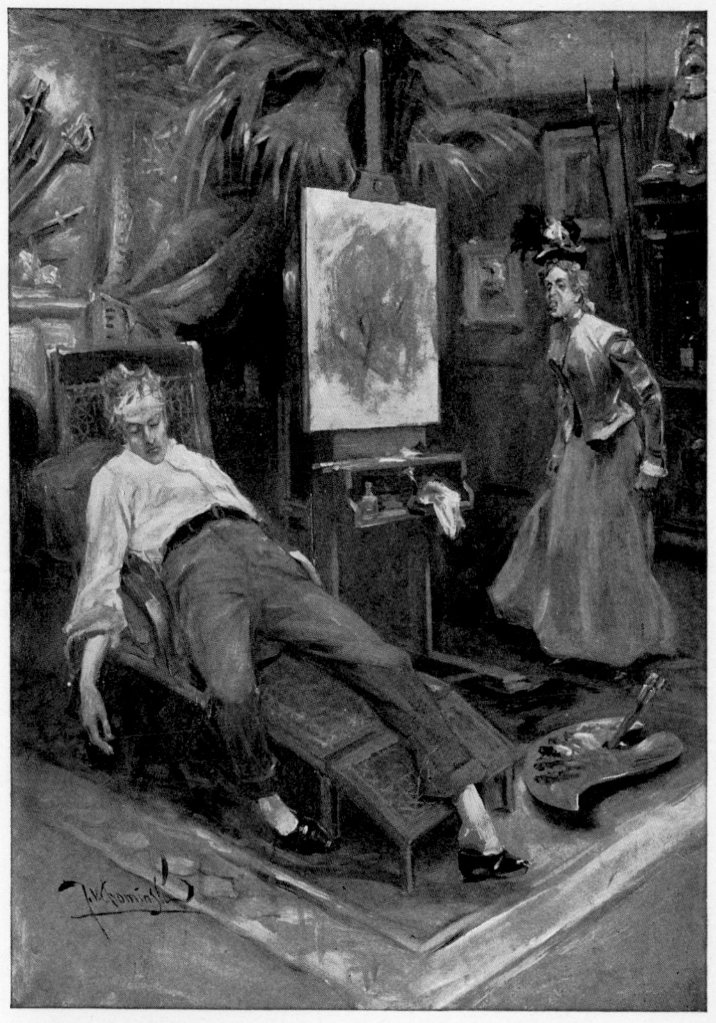

Drawn by T. V. CHOMINSKI.

"In five minutes the picture was a formless, scarred muddle of colors. She stuck out her tongue at the sleeper and whispered 'Bilked!'"

THE LIGHT THAT FAILED—Vol. ii., p. 142.

given her his life—confound him!—and she's given him one kiss apparently."

"Torp," said Dick from the bed, "go out for a walk. You've been here too long. I'll get up. Hi! This is annoying. I can't dress myself. Oh, it's too absurd!"

Torpenhow helped him into his clothes and led him to the big chair in the studio. He sat quietly waiting under strained nerves for the darkness to lift. It did not lift that day, nor the next. Dick adventured on a voyage round the walls. He hit his shins against the stove, and this suggested to him that it would be better to crawl on all-fours, one hand in front of him. Torpenhow found him on the floor.

"I'm trying to get the geography of my new possessions," said he. "D'you remember that nigger you gouged in the square? Pity you didn't keep the odd eye. It would have been useful. Any letters for me? Give me all the ones in fat gray envelopes with a sort of crown thing outside. They're of no importance."

Torpenhow gave him a letter with a black M. on the envelope flap. Dick put it into his pocket. There was nothing in it that Torpenhow might not have read, but it belonged to himself and to Maisie, who would never belong to him.

"When she finds that I don't write, she'll stop writing. It's better so. I couldn't be any use to her now," Dick argued, and the tempter suggested that he should make known his condition. Every nerve in him revolted. "I have fallen low enough already. I'm not going to beg for pity. Besides, it would be cruel to her." He strove to put Maisie out of his thoughts; but the blind have many opportunities for thinking, and as the tides of his strength came back to him in the long employless days of dead darkness, Dick's soul was troubled to the core. Another letter, and another, came from Maisie. Then there was silence, and Dick sat by the window, the pulse of summer in the air, and pictured her being won by another man, stronger than himself. His imagination, the keener for the dark background it worked against, spared him no single detail that might send him raging up and down the studio, to stumble over the stove that seemed to be in four places at once. Worst of all, tobacco would not taste in the darkness. The arrogance of the man had disappeared, and in its place were settled despair that Torpenhow knew, and blind passion that Dick confided to his pillow at night. The intervals between the paroxysms were filled with intolerable waiting and the weight of intolerable darkness.

"Come out into the Park," said Torpenhow. "You haven't stirred out since the beginning of things."

"What's the use? There's no movement in the dark; and, besides"—he paused irresolutely at the head of the stairs—"something will run over me."

"Not if I'm with you. Proceed gingerly."

The roar of the streets filled Dick with nervous terror, and he clung to Torpenhow's arm. "Fancy having to feel for a gutter with your foot!" he said petulantly, as he turned into the Park. "Let's curse God and die."

"Sentries are forbidden to pay unauthorized compliments. By Jove, there are the Guards!"

Dick's figure straightened. "Let's get near 'em. Let's go in and look. Let's get on the grass and run. I can smell the trees."

"Mind the low railing. That's all right!" Torpenhow kicked out a tuft of grass with his heel. "Smell that," he said. "Isn't it good?" Dick snuffed luxuriously. "Now pick up your feet and run." They approached as near to the regiment as was possible. The clank of bayonets being unfixed made Dick's nostrils quiver.

"Let's get nearer. They're in column, aren't they?"

"Yes. How did you know?"

"Felt it. Oh, my men!—my beautiful men!" He edged forward as though he could see. "I could draw those chaps once. Who'll draw 'em now?"

"They'll move off in a minute. Don't jump when the band begins."

"Huh! I'm not a new charger. It's the silences that

hurt. Nearer, Torp!—nearer! Oh, my God, what wouldn't I give to see 'em for a minute!—one half minute!"

He could hear the armed life almost within reach of him, could hear the slings tighten across the bandsman's chest as he heaved the big drum from the ground.

"Sticks crossed above his head," whispered Torpenhow.

"I know. *I* know! Who should know if I don't? H'sh!"

The drum-sticks fell with a boom, and the men swung forward to the crash of the band. Dick felt the wind of the massed movement in his face, heard the maddening tramp of feet and the friction of the pouches on the belts. The big drum pounded out the tune. It was a music-hall refrain that made a perfect quickstep—

"He must be a man of decent height,
He must be a man of weight,
He must come home on a Saturday night
In a thoroughly sober state;
He must know how to love me,
And he must know how to kiss;
And if he's enough to keep us both
I can't refuse him bliss."

"What's the matter?" said Torpenhow, as he saw Dick's head fall when the last of the regiment had departed.

"Nothing. I feel a little bit out of the running—that's all. Torp, take me back. Why did you bring me out?"

CHAPTER TWELVE

There were three friends that buried the fourth,
  The mould in his mouth and the dust in his eyes;
And they went south and east, and north—
  The strong man fights, but the sick man dies.

There were three friends that spoke of the dead—
  The strong man fights, but the sick man dies.—
"And would he were here with us now," they said,
  "The sun in our face and the wind in our eyes."

—Ballad

THE Nilghai was angry with Torpenhow. Dick had been sent to bed—blind men are ever under the orders of those who can see—and since he had returned from the Park had fluently sworn at Torpenhow because he was alive, and all the world because it was alive and could see, while he, Dick, was dead in the death of the blind, who, at the best, are only burdens upon their associates. Torpenhow had said something about a Mrs. Gummidge, and Dick had retired in a black fury to handle and rehandle three unopened letters from Maisie.

The Nilghai, fat, burly, and aggressive, was in Torpenhow's rooms. Behind him sat the Keneu, the Great War Eagle, and between them lay a large map embellished with black and white-headed pins.

"I was wrong about the Balkans," said the Nilghai. "But I'm not wrong about this business. The whole of our work in the Southern Soudan must be done over again. The public doesn't care, of course, but the government does, and they are making their arrangements quietly. You know that as well as I do."

"I remember how the people cursed us when our troops withdrew from Omdurman. It was bound to crop up sooner or later. But I can't go," said Torpenhow. He pointed through the open door; it was a hot night. "Can you blame me?"

The Keneu purred above his pipe like a large and very happy cat—

"Don't blame you in the least. It's uncommonly good of you, and all the rest of it, but every man—even you, Torp—must consider his work. I know it sounds brutal, but Dick's out of the race—down—*gastados*, expended, finished, done for. He has a little money of his own. He won't starve, and you can't pull out of your slide for his sake. Think of your own reputation."

"Dick's was five times bigger than mine and yours put together."

"That was because he signed his name to everything he did. It's all ended now. You must hold yourself in readiness to move out. You can command your own prices, and you do better work than any three of us."

"Don't tell me how tempting it is. I'll stay here to look after Dick for a while. He's as cheerful as a bear with a sore head, but I think he likes to have me near him."

The Nilghai said something uncomplimentary about soft-headed fools who throw away their careers for other fools. Torpenhow flushed angrily. The constant strain of attendance on Dick had worn his nerves thin.

"There remains a third fate," said the Keneu thoughtfully. "Consider this, and be not larger fools than is necessary. Dick is—or rather was—an able-bodied man of moderate attractions and a certain amount of audacity."

"Oho!" said the Nilghai, who remembered an affair at Cairo. "I begin to see.—Torp, I'm sorry."

Torpenhow nodded forgiveness: "You were more sorry when he cut you out, though.—Go on, Keneu."

"I've often thought, when I've seen men die out in the desert, that if the news could be sent through the world, and the means of transport were quick enough, there would be one woman at least at each man's bedside."

"There would be some mighty quaint revelations. Let us be grateful things are as they are," said the Nilghai.

"Let us rather reverently consider whether Torp's three-cornered ministrations are exactly what Dick needs just now.—What do you think yourself, Torp?"

"I know they aren't. But what can I do?"

"Lay the matter before the board. We are all Dick's friends here. You've been most in his life."

"But I picked it up when he was off his head."

"The greater chance of its being true. I thought we should arrive. Who is she?"

Then Torpenhow told a tale in plain words, as a special correspondent who knows how to make a verbal *précis* should tell it. The men listened without interruption.

"Is it possible that a man can come back across the years to his calf-love?" said the Keneu. "Is it possible?"

"I give the facts. He says nothing about it now, but he sits fumbling three letters from her when he thinks I'm not looking. What am I to do?"

"Speak to him," said the Nilghai.

"Oh, yes! Write to her—I don't know her full name, remember—and ask her to accept him out of pity. I believe you once told Dick you were sorry for him, Nilghai. You remember what happened, eh? Go into the bedroom and suggest full confession and an appeal to this Maisie girl, whoever she is. I honestly believe he'd try to kill you; and the blindness has made him rather muscular."

"Torpenhow's course is perfectly clear," said the Keneu. "He will go to Vitry-sur-Marne, which is on the Bézières-Landes Railway—single track from Tourgas. The Prussians shelled it out in '70 because there was a poplar on the top of a hill eighteen hundred yards from the church spire. There's a squadron of cavalry quartered there—or ought to be. Where this studio Torp spoke about may be I cannot tell. That is Torp's business. I have given him his route. He will dispassionately explain the situation to the girl, and she will come back to Dick—the more especially because, to use Dick's words, 'there is nothing but her damned obstinacy to keep them apart.' "

"And they have four hundred and twenty pounds a year between 'em. Dick never lost his head for figures, even in his delirium. You haven't the shadow of an excuse for not going," said the Nilghai.

Torpenhow looked very uncomfortable. "But it's absurd and impossible. I can't drag her back by the hair."

"Our business—the business for which we draw our money—is to do absurd and impossible things—generally with no reason whatever except to amuse the public. Here we have a reason. The rest doesn't matter. I shall share these rooms with the Nilghai till Torpenhow returns. There will be a batch of unbridled 'specials' coming to town in a little while, and these will serve as their headquarters. Another reason for sending Torpenhow away. Thus Providence helps those who help others, and"—here the Keneu dropped his measured speech—"we can't have you tied by the leg to Dick when the trouble begins. It's your only chance of getting away; and Dick will be grateful."

"He will—worse luck! I can but go and try. I can't conceive a woman in her senses refusing Dick."

"Talk that out with the girl. I have seen you wheedle an angry Mahdieh woman into giving you dates. This won't be a tithe as difficult. You had better not be here to-morrow afternoon, because the Nilghai and I will be in possession. It is an order. Obey."

"Dick," said Torpenhow next morning, "can I do anything for you?"

"No! Leave me alone. How often must I remind you that I'm blind?"

"Nothing I could go for to fetch for to carry for to bring."

"No. Take those infernal creaking boots of yours away."

"Poor chap!" said Torpenhow to himself. "I must have been sitting on his nerves lately. He wants a lighter step." Then, aloud, "Very well. Since you're so independent, I'm going off for four or five days. Say good-by at least. The housekeepeı will look after you, and Keneu has my rooms."

Dick's face fell. "You won't be longer than a week at the outside? I know I'm touched in the temper, but I can't get on without you."

"Can't you? You'll have to do without me in a little time, and you'll be glad I'm gone."

Dick felt his way back to the big chair, and wondered what these things might mean. He did not wish to be tended by the housekeeper, and yet Torpenhow's constant tendernesses jarred on him. He did not exactly know what he wanted. The darkness would not lift, and Maisie's unopened letters felt worn and old from much handling. He could never read them for himself as long as life endured; but Maisie might have sent him some fresh ones to play with. The Nilghai entered with a gift—a piece of red modeling wax. He fancied that Dick might find interest in using his hands. Dick poked and patted the stuff for a few minutes, and, "Is it like anything in the world?" he said drearily. "Take it away. I may get the touch of the blind in fifty years. Do you know where Torpenhow has gone?"

The Nilghai knew nothing. "We're staying in his rooms till he comes back. Can we do anything for you?"

"I'd like to be left alone, please. Don't think I'm ungrateful; but I'm best alone."

The Nilghai chuckled, and Dick resumed his drowsy brooding and sullen rebellion against fate. He had long since ceased to think about the work he had done in the old days, and the desire to do more work had departed from him. He was exceedingly sorry for himself, and the completeness of his tender grief soothed him. But his soul and his body cried for Maisie—Maisie who would understand. His mind pointed out that Maisie, having her own work to do, would not care. His experience had taught him that when money was exhausted women went away, and that when a man was knocked out of the race the others trampled on him. "Then at the least," said Dick, in reply, "she could use me as I used

Binat—for some sort of a study. I wouldn't ask more than to be near her again, even though I knew that another man was making love to her. Ugh! what a dog I am!"

A voice on the staircase began to sing joyfully—

"When we go—go—go away from here,
Our creditors will weep and they will wail,
Our absence much regretting when they find
that we've been getting
Out of England by next Tuesday's Indian
mail."

Following the trampling of feet, slamming of Torpenhow's door, and the sound of voices in strenuous debate, some one squeaked, "And see, you good fellows, I have found a new water-bottle—firs'-class patent—eh, how you say? Open himself inside out."

Dick sprang to his feet. He knew the voice well. "That's Cassavetti, come back from the Continent. Now I know why Torp went away. There's a row somewhere, and—I'm out of it!"

The Nilghai commanded silence in vain. "That's for my sake," Dick said bitterly. "The birds are getting ready to fly, and they wouldn't tell me. I can hear Morten-Sutherland and Mackaye. Half the War Correspondents in London are there—and I'm out of it."

He stumbled across the landing and plunged into Torpenhow's room. He could feel that it was full of men. "Where's the trouble?" said he. "In the Balkans at last? Why didn't some one tell me?"

"We thought you wouldn't be interested," said the Nilghai shamefacedly. "It's in the Soudan, as usual."

"You lucky dogs! Let me sit here while you talk. I shan't be a skeleton at the feast.—Cassavetti, where are you? Your English is as bad as ever."

Dick was led into a chair. He heard the rustle of the maps, and the talk swept forward, carrying him with it. Everybody spoke at once, discussing press censorships, railway-routes, transport, water-supply, the capacities of generals—these in language that would have horrified a trusting public—ranting, asserting, denouncing, and laughing at the top of their voices. There was the glorious certainty of war in the Soudan at any moment. The Nilghai said so, and it was well to be in readiness. The Keneu had telegraphed to Cairo for horses; Cassavetti had stolen a perfectly inaccurate list of troops that would be ordered forward, and was reading it out amid profane interruptions, and the Keneu introduced to Dick some man unknown who would be employed as war artist by the Central Southern Syndicate. "It's his first outing," said the Keneu. "Give him some tips—about riding camels."

"Oh, those camels!" groaned Cassavetti. "I shall learn to ride him again, and now I am so much all soft! Listen, you good fellows. I know your military arrangement very well. There will go the Royal Argalshire Sutherlanders. So it was read to me upon best authority."

A roar of laughter interrupted him.

"Sit down," said the Nilghai. "The lists aren't even made out in the War Office."

"Will there be any force at Suakin?" said a voice.

Then the outcries redoubled, and grew mixed, thus: "How many Egyptian troops will they use?—God help the Fellaheen! —There's a railway in Plumstead marshes doing duty as a fives-court.—We shall have the Suakin-Berber line built at last.—Canadian voyageurs are too careful. Give me a half drunk Krooman in a whale-boat.—Who commands the Desert column?—No, they never blew up the big rock in the Ghineh bend. We shall have to be hauled up, as usual.—Somebody tell me if there's an Indian contingent, or I'll break everybody's head.—Don't tear the map in two.—It's a war of occupation, I tell you, to connect with the African companies in the South.—There's Guinea-worm in most of the wells on that route." Then the Nilghai, despairing of peace, bellowed like a fog-horn and beat upon the table with both hands.

"But what becomes of Torpenhow?" said Dick, in the silence that followed.

"Torp's in abeyance just now. He's off love-making somewhere, I suppose," said the Nilghai.

"He said he was going to stay at home," said the Keneu.

"Is he?" said Dick with an oath. "He won't. I'm not much good now, but if you and the Nilghai hold him down I'll engage to trample on him till he sees reason. He stay behind, indeed! He's the best of you all. There'll be some tough work by Omdurman. We shall come there to stay, this time. But I forgot. I wish I were going with you."

"So do we all, Dickie," said the Keneu.

"And I most of all," said the new artist of the Central Southern Syndicate. "Could you tell me—"

"I'll give you one piece of advice," Dick answered, moving toward the door. "If you happen to be cut over the head in a scrimmage, don't guard. Tell the man to go on cutting. You'll find it cheapest in the end. Thanks for letting me look in."

"There's grit in Dick," said the Nilghai, an hour later, when the room was emptied of all save the Keneu.

"It was the sacred call of the war trumpet. Did you notice how he answered to it? Poor fellow! Let's look at him," said the Keneu.

The excitement of the talk had died away. Dick was sitting by the studio table, with his head on his arms, when the men came in. He did not change his position.

"It hurts," he moaned. "God forgive me, but it hurts cruelly; and yet, y'know, the world has a knack of spinning round all by itself. Shall I see Torp before he goes?"

"Oh, yes. You'll see him," said the Nilghai.

CHAPTER THIRTEEN

The sun went down an hour ago,
I wonder if I face toward home,
If I lost my way in the light of day
How shall I find it now night is come?

Old Song

"MAISIE, come to bed."

"It's so hot I can't sleep. Don't worry."

Maisie put her elbows on the window-sill and looked at the moonlight on the straight, poplar-flanked road. Summer had come upon Vitry-sur-Marne and parched it to the bone. The grass was dry-burned in the meadows, the clay by the bank of the river was caked to brick, the roadside flowers were long since dead, and the roses in the garden hung withered on their stalks. The heat in the little low bedroom under the eaves was almost intolerable. The very moonlight on the wall of Kami's studio across the road seemed to make the night hotter, and the shadow of the big bell-handle by the closed gate cast a bar of inky black that caught Maisie's eye and annoyed her.

"Horrid thing! It should be all white," she murmured. "And the gate isn't in the middle of the wall, either. I never noticed that before."

Maisie was hard to please at that hour. First, the heat of the past few weeks had worn her down; secondly, her work, and particularly the study of a female head intended to represent the Melancolia and not finished in time for the Salon, was unsatisfactory; thirdly, Kami had said as much two days before; fourthly—but so completely fourthly that it was hardly worth thinking about—Dick, her property, had not written to her for more than six weeks. She was angry with the heat, with Kami, and with her work, but she was exceedingly angry with Dick.

She had written to him three times—each time proposing a fresh treatment of her Melancolia. Dick had taken no notice of these communications. She had resolved to write no more. When she returned to England in the autumn—for her pride's sake she could not return earlier—she would speak to him. She missed the Sunday afternoon conferences more than she cared to admit. All that Kami said was, "*Continuez, mademoiselle, continuez toujours,*" and he had been repeating his wearisome counsel through the hot summer, exactly like a cicala—an old gray cicala in a black alpaca coat, white trousers, and a huge felt hat. But Dick had tramped masterfully up and down her little studio north of the cool green London park, and had said things ten times worse than *continuez*, before he snatched the brush out of her hand and showed her where her error lay. His last letter, Maisie remembered, contained some trivial advice about not sketching in the sun or drinking water at wayside farmhouses; and he had said that not once, but three times—as if he did not know that Maisie could take care of herself.

But what was he doing, that he could not trouble to write? A murmur of voices in the road made her lean from the window. A cavalryman of the little garrison in the town was talking to Kami's cook. The moonlight glittered on the scabbard of his saber, which he was holding in his hand lest it should clank inopportunely. The cook's cap cast deep shadows on her face, which was close to the conscript's. He slid his arm round her waist, and there followed the sound of a kiss.

"Faugh!" said Maisie, stepping back.

"What's that?" said the red haired girl, who was tossing uneasily outside her bed.

"Only a conscript kissing the cook," said Maisie. "They've gone away now." She leaned out of the window again, and put a shawl over her nightgown to guard against chills. There was a very small night-breeze abroad, and a sun-baked rose below nodded its head as one who knew unutterable secrets. Was it possible that Dick should turn his thoughts from her work and his own and descend to the degradation of Suzanne and the conscript? He could not! The rose nodded its head and one leaf therewith. It looked like a naughty little devil scratching its ear. Dick could not, "because," thought Maisie, "he is mine—mine—mine. He said he was. I'm sure I don't care what he does. It will only spoil his work if he does; and it will spoil mine too."

The rose continued to nod in the futile way peculiar to flowers. There was no earthly reason why Dick should not disport himself as he chose, except that he was called by Providence, which was Maisie, to assist Maisie in her work. And her work was the preparation of pictures that went sometimes to English provincial exhibitions, as the notices in the scrap-book proved, and that were invariably rejected by the Salon when Kami was plagued into allowing her to send them up. Her work in the future, it seemed, would be the preparation of pictures on exactly similar lines which would be rejected in exactly the same way—

The red-haired girl threshed distressfully across the sheets. "It's too hot to sleep," she moaned; and the interruption jarred.

Exactly the same way. Then she would divide her years between the little studio in England and Kami's big studio at Vitry-sur-Marne. No, she would go to another master, who should force her into the success that was her right, if patient toil and desperate endeavor gave one a right to anything. Dick had told her that he had worked ten years to understand his craft. She had worked ten years, and ten years were nothing. Dick had said that ten years were nothing—but that was in regard to herself only. He had said—this very man who could not find time to write—that he would wait ten years for her, and that she was bound to come back to him sooner or later. He had said this in the absurd letter about sunstroke and diphtheria; and then he had stopped writing. He was wandering up and down moonlit streets, kissing cooks. She would like to lecture him now—not in her night-gown of course, but properly dressed, severely and from a height. Yet if he was kissing other girls he certainly would not care whether she lectured him or not. He would laugh at her. Very good. She would go back to her studio and prepare pictures that went, etc., etc. The mill-wheel of thought swung round slowly, that no section of it might be slurred over, and the red-haired girl tossed and turned behind her.

Maisie put her chin in her hands and decided that there could be no doubt whatever of the villainy of Dick. To justify herself, she began, unwomanly, to weigh the evidence. There was a boy, and he had said he loved her. And he kissed her—kissed her on the cheek—by a yellow sea-poppy that nodded its head exactly like the maddening dry rose in the garden. Then there was an interval, and men had told her that they loved her—just when she was busiest with her work. Then the boy came back, and at their very second meeting had told her that he loved her. Then he had— But there was no end to the things he had done. He had given her his time and his powers. He had spoken to her of Art, housekeeping, technique, tea-cups, the abuse of pickles as a stimulant—that was rude—sable hair-brushes—he had given her the best in her stock—she used them daily; he had given her advice that she profited by, and now and again—a look. Such a look! The look of a beaten hound waiting for the word to crawl to his mistress's feet. In return she had given him nothing whatever, except—here she brushed her mouth against the open-work sleeve of her night-gown—the privilege of kissing her once. And on the mouth, too. Disgraceful! Was that not enough, and more than enough? and if it was not, had he not canceled the debt by not writing and—probably kissing other girls?

"Maisie, you'll catch a chill. Do go and lie down," said the wearied voice of her companion. "I can't sleep a wink with you at the window."

Maisie shrugged her shoulders and did not answer. She was reflecting on the meannesses of Dick, and on other meannesses with which he had nothing to do. The remorseless moonlight would not let her sleep. It lay on the skylight of the studio across the road in cold silver; she stared at it intently and her thoughts began to slide one into the other. The shadow of the big bell-handle in the wall grew short, lengthened again, and faded out as the moon went down behind the pasture and a hare came limping home across the road. Then the dawn-wind washed through the upland grasses, and brought coolness with it, and the cattle lowed by the drought-shrunk river. Maisie's head fell forward on the window-sill, and the tangle of black hair covered her arms.

"Maisie, wake up. You'll catch a chill."

"Yes, dear; yes, dear." She staggered to her bed like a wearied child, and as she buried her face in the pillows she muttered, "I think—I think . . . . But he ought to have written."

Day brought the routine of the studio, the smell of paint and turpentine, and the monotonous wisdom of Kami, who was a leaden artist, but a golden teacher if the pupil were only in sympathy with him. Maisie was not in sympathy that day, and she waited impatiently for the end of the work. She knew when it was coming; for Kami would gather his black alpaca coat into a bunch behind him, and, with faded blue eyes that saw neither pupils nor canvas, look back into the past to recall the history of one Binat. "You have all done not so badly," he would say. "But you shall remember that it is not enough to have the method, and the art, and the power, nor even that which is touch, but you shall have also the conviction that nails the work to the wall. Of the so many I have taught"—here the students would begin to unfix drawing-pins or get their tubes together—"the very so many that I have taught, the best was Binat. All that comes of the study and the work and the knowledge was to him even when he came. After he left me he should have done all that could be done with the color, the form, and the knowledge. Only, he had not the conviction. So to-day I hear no more of Binat—the best of my pupils—and that is long ago. So to-day, too, you will be glad to hear no more of me.

Continuez, *mesdemoiselles*, and, above all, with conviction."

He went into the garden to smoke and mourn over the lost Binat as the pupils dispersed to their several cottages or loitered in the studio to make plans for the cool of the afternoon.

Maisie looked at her very unhappy Melancolia, restrained a desire to grimace before it, and was hurrying across the road to write a letter to Dick, when she was aware of a large man on a white troop-horse. How Torpenhow had managed in the course of twenty hours to find his way to the hearts of the cavalry officers in quarters at Vitry-sur-Marne, to discuss with them the certainty of a glorious revenge for France, to reduce the colonel to tears of pure affability, and to borrow the best horse in the squadron for the journey to Kami's studio, is a mystery that only special correspondents can unravel.

"I beg your pardon," said he. "It seems an absurd question to ask, but the fact is that I don't know her by any other name: Is there any young lady here that is called Maisie?"

"I am Maisie," was the answer from the depths of a great sun-hat.

"I ought to introduce myself," he said, as the horse capered in the blinding white dust. "My name is Torpenhow. Dick Heldar is my best friend, and—and—the fact is that he has gone blind."

"Blind!" said Maisie stupidly. "He can't be blind."

"He has been stone-blind for nearly two months."

Maisie lifted up her face, and it was pearly white. "No! No! Not blind! I won't have him blind!"

"Would you care to see for yourself?' said Torpenhow.

"Now—at once?"

"Oh no! The Paris train doesn't go through this place till eight to-night. There will be ample time."

"Did Mr. Heldar send you to me?"

"Certainly not. Dick wouldn't do that sort of thing.

He's sitting in his studio, turning over some letters that he can't read because he's blind."

There was a sound of choking from the sun-hat. Maisie bowed her head and went into the cottage, where the red-haired girl was on a sofa, complaining of a headache.

"Dick's blind!" said Maisie, taking her breath quickly as she steadied herself against a chair-back. "My Dick's blind!"

"What?" The girl was on the sofa no longer.

"A man has come from England to tell me. He hasn't written to me for six weeks."

"Are you going to him?"

"I must think."

"Think! *I* should go back to London and see him, and I should kiss his eyes and kiss them and kiss them until they got well again! If you don't go I shall. Oh, what am I talking about? You wicked little idiot! Go to him at once. Go!"

Torpenhow's neck was blistering, but he preserved a smile of infinite patience as Maisie appeared bare-headed in the sunshine.

"I am coming," said she, her eyes on the ground.

"You will be at Vitry Station, then, at seven this evening." This was an order delivered by one who was used to being obeyed. Maisie said nothing, but she felt grateful that there was no chance of disputing with this big man who took everything for granted and managed a squealing horse with one hand. She returned to the red-haired girl, who was weeping bitterly, and between tears, kisses—very few of those—menthol, packing, and an interview with Kami, the sultry afternoon wore away. Thought might come afterward. Her present duty was to go to Dick—Dick who owned the wondrous friend and sat in the dark playing with her unopened letters.

"But what will you do?" she said to her companion.

"I? Oh, I shall stay here and—finish your Melancolia," she said, smiling pitifully. "Write to me afterward."

That night there ran a legend through Vitry-sur-Marne

of a mad Englishman, doubtless suffering from sunstroke, who had drunk all the officers of the garrison under the table, had borrowed a horse from the lines, and had then and there eloped, after the English custom, with one of those more than mad English girls who drew pictures down there under the care of that good Monsieur Kami.

"They are very droll," said Suzanne to the conscript in the moonlight by the studio wall. "She walked always with those big eyes that saw nothing, and yet she kisses me on both cheeks as though she were my sister, and gives me—see—ten francs!"

The conscript levied a contribution on both gifts; for he prided himself on being a good soldier.

Torpenhow spoke very little to Maisie during the journey to Calais; but he was careful to attend to all her wants, to get her a compartment entirely to herself, and to leave her alone. He was amazed at the ease with which the matter had been accomplished.

"The safest thing would be to let her think things out. By Dick's showing—when he was off his head—she must have ordered him about very thoroughly. Wonder how she likes being under orders."

Maisie never told. She sat in the empty compartment often with her eyes shut, that she might realize the sensation of blindness. It was an order that she should return to London swiftly, and she found herself at last almost beginning to enjoy the situation. This was better than looking after luggage and a red-haired friend who never took any interest in her surroundings. But there appeared to be a feeling in the air that she, Maisie—of all people—was in disgrace. Therefore she justified her conduct to herself with great success, till Torpenhow came up to her on the steamer and without preface began to tell the story of Dick's blindness, suppressing a few details, but dwelling at length on the miseries of delirium. He stopped before he reached the end, as though he had lost interest in the subject, and went forward to smoke. Maisie was furious with him and with herself.

She was hurried on from Dover to London almost before she could ask for breakfast, and—she was past any feeling of indignation now—was bidden curtly to wait in the hall at the foot of some lead-covered stairs while Torpenhow went up to make inquiries. Again the knowledge that she was being treated like a naughty little girl made her pale cheeks flame. It was all Dick's fault for being so stupid as to go blind.

Torpenhow led her up to a shut door, which he opened very softly. Dick was sitting by the window, with his chin on his chest. There were three envelopes in his hand, and he turned them over and over. The big man who gave orders was no longer by her side, and the studio door snapped behind her.

Dick thrust the letters into his pocket as he heard the sound. "Hullo, Torp! Is that you? I've been so lonely."

His voice had taken the peculiar flatness of the blind. Maisie pressed herself up into a corner of the room. Her heart was beating furiously, and she put one hand on her breast to keep it quiet. Dick was staring directly at her, and she realized for the first time that he was blind. Shutting her eyes in a railway-carriage to open them when she pleased was child's play. This man was blind though his eyes were wide open.

"Torp, is that you? They said you were coming." Dick looked puzzled and a little irritated at the silence.

"No: it's only me," was the answer, in a strained little whisper. Maisie could hardly move her lips.

"H'm!" said Dick composedly, without moving. "This is a new phenomenon. Darkness I'm getting used to; but I object to hearing voices."

Was he mad, then, as well as blind, that he talked to himself? Maisie's heart beat more wildly, and she breathed in gasps. Dick rose and began to feel his way across the room, touching each table and chair as he passed. Once he caught his foot on a rug, and swore, dropping on his knees to feel what the obstruction might be. Maisie remembered him walking in the Park as though all the earth belonged to him, tramping up and down her studio two months ago, and flying up the gangway of the Channel steamer. The beating of her heart was making her sick, and Dick was coming nearer, guided by the sound of her breathing. She put out a hand mechanically to ward him off or to draw him to herself, she did not know which. It touched his chest, and he stepped back as though he had been shot.

"It's Maisie!" said he, with a dry sob. "What are you doing here?"

"I came—I came—to see you, please."

Dick's lips closed firmly.

"Won't you sit down, then? You see, I've had some bother with my eyes, and—"

"I know. I know. Why didn't you tell me?"

"I couldn't write."

"You might have told Mr. Torpenhow."

"What has he to do with my affairs?"

"He—he brought me from Vitry-sur-Marne. He thought I ought to see you."

"Why, what has happened? Can I do anything for you? No, I can't. I forgot."

"Oh, Dick, I'm so sorry! I've come to tell you, and—Let me take you back to your chair."

"Don't. I'm not a child. You only do that out of pity. I never meant to tell you anything about it. I'm no good now. I'm down and done for. Let me alone!"

He groped back to his chair, his chest laboring as he sat down.

Maisie watched him, and the fear went out of her heart, to be followed by a very bitter shame. He had spoken a truth that had been hidden from the girl through every step of the impetuous flight to London; for he was, indeed, down and done for—masterful no longer but rather a little abject; neither an artist stronger than she, nor a man to be looked up to—only some blind one that sat in a chair and seemed on the point of crying. She was immensely and unfeignedly sorry for him—more sorry than she had ever been for any one in her life, but not sorry enough to deny his words. So she stood still and felt ashamed and a little hurt, because she had honestly intended that her journey should end triumphantly; and now she was only filled with pity most startlingly distinct from love.

"Well?" said Dick, his face steadily turned away. "I never meant to worry you any more. What's the matter?"

He was conscious that Maisie was catching her breath, but was as unprepared as herself for the torrent of emotion that followed. People who cannot cry easily weep unrestrainedly when the fountains of the great deep are broken up. She had dropped into a chair and was sobbing with her face hidden in her hands.

"I can't—I can't!" she cried desperately. "Indeed, I can't. It isn't my fault. I'm so sorry. Oh, Dickie, I'm so sorry."

Dick's shoulders straightened again, for the words lashed like a whip. Still the sobbing continued. It is not good to realize that you have failed in the hour of trial or flinched before the mere possibility of making sacrifices.

"I do despise myself—indeed I do. But I can't. Oh, Dickie, you wouldn't ask me—would you?" wailed Maisie.

She looked up for a minute, and by chance it happened that Dick's eyes fell on hers. The unshaven face was very white and set, and the lips were trying to force themselves into a smile. But it was the worn-out eyes that Maisie feared. Her Dick had gone blind and left in his place some one that she could hardly recognize till he spoke.

"Who is asking you to do anything, Maisie? I told you how it would be. What's the use of worrying? For pity's sake don't cry like that; it isn't worth it."

"You don't know how I hate myself. Oh, Dick, help me—help me!" The passion of tears had grown beyond her control and was beginning to alarm the man. He stumbled forward and put his arm round her, and her head fell on his shoulder.

"Hush, dear, hush! Don't cry. You're quite right, and

you've nothing to reproach yourself with—you never had. You're only a little upset by the jouney, and I don't suppose you've had any breakfast. What a brute Torp was to bring you over."

"I wanted to come. I did indeed," she protested.

"Very well. And now you've come and seen, and I'm—immensely grateful. When you're better you shall go away and get something to eat. What sort of a passage did you have coming over?"

Maisie was crying more subduedly, for the first time in her life glad that she had something to lean against. Dick patted her on the shoulder tenderly but clumsily, for he was not quite sure where her shoulder might be.

She drew herself out of his arms at last and waited, trembling and most unhappy. He had felt his way to the window to put the width of the room between them, and to quiet a little the tumult in his heart.

"Are you better now?" he said.

"Yes, but—don't you hate me?"

"I hate you? My God! I?"

"Isn't—isn't there anything I could do for you, then? I'll stay here in England to do it, if you like. Perhaps I could come and see you sometimes."

"I think not, dear. It would be kindest not to see me any more, please. I don't want to seem rude, but—don't you think—perhaps you had almost better go now."

He was conscious that he could not bear himself as a man if the strain continued much longer.

"I don't deserve anything else. I'll go, Dick. Oh, I'm so miserable."

"Nonsense. You've nothing to worry about; I'd tell you if you had. Wait a moment, dear. I've got something to give you first. I meant it for you ever since this little trouble began. It's my Melancolia; she was a beauty when I last saw her. You can keep her for me, and if ever you're poor you can sell her. She's worth a few hundreds at any state of the market." He groped among his canvases.

"She's framed in black. Is this a black frame that I have my hand on? There she is. What do you think of her?"

He turned a scarred formless muddle of paint toward Maisie, and the eyes strained as though they would catch her wonder and surprise. One thing and one thing only could she do for him.

"Well?"

The voice was fuller and more rounded, because the man knew he was speaking of his best work. Maisie looked at the blur, and a lunatic desire to laugh caught her by the throat. But for Dick's sake—whatever this mad blankness might mean—she must make no sign. Her voice choked with hard-held tears as she answered, still gazing on the wreck—

"Oh, Dick, it *is* good!"

He heard the little hysterical gulp and took it for tribute. "Won't you have it, then? I'll send it over to your house if you will."

"I? Oh, yes—thank you. Ha! ha!" If she did not fly at once the laughter that was worse than tears would kill her. She turned and ran, choking and blinded, down the staircases that were empty of life to take refuge in a cab and go to her house across the Parks. There she sat down in the almost dismantled drawing-room and thought of Dick in his blindness, useless till the end of life, and of herself in her own eyes. Behind the sorrow, the shame, and the humiliation, lay fear of the cold wrath of the red-haired girl when Maisie should return. Maisie had never feared her companion before. Not until she found herself saying, "Well, he never asked me," did she realize her scorn of herself.

And that is the end of Maisie.

For Dick was reserved more searching torment. He could not realize at first that Maisie, whom he had ordered to go, had left him without a word of farewell. He was savagely angry against Torpenhow, who had brought upon him this humiliation and troubled his miserable peace. Then his dark hour came and he was alone with himself and his desires to get what help he could from the darkness. The queen could do no wrong, but in following the right, so far as it served her work, she had wounded her one subject more than his own brain would let him know.

"It's all I had and I've lost it," he said, as soon as the misery permitted clear thinking. "And Torp will think that he has been so infernally clever that I shan't have the heart to tell him. I must think this out quietly."

"Hullo!" said Torpenhow, entering the studio after Dick had enjoyed two hours of thought. "I'm back. Are you feeling any better?"

"Torp, I don't know what to say. Come here." Dick coughed huskily, wondering, indeed, what he should say, and how to say it temperately.

"What's the need for saying anything? Get up and tramp." Torpenhow was perfectly satisfied.

They walked up and down as of custom, Torpenhow's hand on Dick's shoulder, and Dick buried in his own thoughts.

"How in the world did you find it all out?" said Dick at last.

"You shouldn't go off your head if you want to keep secrets, Dickie. It was absolutely impertinent on my part; but if you'd seen me rocketing about on a half-trained French troop-horse under a blazing sun you'd have laughed. There will be a charivari in my rooms to-night. Seven other devils—"

"I know—the row in the Southern Soudan. I surprised their councils the other day, and it made me unhappy. Have you fixed your flint to go? Who d'you work for?"

"'Haven't signed any contracts yet. I wanted to see how your business would turn out."

"Would you have stayed with me, then, if—things had gone wrong?" He put his question cautiously.

"Don't ask me too much. I'm only a man."

"You've tried to be an angel very successfully."

"Oh, ye—es! . . . Well, do you attend the function to-night? We shall be half screwed before the morning. All the men believe the war's a certainty."

"I don't think I will, old man, if it's all the same to you. I'll stay quiet here."

"And meditate? I don't blame you. You deserve a good time if ever a man did."

That night there was tumult on the stairs. The correspondents poured in from theater, dinner, and music-hall to Torpenhow's room that they might discuss their plan of campaign in the event of military operations being a certainty. Torpenhow, the Keneu, and the Nilghai had bidden all the men they had worked with to the orgy; and Mr. Beeton, the housekeeper, declared that never before in his checkered experience had he seen quite such a fancy lot of gentlemen. They waked the chambers with shoutings and song; and the elder men were quite as bad as the younger. For the chances of war were in front of them, and all knew what those meant.

Sitting in his own room a little perplexed by the noise across the landing, Dick suddenly began to laugh to himself.

"When one comes to think of it the situation is intensely comic. Maisie's quite right—poor little thing. I didn't know she could cry like that before; but now I know what Torp thinks, I'm sure he'd be quite fool enough to stay at home and try to console me—if he knew. Besides, it isn't nice to own that you've been thrown over like a broken chair. I must carry this business through alone—as usual. If there isn't a war, and Torp finds out, I shall look foolish, that's all. If there is a war I mustn't interfere with another man's chances. Business is business, and I want to be alone —I want to be alone. What a row they're making!"

Somebody hammered at the studio door.

"Come out and frolic, Dickie," said the Nilghai.

"I should like to, but I can't. I'm not feeling frolicsome."

"Then I'll tell the boys and they'll draw you like a badger."

"Please not, old man. On my word, I'd sooner be left alone just now."

"Very good. Can we send anything in to you? Fizz, for instance. Cassavetti is beginning to sing songs of the Sunny South already."

For one minute Dick considered the proposition seriously.

"No, thanks. I've a headache already."

"Virtuous child. That's the effect of emotion on the young. All my congratulations, Dick. I also was concerned in the conspiracy for your welfare."

"Go to the devil and—oh, send Binkie in here."

The little dog entered on elastic feet, riotous from having been made much of all the evening. He had helped to sing the choruses; but scarcely inside the studio he realized that this was no place for tail-wagging, and settled himself on Dick's lap till it was bedtime. Then he went to bed with Dick, who counted every hour as it struck, and rose in the morning with a painfully clear head to receive Torpenhow's more formal congratulations and a particular account of the last night's revels.

"You aren't looking very happy for a newly-accepted man," said Torpenhow.

"Never mind that—it's my own affair, and I'm all right. Do you really go?"

"Yes. With the old Central Southern as usual. They wired and I accepted on better terms than before."

"When do you start?"

"The day after to-morrow—for Brindisi."

"Thank God." Dick spoke from the bottom of his heart.

"Well, that's not a pretty way of saying you're glad to get rid of me. But men in your condition are allowed to be selfish."

"I didn't mean that. Will you get a hundred pounds cashed for me before you leave?"

"That's a slender amount for housekeeping, isn't it?"

"Oh, it's only for—marriage expenses."

Torpenhow brought him the money, counted it out in fives and tens, and carefully put it away in the writing-table.

"Now I suppose I shall have to listen to his ravings about his girl until I go. Heaven send us patience with a man in love!" said he to himself.

But never a word did Dick say of Maisie or marriage. He hung in the doorway of Torpenhow's room when the latter was packing and asked innumerable questions about the coming campaign, till Torpenhow began to feel annoyed.

"You're a secretive animal, Dickie, and you consume your own smoke, don't you?" he said on the last evening.

"I—I suppose so. By the way, how long do you think this war will last?"

"Days, weeks, or months. One can never tell. It may go on for years."

"I wish I were going."

"Good heavens! You're the most unaccountable creature! Hasn't it occurred to you that you're going to be married—thanks to me?"

"Of course, yes. I'm going to be married—so I am. Going to be married. I'm awfully grateful to you. Haven't I told you that?"

"You might be going to be hanged by the look of you," said Torpenhow.

And the next day Torpenhow bade him good-by, and left him to the loneliness he had so much desired.

CHAPTER FOURTEEN

Yet at the last, ere our spearmen had found him,
  Yet at the last, ere a sword-thrust could save,
Yet at the last, with his masters around him,
  He of the Faith spoke as master to slave;
Yet at the last, tho' the Kafirs had maimed him,
  Broken by bondage and wrecked by the reiver—
Yet at the last, tho' the darkness had claimed him,
  He called upon Allah and died a believer.

—*Kizilbashi*

"BEG your pardon, Mr. Heldar, but—but isn't nothin' going to happen?" said Mr. Beeton.

"No!" Dick had just waked to another morning of blank despair and his temper was of the shortest.

"'Tain't my regular business o' course, sir; and what I say is, 'Mind your own business and let other people mind theirs'; but just before Mr. Torpenhow went away he give me to understand, like, that you might be moving into a house of your own, so to speak—a sort of house with rooms upstairs and downstairs where you'd be better attended to, though I try to act just by all our tenants. Don't I?"

"Ah! That must have been a mad-house. I shan't trouble you to take me there yet. Get me my breakfast, please, and leave me alone."

"I hope I haven't done anything wrong, sir, but you know I hope that as far as a man can I tries to do the proper thing by all the gentlemen in chambers—and more particular those whose lot is hard—such as you, for instance, Mr. Heldar. You likes soft-roe bloater, don't you? Soft-roe bloaters is scarcer than hard-roe, but what I says is, 'Never mind a little extra trouble so long as you gives satisfaction to the tenants.'"

Mr. Beeton withdrew and left Dick to himself. Torpenhow had been long away; there was no more rioting in the chambers, and Dick had settled down to his new life, which he was weak enough to consider nothing better than death.

It is hard to live alone in the dark, confusing the day and night; dropping to sleep through sheer weariness at mid-day, and rising restless in the chill of the dawn. At first Dick, on his awakenings, would grope along the corridors of the chambers till he heard some one snore. Then he would know that the day had not yet come, and return wearily to his bedroom. Later he learned not to stir till there was a noise and movement in the house and Mr. Beeton advised him to get up. Once dressed—and dressing, now that Torpenhow was away, was a lengthy business, because collars, ties, and the like, hid themselves in far corners of the room, and search meant head-beating against chairs and trunks—once dressed, there was nothing whatever to do except to sit still and brood till the three daily meals came. Centuries separated breakfast from lunch and lunch from dinner, and though a man prayed for hundreds of years that his mind might be taken from him, God would never hear. Rather the mind was quickened and the revolving thoughts ground against each other as millstones grind when there is no corn between; and yet the brain would not wear out and give him rest. It continued to think, at length, with imagery and all manner of reminiscences. It recalled Maisie and past success, reckless travels by land and sea, the glory of doing work and feeling that it was good, and suggested all that might have happened had the eyes only been faithful to their duty. When thinking ceased through sheer weariness, there poured into Dick's soul tide on tide of overwhelming, purposeless fear—dread of starvation always, terror lest the unseen ceiling should crush down upon him, fear of fire in the chambers and a louse's death in red flame, and agonies of fiercer horror that had nothing to do with any fear of death. Then Dick bowed his head, and clutching the arms of his chair fought with his sweating self till the tinkle of plates told him that something to eat was being set before him.

Mr. Beeton would bring the meal when he had time to

spare, and Dick learned to hang upon his speech, which dealt with badly-fitted gas plugs, waste pipes out of repair, little tricks for driving picture nails into walls, and the sins of the char-woman or the housemaids. In the lack of better things the small gossip of a servant's hall becomes immensely interesting, and the screwing of a washer on a tap an event to be talked over for days.

Once or twice a week, too, Mr. Beeton would take Dick out with him when he went marketing in the morning to haggle with tradesmen over fish, lamp-wicks, mustard, tapioca, and so forth, while Dick rested his weight first on one foot and then on the other and played aimlessly with the tins and string-ball on the counter. Then they would perhaps meet one of Mr. Beeton's friends, and Dick, standing aside a little, would hold his peace till Mr. Beeton was willing to go on again.

The life did not increase his self-respect. He abandoned shaving as a dangerous exercise, and being shaved in a barber's shop meant exposure of his infirmity. He could not see that his clothes were properly brushed, and since he had never taken any care of his personal appearance he became every known variety of sloven. A blind man cannot eat with cleanliness till he has been some months used to the darkness. If he demand attendance and grow angry at the want of it, he must assert himself and stand upright. Then the meanest menial can see that he is blind and, therefore, of no consequence. A wise man will keep his eyes on the floor and sit still. For amusement he may pick coal lump by lump out of the scuttle with the tongs and pile it in a little heap in the fender, keeping count of the lumps, which must all be put back again, one by one and very carefully. He may set himself sums if he cares to work them out; he may talk to himself or to the cat if she chooses to visit him; and if his trade has been that of an artist, he may sketch in the air with his forefinger; but that is too much like drawing a pig with the eyes shut. He may go to his bookshelves and count his books, ranging them in order of their size; or to his wardrobe and count his shirts, laying them in piles of two or three on the bed, as they suffer from frayed cuffs or lost buttons. Even this entertainment wearies after a time; and all the times are very, very long.

Dick was allowed to sort a tool-chest where Mr. Beeton kept hammers, taps and nuts, lengths of gas-pipes, oil bottles and string.

"If I don't have everything just where I know where to look for it, why, then, I can't find anything when I do want it. You've no idea, sir, the amount of little things that these chambers uses up," said Mr. Beeton. Fumbling at the handle of the door as he went out: "It's hard on you, sir, I *do* think it's hard on you. Ain't you going to do anything, sir?"

"I'll pay my rent and messing. Isn't that enough?"

"I wasn't doubting for a moment that you couldn't pay your way, sir; but I 'ave often said to my wife, 'It's 'ard on 'im because it isn't as if he was an old man, nor yet a middle-aged one, but quite a young gentleman. *That's* where it comes so 'ard.' "

"I suppose so," said Dick absently. This particular nerve through long battering had ceased to feel—much.

"I was thinking," continued Mr. Beeton, still making as if to go, "that you might like to hear my boy Alf read you the papers sometimes of an evening. He do read beautiful, seeing he's only nine."

"I should be very grateful," said Dick. "Only let me make it worth his while."

"We wasn't thinking of *that*, sir, but of course it's in your own 'ands; but only to 'ear Alf sing 'A Boy's best Friend is 'is Mother!' Ah!"

"I'll hear him sing that too. Let him come in this evening with the newspapers."

Alf was not a nice child, being puffed up with many school-board certificates for good conduct and inordinately proud of his singing. Mr. Beeton remained, beaming, while the child wailed his way through a song of some eight eight-line verses in the usual whine of the young Cockney, and, after compliments, left him to read Dick the foreign telegrams. Ten minutes later Alf returned to his parents rather pale and scared.

"'E said 'e couldn't stand it no more," he explained.

"He never said you read badly, Alf?" Mrs. Beeton spoke.

"No. 'E said I read beautiful. Said 'e never 'eard any one read like that, but 'e said 'e couldn't abide the stuff in the papers."

"P'raps he's lost some money in the Stocks. Were you readin' him about Stocks, Alf?"

"No; it was all about fightin' out there where the soldiers is gone—a great long piece with all the lines close together and very hard words in it. 'E give me 'arf a crown because I read so well. And 'e says the next time there's anything 'e wants read 'e'll send for me."

"That's good hearing, but I do think for all the half-crown—put it into the kicking-donkey money-box, Alf, and let me see you do it—he might have kept you longer. Why, he couldn't have begun to understand how beautiful you read."

"He's best left to hisself—gentlemen always are when they're downhearted," said Mr. Beeton.

Alf's rigorously limited powers of comprehending Torpenhow's special correspondence had waked the devil of unrest in Dick. He could hear, through the boy's nasal chant, the camels grunting in the squares behind the soldiers outside Suakin; could hear the men swearing and chaffing across the cooking pots, and could smell the acrid wood-smoke as it drifted over the camp before the wind of the desert.

That night he prayed to God that his mind might be taken from him, offering for proof that he was worthy of this favor the fact that he had not shot himself long ago. That prayer was not answered, and indeed Dick knew in his heart of hearts that only a lingering sense of humor and no special virtue had kept him alive. Suicide, he had persuaded himself, would be a ludicrous insult to the gravity of the situation as well as a weak-kneed confession of fear.

"Just for the fun of the thing," he said to the cat, who had taken Binkie's place in his establishment, "I should like to know how long this is going to last. I can live for a year on the hundred pounds Torp cashed for me. I must have two or three thousand at least at the Bank—twenty or thirty years more provided for, that is to say. Then I fall back on my hundred and twenty a year, which will be more by that time. Let's consider. Twenty-five—thirty-five—a man's in his prime then, they say—forty-five—a middle-aged man just entering politics—fifty-five—'died at the comparatively early age of fifty-five,' according to the newspapers. Bah! How these Christians funk death! Sixty-five—we're only getting on in years. Seventy-five is just possible though. Great Hell, cat O! fifty years more of solitary confinement in the dark! You'll die, and Beeton will die, and Torp will die, and Mai—everybody else will die, but I shall be alive and kicking with nothing to do. I'm very sorry for myself. I should like some one else to be sorry for me. Evidently I'm not going mad before I die, but the pain's just as bad as ever. Some day when you're vivisected, cat O! they'll tie you down on a little table and cut you open—but don't be afraid; they'll take precious good care that you don't die. You'll live, and you'll be very sorry then that you weren't sorry for me. Perhaps Torp will come back or . . . I wish I could go to Torp and the Nilghai, even though I were in their way."

Pussy left the room before the speech was ended, and Alf, as he entered, found Dick addressing the empty hearth rug.

"There's a letter for you, sir," he said. "Perhaps you'd like me to read it."

"Lend it to me for a minute and I'll tell you."

The outstretched hand shook just a little and the voice was not over-steady. It was within the limits of human possibility that—that was no letter from Maisie. He knew the heft of three closed envelopes only too well. It was a foolish hope that the girl should write to him, for he did not realize that there is a wrong which admits of no reparation though the evildoer may with tears and the heart's best love strive to mend all. It is best to forget that wrong whether it be caused or endured, since it is as remediless as bad work once put forward.

"Read it, then," said Dick, and Alf began intoning according to the rules of the Board School—

"'*I could have given you love, I could have given you loyalty, such as you never dreamed of. Do you suppose I cared* what *you were? But you chose to whistle everything down the wind for nothing. My only excuse for you is that you are so young.*'"

"That's all," he said, returning the paper to be dropped into the fire.

"What was in the letter?" asked Mrs. Beeton when Alf returned.

"I don't know. I think it was a circular or a tract about not whistlin' at everything when you're young."

"I must have stepped on something when I was alive and walking about and it has bounced up and hit me. God help it, whatever it is—unless it was all a joke. But I don't know any one who'd take the trouble to play a joke on me. . . . Love and loyalty for nothing. It sounds tempting enough. I wonder whether I have lost anything really?"

Dick considered for a long time but could not remember when or how he had put himself in the way of winning these trifles at a woman's hands.

Still, the letter, as touching on matters that he preferred not to think about, stung him into a fit of frenzy that lasted for a day and night. When his heart was so full of despair that it would hold no more, body and soul together seemed to be dropping without check through the darkness. Then came fear of darkness and desperate attempts to reach the light again. But there was no light to be reached. When that agony had left him sweating and breathless, the downward flight would recommence till the gathering torture of it spurred him into another fight as hopeless as the first. Followed some few minutes of sleep in which he dreamed that he saw. Then the procession of events would repeat itself till he was utterly worn out and the brain took up its everlasting consideration of Maisie and might-have-beens.

At the end of everything Mr. Beeton came to his room and volunteered to take him out. "Not marketing this time, but we'll go into the Parks if you like."

"Be damned if I do," quoth Dick. "Keep to the streets and walk up and down. I like to hear the people round me."

This was not altogether true. The blind in the first stages of their infirmity dislike those who can move with a free stride and unlifted arms—but Dick had no earthly desire to go to the Parks. Once and only once since Maisie had shut the door he had gone there under Alf's charge. Alf forgot him and fished for minnows in the Serpentine with some companions. After half an hour's waiting Dick, almost weeping with rage and wrath, caught a passer-by who introduced him to a friendly policeman who led him to a four-wheeler opposite the Albert Hall. He never told Mr. Beeton of Alf's forgetfulness, but . . . this was not the manner in which he was used to walk the Parks aforetime.

"What streets would you like to walk down, then?" said Mr. Beeton sympathetically. His own ideas of a riotous holiday meant picnicking on the grass of the Green Park with his family, and half a dozen paper bags full of food.

"Keep to the river," said Dick, and they kept to the river, and the rush of it was in his ears till they came to Blackfriars Bridge and struck thence on to the Waterloo Road, Mr. Beeton explaining the beauties of the scenery as he went on.

"And walking on the other side of the pavement," said he, "unless I'm much mistaken, is the young woman that used to come to your rooms to be drawed. I never forgets a face and I never remembers a name, except paying tenants, o' course!"

"Stop her," said Dick. "It's Bessie Broke. Tell her I'd like to speak to her again. Quick, man!"

Mr. Beeton crossed the road under the noses of the omnibuses and arrested Bessie then on her way northward. She recognized him as the man in authority who used to glare at her when she passed up Dick's staircase, and her first impulse was to run.

"Wasn't you Mr. Heldar's model?" said Mr. Beeton, planting himself in front of her. "You was. He's on the other side of the road and he'd like to see you."

"Why?" said Bessie faintly. She remembered—indeed had never for long forgotten—an affair connected with a newly-finished picture.

"Because he has asked me to do so, and because he's most particular blind."

"Drunk?"

"No. 'Orspital blind. He can't see. That's him over there."

Dick was leaning against the parapet of the bridge as Mr. Beeton pointed him out—a stub-bearded, bowed creature wearing a dirty magenta colored neckcloth outside an unbrushed coat. There was nothing to fear from such a one. Even if he chased her, Bessie thought, he could not follow far. She crossed over and Dick's face lighted up. It was long since a woman of any kind had taken the trouble to speak to him.

"I hope you're well, Mr. Heldar?" said Bessie, a little puzzled. Mr. Beeton stood by with the air of an embassador and breathed responsibly.

"I'm very well indeed, and, by Jove! I'm glad to see—hear you, I mean, Bess. You never thought it worth while to turn up and see us again after you got your money. I don't know why you should. Are you going anywhere in particular just now?"

"I was going for a walk," said Bessie.

"Not the old business?" Dick spoke under his breath.

"Lor', no! I paid my premium"—Bessie was very proud of that word—"for a barmaid, sleeping in, and I'm at the bar now quite respectable. Indeed I am."

Mr. Beeton had no special reason to believe in the loftiness of human nature. Therefore he dissolved himself like a mist and returned to his gas-plugs without a word of apology. Bessie watched the flight with a certain uneasiness; but so long as Dick appeared to be ignorant of the harm that had been done to him. . . .

"It's hard work pulling the beer handles," she went on, "and they've got one of them penny-in-the-slot cash-machines, so if you get wrong by a penny at the end of the day —but then I don't believe the machinery is right. Do you?"

"I've only seen it work. Mr. Beeton."

"He's gone."

"I'm afraid I must ask you to help me home, then. I'll make it worth your while. You see." The sightless eyes turned toward her and Bessie saw.

"It isn't taking you out of your way?" he said hesitatingly. "I can ask a policeman if it is."

"Not at all. I come on at seven and I'm off at four. That's easy hours."

"Good God!—but I'm on all the time. I wish I had some work to do too. Let's go home, Bess."

He turned and cannoned into a man on the sidewalk, recoiling with an oath. Bessie took his arm and said nothing —as she had said nothing when he had ordered her to turn her face a little more to the light. They walked for some time in silence, the girl steering him deftly through the crowd.

"And where's—where's Mr. Torpenhow?" she inquired at last.

"He has gone away to the desert."

"Where's that?"

Dick pointed to the right. "East—out of the mouth of the river," said he. "Then west, then south, and then east again, all along the under-side of Europe. Then south again, God knows how far." The explanation did not enlighten Bessie in the least, but she held her tongue and looked to Dick's path till they came to the chambers.

"We'll have tea and muffins," he said joyously. "I can't tell you, Bessie, how glad I am to find you again. What made you go away so suddenly?"

"I didn't think you'd want me any more," she said, emboldened by his ignorance.

"I didn't as a matter of fact—but afterward— At any rate I'm glad you've come. You know the stairs."

So Bessie led him home to his own place—there was no one to hinder—and shut the door of the studio.

"What a mess!" was her first word. "All these things haven't been looked after for months and months."

"No, only weeks, Bess. You can't expect them to care."

"I don't know what you expect them to do. They ought to know what you've paid them for. The dust's just awful. It's all over the easel."

"I don't use it much now."

"All over the pictures and the floor, and all over your coat. I'd like to speak to them housemaids."

"Ring for tea, then." Dick felt his way to the one chair he used by custom. Bessie saw the action and, as far as in her lay, was touched. But there remained always a keen sense of new-found superiority, and it was in her voice when she spoke.

"How long have you been like this?" she said wrathfully, as though the blindness were some fault of the housemaids.

"How?"

"As you are."

"The day after you went away with the check, almost as soon as my picture was finished; I hardly saw her alive."

"Then they've been cheating you ever since, that's all. I know their nice little ways."

A woman may love one man and despise another, but on general feminine principles she will do her best to save the man she despises from being defrauded. Her loved one can look to himself, but the other man, being obviously an idiot, needs protection.

"I don't think Mr. Beeton cheats much," said Dick. Bessie was flouncing up and down the room, and he was conscious of a keen sense of enjoyment as he heard the swish of her skirts and the light step between.

"Tea *and* muffins," she said shortly, when the ring at the bell was answered; "two teaspoonfuls and one over for the pot. I don't want the old teapot that was here when I used to come. It don't draw. Get another."

The housemaid went away scandalized, and Dick chuckled. Then he began to cough as Bessie banged up and down the studio disturbing the dust.

"What are you trying to do?"

"Put things straight. This is like unfurnished lodgings. How could you let it go so?"

"How could I help it? Dust away."

She dusted furiously, and in the midst of all the pother entered Mrs. Beeton. Her husband on his return had explained the situation, winding up with the peculiarly felicitous proverb, "Do unto others as you would be done by." She had descended to put into her place the person who demanded muffins and an uncracked teapot as though she had a right to both.

"Muffins ready yet?" said Bess, still dusting. She was no longer a drab of the streets but a young lady who, thanks to Dick's check, had paid her premium and was entitled to pull beer-handles with the best. Being neatly dressed in black she did not hesitate to face Mrs. Beeton, and there passed between the two women certain regards that Dick would have appreciated. The situation adjusted itself by eye. Bessie had won, and Mrs. Beeton returned to cook muffins and make scathing remarks about models, hussies, trollops, and the like, to her husband.

"There's nothing to be got of interfering with him, Liza," he said. "Alf, you go along into the street to play. When he isn't crossed he's as kindly as kind, but when he's crossed he's the devil and all. We took too many little things out of his rooms since he was blind to be that particular about what he does. They ain't no objects to a blind man, of course, but if it was to come into court we'd get the sack. Yes, I did introduce him to that girl because I'm a feelin' man myself."

"Much too feelin'!" Mrs. Beeton slapped the muffins into the dish, and thought of comely housemaids long since dismissed on suspicion.

"I ain't ashamed of it, and it isn't for us to judge him hard so long as he pays quiet and regular as he do. I know how to manage young gentlemen, you know how to cook for them, and what I says is, let each stick to his own business and then there won't be any trouble. Take them muffins down, Liza, and be sure you have no words with that young woman. His lot is cruel hard, and if he's crossed he do swear worse than any one I've ever served."

"That's a little better," said Bessie, sitting down to the tea. "You needn't wait, thank you, Mrs. Beeton."

"I had no intention of doing such, I do assure you."

Bessie made no answer whatever. This, she knew, was the way in which real ladies routed their foes, and when one is a barmaid at a first-class public-house one may become a real lady at ten minutes' notice.

Her eyes fell on Dick opposite her and she was both shocked and displeased. There were droppings of food all down the front of his coat; the mouth under the ragged ill-grown beard drooped sullenly; the forehead was lined and contracted; and on the lean temples the hair was a dusty indeterminate color that might or might not have been called gray. The utter misery and self-abandonment of the man appealed to her, and at the bottom of her heart lay the wicked feeling that he was humbled and brought low who had once humbled her.

"Oh! it *is* good to hear you moving about," said Dick, rubbing his hands. "Tell us all about your bar successes, Bessie, and the way you live now."

"Never mind that. I'm quite respectable, as you'd see by looking at me. *You* don't seem to live too well. What made you go blind that sudden? Why isn't there any one to look after you?"

Dick was too thankful for the sound of her voice to resent the tone of it.

"I was cut across the head a long time ago, and that ruined my eyes. I don't suppose anybody thinks it worth while to look after me any more. Why should they?—and Mr. Beeton really does everything I want."

"Don't you know any gentlemen and ladies, then, while you was—well?"

"A few, but I don't care to have them looking at me."

"I suppose that's why you've growed a beard. Take it off, it don't become you."

"Good gracious, child, do you imagine that I think of what becomes me these days?"

"You ought. Get that taken off before I come here again. I suppose I can come, can't I?"

"I'd be only too grateful if you did. I don't think I treated you very well in the old days. I used to make you angry."

"Very angry, you did."

"I'm sorry for it, then. Come and see me when you can and as often as you can. God knows, there isn't a soul in the world to take that trouble except you and Mr. Beeton."

"A lot of trouble *he's* taking and *she* too." This with a toss of the head. "They've let you do anyhow and they haven't done anything for you. I've only to look to see that much. I'll come, and I'll be glad to come, but you must go and be shaved, and you must get some other clothes—those ones aren't fit to be seen."

"I have heaps somewhere," he said helplessly.

"I know you have. Tell Mr. Beeton to give you a new suit and I'll brush it and keep it clean. You may be as blind as a barn-door, Mr. Heldar, but it doesn't excuse you looking like a sweep."

"Do I look like a sweep then?"

"Oh, I'm sorry for you. I'm that sorry for you!" she

cried impulsively, and took Dick's hands. Mechanically, he lowered his head as if to kiss—she was the only woman who had taken pity on him, and he was not too proud for a little pity now. She stood up to go.

"Nothing o' that kind till you look more like a gentleman. It's quite easy when you get shaved, and some clothes."

He could hear her drawing on her gloves and rose to say good-by. She passed behind him, kissed him audaciously on the back of the neck, and ran away as swiftly as on the day when she had destroyed the Melancolia.

"To think of me kissing Mr. Heldar," she said to herself, "after all he's done to me and all! Well, I'm sorry for him, and if he was shaved he wouldn't be so bad to look at, but . . . . Oh them Beetons, how shameful they've treated him! I know Beeton's wearing his shirts on his back to-day just as well as if I'd aired it. To-morrow, I'll see . . . I wonder if he has much of his own. It might be worth more than the bar—I wouldn't have to do any work—and just as respectable if no one knew."

Dick was not grateful to Bessie for her parting gift. He was acutely conscious of it in the nape of his neck throughout the night, but it seemed, among very many other things, to enforce the wisdom of getting shaved. He was shaved accordingly in the morning, and felt the better for it. A fresh suit of clothes, white linen, and the knowledge that some one in the world said that she took an interest in his personal appearance, made him carry himself almost upright; for the brain was relieved for a while from thinking of Maisie, who, under other circumstances, might have given that kiss and a million others.

"Let us consider," said he after lunch. "The girl can't care, and it's a toss-up whether she comes again or not, but if money can buy her to look after me she shall be bought. Nobody else in the world would take the trouble, and I can make it worth her while. She's a child of the gutter holding brevet rank as a barmaid; so she shall have everything she wants if she'll only come and talk and look after me." He rubbed his newly-shorn chin and began to perplex himself with the thought of her not coming. "I suppose I did look rather a sweep," he went on. "I had no reason to look otherwise. I knew things dropped on my clothes, but it didn't matter. It would be cruel if she didn't come. She must. Maisie came once, and that was enough for her. She was quite right. She had something to work for. This creature has only beer-handles to pull, unless she has deluded some young man into keeping company with her. Fancy being cheated for the sake of a counter-jumper! We're falling pretty low."

Something cried aloud within him—This will hurt more than anything that has gone before. It will recall and remind and suggest and tantalize, and in the end drive you mad.

"I know it, I know it!" Dick cried, clinching his hands despairingly; "but, good heavens! is a poor blind beggar never to get anything out of his life except three meals a day and a greasy waistcoat? I wish she'd come."

Early in the afternoon time she came, because there was no young man in her life just then, and she thought of material advantages which would allow her to be idle for the rest of her days.

"I shouldn't have known you," she said approvingly. "You look as you used to look—a gentleman that was proud of himself."

"Don't you think I deserve another kiss then?" said Dick, flushing a little.

"Maybe—but you won't get it yet. Sit down and let's see what I can do for you. I'm certain sure Mr. Beeton cheats you, now that you can't go through the housekeeping books every month. Isn't that true?"

"You'd better come and housekeep for me then, Bessie."

"'Couldn't do it in these chambers—you know that as well as I do."

"I know, but we might go somewhere else, if you thought it worth your while."

"I'd try to look after you, anyhow; but I shouldn't care to have to work for both of us." This was tentative.

Dick laughed.

"Do you remember where I used to keep my bank-book?" said he. "Torp took it to be balanced just before he went away. Look and see."

"It was generally under the tobacco-jar. Ah!"

"Well?"

"Oh! Four thousand two hundred and ten pounds nine shillings and a penny! Oh my!"

"You can have the penny. That's not bad for one year's work. Is that and a hundred and twenty pounds a year good enough?"

The idleness and the pretty clothes were almost within her reach now, but she must, by being housewifely, show that she deserved them.

"Yes; but you'd have to move, and if we took an inventory, I think we'd find that Mr. Beeton has been prigging little things out of the rooms here and there. They don't look as full as they used."

"Never mind, we'll let him have them. The only thing I'm particularly anxious to take away is that picture I used you for—when you used to swear at me. We'll pull out of this place, Bess, and get away as far as ever we can."

"Oh, yes," she said uneasily.

"I don't know where I can go to get away from myself, but I'll try, and you shall have all the pretty frocks that you care for. You'll like that. Give me that kiss now, Bess. Ye gods! it's good to put one's arm round a woman's waist again."

Then came the fulfillment of the prophecy within the brain. If his arm were thus round Maisie's waist and a kiss had just been given and taken between them—why then. . . He pressed the girl more closely to himself because the pain whipped him. She was wondering how to explain a little accident to the Melancolia. At any rate, if this man really desired the solace of her company—and certainly he would relapse into his original slough if she withdrew it—he would not be more than just a little vexed. It would be delightful at least to see what would happen, and by her teachings it was good for a man to stand in certain awe of his companion.

She laughed nervously, and slipped out of his reach.

"I shouldn't worrit about that picture if I was you," she began, in the hope of turning his attention.

"It's at the back of all my canvases somewhere. Find it, Bess; you know it as well as I do."

"I know—but—"

"But what? You've wit enough to manage the sale of it to a dealer. Women haggle much better than men. It might be a matter of eight or nine hundred pounds to—to us. I simply didn't like to think about it for a long time. It was mixed up with my life so.—But we'll cover up our tracks and get rid of everything, eh? Make a fresh start from the beginning, Bess."

Then she began to repent very much indeed, because she knew the value of money. Still, it was probable that the blind man was overestimating the value of his work. Gentlemen, she knew, were absurdly particular about their things. She giggled as a nervous housemaid giggles when she tries to explain the breakage of a pipe.

"I'm very sorry, but you remember I was—I was angry with you before Mr. Torpenhow went away?"

"You were very angry, child; and on my word I think you had some right to be."

"Then I—but aren't you sure Mr. Torpenhow didn't tell you?"

"Tell me what? Good gracious, what are you making such a fuss about when you might just as well be giving me another kiss."

He was beginning to learn, not for the first time in his experience, that kissing is a cumulative poison. The more you get of it, the more you want. Bessie gave the kiss promptly, whispering, as she did so, "I was so angry I rubbed out that picture with the turpentine. You aren't angry, are you?"

"What? Say that again." The man's hand had closed on her wrist.

"I rubbed it out with turps and the knife," faltered Bessie. "I thought you'd only have to do it over again. You did do it over again, didn't you? Oh, let go of my wrist; you're hurting me."

"Isn't there anything left of the thing?"

"N'nothing that looks like anything. I'm sorry—I didn't know you'd take on about it; I only meant to do it in fun. You aren't going to hit me?"

"Hit you! No! Let's think."

He did not relax his hold upon her wrist but stood staring at the carpet. Then he shook his head as a young steer shakes it when the lash of the stock-whip across his nose warns him back to the path to the shambles that he would escape. For weeks he had forced himself not to think of the Melancolia, because she was a part of his dead life. With Bessie's return and certain new prospects that had developed themselves, the Melancolia—lovelier in his imagination than she had ever been on canvas—reappeared. By her aid he might have procured more money wherewith to amuse Bess and to forget Maisie, as well as another taste of an almost forgotten success. Now, thanks to a vicious little housemaid's folly, there was nothing to look for—not even the hope that he might some day take an abiding interest in the housemaid. Worst of all, he had been made to appear ridiculous in Maisie's eyes. A woman will forgive the man who has ruined her life's work so long as he gives her love: a man may forgive those who ruin the love of his life, but he will never forgive the destruction of his work.

"Tck—tck—tck," said Dick between his teeth, and then laughed softly. "It's an omen, Bessie, and—a good many things considered, it serves me right for doing what I have done. By Jove! that accounts for Maisie's running away. She must have thought me perfectly mad—small blame to her! The whole picture ruined, isn't it so? What made you do it?"

"Because I was that angry. I'm not angry now—I'm awful sorry."

"I wonder.—It doesn't matter, anyhow. I'm to blame for making the mistake."

"What mistake?"

"Something you wouldn't understand, dear. Great heavens! to think that a little piece of dirt like you could throw me out of my stride!" Dick was talking to himself as Bessie tried to shake off his grip on her wrist.

"I ain't a piece of dirt, and you shouldn't call me so! I did it 'cause I hated you, and I'm only sorry now 'cause you're—'cause you're—"

"Exactly—because I'm blind. There's nothing like tact in little things."

Bessie began to sob. She did not like being shackled against her will; she was afraid of the blind face and the look upon it, and was sorry too that her great revenge had only made Dick laugh.

"Don't cry," he said, and took her into his arms. "You only did what you thought right."

"I—I ain't a little piece of dirt, and if you say that I'll never come to you again."

"You don't know what you've done to me. I'm not angry—indeed, I'm not. Be quiet for a minute."

Bessie remained in his arms shrinking. Dick's first thought was connected with Maisie, and it hurt him as white-hot iron hurts an open sore.

Not for nothing is a man permitted to ally himself to the wrong woman. The first pang—the first sense of things lost is but the prelude to the play, for the very just Providence who delights in causing pain has decreed that the agony shall return, and that in the midst of keenest pleasure. They know this pain equally who have forsaken or been forsaken by the love of their life, and in their new wives' arms are compelled to realize it. It is better to remain alone and suffer only the misery of being alone, so long as it is possible to find distraction in daily work. When that resource goes the man is to be pitied and left alone.

These things and some others Dick considered while he was holding Bessie to his heart.

"Though you mayn't know it," he said, raising his head, "the Lord is a just and a terrible God, Bess; with a very strong sense of humor. It serves me right—how it serves me right! Torp could understand it if he were here; he must have suffered something at your hands, child, but only for a minute or so. I saved him. Set that to my credit, some one."

"Let me go," said Bess, her face darkening. "Let me go."

"All in good time. Did you ever attend Sunday school?"

"Never. Let me go, I tell you; you're making fun of me."

"Indeed, I'm not. I'm making fun of myself. . . . Thus. 'He saved others, himself he cannot save.' It isn't exactly a school-board text." He released her wrist, but since he was between her and the door, she could not escape. "What an enormous amount of mischief one little woman can do!"

"I'm sorry; I'm awful sorry about the picture."

"I'm not. I'm grateful to you for spoiling it. . . . What were we talking about before you mentioned the thing?"

"About getting away—and money. Me and you going away."

"Of course. We will get away—that is to say, I will."

"And me?"

"You shall have fifty whole pounds for spoiling a picture."

"Then you won't—?"

"I'm afraid not, dear. Think of fifty pounds for pretty things all to yourself."

"You said you couldn't do anything without me."

"That was true a little while ago. I'm better now, thank you. Get me my hat."

"S'pose I don't?"

"Beeton will, and you'll lose fifty pounds. That's all. Get it."

Bessie cursed under her breath. She had pitied the man sincerely, had kissed him with almost equal sincerity, for he was not unhandsome; it pleased her to be in a way and for a time his protector, and above all there were four thousand pounds to be handled by some one. Now through a slip of the tongue and a little feminine desire to give a little, not too much, pain she had lost the money, the blessed idleness and the pretty things, the companionship, and the chance of looking outwardly as respectable as a real lady.

"Now fill me a pipe. Tobacco doesn't taste, but it doesn't matter, and I'll think things out. What's the day of the week, Bess?"

"Tuesday."

"Then Thursday's mail-day. What a fool—what a blind fool I have been! Twenty-two pounds covers my passage home again. Allow ten for additional expenses. We must put up at Madame Binat's for old sake's sake. Thirty-two pounds altogether. Add a hundred for the cost of the last trip—Gad, won't Torp stare to see me!—a hundred and thirty-two leaves seventy-eight for *baksheesh*—I shall need it—and to play with. What are you crying for, Bess? It wasn't your fault, child; it was mine altogether. Oh, you funny little opossum, mop your eyes and take me out! I want the pass-book and the check-book. Stop a minute. Four thousand pounds at four per cent—that's safe interest—means a hundred and sixty pounds a year; one hundred and twenty pounds a year—also safe—is two eighty, and two hundred and eighty pounds added to three hundred a year means gilded luxury for a single woman. Bess, we'll go to the bank."

Richer by two hundred and ten pounds stored in his money belt, Dick caused Bessie, now thoroughly bewildered, to hurry from the bank to the P. and O. offices, where he explained things tersely.

"Port Said, single first; cabin as close to the baggage-hatch as possible. What ship's going?"

"The 'Colgong,'" said the clerk.

"She's a wet little hooker. Is it Tilbury and a tender, or Galleons and the docks?"

"Galleons. Twelve-forty, Thursday."

"Thanks. Change, please. I can't see very well—will you count it into my hand?"

"If they all took their passages like that instead of talking about their trunks, life would be worth something," said the clerk to his neighbor, who was trying to explain to a harassed mother of many that condensed milk is just as good for babes at sea as daily dairy. Being nineteen and unmarried, he spoke with conviction.

"We are now," quoth Dick, as they returned to the studio, patting the place where his money-belt covered ticket and money, "beyond the reach of man, or devil, or woman—which is much more important. I've three little affairs to carry through before Thursday, but I needn't ask you to help, Bess. Come here on Thursday morning at nine. We'll breakfast, and you shall take me down to Galleons Station."

"What are you going to do?"

"Going away of course. What should I stay for?"

"But you can't look after yourself?"

"I can do anything. I didn't realize it before, but I can. I've done a great deal already. Resolution shall be treated to one kiss if Bessie doesn't object." Strangely enough, Bessie objected and Dick laughed. "I suppose you're right. Well, come at nine the day after to-morrow and you'll get your money."

"Shall I sure?"

"I don't bilk, and you won't know whether I do or not unless you come. Oh, but it's long and long to wait! Good-by, Bessie—send Beeton here as you go out."

The housekeeper came.

"What are all the fittings of my rooms worth?" said Dick imperiously.

"'Tisn't for me to say, sir. Some things is very pretty and some is wore out dreadful."

"I'm insured for two hundred and seventy."

"Insurance policies is no criterion, though I don't say—"

"Oh, damn your longwindedness! You've made your pickings out of me and the other tenants. Why, you talked of retiring and buying a public-house the other day. Give a straight answer to a straight question."

"Fifty," said Mr. Beeton, without a moment's hesitation.

"Double it; or I'll break up half my sticks and burn the rest."

He felt his way to a bookstand that supported a pile of sketch-books, and wrenched out one of the mahogany pillars.

"That's sinful, sir," said the housekeeper, alarmed.

"It's my own. One hundred or—"

"One hundred it is. It'll cost me three and six to get that there pilaster mended."

"I thought so. What an out and out swindler you must have been to spring that price at once!"

"I hope I've done nothing to dissatisfy any of the tenants, least of all you, sir."

"Never mind that. Get me the money to-morrow, and see that all my clothes are packed in the little brown bullock-trunk. I'm going."

"But the quarter's notice?"

"I'll pay forfeit. Look after the packing and leave me alone."

Mr. Beeton discussed this new departure with his wife, who decided that Bessie was at the bottom of it all. Her husband took a more charitable view.

"It's very sudden—but then he was always sudden in his ways. Listen to him now!"

There was a sound of chanting from Dick's room.

"We'll never come back any more, boys,
We'll never come back no more;
We'll go to the deuce on any excuse,
And never come back no more!

Oh, say we're afloat or ashore, boys,
Oh, say we're afloat or ashore;
But we'll never come back any more, boys.
We'll never come back no more!"

"Mr. Beeton! Mr. Beeton! Where the deuce is my pistol?"

"Quick, he's going to shoot himself—'avin' gone mad!" said Mrs. Beeton.

Mr. Beeton addressed Dick soothingly, but it was some time before the latter, threshing up and down his bedroom, could realize the intention of the promises to "find everything to-morrow, sir."

"Oh, you copper-nosed old fool—you impotent Academician!" he shouted at last. "Do you suppose I want to shoot myself? Take the pistol in your silly shaking hand then. If *you* touch it, it will go off, because it's loaded. It's among my campaign kit somewhere—in the parcel at the bottom of the trunk."

Long ago Dick had carefully possessed himself of a forty-pound weight field-equipment constructed by the knowledge of his own experience. It was this put-away treasure that he was trying to find and rehandle. Mr. Beeton whipped the revolver out of its place on the top of the package, and Dick drove his hand among the *khaki* coat and breeches, the blue cloth leg-bands, and the heavy flannel shirts doubled over a pair of swan-neck spurs. Under these and the water-bottle lay a sketch book and a pigskin case of stationery.

"These we don't want; you can have them, Mr. Beeton. Everything else I'll keep. Pack 'em on the top right-hand side of my trunk. When you've done that come into the studio with your wife. I want you both. Wait a minute; get me a pen and a sheet of notepaper."

It is not an easy thing to write when you cannot see, and Dick had particular reasons for wishing that his work should be clear. So he began, following his right hand with his left: "'The badness of this writing is because I am blind and cannot see my pen.' H'mph!—Even a lawyer can't mistake that. It must be signed, I suppose, but it needn't be witnessed. Now an inch lower—why did I never learn to use a type-writer?—'This is the last will and testament of me, Richard Heldar. I am in sound bodily and mental health, and there is no previous will to revoke.'—That's all right. Damn the pen! Whereabouts on the paper was I?—'I leave everything that I possess in the world, including four thousand pounds, and two thousand seven hundred and twenty-eight pounds held for me'—Oh, I can't get this straight." He tore off half the sheet and began again with the caution about the handwriting. Then: "I leave all the money I possess in the world to"—here followed Maisie's name, and the names of the two banks that held his money.

"It mayn't be quite regular, but no one has a shadow of a right to dispute it, and I've given Maisie's address. Come in, Mr. Beeton. This is my signature; you've seen it often enough to know it; I want you and your wife to witness it. Thanks. To-morrow you must take me to the landlord and I'll pay forfeit for leaving without notice, and I'll lodge this paper with him in case anything happens when I'm away. Now we're going to light up the studio stove. Stay with me, and give me my papers as I want 'em."

No one knows until he has tried how fine a blaze a year's accumulation of bills, letters, and dockets can make. Dick stuffed into the stove every document in the studio—saving only three unopened letters: destroyed sketch-books, rough note-books, new and half-finished canvases alike.

"What a lot of rubbish a tenant gets about him if he stays long enough in one place, to be sure," said Mr. Beeton at last.

"He does. Is there anything more left?" Dick felt round the walls.

"Not a thing, and the stove's nigh red-hot."

"Excellent, and you've lost about a thousand pounds' worth of sketches. Ho! ho! Quite a thousand pounds' worth, if I can remember what I used to be."

"Yes, sir," politely. Mr. Beeton was quite sure that

Dick had gone mad, otherwise he would have never parted with his excellent furniture for a song. The canvas things took up storage room and were much better out of the way.

There remained only to leave the little will in safe hands: that could not be accomplished till to-morrow. Dick groped about the floor picking up the last pieces of paper, assured himself again and again that there remained no written word or sign of his past life in drawer or desk, and sat down before the stove till the fire died out and the contracting iron cracked in the silence of the night.

CHAPTER FIFTEEN

With a heart of furious fancies,
  Whereof I am commander;
With a burning spear and a horse of air,
  To the wilderness I wander.
With a knight of ghosts and shadows
  I summoned am to tourney—
Ten leagues beyond the wide world's end,
  Methinks it is no journey.

—*Tom a' Bedlam's Song*

"GOOD-BY, Bess; I promised you fifty. Here's a hundred—all that I got for my furniture from Beeton. That will keep you in pretty frocks for some time. You've been a good little girl, all things considered, but you've given me and Torpenhow a fair amount of trouble."

"Give Mr. Torpenhow my love if you see him, won't you?"

"Of course I will, dear. Now take me up the gang-plank and into the cabin. Once aboard the lugger and the maid is—and I am free, I mean."

"Who'll look after you on the ship?"

"The head-steward, if there's any use in money. The doctor when we come to Port Said, if I know anything of P. and O. doctors. After that, the Lord will provide, as He used to do."

Bess found Dick his cabin in the wild turmoil of a ship full of leavetakers and weeping relatives. Then he kissed her, and laid himself down in his bunk until the decks should be clear. He who had taken so long to move about his own darkened rooms well understood the geography of a ship, and the necessity of seeing to his own comforts was as wine to him. Before the screw began to thrash the ship along the Docks he had been introduced to the head-steward, had royally tipped him, secured a good place at table, opened out his baggage, and settled himself down with joy in the cabin. It was scarcely necessary to feel his way as he moved about, for he knew everything so well. Then God was very kind: a deep sleep of weariness came upon him just as he would have thought of Maisie, and he slept till the steamer had cleared the mouth of the Thames and was lifting to the pulse of the Channel.

The rattle of the engines, the reek of oil and paint, and a very familiar sound in the next cabin roused him to his new inheritance.

"Oh, it's good to be alive again!" He yawned, stretched himself vigorously, and went on deck to be told that they were almost abreast of the lights of Brighton. This is no more open water than Trafalgar Square is a common; the free levels begin at Ushant; but none the less Dick could feel the healing of the sea at work upon him already. A boisterous little cross-swell swung the steamer disrespectfully by the nose; and one wave breaking far aft spattered the quarter-deck and the pile of new deck chairs. He heard the foam fall with the clash of broken glass, was stung in the face by a cupful, and, sniffing luxuriously, felt his way to the smoking-room by the wheel. There a strong breeze found him, blew his cap off and left him bareheaded in the doorway, and the smoking-room steward, understanding that he was a voyager of experience, said that the weather would be stiff in the chops off the Channel and more than half a gale in the Bay. These things fell as they were foretold, and Dick enjoyed himself to the utmost. It is allowable and even necessary at sea to lay firm hold upon tables, stanchions, and ropes in moving from place to place. On land the man who feels with his hands is patently blind. At sea even a blind man who is not seasick can jest with the doctor over the weakness of his fellows. Dick told the doctor many tales—and these are coin of more value than silver if properly handled—smoked with him till unholy hours of the night, and so won his shortlived regard that he promised Dick a few hours of his time when they came to Port Said.

And the sea roared or was still as the winds blew, and the engines sang their song day and night, and the sun grew stronger day by day, and Tom the Lascar barber shaved Dick of a morning under the opened hatch-grating where the cool winds blew, and the awnings were spread and the passengers made merry, and at last they came to Port Said.

"Take me," said Dick to the doctor, "to Madame Binat's—if you know where that is."

"Whew!" said the doctor, "I do. There's not much to choose between 'em; but I suppose you're aware that that's one of the worst houses in the place. They'll rob you to begin with, and knife you later."

"Not they. Take me there, and I can look after myself."

So he was brought to Madame Binat's and filled his nostrils with the well-remembered smell of the East, that runs without a change from the Canal head to Hong-Kong, and his mouth with the villainous Lingua Franca of the Levant. The heat smote him between the shoulder-blades with the buffet of an old friend, his feet slipped on the sand, and his coat-sleeve was warm as new-baked bread when he lifted it to his nose.

Madame Binat smiled with the smile that knows no astonishment when Dick entered the drinking-shop which was one source of her gains. But for a little accident of complete darkness he could hardly realize that he had ever quitted the old life that hummed in his ears. Somebody opened a bottle of peculiarly strong Schiedam. The smell reminded Dick of Monsieur Binat, who, by the way, had spoken of art and degradation. Binat was dead; Madame said as much when the doctor departed, scandalized, so far as a ship's doctor can be, at the warmth of Dick's reception. Dick was delighted at it. "They remember me here after a year. They have forgotten me across the water by this time. Madame, I want a long talk with you when you're at liberty. It is good to be back again."

In the evening she set an iron-topped cafe-table out on the sands, and Dick and she sat by it, while the house behind them filled with riot, merriment, oaths, and threats. The stars came out and the lights of the shipping in the harbor twinkled by the head of the Canal.

"Yes. The war is good for trade, my friend; but what dost thou do here? We have not forgotten thee."

"I was over there in England and I went blind."

"But there was the glory first. We heard of it here, even here—I and Binat; and thou hast used the head of Yellow 'Tina—she is still alive—so often and so well that 'Tina laughed when the papers arrived by the mail-boats. It was always something that we here could recognize in the paintings. And then there was always the glory and the money for thee."

"I am not poor—I shall pay you well."

"Not to me. Thou hast paid for everything." Under her breath, "Mon Dieu, to be blind and so young! What horror!"

Dick could not see her face with the pity on it, or his own with the discolored hair at the temples. He did not feel the need of pity; he was too anxious to get to the front once more, and explained his desire.

"And where? The Canal is full of the English ships. Sometimes they fire as they used to do when the war was here—ten years ago. Beyond Cairo there is fighting, but how canst thou go there without a correspondent's passport? And in the desert there is always fighting, but that is impossible also," said she.

"I must go to Suakin." He knew, thanks to Alf's readings, that Torpenhow was at work with the column that was protecting the construction of the Suakin-Berber line. P. and O. steamers do not touch at that port, and, besides, Madame Binat knew everybody whose help or advice was worth anything. They were not respectable folk, but they could cause things to be accomplished, which is much more important when there is work toward.

"But at Suakin they are always fighting. That desert breeds men always—and always more men. And they are so bold! Why to Suakin?"

"My friend is there."

"Thy friend! Chtt! Thy friend is death, then."

Madame Binat dropped a fat arm on the table-top, filled Dick's glass anew, and looked at him closely under the stars. There was no need that he should bow his head in assent and say—

"No. He is a man, but—if it should arrive . . . blamest thou?"

"I blame?" she laughed shrilly. "Who am I that I should blame any one—except those who try to cheat me over their consommations. But it is very terrible."

"I must go to Suakin. Think for me. A great deal has changed within the year, and the men I knew are not here. The Egyptian lighthouse steamer goes down the Canal to Suakin—and the post-boats—But even then—"

"Do not think any longer. *I* know, and it is for me to think. Thou shalt go—thou shalt go and see thy friend. Be wise. Sit here until the house is a little quiet—I must attend to my guests—and afterward go to bed. Thou shalt go, in truth, thou shalt go."

"To-morrow?"

"As soon as may be." She was talking as though he were a child.

He sat at the table listening to the voices in the harbor and the streets, and wondering how soon the end would come, till Madame Binat carried him off to bed and ordered him to sleep. The house shouted and sang and danced and reveled, Madame Binat moving through it with one eye on the liquor payments and the girls and the other on Dick's interests. To this latter end she smiled upon scowling and furtive Turkish officers of fellaheen regiments, was gracious to Cypriote commissariat underlings, and more than kind to camel agents of no nationality whatever.

In the early morning, being then appropriately dressed in a flaming red silk ball-dress, with a front of tarnished gold embroidery and a necklace of plate-glass diamonds, she made chocolate and carried it in to Dick.

"It is only I, and I am of discreet age, eh? Drink and eat the roll too. Thus in France mothers bring their sons, when those behave wisely, the morning chocolate." She sat down on the side of the bed whispering:

"It is all arranged. Thou wilt go by the lighthouse boat. That is a bribe of ten pounds English. The captain is never paid by the Government. The boat comes to Suakin in four days. There will go with thee George, a Greek muleteer. Another bribe of ten pounds. I will pay; they must not know of thy money. George will go with thee as far as he goes with his mules. Then he comes back to me, for his well-beloved is here, and if I do not receive a telegram from Suakin saying that thou art well, the girl answers for George."

"Thank you." He reached out sleepily for the cup. "You are much too kind, Madame."

"If there were anything that I might do I would say, stay here and be wise; but I do not think that would be best for thee." She looked at her liquor-stained dress with a sad smile. "Nay, thou shalt go, in truth, thou shalt go. It is best so. My boy, it is best so."

She stooped and kissed Dick between the eyes. "That is for good-morning," she said, going away. "When thou art dressed we will speak to George and make everything ready. But first we must open the little trunk. Give me the keys."

"The amount of kissing lately has been simply scandalous. I shall expect Torp to kiss me next. He is more likely to swear at me for getting in his way, though. Well, it won't last long—Ohê, Madame, help me to my toilette of the guillotine! There will be no chance of dressing properly out yonder."

He was rummaging among his new campaign-kit, and roweling his hands with the spurs. There are two ways of wearing well-oiled ankle-jacks, spotless blue leg-bands, *khaki* coat and breeches, and a perfectly pipeclayed helmet. The right way is the way of the untired man, master of himself, setting out upon an expedition, well pleased.

"Everything must be very correct," Dick explained. "It will become dirty afterward, but now it is good to feel well dressed. Is everything as it should be?"

He patted the revolver neatly hidden under the fullness of the blouse on the right hip and fingered his collar.

"I can do no more," Madame said, between laughing and crying. "Look at thyself—but I forgot."

"I am very content." He stroked the creaseless spirals of his leggings. "Now let us go and see the captain and George and the lighthouse boat. Be quick, Madame."

"But thou canst not be seen by the harbor walking with me in the daylight. Figure to yourself if some English ladies—"

"There are no English ladies; and if there are, I have forgotten them. Take me there."

In spite of his burning impatience it was nearly evening ere the lighthouse boat began to move. Madame had said a great deal both to George and the captain touching the arrangements that were to be made for Dick's benefit. Very few men who had the honor of her acquaintance cared to disregard Madame's advice. That sort of contempt might end in being knifed by a stranger in a gambling hell upon surprisingly short provocation.

For six days—two of them were wasted in the crowded Canal—the little steamer worked her way to Suakin, where she was to pick up the superintendent of lighthouses; and Dick made it his business to propitiate George, who was distracted with fears for the safety of his light-of-love and half inclined to make Dick responsible for his own discomfort.

When they arrived George took him under his wing, and together they entered the red-hot seaport, encumbered with the material and wastage of the Suakin-Berber line, from locomotives in disconsolate fragments to mounds of chairs and pot-sleepers.

"If you keep with me," said George, "nobody will ask for passports or what you do. They are all very busy."

"Yes; but I should like to hear some of the Englishmen talk. They might remember me. I was known here a long time ago—when I was some one indeed."

"A long time ago is a very long time ago here. The graveyards are full. Now listen. This new railway runs out so far as Tanai-el-Hassan—that is seven miles. Then there is a camp. They say that beyond Tanai-el-Hassan the English troops go forward, and everything that they require will be brought to them by this line."

"Ah! Base camp. I see. That's a better business than fighting Fuzzies in the open."

"For this reason even the mules go up in the iron-train."

"Iron what?"

"It is all covered with iron, because it is still being shot at."

"An armored train. Better and better! Go on, faithful George."

"And I go up with my mules to-night. Only those who particularly require to go to the camp go out with the train. They begin to shoot not far from the city."

"The dears—they always used to!" Dick snuffed the smell of parched dust, heated iron, and flaking paint with delight. Certainly the old life was welcoming him back most generously.

"When I have got my mules together I go up to-night, but you must first send a telegram to Port Said, declaring that I have done you no harm."

"Madame has you well in hand. Would you stick a knife into me if you had the chance?"

"I have no chance," said the Greek. "*She* is there with that woman."

"I see. It's a bad thing to be divided between love of woman and the chance of loot. I sympathize with you, George."

They went to the telegraph-office unquestioned, for all the world was desperately busy and had scarcely time to turn its head, and Suakin was the last place under sky that would be chosen for holiday ground. On their return the voice of an English subaltern asked Dick what he was doing. The blue goggles were over his eyes and he walked with his hand on George's elbow as he replied—

"Egyptian Government—mules. My orders are to give them over to the A. C. G. at Tanai-el-Hassan. 'Any occasion to show my papers?"

"Oh, certainly not. I beg your pardon. I'd no right to ask, but not seeing your face before I—"

"I go out in the train to-night, I suppose," said Dick boldly. "There will be no difficulty in loading up the mules, will there?"

"You can see the horse-platforms from here. You must have them loaded up early." The young man went away wondering what sort of broken-down waif this might be who talked like a gentleman and consorted with Greek muleteers. Dick felt unhappy. To outface an English officer is no small thing, but the bluff loses relish when one plays it from the utter dark, and stumbles up and down rough ways, thinking and eternally thinking of what might have been if things had fallen out otherwise, and all had been as it was not.

George shared his meal with Dick and went off to the mule-lines. His charge sat alone in a shed with his face in his hands. Before his tight-shut eyes danced the face of Maisie, laughing, with parted lips. There was a great bustle and clamor about him. He grew afraid and almost called for George.

"I say, have you got your mules ready?" It was the voice of the subaltern over his shoulder.

"My man's looking after them. The—the fact is I've a touch of ophthalmia and I can't see very well."

"By Jove! that's bad. You ought to lie up in hospital for a while. I've had a turn of it myself. It's as bad as being blind."

"So I find it. When does this armored train go?"

"At six o'clock. It takes an hour to cover the seven miles."

"Are the Fuzzies on the rampage—eh?"

"About three nights a week. 'Fact is I'm in acting command of the night-train. It generally runs back empty to Tanai for the night."

"Big camp at Tanai, I suppose?"

"Pretty big. It has to feed our desert-column somehow."

"Is that far off?"

"Between thirty and forty miles—in an infernal thirsty country."

"Is the country quiet between Tanai and our men?"

"More or less. I shouldn't care to cross it alone, or with a subaltern's command for the matter of that, but the scouts get through in some extraordinary fashion."

"They always did."

"Have you been here before, then?"

"I was through most of the trouble when it first broke out."

"In the service and cashiered," was the subaltern's first thought, so he refrained from putting any questions.

"There's your man coming up with the mules. It seems rather queer—"

"That I should be mule-leading?" said Dick.

"I didn't mean to say so, but it is. Forgive me—it's beastly impertinence I know, but you speak like a man who has been at a public school. There's no mistaking the tone."

"I am a public school man."

"I thought so I say, I don't want to hurt your feelings, but you're a little down on your luck, aren't you? I saw you sitting with your head in your hands, and that's why I spoke."

"Thanks. I am about as thoroughly and completely broke as a man need be."

"Suppose—I mean I'm a public school man myself. Couldn't I perhaps—take it as a loan, y' know and—"

"You're much too good, but on my honor I've as much money as I want. . . . I tell you what you could do for me, though, and put me under an everlasting obligation. Let me come into the bogie truck of the train. There is a fore-truck, isn't there?"

"Yes. How d'you know?"

"I've been in an armored train before. Only let me see—hear some of the fun I mean, and I'll be grateful. I go at my own risk as a non-combatant."

The young man thought for a minute. "All right," he said. "We're supposed to be an empty train, and there's no one to blow me up at the other end."

George and a horde of yelling amateur assistants had loaded up the mules, and the narrow-gauge armored train, plated with three-eighths inch boiler-plate till it looked like one long coffin, stood ready to start.

Two bogie trucks running before the locomotive were com pletely covered in with plating, except that the leading one was pierced in front for the nozzle of a machine-gun, and the second at either side for lateral fire. The trucks together made one long iron vaulted chamber in which a score of artillerymen were rioting.

"Whitechapel—last train! Ah, I see yer kissin' in the first class there!" somebody shouted, just as Dick was clambering into the forward truck.

"Lordy! 'Ere's a real live passenger for the Kew, Tanai, Acton, and Ealin' train. 'Echo,' sir. Speshul edition! 'Star,' sir."—"Shall I get you a foot-warmer?" said another.

"Thanks. I'll pay my footing," said Dick, and relations of the most amicable were established ere silence came with the arrival of the subaltern, and the train jolted out over the rough track.

"This is an immense improvement on shooting the unimpressionable Fuzzy in the open," said Dick from his place in the corner.

"Oh, but he's still unimpressed. There he goes!" said the subaltern, as a bullet struck the outside of the truck. "We always have at least one demonstration against the night-train. Generally they attack the rear-truck where my junior commands. He gets all the fun of the fair."

"Not to-night though! Listen!" said Dick. A flight of heavy-handed bullets was succeeded by yelling and shouts. The children of the desert valued their nightly amusement, and the train was an excellent mark.

"Is it worth while giving them half a hopper full?" the subaltern asked of the engine which was driven by a Lieutenant of Sappers.

"I should just think so! This is my section of the line. They'll be playing Old Harry with my permanent way if we don't stop 'em."

"Right O!"

"*Hrrmph!*" said the machine gun through all its five noses as the subaltern drew the lever home. The empty cartridges clashed on the floor and the smoke blew back through the truck. There was indiscriminate firing at the rear of the train, a return fire from the darkness without, and unlimited howling. Dick stretched himself on the floor, wild with delight at the sounds and the smells.

"God is very good—I never thought I'd hear this again. Give 'em hell, men. Oh, give 'em hell!" he cried.

The train stopped for some obstruction on the line ahead and a party went out to reconnoiter, but came back cursing, for spades. The children of the desert had piled sand and gravel on the rails, and twenty minutes were lost in clearing it away. Then the slow progress recommenced, to be varied with more shots, more shoutings, the steady clack and kick of the machine guns, and a final difficulty with a half-lifted rail ere the train came under the protection of the roaring camp at Tanai-el-Hassan.

"Now, you see why it takes an hour and a half to fetch her through," said the subaltern, unshipping the cartridge hopper above his pet gun.

"It was a lark, though. I only wish it had lasted twice as long. How superb it must have looked from outside!" said Dick, sighing regretfully.

"It palls after the first few nights. By the way, when you've settled about your mules, come and see what we can find to eat in my tent. I'm Bennil of the Gunners—in the artillery lines—and mind you don't fall over my tent-ropes in the dark."

But it was all dark to Dick. He could only smell the camels, the hay-bales, the cooking, the smoky fires, and the tanned canvas of the tents as he stood, where he had dropped from the train, shouting for George. There was a sound of light-hearted kicking on the iron skin of the rear trucks, with squealing and grunting. George was unloading the mules.

The engine was blowing off steam nearly in Dick's ear; a cold wind of the desert danced between his legs; he was hungry, and felt tired and dirty—so dirty that he tried to brush his coat with his hands. That was a hopeless job; he thrust his hands into his pockets and began to count over the many times that he had waited in strange or remote places for trains or camels, mules or horses, to carry him to his business. In those days he could see—few men more clearly—and the spectacle of an armed camp at dinner under the stars was an ever fresh pleasure to the eye. There was color, light, and motion, without which no man has much pleasure in living. This night there remained for him only one more journey through the darkness that never lifts to tell a man how far he has traveled. Then he would grip Torpenhow's hand again—Torpenhow, who was alive and strong, and lived in the midst of the action that had once made the reputation of a man called Dick Heldar: not in the least to be confused with the blind, bewildered vagabond who seemed to answer to the same name. Yes, he would find Torpenhow, and come as near to the old life as might be. Afterward he would forget everything: Bessie, who had wrecked the Melancolia and so nearly wrecked his life; Beeton, who lived in a strange unreal city full of tin-tacks and gas-plugs and matters that no men needed; that irrational being who had offered him love and loyalty for nothing, but had not signed her name; and most of all Maisie, who, from her own point of view, was undeniably right in all she did, but oh, at this distance, so tantalizingly fair.

George's hand on his arm pulled him back to the situation.

"And what now?" said George.

"Oh yes, of course. What now? Take me to the camel-men. Take me to where the scouts sit when they come in from the desert. They sit by their camels, and the camels eat grain out of a black blanket held up at the corners, and the men eat by their side just like camels. Take me there!"

The camp was rough and rutty, and Dick stumbled many times over the stumps of scrub. The scouts were sitting by their beasts, as Dick knew they would. The light of the dung-fires flickered on their bearded faces, and the camels bubbled and mumbled beside them at rest. It was no part of Dick's policy to go into the desert with a convoy of supplies. That would lead to impertinent questions, and since a blind non-combatant is not needed at the front, he would probably be forced to return to Suakin. He must go up alone, and go immediately.

"Now for one last bluff—the biggest of all," he said. "Peace be with you, brethren!" The watchful George steered him to the circle of the nearest fire. The heads of the camel-sheiks bowed gravely, and the camels, scenting a European, looked sidewise curiously like brooding hens, half ready to get to their feet.

"A beast and a driver to go to the fighting line to-night," said Dick.

"A Mulaid?" said a voice, scornfully naming the best baggage-breed that he knew.

"A Bisharin," returned Dick with perfect gravity. "A Bisharin without saddle-galls. Therefore no charge of thine shock-head."

Two or three minutes passed. Then—

"We be knee-haltered for the night. There is no going out from the camp."

"Not for money?"

"H'm! Ah!—English money?"

Another depressing interval of silence.

"How much?"

"Twenty-five pounds English paid into the hand of the driver at my journey's end, and as much more into the hand of the camel-sheik here, to be paid when the driver returns."

This was royal payment, and the sheik, who knew that he would get his commission on the deposit, stirred in Dick's behalf.

"For scarcely one night's journey—fifty pounds. Land and wells and good trees and wives to make a man content for the rest of his days. Who speaks?" said Dick.

"I," said a voice. "I will go—but there is no going from the camp."

"Fool! I know that a camel can break his knee-halter, and the sentries do not fire if one goes in chase. Twenty-five pounds and another twenty-five pounds. But the beast must be a good Bisharin; I will take no baggage-camel."

Then the bargaining began, and at the end of half an hour the first deposit was paid over to the sheik, who talked in low tones to the driver. Dick heard the latter say: "A little way out only. Any baggage-beast will serve. Am I a fool to waste my cattle for a blind man?"

"And though I cannot see"—Dick lifted his voice a little —"yet I carry that which has six eyes, and the driver will sit before me. If we do not reach the English troops in the dawn he will be dead."

"But where, in God's name, are the troops?"

"Unless thou knowest let another man ride. *Dost* thou know? Remember it will be life or death to thee."

"I know," said the driver sullenly. "Stand back from my beast. I am going to slip him."

"Not so swiftly. George, hold the camel's head a moment. I want to feel his cheek." The hands wandered over the hide till they found the branded half-circle that is the mark of the Bisharin, the light-built riding-camel. "That is well. Cut this one loose. Remember no blessing of God comes on those who try to cheat the blind."

The men chuckled by the fires at the camel-driver's discomfiture. He had intended to substitute a slow, saddle-galled baggage-colt.

"Stand back!" one shouted, lashing the Bisharin under the belly with a quirt. Dick obeyed as soon as he felt the nose-string tighten in his hand—and a cry went up, "Illaha! Aho! He is loose."

With a roar and a grunt the Bisharin rose to his feet and plunged forward toward the desert, his driver following with shouts and lamentation. George caught Dick's arm and hurried him stumbling and tripping past a disgusted sentry who was used to stampeding camels.

"What's the row now?" he cried.

"Every stitch of my kit on that blasted dromedary," Dick answered, after the manner of a common soldier.

"Go on, and take care your throat's not cut outside—you and your dromedary's."

The outcries ceased when the camel had disappeared behind a hillock, and his driver had called him back and made him kneel down.

"Mount first," said Dick. Then climbing into the second seat and gently screwing the pistol muzzle into the small of his companion's back, "Go on in God's name, and swiftly. Good-by, George. Remember me to Madame, and have a good time with your girl. Get forward, child of the Pit!"

A few minutes later he was shut up in a great silence, hardly broken by the creaking of the saddle and the soft pad of the tireless feet. Dick adjusted himself comfortably to the rock and pitch of the pace, girthed his belt tighter, and felt the darkness slide past. For an hour he was conscious only of the sense of rapid progress.

"A good camel," he said at last.

"He has never been underfed. He is my own and clean bred," the driver replied.

"Go on."

His head dropped on his chest and he tried to think, but the tenor of his thoughts was broken because he was very sleepy. In the half doze it seemed that he was learning a punishment hymn at Mrs. Jennett's. He had committed some crime as bad as Sabbath-breaking, and she had locked him up in his bedroom. But he could never repeat more than the first two lines of the hymn—

"When Israel of the Lord beloved
Out of the land of bondage came."

He said them over and over thousands of times. The driver turned in the saddle to see if there were any chance of capturing the revolver and ending the ride. Dick roused, struck him over the head with the butt, and stormed himself wide awake. Somebody hidden in a clump of camel-thorn shouted as the camel toiled up rising ground. A shot was fired, and the silence shut down again, bringing the desire to sleep. Dick could think no longer. He was too tired and stiff and cramped to do more than nod uneasily from time to time, waking with a start and punching the driver with the pistol.

"Is there a moon?" he asked drowsily.

"She is near her setting."

"I wish that I could see her. Halt the camel. At least let me hear the desert talk."

The man obeyed. Out of the utter stillness came one breath of wind. It rattled the dead leaves of a shrub some distance away and ceased. A handful of dry earth detached itself from the edge of a rain trench and crumbled softly to the bottom.

"Go on. The night is very cold."

Those who have watched till the morning know how the

last hour before the light lengthens itself into many eternities. It seemed to Dick that he had never since the beginning of original darkness done anything at all save jolt through the air. Once in a thousand years he would finger the nail-heads on the saddle-front and count them all carefully. Centuries later he would shift his revolver from his right hand to his left and allow the eased arm to drop down at his side. From the safe distance of London he was watching himself thus employed—watching critically. Yet whenever he put out his hand to the canvas that he might paint the tawny yellow desert under the glare of the sinking moon, the black shadow of the camel and the two bowed figures atop, that hand held a revolver and the arm was numbed from wrist to collar-bone. Moreover, he was in the dark, and could see no canvas of any kind whatever.

The driver grunted, and Dick was conscious of a change in the air.

"I smell the dawn," he whispered.

"It is here, and yonder are the troops. Have I done well?"

The camel stretched out its neck and roared as there came down wind the pungent reek of camels in square.

"Go on. We must get there swiftly. Go on."

"They are moving in their camp. There is so much dust that I cannot see what they do."

"Am I in better case? Go forward."

They could hear the hum of voices ahead, the howling and the bubbling of the beasts and the hoarse cries of the soldiers girthing up for the day. Two or three shots were fired.

"Is that at us? Surely they can see that I am English," Dick spoke angrily.

"Nay, it is from the desert," the driver answered, cowering in his saddle. "Go forward, my child! Well it is that the dawn did not uncover us an hour ago."

The camel headed straight for the column and the shots behind multiplied. The children of the desert had arranged

Drawn by T. V. CHOMINSKI.

"*That hand held a revolver, and the arm was numbed from wrist to collar-bone.*"

THE LIGHT THAT FAILED—Vol. ii., p. 218.

that most uncomfortable of surprises, a dawn attack for the English troops, and were getting their distance by snap-shots at the only moving object without the square.

"What luck! What stupendous and imperial luck!" said Dick. "It's 'just before the battle, mother.' Oh, God has been most good to me! Only"—the agony of the thought made him screw up his eyes for an instant—"Maisie . . ."

"Allahu! We are in," said the man, as he drove into the rearguard and the camel knelt.

"Who the deuce are you? Dispatches or what? What's the strength of the enemy behind that ridge? How did you get through?" asked a dozen voices.

For all answer Dick took a long breath, unbuckled his belt, and shouted from the saddle at the top of a wearied and dusty voice, "Torpenhow! Ohé, Torp! Coo-ee, Torpen-how."

A bearded man raking in the ashes of a fire for a light to his pipe moved very swiftly toward that cry, as the rearguard, facing about, began to fire at the puffs of smoke from the hillocks around. Gradually the scattered white cloudlets drew out into long lines of banked white that hung heavily in the stillness of the dawn before they turned over wave-like and glided into the valleys. The soldiers in the square were coughing and swearing as their own smoke obstructed their view, and they edged forward to get beyond it. A wounded camel leaped to its feet and roared aloud, the cry ending in a bubbling grunt. Some one had cut its throat to prevent confusion. Then came the thick sob of a man receiving his death-wound from a bullet; then a yell of agony and redoubled firing.

There was no time to ask any questions.

"Get down, man! Get down behind the camel!"

"No. Put me, I pray, in the forefront of the battle." Dick turned his face to Torpenhow and raised his hand to set his helmet straight, but, miscalculating the distance, knocked it off.

Torpenhow saw that his hair was gray on the temples, and that his face was the face of an old man.

"Come down, you damned fool! Dickie, come off!"

And Dick came obediently, but as a tree falls, pitching sidewise from the Bisharin's saddle at Torpenhow's feet. His luck had held to the last, even to the crowning mercy of a kindly bullet through his head. Torpenhow knelt under the lee of the camel, with Dick's body in his arms.

END OF "THE LIGHT THAT FAILED"

PLAIN TALES FROM THE HILLS

To

THE WITTIEST WOMAN IN INDIA

I DEDICATE THIS BOOK

PREFACE

EIGHT-AND-TWENTY of these tales appeared originally in the "Civil and Military Gazette." I am indebted to the kindness of the Proprietors of that paper for permission to reprint them. The remaining tales are, more or less, new.

RUDYARD KIPLING.

LISPETH

Look, you have cast out Love! What Gods are these
You bid me please?
The Three in One, the One in Three? Not so!
To my own Gods I go.
It may be they shall give me greater ease
Than your cold Christ and tangled Trinities.

—*The Convert*

SHE was the daughter of Sonoo, a Hill-man of the Himalayas, and Jadéh his wife. One year their maize failed, and two bears spent the night in their only opium poppy-field just above the Sutlej Valley on the Kotgarh side; so, next season, they turned Christian, and brought their baby to the Mission to be baptized. The Kotgarh Chaplain christened her Elizabeth, and "Lispeth" is the Hill or *pahari* pronunciation.

Later, cholera came into the Kotgarh Valley and carried off Sonoo and Jadéh, and Lispeth became half servant, half companion, to the wife of the then Chaplain of Kotgarh. This was after the reign of the Moravian missionaries in that place, but before Kotgarh had quite forgotten her title of "Mistress of the Northern Hills."

Whether Christianity improved Lispeth, or whether the gods of her own people would have done as much for her under any circumstances, I do not know; but she grew very lovely. When a Hill-girl grows lovely, she is worth traveling fifty miles over bad ground to look upon. Lispeth had a Greek face—one of those faces people paint so often, and see so seldom. She was of a pale, ivory color, and, for her race, extremely tall. Also, she possessed eyes that were wonderful; and, had she not been dressed in the abominable print-cloths affected by Missions, you would, meeting her on the hillside unexpectedly, have thought her the original Diana of the Romans going out to slay.

Lispeth took to Christianity readily, and did not abandon it when she reached womanhood, as do some Hill-girls. Her own people hated her because she had, they said, become a white woman and washed herself daily; and the Chaplain's wife did not know what to do with her. One cannot ask a stately goddess, five foot ten in her shoes, to clean plates and dishes. She played with the Chaplain's children and took classes in the Sunday School, and read all the books in the house, and grew more and more beautiful, like the Princesses in fairy tales. The Chaplain's wife said that the girl ought to take service in Simla as a nurse or something "genteel." But Lispeth did not want to take service. She was very happy where she was.

When travelers—there were not many in those years—came in to Kotgarh, Lispeth used to lock herself into her own room for fear they might take her away to Simla, or out into the unknown world.

One day, a few months after she was seventeen years old, Lispeth went out for a walk. She did not walk in the manner of English ladies—a mile and a half out, with a carriage-ride back again. She covered between twenty and thirty miles in her little constitutionals, all about and about, between Kotgarh and Narkunda. This time she came back at full dusk, stepping down the breakneck descent into Kotgarh with something heavy in her arms. The Chaplain's wife was dozing in the drawing-room when Lispeth came in breathing heavily and very exhausted with her burden. Lispeth put it down on the sofa, and said simply, "This is my husband. I found him on the Bagi Road. He has hurt himself. We will nurse him, and when he is well, your husband shall marry him to me."

This was the first mention Lispeth had ever made of her matrimonial views, and the Chaplain's wife shrieked with horror. However, the man on the sofa needed attention first. He was a young Englishman, and his head had been cut to the bone by something jagged. Lispeth said she had found him down the hillside, and had brought him in. He was breathing queerly and was unconscious.

He was put to bed and tended by the Chaplain, who knew something of medicine; and Lispeth waited outside the door in case she could be useful. She explained to the Chaplain that this was the man she meant to marry; and the Chaplain and his wife lectured her severely on the impropriety of her conduct. Lispeth listened quietly, and repeated her first proposition. It takes a great deal of Christianity to wipe out uncivilized Eastern instincts, such as falling in love at first sight. Lispeth, having found the man she worshiped, did not see why she should keep silent as to her choice. She had no intention of being sent away, either. She was going to nurse that Englishman until he was well enough to marry her. This was her programme.

After a fortnight of slight fever and inflammation, the Englishman recovered coherence and thanked the Chaplain and his wife, and Lispeth—especially Lispeth—for their kindness. He was a traveler in the East, he said—they never talked about "globe-trotters" in those days, when the P. & O. fleet was young and small—and had come from Dehra Dun to hunt for plants and butterflies among the Simla hills. No one at Simla, therefore, knew anything about him. He fancied that he must have fallen over the cliff while reaching out for a fern on a rotten tree-trunk, and that his coolies must have stolen his baggage and fled. He thought he would go back to Simla when he was a little stronger. He desired no more mountaineering.

He made small haste to go away, and recovered his strength slowly. Lispeth objected to being advised either by the Chaplain or his wife; therefore the latter spoke to the Englishman, and told him how matters stood in Lispeth's heart. He laughed a good deal, and said it was very pretty and romantic, but, as he was engaged to a girl at Home, he fancied that nothing would happen. Certainly he would behave with discretion. He did that. Still he found it very pleasant to talk to Lispeth, and walk with Lispeth, and say nice things to her, and call her pet names while he was getting strong enough to go away. It meant nothing at all to him, and everything in the world to Lispeth. She was very happy while the fortnight lasted, because she had found a man to love.

Being a savage by birth, she took no trouble to hide her feelings, and the Englishman was amused. When he went away, Lispeth walked with him up the Hill as far as Narkunda, very troubled and very miserable. The Chaplain's wife, being a good Christian and disliking anything in the shape of fuss or scandal—Lispeth was beyond her management entirely—had told the Englishman to tell Lispeth that he was coming back to marry her. "She is but a child, you know, and, I fear, at heart a heathen," said the Chaplain's wife. So all the twelve miles up the Hill the Englishman, with his arm round Lispeth's waist, was assuring the girl that he would come back and marry her; and Lispeth made him promise over and over again. She wept on the Narkunda Ridge till he had passed out of sight along the Muttiani path.

Then she dried her tears and went in to Kotgarh again, and said to the Chaplain's wife, "He will come back and marry me. He has gone to his own people to tell them so." And the Chaplain's wife soothed Lispeth and said, "He will come back." At the end of two months, Lispeth grew impatient, and was told that the Englishman had gone over the seas to England. She knew where England was, because she had read little geography primers; but, of course, she had no conception of the nature of the sea, being a Hill-girl. There was an old puzzle-map of the World in the house. Lispeth had played with it when she was a child. She unearthed it again, and put it together of evenings, and cried to herself, and tried to imagine where her Englishman was. As she had no ideas of distance or steamboats, her notions were somewhat wild. It would not have made the least difference had she been perfectly correct; for the Englishman had no intention of coming back to marry a Hill-girl. He forgot all about her by the time he was butterfly-hunting in Assam. He wrote a book on the East afterward. Lispeth's name did not appear there.

At the end of three months, Lispeth made daily pilgrimage to Narkunda to see if her Englishman was coming along the road. It gave her comfort, and the Chaplain's wife finding her happier thought that she was getting over her "barbarous and most indelicate folly." A little later, the walks ceased to help Lispeth and her temper grew very bad. The Chaplain's wife thought this a profitable time to let her know the real state of affairs—that the Englishman had only promised his love to keep her quiet—that he had never meant anything, and that it was wrong and improper of Lispeth to think of marriage with an Englishman, who was of a superior clay, besides being promised in marriage to a girl of his own people. Lispeth said that all this was clearly impossible because he had said he loved her, and the Chaplain's wife had, with her own lips, asserted that the Englishman was coming back.

"How can what he and you said be untrue?" asked Lispeth.

"We said it as an excuse to keep you quiet, child," said the Chaplain's wife.

"Then you have lied to me," said Lispeth, "you and he?"

The Chaplain's wife bowed her head, and said nothing. Lispeth was silent, too, for a little time; then she went out down the valley, and returned in the dress of a Hill-girl—infamously dirty, but without the nose-stud and ear-rings. She had her hair braided into the long pigtail, helped out with black thread, that Hill-women wear.

"I am going back to my own people," said she. "You have killed Lispeth. There is only left old Jadeh's daughter—the daughter of a *pahari* and the servant of *Tarka Devi*. You are all liars, you English."

By the time that the Chaplain's wife had recovered from the shock of the announcement that Lispeth had 'verted to her mother's gods, the girl had gone; and she never came back.

She took to her own unclean people savagely, as if to make up the arrears of the life she had stepped out of; and, in a little time, she married a woodcutter who beat her after the manner of *paharis*, and her beauty faded soon.

"There is no law whereby you can account for the vagaries of the heathen," said the Chaplain's wife, "and I believe that Lispeth was always at heart an infidel." Seeing she had been taken into the Church of England at the mature age of five weeks, this statement does not do credit to the Chaplain's wife.

Lispeth was a very old woman when she died. She had always a perfect command of English, and when she was sufficiently drunk, could sometimes be induced to tell the story of her first love-affair.

It was hard then to realize that the bleared, wrinkled creature, exactly like a wisp of charred rag, could ever have been "Lispeth of the Kotgarh Mission."

THREE AND—AN EXTRA

When halter and heel-ropes are slipped, do not give chase with sticks, but with *gram*.—*Punjabi Proverb*

After marriage arrives a reaction, sometimes a big, sometimes a little one; but it comes sooner or later, and must be tided over by both parties if they desire the rest of their lives to go with the current.

In the case of the Cusack-Bremmils this reaction did not set in till the third year after the wedding. Bremmil was hard to hold at the best of times; but he was a beautiful husband until the baby died and Mrs. Bremmil wore black, and grew thin, and mourned as though the bottom of the Universe had fallen out. Perhaps Bremmil ought to have comforted her. He tried to do so, but the more he comforted the more Mrs. Bremmil grieved, and, consequently, the more uncomfortable grew Bremmil. The fact was that they both needed a tonic. And they got it. Mrs. Bremmil can afford to laugh now, but it was no laughing matter to her at the time.

Mrs. Hauksbee appeared on the horizon; and where she existed was fair chance of trouble. At Simla her by-name was the "Stormy Petrel." She had won that title five times to my own certain knowledge. She was a little, brown, thin, almost skinny, woman, with big, rolling, violet-blue eyes, and the sweetest manners in the world. You had only to mention her name at afternoon teas for every woman in the room to rise up, and call her not blessed. She was clever, witty, brilliant, and sparkling beyond most of her kind; but possessed of many devils of malice and mischievousness. She could be nice, though, even to her own sex. But that is another story.

Bremmil went off at score after the baby's death and the general discomfort that followed, and Mrs. Hauksbee annexed him. She took no pleasure in hiding her captives. She annexed him publicly, and saw that the public saw it. He rode with her, and walked with her, and talked with her, and picnicked with her, and tiffined at Peliti's with her, till people put up their eyebrows and said, "Shocking!" Mrs. Bremmil stayed at home turning over the dead baby's frocks and crying into the empty cradle. She did not care to do anything else. But some eight dear, affectionate lady-friends explained the situation at length to her in case she should miss the cream of it. Mrs. Bremmil listened quietly, and thanked them for their good offices. She was not as clever as Mrs. Hauksbee, but she was no fool. She kept her own counsel, and did not speak to Bremmil of what she had heard. This is worth remembering. Speaking to, or crying over, a husband never did any good yet.

When Bremmil was at home, which was not often, he was more affectionate than usual; and that showed his hand. The affection was forced partly to soothe his own conscience and partly to soothe Mrs. Bremmil. It failed in both regards. Then "the A.-D.-C. in Waiting was commanded by Their Excellencies, Lord and Lady Lytton, to invite Mr. and Mrs. Cusack-Bremmil to Peterhoff on July 26 at 9:30 P.M."—"Dancing" in the bottom-left-hand corner.

"I can't go," said Mrs. Bremmil, "it is too soon after poor little Florrie . . . but it need not stop you, Tom."

She meant what she said then, and Bremmil said that he would go just to put in an appearance. Here he spoke the thing which was not; and Mrs. Bremmil knew it. She guessed—a woman's guess is much more accurate than a man's certainty—that he had meant to go from the first, and with Mrs. Hauksbee. She sat down to think, and the outcome of her thoughts was that the memory of a dead child was worth considerably less than the affections of a living husband. She made her plan and staked her all upon it. In that hour she discovered that she knew Tom Bremmil thoroughly, and this knowledge she acted on.

"Tom," said she, "I shall be dining out at the Longmores' on the evening of the 26th. You'd better dine at the Club."

This saved Bremmil from making an excuse to get away and dine with Mrs. Hauksbee, so he was grateful, and felt small and mean at the same time—which was wholesome. Bremmil left the house at five for a ride. About half-past five in the evening a large leather-covered basket came in from Phelps's for Mrs. Bremmil. She was a woman who knew how to dress; and she had not spent a week on designing that dress and having it gored, and hemmed, and herring-boned, and tucked and rucked (or whatever the terms are), for nothing. It was a gorgeous dress—slight mourning. I can't describe it, but it was what "The Queen" calls "a creation"—a thing that hit you straight between the eyes and made you gasp. She had not much heart for what she was going to do; but as she glanced at the long mirror she had the satisfaction of knowing that she had never looked so well in her life. She was a large blonde and, when she chose, carried herself superbly.

After the dinner at the Longmores', she went on to the dance—a little late—and encountered Bremmil with Mrs. Hauksbee on his arm. That made her flush, and as the men crowded round her for dances she looked magnificent. She filled up all her dances except three, and those she left blank. Mrs. Hauksbee caught her eye once; and she knew it was war—real war—between them. She started handicapped in the struggle, for she had ordered Bremmil about just the least little bit in the world too much; and he was beginning to resent it. Moreover, he had never seen his wife look so lovely. He stared at her from doorways, and glared at her from passages as she went about with her partners; and the more he stared, the more taken was he. He could scarcely believe that this was the woman with the red eyes and the black stuff gown who used to weep over the eggs at breakfast.

Mrs. Hauksbee did her best to hold him in play, but, after two dances, he crossed over to his wife and asked for a dance.

"I'm afraid you've come too late, *Mister* Bremmil," she said, with her eyes twinkling.

Then he begged her to give him a dance, and, as a great favor, she allowed him the fifth waltz. Luckily Five stood vacant on his programme. They danced it together, and there was a little flutter round the room. Bremmil had a sort of a notion that his wife could dance, but he never knew she danced so divinely. At the end of that waltz he asked for another—as a favor, not as a right; and Mrs. Bremmil said, "Show me your programme, dear!" He showed it as a naughty little schoolboy hands up contraband sweets to a master. There was a fair sprinkling of "H" on it, besides "H" at supper. Mrs. Bremmil said nothing, but she smiled contemptuously, ran her pencil through Seven and Nine—two "H's"—and returned the card with her own name written above—a pet name that only she and her husband used. Then she shook her finger at him, and said laughing, "Oh, you silly, *silly* boy!"

Mrs. Hauksbee heard that, and—she owned as much—felt she had the worst of it. Bremmil accepted Seven and Nine gratefully. They danced Seven, and sat out Nine in one of the little tents. What Bremmil said and what Mrs. Bremmil did is no concern of any one.

When the band struck up "The Roast Beef of Old England," the two went out into the veranda, and Bremmil began looking for his wife's dandy (this was before 'rickshaw days) while she went into the cloak-room. Mrs. Hauksbee came up and said, "You take me in to supper, I think, Mr. Bremmil?" Bremmil turned red and looked foolish, "Ah—h'm! I'm going home with my wife, Mrs. Hauksbee. I think there has been a little mistake." Being a man, he spoke as though Mrs. Hauksbee were entirely responsible.

Mrs. Bremmil came out of the cloak room in a swansdown cloak with a white "cloud" round her head. She looked radiant; and she had a right to.

The couple went off into the darkness together, Bremmil riding very close to the dandy.

Then said Mrs. Hauksbee to me—she looked a trifle faded and jaded in the lamplight—"Take my word for it, the silliest woman can manage a clever man; but it needs a very clever woman to manage a fool."

Then we went in to supper.

THROWN AWAY

And some are sulky, while some will plunge.
  [*So ho! Steady! Stand still, you!*]
Some you must gentle, and some you must lunge.
  [*There! There! Who wants to kill you?*]
Some—there are losses in every trade—
Will break their hearts ere bitted and made,
Will fight like fiends as the rope cuts hard,
And die dumb-mad in the breaking-yard.
—Toolungala Stockyard Chorus

To rear a boy under what parents call the "sheltered life system" is, if the boy must go into the world and fend for himself, not wise. Unless he be one in a thousand he has certainly to pass through many unnecessary troubles; and may, possibly, come to extreme grief simply from ignorance of the proper proportions of things.

Let a puppy eat the soap in the bath-room or chew a newly-blacked boot. He chews and chuckles until, by-and-by, he finds out that blacking and Old Brown Windsor make him very sick; so he argues that soap and boots are not wholesome. Any old dog about the house will soon show him the unwisdom of biting big dogs' ears. Being young, he remembers and goes abroad, at six months, a well-mannered little beast with a chastened appetite. If he had been kept away from boots, and soap, and big dogs till he came to the trinity full-grown and with developed teeth, consider how fearfully sick and thrashed he would be! Apply that notion to the "sheltered life," and see how it works. It does not sound pretty, but it is the better of two evils.

There was a Boy once who had been brought up under the "sheltered life" theory; and the theory killed him dead. He stayed with his people all his days, from the hour he was born till the hour he went into Sandhurst nearly at the top of the list. He was beautifully taught in all that wins marks by a private tutor, and carried the extra weight of "never having given his parents an hour's anxiety in his life." What he learned at Sandhurst beyond the regular routine is of no great consequence. He looked about him, and he found soap and blacking, so to speak, very good. He ate a little, and came out of Sandhurst not so high as he went in. Then there was an interval and a scene with his people, who expected much from him. Next a year of living unspotted from the world in a third-rate depot battalion where all the juniors were children and all the seniors old women; and lastly he came out to India, where he was cut off from the support of his parents, and had no one to fall back on in time of trouble except himself.

Now India is a place beyond all others where one must not take things too seriously—the mid-day sun always excepted.

Too much work and too much energy kill a man just as effectively as too much assorted vice or too much drink. Flirtation does not matter, because every one is being transferred, and either you or she leave the Station and never return. Good work does not matter, because a man is judged by his worst output and another man takes all the credit of his best as a rule. Bad work does not matter, because other men do worse and incompetents hang on longer in India than anywhere else. Amusements do not matter, because you must repeat them as soon as you have accomplished them once, and most amusements only mean trying to win another person's money. Sickness does not matter, because it's all in the day's work, and if you die, another man takes over your place and your office in the eight hours between death and burial. Nothing matters except Home-furlough and acting allowances, and these only because they are scarce. It is a slack country where all men work with imperfect instruments; and the wisest thing is to escape as soon as ever you can to some place where amusement is amusement and a reputation worth the having.

But this Boy—the tale is as old as the Hills—came out, and took all things seriously. He was pretty and was petted. He took the pettings seriously and fretted over women not worth saddling a pony to call upon. He found his new free life in India very good. It does look attractive in the beginning, from a subaltern's point of view—all ponies, partners, dancing, and so on. He tasted it as the puppy tastes the soap. Only he came late to the eating, with a grown set of teeth. He had no sense of balance—just like the puppy—and could not understand why he was not treated with the consideration he received under his father's roof. This hurt his feelings.

He quarreled with other boys and, being sensitive to the marrow, remembered these quarrels, and they excited him. He found whist, and gymkhanas, and things of that kind (meant to amuse one after office), good; but he took them seriously too, just as seriously as he took the "head" that followed after drink. He lost his money over whist and gymkhanas because they were new to him.

He took his losses seriously, and wasted as much energy and interest over a two-goldmohur race for maiden *ekka*-ponies with their manes hogged, as if it had been the Derby. One half of this came from inexperience—much as the puppy squabbles with the corner of the heartrug—and the other half from the dizziness bred by stumbling out of his quiet life into the glare and excitement of a livelier one. No one told him about the soap and the blacking, because an average man takes it for granted that an average man is ordinarily careful in regard to them. It was pitiful to watch The Boy knocking himself to pieces, as an over-handled colt falls down and cuts himself when he gets away from the groom.

This unbridled license in amusements not worth the trouble of breaking line for, much less rioting over, endured for six months—all through one cold weather—and then we thought that the heat and the knowledge of having lost his money and health and lamed his horses would sober The Boy down, and he would stand steady. In ninety-nine cases out of a hundred this would have happened. You can see the principle working in any Indian Station. But this particular case fell through because The Boy was sensitive and took things seriously—as I may have said some seven times before. Of course, we could not tell how his excesses struck him personally. They were nothing very heartbreaking or above the average. He might be crippled for life financially, and want a little nursing. Still the memory of his performances would wither away in one hot weather, and the bankers would help him to tide over the money-troubles. But he must have taken another view altogether and have believed himself ruined beyond redemption. His Colonel talked to him severely when the cold weather ended. That made him more wretched than ever; and it was only an ordinary "Colonel's wigging!"

What follows is a curious instance of the fashion in which we are all linked together and made responsible for one another. *The* thing that kicked the beam in The Boy's mind was a remark that a woman made when he was talking to her. There is no use in repeating it, for it was only a cruel little sentence, rapped out before thinking, that made him flush to the roots of his hair. He kept himself to himself for three days, and then put in for two days' leave to go shooting near a Canal Engineer's Rest House about thirty miles out. He got his leave, and that night at mess was noisier and more offensive than ever. He said that he was "going to shoot big game," and left at half-past ten o'clock in an *ekka*. Partridge—which was the only thing a man could get near the Rest House—is not big game; so every one laughed.

Next morning one of the Majors came in from short leave, and heard that The Boy had gone out to shoot "big game." The Major had taken an interest in The Boy, and had, more than once, tried to check him. The Major put up his eyebrows when he heard of the expedition and went to The Boy's rooms where he rummaged.

Presently he came out and found me leaving cards on the Mess. There was no one else in the ante-room.

He said, "The Boy has gone out shooting. *Does* a man shoot *tetur* with a revolver and writing-case?"

I said, "Nonsense, Major!" for I saw what was in his mind.

He said, "Nonsense or no nonsense, I'm going to the Canal now—at once. I don't feel easy."

Then he thought for a minute, and said, "Can you lie?"

"You know best," I answered. "It's my profession."

"Very well," said the Major, "you must come out with me now—at once—in an *ekka* to the Canal to shoot black-buck. Go and put on *shikar*-kit—*quick*—and drive here with a gun."

The Major was a masterful man; and I knew that he would not give orders for nothing. So I obeyed, and on return found the Major packed up in an *ekka*—gun-cases and food slung below—all ready for a shooting-trip.

He dismissed the driver and drove himself. We jogged along quietly while in the station; but, as soon as we got to the dusty road across the plains, he made that pony fly. A country-bred can do nearly anything at a pinch. We covered the thirty miles in under three hours, but the poor brute was nearly dead.

Once I said, "What's the blazing hurry, Major?"

He said quietly, "The Boy has been alone, by himself for —one, two, five—fourteen hours now! I tell you, I don't feel easy."

This uneasiness spread itself to me, and I helped to beat the pony.

When we came to the Canal Engineer's Rest House the Major called for The Boy's servant; but there was no answer. Then we went up to the house, calling for The Boy by name; but there was no answer.

"Oh, he's out shooting," said I.

Just then, I saw through one of the windows a little hurricane-lamp burning. This was at four in the afternoon. We both stopped dead in the veranda, holding our breath to catch every sound; and we heard, inside the room, the "*brr—brr—brr*" of a multitude of flies. The Major said nothing, but he took off his helmet and we entered very softly.

The Boy was dead on the bed in the center of the bare, lime-washed room. He had shot his head nearly to pieces with his revolver. The gun-cases were still strapped, so was the bedding, and on the table lay The Boy's writing-case with photographs. He had gone away to die like a poisoned rat!

The Major said to himself softly, "Poor Boy! Poor, *poor* devil!" Then he turned away from the bed and said, "I want your help in this business."

Knowing The Boy was dead by his own hand, I saw exactly what that help would be, so I passed over to the table, took a chair, lighted a cheroot, and began to go through the writing-case; the Major looking over my shoulder and repeating to himself, "We came too late!—Like a rat in a hole!—Poor, *poor* devil!"

The Boy must have spent half the night in writing to his

people, to his Colonel, and to a girl at Home; and as soon as he had finished, must have shot himself, for he had been dead a long time when we came in.

I read all that he had written, and passed over each sheet to the Major as I finished it.

We saw from his accounts how very seriously he had taken everything. He wrote about "disgrace which he was unable to bear"—"indelible shame"—"criminal folly"—"wasted life," and so on; besides a lot of private things to his father and mother much too sacred to put into print. The letter to the girl at Home was the most pitiful of all; and I choked as I read it. The Major made no attempt to keep dry-eyed. I respected him for that. He read and rocked himself to and fro, and simply cried like a woman without caring to hide it. The letters were so dreary and hopeless and touching. We forgot all about The Boy's follies, and only thought of the poor Thing on the bed and the scrawled sheets in our hands. It was utterly impossible to let the letters go Home. They would have broken his father's heart and killed his mother after killing her belief in her son.

At last the Major dried his eyes openly, and said, "Nice sort of thing to spring on an English family! What shall we do?"

I said, knowing what the Major had brought me out for —"The Boy died of cholera. We were with him at the time. We can't commit ourselves to half-measures. Come along."

Then began one of the most grimly comic scenes I have ever taken part in—the concoction of a big, written lie, bolstered with evidence, to soothe The Boy's people at Home. I began the rough draft of the letter, the Major throwing in hints here and there while he gathered up all the stuff that The Boy had written and burned it in the fireplace. It was a hot, still evening when we began, and the lamp burned very badly. In due course I made the draft to my satisfaction, setting forth how The Boy was the pattern of all virtues, beloved by his regiment, with every promise of a great career before him, and so on; how we had helped him through the sickness—it was no time for little lies you will understand—and how he had died without pain. I choked while I was putting down these things and thinking of the poor people who would read them. Then I laughed at the grotesqueness of the affair, and the laughter mixed itself up with the choke—and the Major said that we both wanted drinks.

I am afraid to say how much whisky we drank before the letter was finished. It had not the least effect on us. Then we took off The Boy's watch, locket, and rings.

Lastly, the Major said, "We must send a lock of hair too. A woman values that."

But there were reasons why we could not find a lock fit to send. The Boy was black-haired, and so was the Major, luckily. I cut off a piece of the Major's hair above the temple with a knife, and put it into the packet we were making. The laughing-fit and the chokes got hold of me again, and I had to stop. The Major was nearly as bad; and we both knew that the worst part of the work was to come.

We sealed up the packet, photographs, locket, seals, ring, letter, and lock of hair with The Boy's sealing-wax and The Boy's seal.

Then the Major said, "For God's sake let's get outside—away from the room—and think!"

We went outside, and walked on the banks of the Canal for an hour, eating and drinking what we had with us, until the moon rose. I know now exactly how a murderer feels. Finally, we forced ourselves back to the room with the lamp and the Other Thing in it, and began to take up the next piece of work. I am not going to write about this. It was too horrible. We burned the bedstead and dropped the ashes into the Canal; we took up the matting of the room and treated that in the same way. I went off to a village and borrowed two big hoes—I did not want the villagers to help—while the Major arranged—the other matters. It took us four hours' hard work to make the grave. As we worked, we argued out whether it was right to say as much as we remembered of the Burial of the Dead. We compromised things by saying the Lord's Prayer with a private unofficial prayer for the peace of the soul of The Boy. Then we filled in the grave and went into the veranda—not the house—to lie down to sleep. We were dead-tired.

When we woke the Major said wearily, "We can't go back till to-morrow. We must give him a decent time to die in. He died early *this* morning, remember. That seems more natural." So the Major must have been lying awake all the time, thinking.

I said, "Then why didn't we bring the body back to cantonments?"

The Major thought for a minute. "Because the people bolted when they heard of the cholera. And the *ekka* has gone!"

That was strictly true. We had forgotten all about the *ekka*-pony, and he had gone home.

So we were left there alone, all that stifling day, in the Canal Rest House, testing and retesting our story of The Boy's death to see if it was weak in any point. A native appeared in the afternoon, but we said that a *Sahib* was dead of cholera, and he ran away. As the dusk gathered, the Major told me all his fears about The Boy, and awful stories of suicide or nearly-carried-out suicide—tales that made one's hair crisp. He said that he himself had once gone into the same Valley of the Shadow as The Boy, when he was young and new to the country; so he understood how things fought together in The Boy's poor jumbled head. He also said that youngsters, in their repentant moments, consider their sins much more serious and ineffaceable than they really are. We talked together all through the evening and rehearsed the story of the death of The Boy. As soon as the moon was up, and The Boy, theoretically, just buried, we struck across country for the Station. We walked from eight till six o'clock in the morning; but though we were dead-tired, we did not forget to go to The Boy's rooms and put away his revolver with the proper amount of cartridges in the pouch. Also to set his writing-case on the table. We found the Colonel and reported the death, feeling more like murderers than ever. Then we went to bed and slept the clock round; for there was no more in us.

The tale had credence as long as was necessary; for every one forgot about The Boy before a fortnight was over. Many people, however, found time to say that the Major had behaved scandalously in not bringing in the body for a regimental funeral. The saddest thing of all was the letter from The Boy's mother to the Major and me—with big inky blisters all over the sheet. She wrote the sweetest possible things about our great kindness, and the obligation she would be under to us as long as she lived.

All things considered, she was under an obligation; but not exactly as she meant.

MISS YOUGHAL'S SAIS

When Man and Woman are agreed, what can the Kazi do?—*Proverb*

SOME people say that there is no romance in India. Those people are wrong. Our lives hold quite as much romance as is good for us. Sometimes more.

Strickland was in the Police, and people did not understand him; so they said he was a doubtful sort of man and passed by on the other side. Strickland had himself to thank for this. He held the extraordinary theory that a Policeman in India should try to know as much about the natives as the natives themselves. Now, in the whole of Upper India, there is only one man who can pass for Hindu or Mohammedan, hide-dresser or priest, as he pleases. He is feared and respected by the natives from the Ghor Kathri to the Jamma Musjid; and he is supposed to have the gift of invisibility and executive control over many Devils. But this has done him no good in the eyes of the Indian Government.

Strickland was foolish enough to take that man for his model; and, following out his absurd theory, dabbled in unsavory places no respectable man would think of exploring—all among the native riff-raff. He educated himself in this peculiar way for seven years, and people could not appreciate it. He was perpetually "going Fantee" among natives, which, of course, no man with any sense believes in. He was initiated into the Sat Bhai at Allahabad once, when he was on leave; he knew the Lizard-Song of the Sansis, and the Hálli-Hukk dance, which is a religious can-can of a startling kind. When a man knows who dance the Hálli-Hukk, and how, and when, and where, he knows something to be proud of. He has gone deeper than the skin. But Strickland was not proud, though he had helped once, at Jagadhri, at the Painting of the Death Bull, which no Englishman must even look upon; had mastered the thieves-patter of the *chángars;* had taken a Eusufzai horse-thief alone near Attock; and had stood under the sounding-board of a Border mosque and conducted service in the manner of a Sunni Mollah.

His crowning achievement was spending eleven days as a *faquir* or priest in the gardens of Baba Atal at Amritsar, and there picking up the threads of the great Nasiban Murder Case. But people said, justly enough, "Why on earth can't Strickland sit in his office and write up his diary, and recruit, and keep quiet, instead of showing up the incapacity of his seniors?" So the Nasiban Murder Case did him no good departmentally; but, after his first feeling of wrath, he returned to his outlandish custom of prying into native life. When a man once acquires a taste for this particular amusement, it abides with him all his days. It is the most fascinating thing in the world; Love not excepted. Where other men took ten days to the Hills, Strickland took leave for what he called *shikar*, put on the disguise that appealed to him at the time, stepped down into the brown crowd, and was swallowed up for a while. He was a quiet, dark young fellow—spare, black-eyed—and, when he was not thinking of something else, a very interesting companion. Strickland on Native Progress as he had seen it was worth hearing. Natives hated Strickland; but they were afraid of him. He knew too much.

When the Youghals came into the Station, Strickland—very gravely, as he did everything—fell in love with Miss Youghal; and she, after a while, fell in love with him because she could not understand him. Then Strickland told the parents; but Mrs. Youghal said she was not going to throw her daughter into the worst paid Department in the Empire, and old Youghal said, in so many words, that he mistrusted Strickland's ways and works, and would thank him not to speak or write to his daughter any more. "Very well," said Strickland, for he did not wish to make his lady-love's life a burden. After one long talk with Miss Youghal he dropped the business entirely.

The Youghals went up to Simla in April.

In July Strickland secured three months' leave on "urgent private affairs." He locked up his house—though not a native in the Province would wittingly have touched "Estreekin Sahib's" gear for the world—and went down to see a friend of his, an old dyer, at Tarn Taran.

Here all trace of him was lost, until a *sais* or groom met me on the Simla Mall with this extraordinary note:

"DEAR OLD MAN—Please give bearer a box of cheroots—Supers, No. 1, for preference. They are freshest at the Club. I'll repay when I reappear; but at present I'm out of society.
"Yours, E. STRICKLAND."

I ordered two boxes, and handed them over to the *sais* with my love. That *sais* was Strickland, and he was in old Youghal's employ, attached to Miss Youghal's Arab. The poor fellow was suffering for an English smoke, and knew that, whatever happened, I should hold my tongue till the business was over.

Later on, Mrs. Youghal, who was wrapped up in her servants, began talking at houses where she called of her paragon among *saises*—the man who was never too busy to get up in the morning and pick flowers for the breakfast-table, and who blacked—actually *blacked*—the hoofs of his horse like a London coachman! The turn-out of Miss Youghal's Arab was a wonder and a delight. Strickland—Dulloo, I mean—found his reward in the pretty things that Miss Youghal said to him when she went out riding. Her parents were pleased to find she had forgotten all her foolishness for young Strickland and said she was a good girl.

Strickland vows that the two months of his service were the most rigid mental discipline he has ever gone through. Quite apart from the little fact that the wife of one of his fellow-*saises* fell in love with him and then tried to poison him with arsenic because he would have nothing to do with her, he had to school himself into keeping quiet when Miss Youghal went out riding with some man who tried to flirt with her, and he was forced to trot behind carrying the blanket and hearing every word! Also, he had to keep his temper when he was slanged in the theater porch by a policeman—especially once when he was abused by a Naik he had himself recruited from Isser Jang village—or, worse still, when a young subaltern called him a pig for not making way quickly enough.

But the life had its compensations. He obtained great insight into the ways and thefts of *saises*—enough he says to have summarily convicted half the population of the Punjab if he had been on business. He became one of the leading players at knuckle-bones, which all *jhampanis* and many *saises* play while they are waiting outside the Government House or the Gaiety Theater of nights; he learned to smoke tobacco that was three-fourths cowdung; and he heard the wisdom of the grizzled Jemadar of the Government House grooms. Whose words are valuable. He saw many things which amused him; and he states, on honor, that no man can appreciate Simla properly till he has seen it from the *sais's* point of view. He also says that, if he chose to write all he saw, his head would be broken in several places.

Strickland's account of the agony he endured on wet nights, hearing the music and seeing the lights in "Benmore," with his toes tingling for a waltz and his head in a horse-blanket, is rather amusing. One of these days, Strickland is going to write a little book on his experiences. That book will be worth buying; and even more worth suppressing.

Thus, he served faithfully as Jacob served for Rachel; and his leave was nearly at an end when the explosion came. He had really done his best to keep his temper in the hearing of the flirtations I have mentioned; but he broke down at last. An old and very distinguished General took Miss Youghal for a ride, and began that specially offensive "you're-only-a-little-girl" sort of flirtation—most difficult for a woman to turn aside deftly, and most maddening to listen to. Miss Youghal was shaking with fear at the things he said in the hearing of her *sais*. Dulloo—Strickland—stood it as long as he could. Then he caught hold of the General's bridle, and, in most fluent English, invited him to step off and be flung over the cliff. Next minute, Miss Youghal began to cry; and Strickland saw that he had hopelessly given himself away, and everything was over.

The General nearly had a fit, while Miss Youghal was sobbing out the story of the disguise and the engagement that was not recognized by the parents. Strickland was furiously angry with himself, and more angry with the General for forcing his hand; so he said nothing, but held the horse's head and prepared to thrash the General as some sort of satisfaction. But when the General had thoroughly grasped the story, and knew who Strickland was, he began to puff and blow in the saddle, and nearly rolled off with laughing. He said Strickland deserved a V.C., if it were only for putting on a *sais's* blanket. Then he called himself names, and vowed that he deserved a thrashing, but he was too old to take it from Strickland. Then he complimented Miss Youghal on her lover. The scandal of the business never struck him; for he was a nice old man, with a weakness for flirtations. Then he laughed again, and said that old Youghal was a fool. Strickland let go of the cob's head, and suggested that the General had better help them, if that was his opinion. Strickland knew Youghal's weakness for men with titles and letters after their names and high official position. "It's rather like a forty-minute farce," said the General, "but, begad, I *will* help, if it's only to escape that tremendous thrashing I deserve. Go along to your home, my *sais*-Policeman, and change into decent kit, and I'll attack Mr. Youghal. Miss Youghal, may I ask you to canter home and wait?"

. . . .

About seven minutes later, there was a wild hurroosh at the Club. A *sais*, with blanket and head-rope, was asking all the men he knew: "For Heaven's sake lend me decent clothes!" As the men did not recognize him, there were some peculiar scenes before Strickland could get a hot bath, with soda in it, in one room, a shirt here, a collar there, a pair of trousers elsewhere, and so on. He galloped off, with half the Club wardrobe on his back, and an utter stranger's pony under him, to the house of old Youghal. The General, arrayed in purple and fine linen, was before him. What the General had said Strickland never knew, but Youghal received Strickland with moderate civility; and Mrs. Youghal, touched by the devotion of the transformed Dulloo, was almost kind. The General beamed and chuckled, and Miss Youghal came in, and, almost before old Youghal knew where he was, the parental consent had been wrenched out, and Strickland had departed with Miss Youghal to the Telegraph Office to wire for his European kit. The final embarrassment was when a stranger attacked him on the Mall and asked for the stolen pony.

In the end, Strickland and Miss Youghal were married, on the strict understanding that Strickland should drop his old ways, and stick to Departmental routine, which pays best and leads to Simla. Strickland was far too fond of his wife, just then, to break his word, but it was a sore trial to him; for the streets and the bazaars, and the sounds in them, were full of meaning to Strickland, and these called to him to come back and take up his wanderings and his discoveries. Some day, I will tell you how he broke his promise to help a friend. That was long since, and he has, by this time, been nearly spoiled for what he would call *shikar*. He is forgetting the slang, and the beggar's cant, and the marks, and the signs, and the drift of the under-currents, which, if a man would master, he must always continue to learn.

But he fills in his Departmental returns beautifully.

"YOKED WITH AN UNBELIEVER"

I am dying for you, and you are dying for another.—*Punjabi Proverb*

When the Gravesend tender left the P. & O. steamer for Bombay and went back to catch the train to Town, there were many people in it crying. But the one who wept most, and most openly, was Miss Agnes Laiter. She had reason to cry, because the only man she ever loved—or ever could love, so she said—was going out to India; and India, as every one knows, is divided equally between jungle, tigers, cobras, cholera, and sepoys.

Phil Garron, leaning over the side of the steamer in the rain, felt very unhappy too; but he did not cry. He was sent out to "tea." What "tea" meant he had not the vaguest idea, but fancied that he would have to ride on a prancing horse over hills covered with tea-vines, and draw a sumptuous salary for doing so; and he was very grateful to his uncle for getting him the berth. He was really going to reform all his slack, shiftless ways, save a large proportion of his magnificent salary yearly, and, in a very short time, return to marry Agnes Laiter. Phil Garron had been lying loose on his friends' hands for three years, and, as he had nothing to do, he naturally fell in love. He was very nice; but he was not strong in his views and opinions and principles, and though he never came to actual grief his friends were thankful when he said good-by, and went out to this mysterious "tea" business near Darjiling. They said, "God bless you, dear boy! Let us never see your face again"—or at least that was what Phil was given to understand.

When he sailed, he was very full of a great plan to prove himself several hundred times better than any one had given him credit for—to work like a horse, and triumphantly marry Agnes Laiter. He had many good points besides his good looks; his only fault being that he was weak, the least little bit in the world weak. He had as much notion of economy as the Morning Sun; and yet you could not lay your hand on any one item, and say, "Herein Phil Garron is extravagant or reckless." Nor could you point out any particular vice in his character; but he was "unsatisfactory" and as workable as putty.

Agnes Laiter went about her duties at home—her family objected to the engagement—with red eyes, while Phil was sailing to Darjiling—a "port on the Bengal Ocean," as his mother used to tell her friends. He was popular enough on boardship, made many acquaintances and a moderately large liquor-bill, and sent off huge letters to Agnes Laiter at each port. Then he fell to work on this plantation, somewhere between Darjiling and Kangra, and, though the salary and the horse and the work were not quite all he had fancied, he succeeded fairly well, and gave himself much unnecessary credit for his perseverance.

In the course of time, as he settled more into collar, and his work grew fixed before him, the face of Agnes Laiter went out of his mind and only came when he was at leisure, which was not often. He would forget all about her for a fortnight, and remember her with a start, like a schoolboy who has forgotten to learn his lesson. She did not forget Phil, because she was of the kind that never forgets. Only, another man—a really desirable young man—presented himself before Mrs. Laiter; and the chance of a marriage with Phil was as far off as ever; and his letters were so unsatisfactory; and there was a certain amount of domestic pressure brought to bear on the girl; and the young man really was an eligible person as incomes go; and the end of all things was that Agnes married him, and wrote a tempestuous whirlwind of a letter to Phil in the wilds of Darjiling, and said she should never know a happy moment all the rest of her life. Which was a true prophecy.

Phil received that letter, and held himself ill-treated. This was two years after he had come out; but by dint of thinking fixedly of Agnes Laiter, and looking at her photograph, and patting himself on the back for being one of the most constant lovers in history, and warming to the work as he went on, he really fancied that he had been very hardly used. He sat down and wrote one final letter—a really pathetic "world without end, amen," epistle; explaining how he would be true to Eternity, and that all women were very much alike, and he would hide his broken heart, etc., etc.; but if, at any future time, etc., etc., he could afford to wait, etc., etc., unchanged affections, etc., etc., return to her old love, etc., etc., for eight closely-written pages. From an artistic point of view, it was very neat work, but an ordinary Philistine, who knew the state of Phil's real feelings—not the ones he rose to as he went on writing—would have called it the thoroughly mean and selfish work of a thoroughly mean and selfish weak man. But this verdict would have been incorrect. Phil paid for the postage, and felt every word he had written for at least two days and a half. It was the last flicker before the light went out.

That letter made Agnes Laiter very unhappy, and she cried and put it away in her desk, and became Mrs. Somebody Else for the good of her family. Which is the first duty of every Christian maid.

Phil went his ways, and thought no more of his letter, except as an artist thinks of a neatly touched-in sketch. His ways were not bad, but they were not altogether good until they brought him across Dunmaya, the daughter of a Rajput ex-Subadar-Major of our Native Army. The girl had a strain of Hill blood in her, and like the Hill-women, was not a *purdah-nashin* or woman who lives behind the veil.

Where Phil met her, or how he heard of her, does not matter. She was a good girl and handsome, and, in her way, very clever and shrewd; though, of course, a little hard. It is to be remembered that Phil was living very comfortably, denying himself no small luxury, never putting by a penny, very satisfied with himself and his good intentions, was dropping all his English correspondents one by one, and beginning more and more to look upon India as his home. Some men fall this way; and they are of no use afterward. The climate where he was stationed was good, and it really did not seem to him that there was any reason to return to England.

He did what many planters have done before him—that is to say, he made up his mind to marry a Hill-girl and settle down. He was seven-and-twenty then, with a long life before him, but no spirit to go through with it. So he married Dunmaya by the forms of the English Church, and some fellow-planters said he was a fool, and some said he was a wise man. Dunmaya was a thoroughly honest girl, and, in spite of her reverence for an Englishman, had a reasonable estimate of her husband's weaknesses. She managed him tenderly, and became, in less than a year, a very passable imitation of an English lady in dress and carriage. It is curious to think that a Hill-man after a lifetime's education is a Hill-man still; but a Hill-woman can in six months master most of the ways of her English sisters. There was a coolie-woman once. But that is another story. Dunmaya dressed by preference in black and yellow and looked well.

Meantime Phil's letter lay in Agnes Laiter's desk, and now and again she would think of poor, resolute, hard-working Phil among the cobras and tigers of Darjiling, toiling in the vain hope that she might come back to him. Her husband was worth ten Phils, except that he had rheumatism of the heart. Three years after he was married—and after he had tried Nice and Algeria for his complaint—he went to Bombay, where he died, and set Agnes free. Being a devout woman, she looked on his death and the place of it as a direct interposition of Providence, and when she had recovered from the shock, she took out and re-read Phil's letter with the "etc., etc.," and the big dashes, and the little dashes, and kissed it several times. No one knew her in Bombay; she had her husband's income, which was a large one, and Phil was close at hand. It was wrong and improper, of course, but she decided, as heroines do in novels, to find her old lover, to offer him her hand and her gold, and with him spend the rest of her life in some spot far from unsympathetic souls. She sat for two months, alone in Watson's Hotel, elaborating this decision, and the picture was a pretty one. Then she set out in search of Phil Garron, assistant on a tea plantation with a more than usually unpronounceable name.

. . . .

She found him. She spent a month over it, for his plantation was not in the Darjiling district at all, but nearer Kangra. Phil was very little altered, and Dunmaya was very nice to her.

Now the particular sin and shame of the whole business is that Phil, who really is not worth thinking of twice, was and is loved by Dunmaya, and more than loved by Agnes, the whole of whose life he seems to have spoiled.

Worst of all, Dunmaya is making a decent man of him; and he will ultimately be saved from perdition through her training.

Which is manifestly unfair.

———

FALSE DAWN

> To-night God knows what thing shall tide,
> The Earth is racked and faint—
> Expectant, sleepless, open-eyed;
> And we, who from the Earth were made,
> Thrill with our Mother's pain.
>
> —*In Durance*

No man will ever know the exact truth of this story; though women may sometimes whisper it to one another after a dance, when they are putting up their hair for the night and comparing lists of victims. A man, of course, cannot assist at these functions. So the tale must be told from the outside—in the dark—all wrong.

Never praise a sister to a sister, in the hope of your compliments reaching the proper ears, and so preparing the way for you later on. Sisters are women first, and sisters afterward; and you will find that you do yourself harm.

Saumarez knew this when he made up his mind to propose to the elder Miss Copleigh. Saumarez was a strange man, with few merits so far as men could see, though he was popular with women, and carried enough conceit to stock a Viceroy's Council and leave a little over for the Commander-in-Chief's Staff. He was a Civilian. Very many women took an interest in Saumarez, perhaps, because his manner to them was offensive. If you hit a pony over the nose at the outset of your acquaintance, he may not love you, but he will take a deep interest in your movements ever afterward. The elder Miss Copleigh was nice, plump, winning, and pretty. The younger was not so pretty, and, from men disregarding the hint set forth above, her style was repellent and unattractive. Both girls had, practically, the same figure, and there was a strong likeness between them in look and voice; though no one could doubt for an instant which was the nicer of the two.

Saumarez made up his mind, as soon as they came into the station from Behar, to marry the elder one. At least, we all made sure that he would, which comes to the same thing. She was two-and-twenty, and he was thirty-three, with pay and allowances of nearly fourteen hundred rupees a month. So the match, as we arranged it, was in every way a good one. Saumarez was his name, and summary was his nature, as a man once said. Having drafted his Resolution, he formed a Select Committee of One to sit upon it, and resolved to take his time. In our unpleasant slang, the Copleigh girls "hunted in couples." That is to say, you could do nothing with one without the other. They were very loving sisters; but their mutual affection was sometimes inconvenient. Saumarez held the balance-hair true between them, and none but himself could have said to which side his heart inclined; though every one guessed. He rode with them a good deal and danced with them, but he never succeeded in detaching them from each other for any length of time.

Women said that the two girls kept together through deep mistrust, each fearing that the other would steal a march on her. But that has nothing to do with a man. Saumarez was silent for good or bad, and as business-likely attentive as he could be, having due regard to his work and his polo. Beyond doubt both girls were fond of him.

As the hot weather drew nearer and Saumarez made no sign, women said that you could see their trouble in the eyes of the girls—that they were looking strained, anxious, and irritable. Men are quite blind in these matters unless they have more of the woman than the man in their composition, in which case it does not matter what they say or think. I maintain it was the hot April days that took the color out of the Copleigh girls' cheeks. They should have been sent to the Hills early. No one—man or woman—feels an angel when the hot weather is approaching. The younger sister grew more cynical, not to say acid, in her ways; and the winningness of the elder wore thin. There was effort in it.

The Station wherein all these things happened was, though not a little one, off the line of rail, and suffered through want of attention. There were no gardens, or bands or amusements worth speaking of, and it was nearly a day's journey to come into Lahore for a dance. People were grateful for small things to interest them.

About the beginning of May, and just before the final exodus of Hill-goers, when the weather was very hot and there were not more than twenty people in the Station, Saumarez gave a moonlight riding-picnic at an old tomb, six miles away, near the bed of the river. It was a "Noah's Ark" picnic; and there was to be the usual arrangement of quarter-mile intervals between each couple, on account of the dust. Six couples came altogether, including chaperones. Moonlight picnics are useful just at the very end of the season, before all the girls go away to the Hills. They lead to understandings, and should be encouraged by chaperones; especially those whose girls look sweetest in riding-habits. I knew a case once. But that is another story. That picnic was called the "Great Pop Picnic," because every one knew Saumarez would propose then to the elder Miss Copleigh; and, besides his affair, there was another which might possibly come to happiness. The social atmosphere was heavily charged and wanted clearing.

We met at the parade-ground at ten: the night was fearfully hot. The horses sweated even at walking-pace, but anything was better than sitting still in our own dark houses. When we moved off under the full moon we were four couples, one triplet, and Me. Saumarez rode with the Copleigh girls, and I loitered at the tail of the procession wondering with whom Saumarez would ride home. Every one was happy and contented; but we all felt that things were going to happen. We rode slowly; and it was nearly midnight before we reached the old tomb, facing the ruined tank, in the decayed gardens where we were going to eat and drink. I was late in coming up; and, before I went in to the garden, I saw that the horizon to the north carried a faint, dun-colored feather. But no one would have thanked me for spoiling so well-managed an entertainment as this picnic—and a dust-storm, more or less, does no great harm.

We gathered by the tank. Some one had brought out a banjo—which is a most sentimental instrument—and three or four of us sang. You must not laugh at this. Our amusements in out-of-the-way Stations are very few indeed. Then we talked in groups or together, lying under the trees, with the sun-baked roses dropping their petals on our feet, until supper was ready. It was a beautiful supper, as cold and as iced as you could wish; and we stayed long over it.

I had felt that the air was growing hotter and hotter; but nobody seemed to notice it until the moon went out and a burning hot wind began lashing the orange-trees with a sound like the noise of the sea. Before we knew where we were, the dust-storm was on us and everything was roaring, whirling darkness. The supper-table was blown bodily into the tank. We were afraid of staying anywhere near the old tomb for fear it might be blown down. So we felt our way to the orange-trees where the horses were picketed and waited for the storm to blow over. Then the little light that was left vanished, and you could not see your hand before your face. The air was heavy with dust and sand from the bed of the river, that filled boots and pockets and drifted down necks and coated eyebrows and mustaches. It was one of the worst dust-storms of the year. We were all huddled together close to the trembling horses, with the thunder chattering overhead, and the lightning spurting like water from a sluice, all ways at once. There was no danger, of course, unless the horses broke loose. I was standing with my head downward and my hands over my mouth, hearing the trees thrashing each other. I could not see who was next me till the flashes came. Then I found that I was packed near Saumarez and the elder Miss Copleigh, with my own horse just in front of me. I recognized the elder Miss Copleigh, because she had a puggree round her helmet, and the younger had not. All the electricity in the air had gone into my body and I was quivering and tingling from head to foot—exactly as a corn shoots and tingles before rain. It was a grand storm. The wind seemed to be picking up the earth and pitching it to leeward in great heaps; and the heat beat up from the ground like the heat of the Day of Judgment.

The storm lulled slightly after the first half-hour, and I heard a despairing little voice close to my ear, saying to itself, quietly and softly, as if some lost soul were flying about with the wind, "O my God!" Then the younger Miss Copleigh stumbled into my arms, saying, "Where is my horse? Get my horse. I want to go home. I want to go home. Take me home."

I thought that the lightning and the black darkness had frightened her; so I said there was no danger, but she must wait till the storm blew over. She answered, "It is not that! I want to go home! Oh, take me away from here!"

I said that she could not go till the light came; but I felt her brush past me and go away. It was too dark to see where. Then the whole sky was split open with one tremendous flash, as if the end of the world were coming, and all the women shrieked.

Almost directly after this, I felt a man's hand on my shoulder and heard Saumarez bellowing in my ear. Through the rattling of the trees and howling of the wind, I did not catch his words at once, but at last I heard him say, "I've proposed to the wrong one! What shall I do?" Saumarez had no occasion to make this confidence to me. I was never a friend of his, nor am I now; but I fancy neither of us were ourselves just then. He was shaking as he stood with excitement, and I was feeling queer all over with the electricity. I could not think of anything to say except, "More fool you for proposing in a dust-storm." But I did not see how that would improve the mistake.

Then he shouted, "Where's Edith—Edith Copleigh?" Edith was the younger sister. I answered out of my astonishment, "What do you want with *her?*" For the next two minutes, he and I were shouting at each other like maniacs—he vowing that it was the younger sister he had meant to propose to all along, and I telling him till my throat was hoarse that he must have made a mistake! I cannot account for this except, again, by the fact that we were neither of us ourselves. Everything seemed to me like a bad dream—from the stamping of the horses in the darkness to Saumarez telling me the story of his loving Edith Copleigh from the first. He was still clawing my shoulder and begging me to tell him where Edith Copleigh was, when another lull came and brought light with it, and we saw the dust-cloud forming on the plain in front of us. So we knew the worst was over. The moon was low down, and there was just the glimmer of the false dawn that comes about an hour before the real one. But the light was very faint, and the dun cloud roared like a bull. I wondered where Edith Copleigh had gone; and as I was wondering I saw three things together: First, Maud Copleigh's face come smiling out of the darkness and move toward Saumarez who was standing by me. I heard the girl whisper, "George," and slide her arm through the arm that was not clawing my shoulder, and I saw that look on her face which only comes once or twice in a lifetime—when a woman is perfectly happy and the air is full of trumpets and gorgeously-colored fire and the Earth turns into cloud because she loves and is loved. At the same time, I saw Saumarez's face as he heard Maud Copleigh's voice, and fifty yards away from the clump of orange-trees I saw a brown holland habit getting upon a horse.

It must have been my state of over-excitement that made me so ready to meddle with what did not concern me. Saumarez was moving off to the habit; but I pushed him back and said, "Stop here and explain. I'll fetch her back!" And I ran out to get at my own horse. I had a perfectly unnecessary notion that everything must be done decently and in order, and that Saumarez's first care was to wipe the happy look out of Maud Copleigh's face. All the time I was linking up the curb-chain I wondered how he would do it.

I cantered after Edith Copleigh, thinking to bring her back slowly on some pretense or another. But she galloped away as soon as she saw me, and I was forced to ride after her in earnest. She called back over her shoulder—"Go away! I'm going home. Oh, go away!" two or three times; but my business was to catch her first and argue later. The ride fitted in with the rest of the evil dream. The ground was very rough, and now and again we rushed through the whirling, choking "dust-devils" in the skirts of the flying storm. There was a burning hot wind blowing that brought up a stench of stale brick kilns with it; and through the half light and through the dust-devils, across that desolate plain, flickered the brown holland habit on the gray horse. She headed for the Station at first. Then she wheeled round and set off for the river through beds of burned-down jungle-grass, bad even to ride pig over. In cold blood I should never have dreamed of going over such a country at night, but it seemed quite right and natural with the lightning crackling overhead, and a reek like the smell of the Pit in my nostrils. I rode and shouted, and she bent forward and lashed her horse, and the aftermath of the dust-storm came up, and caught us both, and drove us downwind like pieces of paper.

I don't know how far we rode; but the drumming of the horse-hoofs and the roar of the wind and the race of the faint blood-red moon through the yellow mist seemed to have gone on for years and years, and I was literally drenched with sweat from my helmet to my gaiters when the gray stumbled, recovered himself and pulled up dead lame. My brute was used up altogether. Edith Copleigh was bare-headed, plastered with dust, and crying bitterly. "Why can't you let me alone?" she said. "I only wanted to get away and go home. Oh, *please* let me go!"

"You have got to come back with me, Miss Copleigh. Saumarez has something to say to you."

It was a foolish way of putting it; but I hardly knew Miss Copleigh, and, though I was playing Providence at the cost of my horse, I could not tell her in as many words what Saumarez had told me. I thought he could do that better himself. All her pretense about being tired and wanting to go home broke down, and she rocked herself to and fro in the saddle as she sobbed, and the hot wind blew her black hair to leeward. I am not going to repeat what she said, because she was utterly unstrung.

This was the cynical Miss Copleigh, and I, almost an utter stranger to her, was trying to tell her that Saumarez loved her and she was to come back to hear him say so. I believe I made myself understood, for she gathered the gray together and made him hobble somehow, and we set off for the tomb, while the storm went thundering down to Umballa and a few big drops of warm rain fell. I found out that she had been standing close to Saumarez when he proposed to her sister, and had wanted to go home to cry in peace, as an English girl should. She dabbed her eyes with her pocket-handkerchief as we went along, and babbled to me out of sheer lightness of heart and hysteria. That was perfectly unnatural; and yet, it seemed all right at the time and in the place. All the world was only the two Copleigh girls, Saumarez and I, ringed in with the lightning and the dark; and the guidance of this misguided world seemed to lie in my hands.

When we returned to the tomb in the deep dead stillness that followed the storm, the dawn was just breaking and nobody had gone away. They were waiting for our return. Saumarez most of all. His face was white and drawn. As Miss Copleigh and I limped up, he came forward to meet us, and, when he helped her down from her saddle, he kissed her before all the picnic. It was like a scene in a theater, and the likeness was heightened by all the dust-white, ghostly-looking men and women under the orange-trees clapping their hands—as if they were watching a play—at Saumarez's choice. I never knew anything so un-English in my life.

Lastly, Saumarez said we must all go home or the Station

would come out to look for us, and would I be good enough to ride home with Maud Copleigh? Nothing would give me greater pleasure, I said.

So we formed up, six couples in all, and went back two by two; Saumarez walking at the side of Edith Copleigh, who was riding his horse. Maud Copleigh did not talk to me at any length.

The air was cleared; and, little by little, as the sun rose, I felt we were all dropping back again into ordinary men and women, and that the "Great Pop Picnic" was a thing altogether apart and out of the world—never to happen again. It had gone with the dust-storm and the tingle in the hot air.

I felt tired and limp, and a good deal ashamed of myself as I went in for a bath and some sleep.

There is a woman's version of this story, but it will never be written . . . unless Maud Copleigh cares to try.

THE RESCUE OF PLUFFLES

Thus, for a season, they fought it fair—
She and his cousin May—
Tactful, talented, debonnaire,
Decorous foes were they;
But never can battle of man compare
With merciless feminine fray.
—*Two and One*

MRS. HAUKSBEE was sometimes nice to her own sex. Here is a story to prove this; and you can believe just as much as ever you please.

Pluffles was a subaltern in the "Unmentionables." He was callow, even for a subaltern. He was callow all over—like a canary that had not finished fledging itself. The worst of it was that he had three times as much money as was good for him; Pluffles' Papa being a rich man and Pluffles being the only son. Pluffles' Mamma adored him. She was only a little less callow than Pluffles, and she believed everything he said.

Pluffles' weakness was not believing what people said. He preferred what he called trusting to his own judgment. He had as much judgment as he had seat or hands; and this preference tumbled him into trouble once or twice. But the biggest trouble Pluffles ever manufactured came about at Simla—some years ago, when he was four-and-twenty.

He began by trusting to his own judgment as usual, and the result was that, after a time, he was bound hand and foot to Mrs. Reiver's 'rickshaw wheels.

There was nothing good about Mrs. Reiver, unless it was her dress. She was bad from her hair—which started life on a Brittany girl's head—to her boot-heels, which were two and three-eighths inches high. She was not honestly mischievous like Mrs. Hauksbee; she was wicked in a business-like way.

There was never any scandal—she had not generous impulses enough for that. She was the exception which proved the rule that Anglo-Indian ladies are in every way as nice as their sisters at Home. She spent her life in proving that rule.

Mrs. Hauksbee and she hated each other fervently. They hated far too much to clash; but the things they said of each other were startling—not to say original. Mrs. Hauksbee was honest—honest as her own front-teeth—and, but for her love of mischief, would have been a woman's woman. There was no honesty about Mrs. Reiver; nothing but selfishness. And at the beginning of the season, poor little Pluffles fell a prey to her. She laid herself out to that end, and who was Pluffles to resist? He trusted to his judgment, and he got judged.

I have seen Captain Hayes argue with a tough horse—I have seen a tonga-driver coerce a stubborn pony—I have seen a riotous setter broken to gun by a hard keeper—but the breaking-in of Pluffles of the "Unmentionables" was beyond all these. He learned to fetch and carry like a dog, and to wait like one, too, for a word from Mrs. Reiver. He learned to keep appointments which Mrs. Reiver had no intention of keeping. He learned to take thankfully dances which Mrs. Reiver had no intention of giving him. He learned to shiver for an hour and a quarter on the windward side of Elysium while Mrs. Reiver was making up her mind to come for a ride. He learned to hunt for a 'rickshaw, in a light dress-suit under pelting rain, and to walk by the side of that 'rickshaw when he had found it. He learned what it was to be spoken to like a coolie and ordered about like a cook. He learned all this and many other things besides. And he paid for his schooling.

Perhaps, in some hazy way, he fancied that it was fine and impressive, that it gave him a status among men, and was altogether the thing to do. It was nobody's business to warn Pluffles that he was unwise. The pace that season was too good to inquire; and meddling with another man's folly is always thankless work. Pluffles' Colonel should have ordered him back to his regiment when he heard how things were going. But Pluffles had got himself engaged to a girl in England the last time he went Home; and, if there was one thing more than another that the Colonel detested, it was a married subaltern. He chuckled when he heard of the education of Pluffles, and said it was good training for the boy. But it was not good training in the least. It led him into spending money beyond his means, which were good; above that, the education spoiled an average boy and made it a tenth-rate man of an objectionable kind. He wandered into a bad set, and his little bill at the jewelers was a thing to wonder at.

Then Mrs. Hauksbee rose to the occasion. She played her game alone, knowing what people would say of her; and she played it for the sake of a girl she had never seen. Pluffles' *fiancée* was to come out, under chaperonage of an aunt, in October, to be married to Pluffles.

At the beginning of August, Mrs. Hauksbee discovered that it was time to interfere. A man who rides much knows exactly what a horse is going to do next before he does it. In the same way, a woman of Mrs. Hauksbee's experience knows accurately how a boy will behave under certain circumstances—notably when he is infatuated with one of Mrs. Reiver's stamp. She said that, sooner or later, little Pluffles would break off that engagement for nothing at all—simply to gratify Mrs. Reiver, who, in return, would keep him at her feet and in her service just so long as she found it worth her while. She said she knew the signs of these things. If she did not no one else could.

Then she went forth to capture Pluffles under the guns of the enemy; just as Mrs. Cusack-Bremmil carried away Bremmil under Mrs. Hauksbee's eyes.

This particular engagement lasted seven weeks—we called it the Seven Weeks' War—and was fought out inch by inch on both sides. A detailed account would fill a book, and would be incomplete then. Any one who knows about these things can fit in the details for himself. It was a superb fight—there will never be another like it as long as Jakko Hill stands—and Pluffles was the prize of victory. People said shameful things about Mrs. Hauksbee. They did not know what she was playing for. Mrs. Reiver fought partly because Pluffles was useful to her, but mainly because she hated Mrs. Hauksbee, and the matter was a trial of strength between them. No one knows what Pluffles thought. He had not many ideas at the best of times, and the few he possessed made him conceited. Mrs. Hauksbee said, "The boy must be caught; and the only way of catching him is by treating him well."

So she treated him as a man of the world and of experience so long as the issue was doubtful. Little by little Pluffles fell away from his old allegiance and came over to the enemy, by whom he was made much of. He was never sent on outpost duty after 'rickshaws any more, nor was he given dances which never came off, nor were the drains on his purse continued. Mrs. Hauksbee held him on the snaffle; and, after his treatment at Mrs. Reiver's hands, he appreciated the change.

Mrs. Reiver had broken him of talking about himself,

and made him talk about her own merits. Mrs. Hauksbee acted otherwise, and won his confidence, till he mentioned his engagement to the girl at Home, speaking of it in a high and mighty way as a piece of boyish folly. This was when he was taking tea with her one afternoon, and discoursing in what he considered a gay and fascinating style. Mrs. Hauksbee had seen an earlier generation of his stamp bud and blossom, and decay into fat Captains and tubby Majors.

At a moderate estimate there were about three-and-twenty sides to that lady's character. Some men say more. She began to talk to Pluffles after the manner of a mother, and as if there had been three hundred years, instead of fifteen, between them. She spoke with a sort of throaty quaver in her voice which had a soothing effect, though what she said was anything but soothing. She pointed out the exceeding folly, not to say meanness, of Pluffles' conduct, and the smallness of his views. Then he stammered something about "trusting to his own judgment as a man of the world"; and this paved the way for what she wanted to say next. It would have withered up Pluffles had it come from any other woman; but, in the soft cooing style in which Mrs. Hauksbee put it, it only made him feel limp and repentant—as if he had been in some superior kind of church. Little by little, very softly and pleasantly, she began taking the conceit out of Pluffles, as they take the ribs out of an umbrella before re-covering it. She told him what she thought of him and his judgment and his knowledge of the world; and how his performances had made him ridiculous to other people; and how it was his intention to make love to herself if she gave him the chance. Then she said that marriage would be the making of him; and drew a pretty little picture—all rose and opal—of the Mrs. Pluffles of the future going through life relying on the judgment and knowledge of the world of a husband who had nothing to reproach himself with. How she reconciled these two statements she alone knew. But they did not strike Pluffles as conflicting.

Hers was a perfect little homily—much better than any

clergyman could have given—and it ended with touching allusions to Pluffles' Mamma and Papa, and the wisdom of taking his bride Home.

Then she sent Pluffles out for a walk, to think over what she had said. Pluffles left, blowing his nose very hard and holding himself very straight. Mrs. Hauksbee laughed. What Pluffles had intended to do in the matter of the engagement only Mrs. Reiver knew, and she kept her own counsel to her death. She would have liked it spoiled as a compliment, I fancy.

Pluffles enjoyed many talks with Mrs. Hauksbee during the next few days. They were all to the same end, and they helped Pluffles in the path of Virtue.

Mrs. Hauksbee wanted to keep him under her wing to the last. Therefore she discountenanced his going down to Bombay to get married. "Goodness only knows what might happen by the way!" she said. "Pluffles is cursed with the curse of Reuben, and India is no fit place for him!"

In the end, the fiancée arrived with her aunt; and Pluffles, having reduced his affairs to some sort of order—here again Mrs. Hauksbee helped him—was married.

Mrs. Hauksbee gave a sigh of relief when both the "I wills" had been said, and went her way.

Pluffles took her advice about going Home. He left the Service and is now raising speckled cattle inside green painted fences somewhere in England. I believe he does this very judiciously. He would have come to extreme grief in India.

For these reasons, if any one says anything more than usually nasty about Mrs. Hauksbee, tell him the story of the Rescue of Pluffles.

CUPID'S ARROWS

Pit where the buffalo cooled his hide,
By the hot sun emptied and blistered and dried;
Log in the plume-grass, hidden and lone;
Dam where the earth-rat's mounds are strown;
Cave in the bank where the sly stream steals·
Aloe that stabs at the belly and heels,
Jump if you dare on a steed untried—
Safer it is to go wide—go wide!
Hark, from in front where the best men ride:
"Pull to the off, boys! Wide! Go wide!"
—The Peora Hunt

Once upon a time there lived at Simla a very pretty girl, the daughter of a poor but honest District and Sessions Judge. She was a good girl, but could not help knowing her power and using it. Her Mamma was very anxious about her daughter's future, as all good Mammas should be.

When a man is a Commissioner and a bachelor and has the right of wearing open-work jam-tart jewels in gold and enamel on his clothes, and of going through a door before every one except a Member of Council, a Lieutenant-Governor, or a Viceroy, he is worth marrying. At least, that is what ladies say. There was a Commissioner in Simla, in those days, who was, and wore and did all I have said. He was a plain man—an ugly man—the ugliest man in Asia with two exceptions. His was a face to dream about and try to carve on a pipe-head afterward. His name was Saggott—Barr-Saggott—Anthony Barr-Saggott and six letters to follow. Departmentally, he was one of the best men the Government of India owned. Socially, he was like unto a blandishing gorilla.

When he turned his attentions to Miss Beighton, I believe

that Mrs. Beighton wept with delight at the reward Providence had sent her in her old age.

Mr. Beighton held his tongue. He was an easy-going man.

A Commissioner is very rich. His pay is beyond the dreams of avarice—is so enormous that he can afford to save and scrape in a way that would almost discredit a Member of Council. Most Commissioners are mean; but Barr-Saggott was an exception. He entertained royally; he horsed himself well; he gave dances; he was a power in the land; and he behaved as such.

Consider that everything I am writing of took place in an almost pre-historic era in the history of British India. Some folk may remember the years before lawn-tennis was born when we all played croquet. There were seasons before that, if you will believe me, when even croquet had not been invented, and archery—which was revived in England in 1844—was as great a pest as lawn-tennis is now. People talked learnedly about "holding" and "loosing," "steles," "reflexed bows," "56-pound bows," "backed" or "self-yew bows," as we talk about "rallies," "volleys," "smashes," "returns," and "16-ounce rackets."

Miss Beighton shot divinely over ladies' distance—60 yards, that is—and was acknowledged the best lady archer in Simla. Men called her "Diana of Tara-Devi."

Barr-Saggott paid her great attention; and, as I have said, the heart of her mother was uplifted in consequence. Kitty Beighton took matters more calmly. It was pleasant to be singled out by a Commissioner with letters after his name, and to fill the hearts of other girls with bad feelings. But there was no denying the fact that Barr-Saggott was phenomenally ugly; and all his attempts to adorn himself only made him more grotesque. He was not christened "The *Langur*"—which means gray ape—for nothing. It was pleasant, Kitty thought, to have him at her feet, but it was better to escape from him and ride with the graceless Cubbon—the man in a Dragoon Regiment at Umballa—the boy with a handsome face and no prospects. Kitty liked Cubbon more than a little. He never pretended for a moment that he was anything less than head over heels in love with her; for he was an honest boy. So Kitty fled, now and again, from the stately wooings of Barr-Saggott to the company of young Cubbon, and was scolded by her Mamma in consequence. "But, Mother," she said, "Mr. Saggott is such—such a—is so *fearfully* ugly, you know!"

"My dear," said Mrs. Beighton piously, "we cannot be other than an all-ruling Providence has made us. Besides, you will take precedence of your own Mother, you know! Think of that and be reasonable."

Then Kitty put up her little chin and said irreverent things about precedence, and Commissioners, and matrimony. Mr. Beighton rubbed the top of his head; for he was an easy-going man.

Late in the season, when he judged that the time was ripe, Barr-Saggott developed a plan which did great credit to his administrative powers. He arranged an archery-tournament for ladies, with a most sumptuous diamond-studded bracelet as prize. He drew up his terms skillfully, and every one saw that the bracelet was a gift to Miss Beighton; the acceptance carrying with it the hand and the heart of Commissioner Barr-Saggott. The terms were a St. Leonard's Round—thirty-six shots at sixty yards—under the rules of the Simla Toxophilite Society.

All Simla was invited. There were beautifully arranged tea-tables under the deodars at Annandale, where the Grand Stand is now; and, alone in its glory, winking in the sun, sat the diamond bracelet in a blue velvet case. Miss Beighton was anxious—almost too anxious—to compete. On the appointed afternoon all Simla rode down to Annandale to witness the Judgment of Paris turned upside down. Kitty rode with young Cubbon, and it was easy to see that the boy was troubled in his mind. He must be held innocent of everything that followed. Kitty was pale and nervous, and looked long at the bracelet. Barr-Saggott was gorgeously dressed, even more nervous than Kitty, and more hideous than ever.

Mrs. Beighton smiled condescendingly, as befitted the mother of a potential Commissioneress, and the shooting began; all the world standing a semicircle as the ladies came out one after the other.

Nothing is so tedious as an archery competition. They shot, and they shot, and they kept on shooting, till the sun left the valley, and little breezes got up in the deodars, and people waited for Miss Beighton to shoot and win. Cubbon was at one horn of the semicircle round the shooters, and Barr-Saggott at the other. Miss Beighton was last on the list. The scoring had been weak, and the bracelet, with Commissioner Barr-Saggott, was hers to a certainty.

The Commissioner strung her bow with his own sacred hands. She stepped forward, looked at the bracelet, and her first arrow went true to a hair—full into the heart of the "gold"—counting nine points.

Young Cubbon on the left turned white, and his Devil prompted Barr-Saggott to smile. Now horses used to shy when Barr-Saggott smiled. Kitty saw that smile. She looked to her left-front, gave an almost imperceptible nod to Cubbon, and went on shooting.

I wish I could describe the scene that followed. It was out of the ordinary and most improper. Miss Kitty fitted her arrows with immense deliberation, so that every one might see what she was doing. She was a perfect shot; and her 46-pound bow suited her to a nicety. She pinned the wooden legs of the target with great care four successive times. She pinned the wooden top of the target once, and all the ladies looked at each other. Then she began some fancy shooting at the white, which if you hit it counts exactly one point. She put five arrows into the white. It was wonderful archery; but, seeing that her business was to make "golds" and win the bracelet, Barr-Saggott turned a delicate green like young water-grass. Next, she shot over the target twice, then wide to the left twice—always with the same deliberation—while a chilly hush fell over the company, and Mrs. Beighton took out her handkerchief. Then Kitty shot at the ground in front of the target, and split several arrows. Then she made a red—or seven points—just to show what she could do if she liked, and she finished up her amazing performance with some more fancy shooting at the target supports. Here is her score as it was pricked of:

	Gold.	Red.	Blue.	Black.	White.	Total Hits.	Total Score.
Miss Beighton	1	1	0	0	5	7	21

Barr-Saggott looked as if the last few arrow-heads had been driven into his legs instead of the target's, and the deep stillness was broken by a little snubby, mottled, half-grown girl saying in a shrill voice of triumph, "Then *I've* won!"

Mrs. Beighton did her best to bear up; but she wept in the presence of the people. No training could help her through such a disappointment. Kitty unstrung her bow with a vicious jerk, and went back to her place, while Barr-Saggott was trying to pretend that he enjoyed snapping the bracelet on the snubby girl's raw, red wrist. It was an awkward scene—most awkward. Every one tried to depart in a body and leave Kitty to the mercy of her Mamma.

But Cubbon took her away instead, and—the rest isn't worth printing.

THE THREE MUSKETEERS

An' when the war began, we chased the bold Afghan,
An' we made the bloomin' Ghazi for to flee, boys O!
An' we marched into Ka*bul*, an' we tuk the Balar 'Issar
An' we taught 'em to respec' the British Soldier.

—*Barrack-Room Ballad.*

MULVANEY, Ortheris and Learoyd are Privates in B Company of a Line Regiment, and personal friends of mine. Collectively I think, but am not certain, they are the worst men in the regiment so far as genial blackguardism goes.

They told me this story, in the Umballa Refreshment Room while we were waiting for an up-train. I supplied the beer. The tale was cheap at a gallon and a half.

All men know Lord Benira Trig. He is a Duke, or an Earl, or something unofficial; also a Peer; also a Globe-trotter. On all three counts, as Ortheris says, "'e didn't deserve no consideration." He was out in India for three months collecting materials for a book on "Our Eastern Impedimenta," and quartering himself upon everybody, like a Cossack in evening-dress.

His particular vice—because he was a Radical, men said—was having garrisons turned out for his inspection. He would then dine with the Officer Commanding, and insult him, across the Mess table, about the appearance of the troops. That was Benira's way.

He turned out troops once too often. He came to Helanthami Cantonment on a Tuesday. He wished to go shopping in the bazaars on Wednesday, and he "desired" the troops to be turned out on a Thursday. *On—a—Thursday.* The Officer Commanding could not well refuse; for Benira was a Lord. There was an indignation meeting of subalterns in the Mess Room, to call the Colonel pet names.

"But the rale dimonstrashin," said Mulvaney, "was in B Comp'ny barrick; we three headin' it."

Mulvaney climbed on to the refreshment-bar, settled himself comfortably by the beer, and went on: "Whin the row was at ut's foinest an' B Comp'ny was fur goin' out to murther this man Thrigg on the p'rade-groun', Learoyd here takes up his helmut an' sez—fwhat was ut ye said?"

"Ah said," said Learoyd, "gie us t' brass. Tak oop a subscripshun, lads, for to put off t' p'rade, an, if t' p'rade's not put off, ah'll gie t' brass back agean. Thot's wot ah said. All B Coomp'ny knawed me. Ah took oop a big subscripshun—fower rupees eight annas 'twas—an' ah went oot to turn t' job over. Mulvaney an' Orth'ris coom with me."

"We three raises the Divil in couples gin'rally," explained Mulvaney.

Here Ortheris interrupted. "'Ave you read the papers?" said he.

"Sometimes," I said.

"We 'ad read the papers, an' we put hup a faked decoity, a—a sedukshun."

"*Ab*dukshin, ye cockney," said Mulvaney.

"*Ab*dukshun or *se*dukshun—no great odds. Any'ow, we arranged to taik an' put Mister Benhira out o' the way till Thursday was hover, or 'e too busy to rux 'isself about p'raids. *Hi* was the man wot said, 'We'll make a few rupees off o' the business.' "

"We hild a Council av War," continued Mulvaney, "walkin' roun' by the Artill'ry Lines. I was Prisidint, Learoyd was Minister av Finance, an' little Orth'ris here was—"

"A bloomin' Bismarck! *Hi* made the 'ole show pay."

"This interferin' bit av a Benira man," said Mulvaney, "did the thrick for us himself; for, on me sowl, we hadn't a notion av what was to come afther the next minut. He was shoppin' in the bazaar on fut. 'Twas dhrawin' dusk thin, an' we stud watchin' the little man hoppin' in an 'out av the shops, thryin' to injuce the naygurs to *mallum* his *bat*. Prisintly, he sthrols up, his arrums full av thruck, an' he sez in a consiquinshal way, shticking out his little belly, 'Me good men,' sez he, 'have ye seen the Kernel's b'roosh?'—'B'roosh?' says Learoyd. 'There's no b'roosh here —nobbut a *hekka*.'—'Fwhat's that?' sez Thrigg. Learoyd shows him wan down the sthreet, an' he sez, 'How thruly Orientil! I will ride on a *hekka*.' I saw thin that our Rigimintal Saint was for givin' Thrigg over to us neck an' brisket. I purshued a *hekka*, an' I sez to the dhriver-divil, I sez, 'Ye black limb, there's a *Sahib* comin' for this *hekka*. He wants to go *jildi* to the Padsahi Jhil'—'twas about tu moiles away —'to shoot snipe—*chirria*. You dhrive *Jehannum ke marfik*, *mallum*—like Hell? 'Tis no manner av use *bukkin'* to the *Sahib*, bekase he doesn't *samjao* your talk. Av he *bolos* anything, just you *choop* and *chel*. *Dekker?* Go *arsty* for the first *arder*-mile from cantonmints. Thin *chel*, *Shaitan ke marfik*, an' the *chooper* you *choops* an' the *jildier* you *chels* the better *kooshy* will that *Sahib* be; an' here's a rupee for ye?'

"The *hekka*-man knew there was somethin' out av the common in the air. He grinned an' sez, '*Bote achee!* I goin' damn fast.' I prayed that the Kernel's b'roosh wudn't arrive till me darlin' Benira by the grace av God was undher weigh. The little man puts his thruck into the *hekka* an' scuttles in like a fat guinea-pig; niver offerin' us the price av a dhrink for our services in helpin' him home. 'He's off to the Padsahi *jhil*,' sez I to the others."

Ortheris took up the tale—

"Jist then, little Buldoo kim up, 'oo was the son of one of the Artillery grooms—'e would 'ave made a 'evinly newspaper-boy in London, bein' sharp an' fly to all manner o' games. 'E 'ad bin watchin' us puttin' Mister Benhira into 'is temporary baroush, an' 'e sez, 'What '*ave* you been a doin' of, *Sahibs?*' sez 'e. Learoyd 'e caught 'im by the ear an 'e sez—"

"Ah says," went on Learoyd, "'Young mon, that mon's gooin' to have t' goons out o' Thursday—to-morrow—an' thot's more work for you, young mon. Now, sitha, tak' a *tat* an' a *lookri*, an' ride tha domdest to t' Padsahi Jhil. Cotch thot there *hekka*, and tell t' driver iv your lingo that you've coom to tak' his place. T' *Sahib* doesn't speak t' *bat*, an' he's a little mon. Drive t' *hekka* into t' Padsahi Jhil into t' watter. Leave t' *Sahib* theer an' roon hoam; an' here's a rupee for tha.' "

Then Mulvaney and Ortheris spoke together in alternate fragments: Mulvaney leading [You must pick out the two speakers as best you can]:—"He was a knowin' little divil was Bhuldoo—'e sez *bote achee* an' cuts—wid a wink in his oi—but *Hi* sez there's money to be made—an' I wanted to see the ind av the campaign—so *Hi* says we'll double hout to the Padsahi Jhil—an' save the little man from bein' dacoited by the murtherin' Bhuldoo—an' turn hup like reskooers in a

Vic'oria Melodrama—so we doubled for the *jhil*, an' prisintly there was the divil av a hurroosh behind us an' three bhoys on grasscuts' ponies come by, poundin' along for the dear life—s'elp me Bob, hif Buldoo 'adn't raised a rig'lar *harmy* of decoits—to do the job in shtile. An' we ran, an' they ran, shplittin' with laughin', till we gets near the *jhil*—and 'ears sounds of distress floatin' molloncolly on the hevenin' hair." [Ortheris was growing poetical under the influence of the beer. The duet recommenced: Mulvaney leading again.]

"Thin we heard Bhuldoo, the dacoit, shoutin' to the *hekka* man, an' wan of the young divils brought his stick down on the top av the *hekka* cover, an' Benira Thrigg inside howled 'Murther an' Death.' Bhuldoo takes the reins and dhrives like mad for the *jhil*, havin' dishpersed the *hekka* dhriver—'oo cum up to us an' 'e sez, sez 'e, 'That *Sahib's* nigh mad with funk! Wot devil's work 'ave you led me into?'—'Hall right,' sez we, 'you catch that there pony an' come along. This *Sahib's* been decoited, an' we're going to resky 'im!' Says the driver, 'Decoits! Wot decoits? That's Buldoo the *budmash.*'—'Bhuldoo be shot!' sez we. ''Tis a woild dissolute Pathan frum the hills. There's about eight av thim coercin' the *Sahib*. You remimber that an' you'll get another rupee!' Thin we heard the *whop-whop-whop* av the *hekka* turnin' over, an' a splash av water an' the voice av Benira Thrigg callin' upon God to forgive his sins—an' Buldoo an' 'is friends squotterin' in the water like boys in the Serpentine."

Here the three musketeers retired simultaneously into the beer.

"Well? What came next?" said I.

"Fwhat nex'?" answered Mulvaney, wiping his mouth. "Wud ye let three bould sodger-bhoys lave the ornamint av the House av Lords to be dhrowned an' dacoited in a *jhil?* We formed line av quarther-column an' we discinded upon the inimy. For the better part av tin minutes you could not hear yerself spake. The *tattoo* was screamin' in chune wid Benira Thrigg an' Bhuldoo's army, an' the shticks was whistlin' roun' the *hekka*, an' Orth'ris was beatin' the *hekka*-

cover wid his fistes, an' Learoyd yellin', 'Look out for their knives!' an' me cuttin' into the dark, right an' lef', dishpersin' arrmy corps av Pathans. Holy Mother av Moses! 'twas more disp'rit than Ahmid Kheyl wid Maiwund thrown in. Afther a while Bhuldoo an' his bhoys flees. Have ye iver seen a rale live Lord thryin' to hide his nobility undher a fut an' a half av brown swamp wather? 'Tis the livin' image av a water-carrier's goatskin wid the shivers. It tuk toime to pershuade me frind Benira he was not disimbowiled: an' more toime to get out the *hekka*. The dhriver come up afther the battle, swearin' he tuk a hand in repulsin' the inimy. Benira was sick wid the fear. We escorted him back, very slow, to cantonmints, for that an' the chill to soak into him. It suk! Glory be to the Rigimintil Saint, but it suk to the marrow av Lord Benira Thrigg!"

Here Ortheris, slowly, with immense pride—"'E sez, 'You har my noble preservers,' sez 'e. 'You har a *h*onor to the British Harmy,' sez 'e. With that 'e describes the hawful band of dacoits wot set on 'im. There was about forty of 'em an' 'e was hoverpowered by numbers, so 'e was; but 'e never lorst 'is presence of mind, so 'e didn't. 'E guv the *hekka*-driver five rupees for 'is noble assistance, an' 'e said 'e would see to us after 'e 'ad spoken to the Kernul. For we was a *h*onor to the Regiment, we was."

"An' we three," said Mulvaney, with a seraphic smile, "have dhrawn the par-ti-cu-lar attinshin av Bobs Bahadur more than wanst. But he's a rale good little man is Bobs. Go on, Orth'ris, my son."

"Then we leaves 'im at the Kernul's 'ouse, werry sick, an' we cuts hover to B Comp'ny barrick an' we sez we 'ave saved Benira from a bloody doom, an' the chances was agin there bein' p'raid on Thursday. About ten minutes later come three envelicks, one for each of us. S'elp me Bob, if the old bloke 'adn't guv us a fiver apiece—sixty-four rupees in the bazaar! On Thursday 'e was in 'orspital recoverin' from 'is sanguinary encounter with a gang of Pathans, an' B Comp'ny was drinkin' 'emselves into Clink by squads. So there never was no Thursday p'raid. But the Kernul, when 'e 'eard of our galliant conduct, 'e sez, 'Hi know there's been some devilry somewheres,' sez 'e, 'but I can't bring it 'ome to you three.'"

"An' my privit imprisshin is," said Mulvaney, getting off the bar and turning his glass upside down, "that, av they had known they wudn't have brought ut home. 'Tis flyin' in the face, firstly av Nature, secon' av the Rig'lations, an' third the will av Terence Mulvaney, to hold p'rades av Thursdays."

"Good, ma son!" said Learoyd; "but, young mon, what's t' notebook for?"

"Let be," said Mulvaney; "this time next month we're in the 'Sherapis'. 'Tis immortial fame the gentleman's goin' to give us. But kape it dhark till we're out av the range av me little frind Bobs Bahadur."

And I have obeyed Mulvaney's order.

HIS CHANCE IN LIFE

Then a pile of heads he laid—
Thirty thousands heaped on high—
All to please the Kafir maid,
Where the Oxus ripples by.
Grimly spake Atulla Khan:
"Love hath made this thing a Man."
—*Oatta's Story*

If you go straight away from Levees and Government House Lists, past Trades' Balls—far beyond everything and everybody you ever knew in your respectable life—you cross, in time, the Borderline where the last drop of White blood ends and the full tide of Black sets in. It would be easier to talk to a new-made Duchess on the spur of the moment than to the Borderline folk without violating some of their conventions or hurting their feelings. The Black and the White mix very quaintly in their ways. Sometimes the White shows in spurts of fierce, childish pride—which is Pride of Race run crooked—and sometimes the Black in still fiercer abasement and humility, half-heathenish customs and strange, unaccountable impulses to crime. One of these days, this people—understand they are far lower than the class whence Derozio, the man who imitated Byron, sprung—will turn out a writer or a poet; and then we shall know how they live and what they feel. In the meantime, any stories about them cannot be absolutely correct in fact or inference.

Miss Vezzis came from across the Borderline to look after some children who belonged to a lady until a regularly ordained nurse could come out. The lady said Miss Vezzis was a bad, dirty nurse and inattentive. It never struck her that Miss Vezzis had her own life to lead and her own affairs to worry over, and that these affairs were the most important things in the world to Miss Vezzis. Very few mistresses admit this sort of reasoning. Miss Vezzis was as black as a boot, and, to our standard of taste, hideously ugly. She wore cotton-print gowns and bulged shoes; and when she lost her temper with the children, she abused them in the language of the Borderline—which is part English, part Portuguese, and part Native. She was not attractive; but she had her pride, and she preferred being called "Miss Vezzis."

Every Sunday, she dressed herself wonderfully and went to see her Mamma, who lived, for the most part, on an old cane chair in a greasy *tussur*-silk dressing-gown and a big rabbit-warren of a house full of Vezzises, Pereiras, Ribieras, Lisboas and Gonsalveses, and a floating population of loafers; besides fragments of the day's market, garlic, stale incense, clothes thrown on the floor, petticoats hung on strings for screens, old bottles, pewter crucifixes, dried *immortelles*, pariah puppies, plaster images of the Virgin, and hats without crowns. Miss Vezzis drew twenty rupees a month for acting as nurse, and she squabbled weekly with her Mamma as to the percentage to be given toward housekeeping. When the quarrel was over, Michele D'Cruze used to shamble across the low mud wall of the compound and make love to Miss Vezzis after the fashion of the Borderline, which is hedged about with much ceremony. Michele was a poor, sickly weed and very black; but he had his pride. He would not be seen smoking a *huqa* for anything; and he looked down on natives as only a man with seven-eighths native blood in his veins can. The Vezzis Family had their pride too. They traced their descent from a mythical platelayer who had worked on the Sone Bridge when railways were new in India, and they valued their English origin. Michele was a Telegraph Signaler on Rs. 35 a month. The fact that he was in Government employ made Mrs. Vezzis lenient to the shortcomings of his ancestors.

There was a compromising legend—Dom Anna the tailor brought it from Poonani—that a black Jew of Cochin had once married into the D'Cruze family; while it was an open secret that an uncle of Mrs. D'Cruze was, at that very time, doing menial work, connected with cooking, for a Club in Southern India! He sent Mrs. D'Cruze seven rupees eight annas a month; but she felt the disgrace to the family very keenly all the same.

However, in the course of a few Sundays, Mrs. Vezzis brought herself to overlook these blemishes and gave her consent to the marriage of her daughter with Michele, on condition that Michele should have at least fifty rupees a month to start married life upon. This wonderful prudence must have been a lingering touch of the mythical platelayer's Yorkshire blood; for across the Borderline people take a pride in marrying when they please—not when they can.

Having regard to his departmental prospects, Miss Vezzis might as well have asked Michele to go away and come back with the Moon in his pocket. But Michele was deeply in love with Miss Vezzis, and that helped him to endure. He accompanied Miss Vezzis to Mass one Sunday, and after Mass, walking home through the hot stale dust with her hand in his, he swore by several Saints whose names would not interest you, never to forget Miss Vezzis; and she swore by her Honor and the Saints—the oath runs rather curiously: "In nomine Sanctissimæ—" (whatever the name of the she-Saint is) and so forth, ending with a kiss on the forehead, a kiss on the left cheek, and a kiss on the mouth—never to forget Michele.

Next week Michele was transferred, and Miss Vezzis dropped tears upon the window-sash of the "Intermediate" compartment as he left the Station.

If you look at the telegraph-map of India you will see a long line skirting the coast from Backergunge to Madras. Michele was ordered to Tibasu, a little Sub-office one-third down this line, to send messages on from Berhampur to Chicacola, and to think of Miss Vezzis and his chances of getting fifty rupees a month out of office-hours. He had the noise of the Bay of Bengal and a Bengali Babu for company; nothing more. He sent foolish letters, with crosses tucked inside the flaps of the envelopes, to Miss Vezzis.

When he had been at Tibasu for nearly three weeks his chance came.

Never forget that unless the outward and visible signs of Our Authority are always before a native he is as incapable as a child of understanding what authority means, or where is the danger of disobeying it. Tibasu was a forgotten little place with a few Orissa Mohammedans in it. These, hearing nothing of the Collector-*Sahib* for some time and heartily despising the Hindu Sub-Judge, arranged to start a little Mohurrum riot of their own. But the Hindus turned out and broke their heads; when, finding lawlessness pleasant, Hindus and Mohammedans together raised an aimless sort of Donnybrook just to see how far they could go. They looted each others' shops, and paid off private grudges in the regular way. It was a nasty little riot, but not worth putting in the newspapers.

Michele was working in his office when he heard the sound that a man never forgets all his life—the "*ah-yah*" of an angry crowd. [When that sound drops about three tones, and changes to a thick, droning *ut*, the man who hears it had better go away if he is alone.] The Native Police Inspector ran in and told Michele that the town was in an uproar and coming to wreck the Telegraph Office. The Babu put on his cap and quietly dropped out of the window; while the Police Inspector, afraid, but obeying the old race-instinct which recognizes a drop of White blood as far as it can be diluted, said, "What orders does the *Sahib* give?"

The "*Sahib*" decided Michele. Though horribly frightened, he felt that, for the hour, he, the man with the Cochin Jew and the menial uncle in his pedigree, was the only representative of English authority in the place. Then he thought of Miss Vezzis and the fifty rupees, and took the situation on himself. There were seven native policemen in Tibasu, and four crazy smooth-bore muskets among them. All the men were gray with fear, but not beyond leading. Michele dropped the key of the telegraph instrument, and went out, at the head of his army, to meet the mob. As the shouting crew came round a corner of the road, he dropped and fired; the men behind him loosing instinctively at the same time.

The whole crowd—curs to the backbone—yelled and ran; leaving one man dead, and another dying in the road. Michele was sweating with fear; but he kept his weakness under, and went down into the town, past the house where the Sub-Judge had barricaded himself. The streets were empty. Tibasu was more frightened than Michele, for the mob had been taken at the right time.

Michele returned to the Telegraph-Office, and sent a message to Chicacola asking for help. Before an answer came, he received a deputation of the elders of Tibasu telling him that the Sub-Judge said his actions generally were "unconstitutional," and trying to bully him. But the heart of Michele D'Cruze was big and white in his breast, because of his love for Miss Vezzis, the nurse-girl, and because he had tasted for the first time Responsibility and Success. Those two make an intoxicating drink, and have ruined more men than ever has Whisky. Michele answered that the Sub-Judge might say what he pleased, but, until the Assistant Collector came, the Telegraph Signaler was the Government of India in Tibasu, and the elders of the town would be held accountable for further rioting. Then they bowed their heads and said, "Show mercy!" or words to that effect, and went back in great fear; each accusing the other of having begun the rioting.

Early in the dawn, after a night's patrol with his seven policemen, Michele went down the road, musket in hand, to meet the Assistant Collector who had ridden in to quell Tibasu. But, in the presence of this young Englishman, Michele felt himself slipping back more and more into the native; and the tale of the Tibasu Riots ended, with the strain on the teller, in a hysterical outburst of tears, bred by sorrow that he had killed a man, shame that he could not feel as uplifted as he had felt through the night, and childish anger that his tongue could not do justice to his great deeds. It was the White drop in Michele's veins dying out, though he did not know it.

But the Englishman understood; and, after he had schooled those men of Tibasu, and had conferred with the Sub-Judge till that excellent official turned green, he found time to draft an official letter describing the conduct of Michele. Which letter filtered through the Proper Channels, and ended in the transfer of Michele up-country once more, on the Imperial salary of sixty-six rupees a month.

So he and Miss Vezzis were married with great state and ancientry; and now there are several little D'Cruzes sprawling about the verandas of the Central Telegraph Office.

But, if the whole revenue of the Department he serves were to be his reward, Michele could never, never repeat what he did at Tibasu for the sake of Miss Vezzis the nurse-girl.

Which proves that, when a man does good work out of all proportion to his pay, in seven cases out of nine there is a woman at the back of the virtue.

The two exceptions must have suffered from sunstroke.

WATCHES OF THE NIGHT

What is in the Brahman's books that is in the Brahman's heart. Neither you nor I knew there was so much evil in the world.

—*Hindu Proverb*

THIS began in a practical joke; but it has gone far enough now, and is getting serious.

Platte, the Subaltern, being poor, had a Waterbury watch and a plain leather guard.

The Colonel had a Waterbury watch also, and, for guard, the lip-strap of a curb-chain. Lip-straps make the best watch-guards. They are strong and short. Between a lip-strap and an ordinary leather-guard there is no great difference; between one Waterbury watch and another none at all. Every one in the Station knew the Colonel's lip-strap. He was not a horsey man, but he liked people to believe he had been one once; and he wove fantastic stories of the hunting-bridle to which this particular lip-strap had belonged. Otherwise he was painfully religious.

Platte and the Colonel were dressing at the Club—both late for their engagements, and both in a hurry. That was *Kismet*. The two watches were on a shelf below the looking-glass—guards hanging down. That was carelessness. Platte changed first, snatched a watch, looked in the glass, settled his tie, and ran. Forty seconds later, the Colonel did exactly the same thing; each man taking the other's watch.

You may have noticed that many religious people are deeply suspicious. They seem—for purely religious purposes, of course—to know more about iniquity than the Unregenerate. Perhaps they were specially bad before they became converted! At any rate, in the imputation of things evil and in putting the worst construction on things innocent, a certain type of good people may be trusted to surpass all others. The Colonel and his Wife were of that type. But the Colonel's Wife was the worst. She manufactured the Station scandal, and—talked to her ayah. Nothing more need be said. The Colonel's Wife broke up the Laplaces' home. The Colonel's Wife stopped the Ferris-Haughtrey engagement. The Colonel's Wife induced young Buxton to keep his wife down in the Plains through the first year of the marriage. Wherefore little Mrs. Buxton died, and the baby with her. These things will be remembered against the Colonel's Wife so long as there is a regiment in the country.

But to come back to the Colonel and Platte. They went their several ways from the dressing-room. The Colonel dined with two Chaplains, while Platte went to a bachelor-party, and whist to follow.

Mark how things happen! If Platte's groom had put the new saddle-pad on the mare, the butts of the territs would not have worked through the worn leather and the old pad into the mare's withers, when she was coming home at two o'clock in the morning. She would not have reared, bolted, fallen into a ditch, upset the cart, and sent Platte flying over an aloe-hedge on to Mrs. Larkyn's well-kept lawn; and this tale would never have been written. But the mare did all these things, and while Platte was rolling over and over on the turf, like a shot rabbit, the watch and guard flew from his waistcoat—as an Infantry Major's sword hops out of the scabbard when they are firing a *feu-de-joie*—and rolled and rolled in the moonlight, till it stopped under a window.

Platte stuffed his handkerchief under the pad, put the cart straight, and went home.

Mark again how *Kismet* works! This would not arrive once in a hundred years. Toward the end of his dinner with the two Chaplains, the Colonel let out his waistcoat and leaned over the table to look at some Mission Reports. The bar of the watch-guard worked through the buttonhole, and the watch—Platte's watch—slid quietly on to the carpet. Where the bearer found it next morning and kept it.

Then the Colonel went home to the wife of his bosom; but the driver of the carriage was drunk and lost his way. So the Colonel returned at an unseemly hour and his excuses were not accepted. If the Colonel's Wife had been an ordinary vessel of wrath appointed for destruction, she would have known that when a man stays away on purpose, his excuse is always sound and original. The very baldness of the Colonel's explanation proved its truth.

See once more the workings of *Kismet.* The Colonel's watch which came with Platte hurriedly on to Mrs. Larkyn's lawn, chose to stop just under Mrs. Larkyn's window, where she saw it early in the morning, recognized it and picked it up. She had heard the crash of Platte's cart at two o'clock that morning, and his voice calling the mare names. She knew Platte and liked him. That day she showed him the watch and heard his story. He put his head on one side, winked and said, "How disgusting! Shocking old man! With his religious training, too! I should send the watch to the Colonel's Wife and ask for explanations."

Mrs. Larkyn thought for a minute of the Laplaces—whom she had known when Laplace and his wife believed in each other—and answered, "I will send it. I think it will do her good. But, remember, we must never tell her the truth."

Platte guessed that his own watch was in the Colonel's possession, and thought that the return of the lip-strapped Waterbury with a soothing note from Mrs. Larkyn would merely create a small trouble for a few minutes. Mrs. Larkyn knew better. She knew that any poison dropped would find good holding-ground in the heart of the Colonel's Wife.

The packet, and a note containing a few remarks on the Colonel's calling hours, were sent over to the Colonel's Wife, who wept in her own room and took counsel with herself.

If there was one woman under Heaven whom the Colonel's Wife hated with holy fervor, it was Mrs. Larkyn. Mrs. Larkyn was a frivolous lady, and called the Colonel's Wife "old cat." The Colonel's Wife said that somebody in Revelations was remarkably like Mrs. Larkyn. She mentioned other Scripture people as well. From the Old Testament. But the Colonel's Wife was the only person who cared or dared to say anything against Mrs. Larkyn. Every one else accepted her as an amusing, honest little body. Wherefore, to believe that her husband had been shedding watches under that "Thing's" window at ungodly hours, coupled with the fact of his late arrival on the previous night, was . . . .

At this point she rose up and sought her husband. He denied everything except the ownership of the watch. She besought him, for his Soul's sake, to speak the truth. He denied afresh, with two bad words. Then a stony silence held the Colonel's Wife, while a man could draw his breath five times.

The speech that followed is no affair of mine or yours. It was made up of wifely and womanly jealousy; knowledge of old age and sunk cheeks; deep mistrust born of the text that says even little babies' hearts are as bad as they make them; rancorous hatred of Mrs. Larkyn, and the tenets of the creed of the Colonel's Wife's up-bringing.

Over and above all, was the damning lip-strapped Waterbury, ticking away in the palm of her shaking, withered hand. At that hour, I think, the Colonel's Wife realized a little of the restless suspicion she had injected into old Laplace's mind, a little of poor Miss Haughtrey's misery, and some of the canker that ate into Buxton's heart as he watched his wife dying before his eyes. The Colonel stammered and tried to explain. Then he remembered that his watch had disappeared; and the mystery grew greater. The Colonel's Wife talked and prayed by turns till she was tired, and went away to devise means for chastening the stubborn heart of her husband. Which, translated, means, in our slang, "tail-twisting."

Being deeply impressed with the doctrine of Original Sin, she could not believe in the face of appearances. She knew too much, and jumped to the wildest conclusions.

But it was good for her. It spoiled her life, as she

had spoiled the life of the Laplaces. She had lost her faith in the Colonel, and—here the creed-suspicion came in—he might, she argued, have erred many times, before a merciful Providence, at the hands of so unworthy an instrument as Mrs. Larkyn, had established his guilt. He was a bad, wicked, gray-haired profligate. This may sound too sudden a revulsion for a long wedded wife; but it is a venerable fact that, if a man or woman makes a practice of, and takes a delight in, believing and spreading evil of people indifferent to him or her, he or she will end in believing evil of folk very near and dear. You may think, also, that the mere incident of the watch was too small and trivial to raise this misunderstanding. It is another aged fact that, in life as well as racing, all the worst accidents happen at little ditches and cut-down fences. In the same way, you sometimes see a woman who would have made a Joan of Arc in another century and climate, threshing herself to pieces over all the mean worry of housekeeping. But that is another story.

Her belief only made the Colonel's Wife more wretched, because it insisted so strongly on the villainy of men. Remembering what she had done, it was pleasant to watch her unhappiness, and the penny-farthing attempts she made to hide it from the Station. But the Station knew and laughed heartlessly; for they had heard the story of the watch, with much dramatic gesture, from Mrs. Larkyn's lips.

Once or twice Platte said to Mrs. Larkyn, seeing that the Colonel had not cleared himself, "This thing has gone far enough. I move we tell the Colonel's Wife how it happened." Mrs. Larkyn shut her lips and shook her head, and vowed that the Colonel's Wife must bear her punishment as best she could. Now Mrs. Larkyn was a frivolous woman, in whom none would have suspected deep hate. So Platte took no action, and came to believe gradually, from the Colonel's silence, that the Colonel must have run off the line somewhere that night, and, therefore, preferred to stand sentence on the lesser count of rambling into other people's compounds out of calling-hours. Platte forgot about the watch business after a while, and moved down-country with his regiment. Mrs. Larkyn went home when her husband's tour of Indian service expired. She never forgot.

But Platte was quite right when he said that the joke had gone too far. The mistrust and the tragedy of it—which we outsiders cannot see and do not believe in—are killing the Colonel's Wife, and are making the Colonel wretched. If either of them read this story, they can depend upon its being a fairly true account of the case, and can kiss and make friends.

Shakespeare alludes to the pleasure of watching an Engineer being shelled by his own Battery. Now this shows that poets should not write about what they do not understand. Any one could have told him that Sappers and Gunners are perfectly different branches of the Service. But, if you correct the sentence, and substitute Gunner for Sapper, the moral comes just the same.

THE OTHER MAN

When the Earth was sick and the Skies were gray,
And the woods were rotted with rain,
The Dead Man rode through the autumn day
To visit his love again.—*Old Ballad*

Far back in the "seventies," before they had built any Public-Offices at Simla, and the broad road round Jakko lived in a pigeon-hole in the P. W. D. hovels, her parents made Miss Gaurey marry Colonel Schreiderling. He could not have been much more than thirty-five years her senior; and, as he lived on two hundred rupees a month and had money of his own, he was well off. He belonged to good people, and suffered in the cold weather from lung-complaints. In the hot weather he dangled on the brink of heat-apoplexy; but it never quite killed him.

Understand, I do not blame Schreiderling. He was a

good husband according to his lights, and his temper only failed him when he was being nursed. Which was some seventeen days in each month. He was almost generous to his wife about money-matters, and that, for him, was a concession. Still Mrs. Schreiderling was not happy. They married her when she was this side of twenty and had given all her poor little heart to another man. I have forgotten his name, but we will call him the Other Man. He had no money and no prospects. He was not even good-looking; and I think he was in the Commissariat or Transport. But, in spite of all these things, she loved him very badly; and there was some sort of an engagement between the two when Schreiderling appeared and told Mrs. Gaurey that he wished to marry her daughter. Then the other engagement was broken off—washed away by Mrs. Gaurey's tears, for that lady governed her house by weeping over disobedience to her authority and the lack of reverence she received in her old age. The daughter did not take after her mother. She never cried. Not even at the wedding.

The Other Man bore his loss quietly, and was transferred to as bad a station as he could find. Perhaps the climate consoled him. He suffered from intermittent fever, and that may have distracted him from his other trouble. He was weak about the heart also. Both ways. One of the valves was affected, and the fever made it worse. This showed itself later on.

Then many months passed, and Mrs Schreiderling took to being ill. She did not pine away like people in story-books, but she seemed to pick up every form of illness that went about a Station, from simple fever upward. She was never more than ordinarily pretty at the best of times; and the illnesses made her ugly. Schreiderling said so. He prided himself on speaking his mind.

When she ceased being pretty, he left her to her own devices, and went back to the lairs of his bachelordom. She used to trot up and down Simla Mall in a forlorn sort of way, with a gray Terai hat well on the back of her head, and a shocking bad saddle under her. Schreiderling's generosity stopped at the horse. He said that any saddle would do for a woman as nervous as Mrs. Schreiderling. She never was asked to dance, because she did not dance well; and she was so dull and uninteresting that her box very seldom had any cards in it. Schreiderling said that if he had known she was going to be such a scarecrow after her marriage, he would never have married her. He always prided himself on speaking his mind, did Schreiderling.

He left her at Simla one August, and went down to his regiment. Then she revived a little, but she never recovered her looks. I found out at the Club that the Other Man was coming up sick—very sick—on an off chance of recovery. The fever and the heart valves had nearly killed him. She knew that too, and she knew—what I had no interest in knowing—when he was coming up. I suppose he wrote to tell her. They had not seen each other since a month before the wedding. And here comes the unpleasant part of the story.

A late call kept me down at the Dovedell Hotel till dusk one evening. Mrs. Schreiderling had been flitting up and down the Mall all the afternoon in the rain. Coming up along the Cart-road, a tonga passed me, and my pony, tired with standing so long, set off at a canter. Just by the road down to the Tonga Office Mrs. Schreiderling, dripping from head to foot, was waiting for the tonga. I turned uphill, as the tonga was no affair of mine; and just then she began to shriek. I went back at once and saw, under the Tonga Office lamps, Mrs. Schreiderling kneeling in the wet road by the back seat of the newly-arrived tonga, screaming hideously. Then she fell face down in the dirt as I came up.

Sitting in the back seat, very square and firm, with one hand on the awning-stanchion and the wet pouring off his hat and mustache, was the Other Man—dead. The sixty-mile uphill jolt had been too much for his valve, I suppose. The tonga-driver said, "This Sahib died two stages out of Solon. Therefore, I tied him with a rope, lest he should fall out by the way, and so came to Simla. Will the Sahib give me *bukshish? It*," pointing to the Other Man, "should have given one rupee."

The Other Man sat with a grin on his face, as if he enjoyed the joke of his arrival; and Mrs. Schreiderling, in the mud, began to groan. There was no one except us four in the office and it was raining heavily. The first thing was to take Mrs. Schreiderling home, and the second was to prevent her name from being mixed up with the affair. The tonga-driver received five rupees to find a bazaar 'rickshaw for Mrs. Schreiderling. He was to tell the Tonga Babu afterward of the Other Man, and the Babu was to make such arrangements as seemed best.

Mrs. Schreiderling was carried into the shed out of the rain, and for three-quarters of an hour we two waited for the 'rickshaw. The Other Man was left exactly as he had arrived. Mrs. Schreiderling would do everything but cry, which might have helped her. She tried to scream as soon as her senses came back, and then she began praying for the Other Man's soul. Had she not been as honest as the day, she would have prayed for her own soul too. I waited to hear her do this, but she did not. Then I tried to get some of the mud off her habit. Lastly, the 'rickshaw came, and I got her away—partly by force. It was a terrible business from beginning to end; but most of all when the 'rickshaw had to squeeze between the wall and the tonga, and she saw by the lamplight that thin, yellow hand grasping the awning-stanchion.

She was taken home just as every one was going to a dance at Viceregal Lodge—"Peterhoff" it was then—and the doctor found out that she had fallen from her horse, that I had picked her up at the back of Jakko, and really deserved great credit for the prompt manner in which I had secured medical aid. She did not die—men of Schreiderling's stamp marry women who don't die easily. They live and grow ugly.

She never told of her one meeting, since her marriage,

with the Other Man; and, when the chill and cough following the exposure of that evening allowed her abroad, she never by word or sign alluded to having met me by the Tonga Office. Perhaps she never knew.

She used to trot up and down the Mall, on that shocking bad saddle, looking as if she expected to meet some one round the corner every minute. Two years afterward she went Home, and died—at Bournemouth, I think.

Schreiderling, when he grew maudlin at Mess, used to talk about "my poor dear wife." He always set great store on speaking his mind, did Schreiderling.

CONSEQUENCES

Rosicrucian subtleties
In the Orient had rise;
Ye may find their teachers still
Under Jacatâlâ's Hill.
Seek ye Bombast Paracelsus,
Read what Flood the Seeker tells us
Of the Dominant that runs
Through the Cycles of the Suns—
Read my story last, and see
Luna at her apogee.

THERE are yearly appointments, and two-yearly appointments, and five-yearly appointments at Simla, and there are, or used to be, permanent appointments, whereon you stayed up for the term of your natural life and secured red cheeks and a nice income. Of course, you could descend in the cold weather; for Simla is rather dull then.

Tarrion came from goodness knows where—all away and away in some forsaken part of Central India, where they call Pachmari a Sanitarium, and drive behind trotting-bullocks, I believe. He belonged to a regiment; but what he really wanted to do was to escape from his regiment and live in

Simla for ever and ever. He had no preference for anything in particular, beyond a good horse and a nice partner. He thought he could do everything well; which is a beautiful belief when you hold it with all your heart. He was clever in many ways, and good to look at, and always made people round him comfortable—even in Central India.

So he went up to Simla, and, because he was clever and amusing, he gravitated naturally to Mrs. Hauksbee, who could forgive everything but stupidity. Once he did her great service by changing the date on an invitation-card for a big dance which Mrs. Hauksbee wished to attend, but couldn't because she had quarreled with the A.-D.-C., who took care, being a mean man, to invite her to a small dance on the 6th instead of the big Ball of the 26th. It was a very clever piece of forgery; and when Mrs. Hauksbee showed the A.-D.-C. her invitation-card, and chaffed him mildly for not better managing his vendettas, he really thought that he had made a mistake; and—which was wise—realized that it was no use to fight with Mrs. Hauksbee. She was grateful to Tarrion and asked what she could do for him. He said simply, "I'm a Freelance up here on leave, on the lookout for what I can loot. I haven't a square inch of interest in all Simla. My name isn't known to any man with an appointment in his gift, and I want an appointment—a good, sound one. I believe you can do anything you turn yourself to. Will you help me?" Mrs. Hauksbee thought for a minute, and passed the lash of her riding-whip through her lips, as was her custom when thinking. Then her eyes sparkled and she said, "I will"; and she shook hands on it. Tarrion, having perfect confidence in this great woman, took no further thought of the business at all. Except to wonder what sort of an appointment he would win.

Mrs. Hauksbee began calculating the prices of all the Heads of Departments and Members of Council she knew, and the more she thought the more she laughed, because her heart was in the game and it amused her. Then she took a Civil List and ran over a few of the appointments. There are some beautiful appointments in the Civil List. Eventually, she decided that, though Tarrion was too good for the Political Department, she had better begin by trying to place him there. Her own plans to this end do not matter in the least, for Luck or Fate played into her hands and she had nothing to do but to watch the course of events and take the credit of them.

All Viceroys, when they first come out, pass through the Diplomatic Secrecy craze. It wears off in time; but they all catch it in the beginning, because they are new to the country. The particular Viceroy who was suffering from the complaint just then—this was a long time ago, before Lord Dufferin ever came from Canada, or Lord Ripon from the bosom of the English Church—had it very badly; and the result was that men who were new to keeping official secrets went about looking unhappy; and the Viceroy plumed himself on the way in which he had instilled notions of reticence into his Staff.

Now, the Supreme Government have a careless custom of committing what they do to printed papers. These papers deal with all sorts of things—from the payment of Rs.200 to a "secret service" native, up to rebukes administered to Vakils and Motamids of Native States, and rather brusque letters to Native Princes, telling them to put their houses in order, to refrain from kidnapping women, or filling offenders with pounded red pepper, and eccentricities of that kind. Of course, these things could never be made public, because Native Princes never err officially, and their States are officially as well administered as Our territories. Also, the private allowances to various queer people are not exactly matters to put into newspapers, though they give quaint reading sometimes. When the Supreme Government is at Simla, these papers are prepared there, and go round to the people who ought to see them in office-boxes or by post. The principle of secrecy was to that Viceroy quite as important as the practice, and he held that a benevolent despotism like Ours should never allow even little things, such as appointments of subordinate clerks, to leak out till the proper time. He was always remarkable for his principles.

There was a very important batch of papers in preparation at that time. It had to travel from one end of Simla to the other by hand. It was not put into an official envelope, but a large, square, pale pink one; the matter being in MS. on soft crinkley paper. It was addressed to "The Head Clerk, etc., etc." Now, between "The Head Clerk, etc., etc.," and "Mrs. Hauksbee" and a flourish, is no very great difference, if the address be written in a very bad hand, as this was. The orderly who took the envelope was not more of an idiot than most orderlies. He merely forgot where this most unofficial cover was to be delivered, and so asked the first Englishman he met, who happened to be a man riding down to Annandale in a great hurry. The Englishman hardly looked at it, said, "Mrs. Hauksbee," and went on. So did the orderly, because that letter was the last in stock and he wanted to get his work over. There was no book to sign; he thrust the letter into Mrs. Hauksbee's bearer's hands and went off to smoke with a friend. Mrs. Hauksbee was expecting some cut-out pattern things in flimsy paper from a friend. As soon as she got the big square packet, therefore, she said, "Oh, the dear creature!" and tore it open with a paper-knife, and all the MS. inclosures tumbled out on the floor.

Mrs. Hauksbee began reading. I have said the batch was rather important. That is quite enough for you to know. It referred to some correspondence, two measures, a peremptory order to a native chief, and two dozen other things. Mrs. Hauksbee gasped as she read, for the first glimpse of the naked machinery of the Great Indian Government, stripped of its casings, and lacquer, and paint, and guard-rails, impresses even the most stupid man. And Mrs. Hauksbee was a clever woman. She was a little afraid at first, and felt as if she had taken hold of a lightning-flash by the tail, and did not quite know what to do with it. There were remarks and initials at the side of the papers; and some of the remarks were rather more severe than the papers. The initials belonged to men who are all dead or gone now; but they were great in their day. Mrs. Hauksbee read on and thought calmly as she read. Then the value of her trove struck her, and she cast about for the best method of using it. Then Tarrion dropped in, and they read through all the papers together, and Tarrion, not knowing how she had come by them, vowed that Mrs. Hauksbee was the greatest woman on earth. Which I believe was true or nearly so.

"The honest course is always the best," said Tarrion after an hour and a half of study and conversation. "All things considered, the Intelligence Branch is about my form. Either that or the Foreign Office. I go to lay siege to the High Gods in their Temples."

He did not seek a little man, or a little big man, or a weak Head of a strong Department, but he called on the biggest and strongest man that the Government owned, and explained that he wanted an appointment at Simla on a good salary. The compound insolence of this amused the Strong Man, and, as he had nothing to do for the moment, he listened to the proposals of the audacious Tarrion. "You have, I presume, some special qualifications, besides the gift of self-assertion, for the claims you put forward?" said the Strong Man. "That, Sir," said Tarrion, "is for you to judge." Then he began, for he had a good memory, quoting a few of the more important notes in the papers—slowly and one by one as a man drops chlorodyne into a glass. When he had reached the peremptory order—and it was a very peremptory order—the Strong Man was troubled. Tarrion wound up—"And I fancy that special knowledge of this kind is at least as valuable for, let us say, a berth in the Foreign Office, as the fact of being the nephew of a distinguished officer's wife." That hit the Strong Man hard, for the last appointment to the Foreign Office had been by black favor, and he knew it.

"I'll see what I can do for you," said the Strong Man.

"Many thanks," said Tarrion. Then he left, and the

Strong Man departed to see how the appointment was to be blocked.

. . . .

Followed a pause of eleven days; with thunders and lightnings and much telegraphing. The appointment was not a very important one, carrying only between Rs.500 and Rs.700 a month; but, as the Viceroy said, it was the principle of diplomatic secrecy that had to be maintained, and it was more than likely that a boy so well supplied with special information would be worth translating. So they translated Tarrion. They must have suspected him, though he protested that his information was due to singular talents of his own. Now, much of this story, including the after-history of the missing envelope, you must fill in for yourself, because there are reasons why it cannot be written. If you do not know about things Up Above, you won't understand how to fill in, and you will say it is impossible.

What the Viceroy said when Tarrion was introduced to him was—"This is the boy who 'rushed' the Government of India, is it? Recollect, Sir, that is not done twice." So he must have known something.

What Tarrion said when he saw his appointment gazetted was—"If Mrs. Hauksbee were twenty years younger, and I her husband, I should be Viceroy of India in fifteen years."

What Mrs. Hauksbee said, when Tarrion thanked her, almost with tears in his eyes, was first—"I told you so!" and next, to herself—"What fools men are!"

THE CONVERSION OF AURELIAN McGOGGIN

Ride with an idle whip, ride with an unused heel,
But, once in a way, there will come a day
When the colt must be taught to feel
The lash that falls, and the curb that galls, and the sting of the roweled steel.—*Life's Handicap*

THIS is not a tale exactly. It is a Tract; and I am immensely proud of it. Making a Tract is a Feat.

Every man is entitled to his own religious opinions; but no man—least of all a junior—has a right to thrust these down other men's throats. The Government sends out weird Civilians now and again; but McGoggin was the queerest exported for a long time. He was clever—brilliantly clever—but his cleverness worked the wrong way. Instead of keeping to the study of the vernaculars, he had read some books written by a man called Comte, I think, and a man called Spencer. [You will find these books in the Library.] They deal with people's insides from the point of view of men who have no stomachs. There was no order against his reading them; but his Mamma should have smacked him. They fermented in his head, and he came out to India with a rarefied religion over and above his work. It was not much of a creed. It only proved that men had no souls, and there was no God and no hereafter, and that you must worry along somehow for the good of Humanity.

One of its minor tenets seemed to be that the one thing more sinful than giving an order was obeying it. At least, that was what McGoggin said; but I suspect he had misread his primers.

I do not say a word against this creed. It was made up in Town where there is nothing but machinery and asphalt and building—all shut in by the fog. Naturally, a man grows to think that there is no one higher than himself, and that the Metropolitan Board of Works made everything. But in India, where you really see humanity—raw, brown, naked humanity—with nothing between it and the blazing sky, and only the used-up, over-handled earth underfoot, the notion somehow dies away, and most folk come back to simpler theories. Life, in India, is not long enough to waste in proving that there is no one in particular at the head of affairs. For this reason. The Deputy is above the Assistant, the Commissioner above the Deputy, the Lieutenant-Governor above the Commissioner, and the Viceroy above all four, under the orders of the Secretary of State who is responsible to the Empress. If the Empress be not responsible to her Maker—if there is no Maker for her to be responsible to—the entire system of Our administration must be wrong. Which is manifestly impossible. At Home men are to be excused. They are stalled up a good deal and get intellectually "beany." When you take a gross, "beany" horse to exercise, he slavers and slobbers over the bit till you can't see the horns. But the bit is there just the same. Men do not get "beany" in India. The climate and the work are against playing bricks with words.

If McGoggin had kept his creed, with the capital letters and the endings in "isms," to himself, no one would have cared; but his grandfathers on both sides had been Wesleyan preachers, and the preaching strain came out in his mind. He wanted every one at the Club to see that they had no souls too, and to help him to eliminate his Creator. As a good many men told him, *he* undoubtedly had no soul, because he was so young, but it did not follow that his seniors were equally undeveloped; and, whether there was another world or not, a man still wanted to read his papers in this. "But that is not the point—that is not the point!" Aurelian used to say. Then men threw sofa-cushions at him and told him to go to any particular place he might believe in. They christened him the "Blastoderm"—he said he came from a family of that name somewhere, in the prehistoric ages—and, by insult and laughter strove to choke him dumb, for he was an unmitigated nuisance at the Club; besides being an offense to the older men. His Deputy Commissioner, who was working on the Frontier when Aurelian was rolling on a bed-quilt, told him that, for a clever boy, Aurelian was a very big idiot. And, if he had gone on with his work, he would have been caught up to the Secretariat in a few years. He was of the type that goes there—all head, no physique and a hundred theories. Not a soul was interested in McGoggin's soul. He might have had two, or none, or somebody else's. His business was to obey orders and keep abreast of his files, instead of devastating the Club with "isms."

He worked brilliantly; but he could not accept any order without trying to better it. That was the fault of his creed. It made men too responsible and left too much to their honor. You can sometimes ride an old horse in a halter; but never a colt. McGoggin took more trouble over his cases than any of the men of his year. He may have fancied that thirty-page judgments on fifty-rupee cases—both sides perjured to the gullet—advanced the cause of Humanity. At any rate, he worked too much, and worried and fretted over the rebukes he received, and lectured away on his ridiculous creed out of office, till the Doctor had to warn him that he was overdoing it. No man can toil eighteen annas in the rupee in June without suffering. But McGoggin was still intellectually "beany" and proud of himself and his powers, and he would take no hint. He worked nine hours a day steadily.

"Very well," said the Doctor, "you'll break down, because you are over-engined for your beam." McGoggin was a little man.

One day, the collapse came—as dramatically as if it had been meant to embellish a Tract.

It was just before the Rains. We were sitting in the veranda in the dead, hot, close air, gasping and praying that the black-blue clouds would let down and bring the cool.

Very, very far away, there was a faint whisper, which was the roar of the Rains breaking over the river. One of the men heard it, got out of his chair, listened and said, naturally enough, "Thank God!"

Then the Blastoderm turned in his place and said, "Why? I assure you it's only the result of perfectly natural causes—atmospheric phenomena of the simplest kind. Why you should, therefore, return thanks to a Being who never did exist—who is only a figment—"

"Blastoderm," grunted the man in the next chair, "dry up, and throw me over the 'Pioneer.' We know all about your figments." The Blastoderm reached out to the table, took up one paper, and jumped as if something had stung him. Then he handed the paper.

"As I was saying," he went on slowly and with an effort —"due to perfectly natural causes—perfectly natural causes. I mean—"

"Hi! Blastoderm, you've given me the 'Calcutta Mercantile Advertiser.'"

The dust got up in little whorls, while the treetops rocked and the kites whistled. But no one was looking at the coming of the Rains. We were all staring at the Blastoderm, who had risen from his chair and was fighting with his speech. Then he said, still more slowly—

"Perfectly conceivable —— dictionary —— red oak —— amenable——cause——retaining——shuttlecock——alone."

"Blastoderm's drunk," said one man. But the Blastoderm was not drunk. He looked at us in a dazed sort of way, and began motioning with his hands in the half light as the clouds closed overhead. Then—with a scream—

"What is it?——Can't——reserve——attainable——market——obscure—"

But his speech seemed to freeze in him, and—just as the lightning shot two tongues that cut the whole sky into three pieces and the rain fell in quivering sheets—the Blastoderm was struck dumb. He stood pawing and champing like a hard-held horse, and his eyes were full of terror.

The Doctor came over in three minutes, and heard the story. "It's *aphasia*," he said. "Take him to his room. I knew the smash would come." We carried the Blastoderm across in the pouring rain to his quarters, and the Doctor gave him bromide of potassium to make him sleep.

Then the Doctor came back to us and told us that *aphasia* was like all the arrears of "Punjab Head" falling in a lump; and that only once before—in the case of a sepoy—had he met with so complete a case. I have seen mild *aphasia* in an overworked man, but this sudden dumbness was uncanny—though, as the Blastoderm himself might have said, due to "perfectly natural causes."

"He'll have to take leave after this," said the Doctor. "He won't be fit for work for another three months. No; it isn't insanity or anything like it. It's only complete loss of control over the speech and memory. I fancy it will keep the Blastoderm quiet, though."

Two days later, the Blastoderm found his tongue again. The first question he asked was—"What was it?" The Doctor enlightened him. "But I can't understand it!" said the Blastoderm. "I'm quite sane; but I can't be sure of my mind, it seems—my *own* memory—can I?"

"Go up into the Hills for three months, and don't think about it," said the Doctor.

"But I can't understand it," repeated the Blastoderm. "It was my *own* mind and memory."

"I can't help it," said the Doctor; "there are a good many things you can't understand; and, by the time you have put in my length of service, you'll know exactly how much a man dare call his own in this world."

The stroke cowed the Blastoderm. He could not understand it. He went into the Hills in fear and trembling, wondering whether he would be permitted to reach the end of any sentence he began.

This gave him a wholesome feeling of mistrust. The legitimate explanation, that he had been over-working himself, failed to satisfy him. Something had wiped his lips of speech, as a mother wipes the milky lips of her child, and he was afraid—horribly afraid.

So the Club had rest when he returned; and if ever you come across Aurelian McGoggin laying down the law on things Human—he doesn't seem to know as much as he used to about things Divine—put your forefinger to your lip for a moment, and see what happens.

Don't blame me if he throws a glass at your head.

THE TAKING OF LUNGTUNGPEN

So we loosed a bloomin' volley,
An' we made the beggars cut,
An' when our pouch was emptied out,
We used the bloomin' butt,
Ho! My!
Don't yer come anigh,
When Tommy is a playin' with the baynit an'
the butt.—*Barrack-Room Ballad*

My friend Private Mulvaney told me this, sitting on the parapet of the road to Dagshai, when we were hunting butterflies together. He had theories about the Army, and colored clay pipes perfectly. He said that the young soldier is the best to work with, "on account av the surpassing innocinse av the child."

"Now, listen!" said Mulvaney, throwing himself full length on the wall in the sun. "I'm a born scutt av the barrick-room! The Army's mate an' dhrink to me, bekase I'm wan av the few that can't quit ut. I've put in sivinteen years, an' the pipeclay's in the marrow av me. Av I cud have kept out av wan big dhrink a month, I wud have been a Hon'ry Lift'nint by this time—a nuisance to my betthers, a laughin'-shtock to my equils, an' a curse to meself. Bein' fwhat I am, I'm Privit Mulvaney, wid no good-conduc' pay an' a devourin' thirst. Always barrin' me little frind Bobs Bahadur, I know as much about the Army as most men."

I said something here.

"Wolseley be shot! Betune you an' me an' that butterfly net, he's a ramblin', incoherint sort av a divil, wid wan oi on the Quane an' the Coort, an' the other on his blessed silf—everlastin'ly playing Saysar an' Alexandrier rowled into a lump. Now Bobs is a sensible little man. Wid Bobs an' a few three-year-olds, I'd swape any army av the earth into a towel, an' throw it away aftherwards. Faith, I'm not jokin'! 'Tis the bhoys—the raw bhoys—that don't know fwhat a bullut manes, an' wudn't care av they did—that dhu the work. They're crammed wid bull-mate till they fairly *ramps* wid good livin'; and thin, av they don't fight, they blow each other's hids off. 'Tis the trut' I'm tellin' you. They shud be kept on water an' rice in the hot weather; but there'd be a mut'ny av 'twas done.

"Did ye iver hear how Privit Mulvaney tuk the town av Lungtungpen? I thought not! 'Twas the Lift'nint got the credit; but 'twas me planned the schame. A little before I was inviladed from Burma, me an' four-an'-twenty young wans undher a Lift'nint Brazenose, was ruinin' our dijeshins thryin' to catch dacoits. An' such double-ended divils I niver knew! 'Tis only a *dah* an' a Snider that makes a dacoit. Widout thim, he's a paceful cultivator, an' felony for to shoot. We hunted, an' we hunted, an' tuk fever an' elephints now an' again; but no dacoits. Evenshually, we *puckarowed* wan man. 'Trate him tinderly,' sez the Lift'nint. So I tuk him away into the jungle, wid the Burmese Interprut'r an' my clanin'-rod. Sez I to the man, 'My paceful squireen,' sez I, 'you shquot on your hunkers an' dimonstrate to *my* frind here, where *your* frinds are whin they're at home?' Wid that I introjuced him to the clanin'-rod, an' he comminst to jabber; the Interprut'r interprutin' in betweens, an' me helpin' the Intilligince Departmint wid my clanin'-rod whin the man misremimbered.

"Prisintly, I learn that, acrost the river, about nine miles away, was a town just dhrippin' wid dahs, an' bohs an' arrows, an' dacoits, an' elephints, an' *jingles.* 'Good!' sez I; 'this office will now close!'

"That night, I went to the Lift'nint an' communicates my information. I never thought much of Lift'nint Brazenose till that night. He was shtiff wid books an' the-ouries, an' all manner av thrimmin's no manner av use. 'Town did ye say?' sez he. 'Accordin' to the the-ouries av War, we shud wait for reinforcemints.'—'Faith!' thinks I, 'we'd betther dig our graves thin'; for the nearest throops was up to their shtocks in the marshes out Mimbu way. 'But,' says the Lift'nint, 'since 'tis a speshil case, I'll make an excepshin. We'll visit this Lungtungpen to-night.'

"The bhoys was fairly woild wid deloight whin I tould 'em; an', by this an' that, they wint through the jungle like buck-rabbits. About midnight we come to the shtrame which I had clane forgot to minshin to my orficer. I was on, ahead, wid four bhoys, an' I thought that the Lift'nint might want to the-ourise. 'Shtrip, bhoys!' sez I. 'Shtrip to the buff, an' shwim in where glory waits!'—'But I *can't* shwim!' sez two av thim. 'To think I should live to hear that from a bhoy wid a board-school edukashin!' sez I. 'Take a lump av thimber, an' me an' Conolly here will ferry ye over, ye young ladies!'

"We got an ould tree-trunk, an' pushed off wid the kits an' the rifles on it. The night was chokin' dhark, an' just as we was fairly embarked, I heard the Lift'nint behind av me callin' out. 'There's a bit av a *nullah* here, Sorr,' sez I, 'but I can feel the bottom already.' So I cud, for I was not a yard from the bank.

"'Bit av a *nullah!* Bit av an eshtuary!' sez the Lift'nint. 'Go on, ye mad Irishman! Shtrip, bhoys!' I heard him laugh; an' the bhoys begun shtrippin' an' rollin' a log into the wather to put their kits on. So me an' Conolly shtruck out through the warm wather wid our log, an' the rest come on behind.

"That shtrame was miles woide! Orth'ris, on the rear-rank log, whispers we had got into the Thames below Sheerness by mistake. 'Kape on shwimmin', ye little blayguard,' sez I, 'an' don't go pokin' your dirty jokes at the Irriwaddy.' —'Silince, men!' sings out the Lift'nint. So we shwum on into the black dhark, wid our chests on the logs, trustin' in the Saints an' the luck av the British Army.

"Evenshually, we hit ground—a bit av sand—an' a man. I put my heel on the back av him. He screeched an' ran.

" '*Now* we've done it!' sez Lift'nint Brazenose. 'Where the Divil *is* Lungtungpen?' There was about a minute and a half to wait. The bhoys laid a hould av their rifles an' some thried to put their belts on; we was marchin' wid fixed baynits av coorse. Thin we knew where Lungtungpen was; for we had hit the river-wall av it in the dhark, an' the whole town blazed wid thim messin' *jingles* an' Sniders like a cat's back on a frosty night. They was firin' all ways at wanst; but over our hids into the shtrame.

" 'Have you got your rifles?' sez Brazenose. 'Got 'em! sez Orth'ris. 'I've got that thief Mulvaney's for all my back-pay, an' she'll kick my heart sick wid that blunderin' long shtock av hers.'—'Go on!' yells Brazenose, whippin' his sword out. 'Go on an' take the town! An' the Lord have mercy on our sowls!'

"Thin the bhoys gave wan divastatin' howl, an' pranced into the dhark, feelin' for the town, an' blindin' an' stiffin' like Cavalry Ridin' Masters whin the grass pricked their bare legs. I hammered wid the butt at some bamboo-thing that felt wake, an' the rest come an' hammered contagious, while the *jingles* was jingling, an' feroshus yells from inside was shplittin' our ears. We was too close under the wall for thim to hurt us.

"Evenshually, the thing, whatever ut was, bruk; an' the six-and-twinty av us tumbled, wan after the other, naked as we was borrun, into the town of Lungtungpen. There was a *melly* av a sumpshus kind for a whoile; but whether they tuk us, all white an' wet, for a new breed av divil, or a new kind av dacoit, I don't know. They ran as though we was both, an' we wint into thim, baynit an' butt, shriekin' wid laughin'. There was torches in the shtreet, an' I saw little Orth'ris rubbin' his showlther ivry time he loosed my long-shtock Martini; an' Brazenose walkin' into the gang wid his sword, like Diarmid av the Gowlden Collar—barring he hadn't a stitch av clothin' on him. We diskivered elephints wid dacoits under their bellies, an', what wid wan thing an' another, we was busy till mornin' takin' possession av the town of Lungtungpen.

"Thin we halted an' formed up, the wimmen howlin' in the houses an' Lift'nint Brazenose blushin' pink in the light av the mornin' sun. 'Twas the most ondasint p'rade I iver tuk a hand in. Foive and-twenty privits an' a orficer av the Line in review ordher, an' not as much as wud dust a fife betune 'em all in the way of clothin'! Eight av us had their belts an' pouches on; but the rest had gone in wid a handful av cartridges an' the skin God gave thim. *They* was as nakid as Vanus.

"'Number off from the right!' sez the Lift'nint. 'Odd numbers fall out to dress; even numbers pathrol the town till relieved by the dressing party.' Let me tell you, pathrollin' a town wid nothing on is an ex*pay*rience. I pathrolled for tin minutes, an' begad, before 'twas over, I blushed. The women laughed so. I niver blushed before or since; but I blushed all over my carkiss thin. Orth'ris didn't pathrol. He sez only, 'Portsmith Barricks an' the 'Ard av a Sunday!' Thin he lay down an' rowled any ways wid laughin'.

"Whin we was all dhressed, we counted the dead—sivinty-foive dacoits besides wounded. We tuk five elephints, a hunder' an' sivinty Sniders, two hunder' dahs, and a lot av other burglarious thruck. Not a man av us was hurt—excep' maybe the Lift'nint, an' he from the shock to his dasincy.

"The Headman av Lungtungpen, who surrinder'd him-self, asked the Interprut'r—'Av the English fight like that wid their clo'es off, what in the wurruld do they do wid their clo'es on?' Orth'ris began rowlin' his eyes an' crackin' his fingers an' dancin' a step-dance for to impress the Headman. He ran to his house; an' we spint the rest av the day carryin' the Lift'nint on our showlthers round the town, an' playin' wid the Burmese babies—fat, little, brown little divils, as pretty as picturs.

"Whin I was inviladed for the dysent'ry to India, I sez to the Lift'nint, 'Sorr,' sez I, 'you've the makin's in you av a great man; but, av you'll let an ould sodger spake, you're too fond of the-ourisin.' He shuk hands wid me and sez, 'Hit high, hit low, there's no plasin' you, Mulvaney. You've seen me waltzin' through Lungtungpen like a Red Injin widout the war-paint, an' you say I'm too fond av the-ourisin'?' —'Sorr,' sez I, for I loved the bhoy; 'I wud waltz wid you in that condishin through *Hell*, an' so wud the rest av the men!' Thin I wint downshtrame in the flat an' left him my blessin'. May the Saints carry ut where ut shud go, for he was a fine upstandin' young orficer.

"To reshume. Fwhat I've said jist shows the use av three-year-olds. Wud fifty seasoned sodgers have taken Lungtungpen in the dhark that way? No! They'd know the risk av fever and chill. Let alone the shootin'. Two hundher' might have done ut. But the three-year-olds know little an' care less; an' where there's no fear, there's no danger. Catch thim young, feed thim high, an' by the honor av that great, little man Bobs, behind a good orficer 'tisn't only dacoits they'd smash wid their clo'es off—'tis Con-ti-nental Ar-r-r-mies! They tuk Lungtungpen nakid; an' they'd take St. Pethersburg in their dhrawers! Begad, they would that!

"Here's your pipe, Sorr. Shmoke her tinderly wid honey-dew, afther letting the reek av the Canteen plug die away. But 'tis no good, thanks to you all the same, fillin' my pouch wid your chopped hay. Canteen baccy's like the Army. It shpoils a man's taste for moilder things."

So saying, Mulvaney took up his butterfly-net, and returned to barracks.

A GERM-DESTROYER

Pleasant it is for the Little Tin Gods
  When great Jove nods;
But Little Tin Gods make their little mistakes
In missing the hour when great Jove wakes.

As a general rule, it is inexpedient to meddle with questions of State in a land where men are highly paid to work them out for you. This tale is a justifiable exception.

Once in every five years, as you know, we indent for a new Viceroy; and each Viceroy imports, with the rest of his baggage, a Private Secretary, who may or may not be the real Viceroy, just as Fate ordains. Fate looks after the Indian Empire because it is so big and so helpless.

There was a Viceroy once, who brought out with him a turbulent Private Secretary—a hard man with a soft manner and a morbid passion for work. This Secretary was called Wonder—John Fennil Wonder. The Viceroy possessed no name—nothing but a string of counties and two-thirds of the alphabet after them. He said, in confidence, that he was the electro-plated figure-head of a golden administration, and he watched in a dreamy, amused way Wonder's attempts to draw matters which were entirely outside his province into his own hands. "When we are all cherubims together," said His Excellency once, "my dear, good friend Wonder will head the conspiracy for plucking out Gabriel's tail-feathers or stealing Peter's keys. *Then* I shall report him."

But, though the Viceroy did nothing to check Wonder's officiousness, other people said unpleasant things. Maybe the Members of Council began it; but finally all Simla agreed that there was "too much Wonder, and too little Viceroy" in that rule. Wonder was always quoting "His Excellency." It was "His Excellency this," "His Excellency that," "In the opinion of His Excellency," and so on. The Viceroy smiled; but he did not heed. He said that, so long as his old men squabbled with his "dear, good Wonder," they might be induced to leave the Immemorial East in peace.

"No wise man has a Policy," said the Viceroy. "A Policy is the blackmail levied on the Fool by the Unforeseen. I am not the former, and I do not believe in the latter."

I do not quite see what this means, unless it refers to an Insurance Policy. Perhaps it was the Viceroy's way of saying, "Lie low."

That season, came up to Simla one of these crazy people with only a single idea. These are the men who make things move; but they are not nice to talk to. This man's name was Mellish, and he had lived for fifteen years on land of his own, in Lower Bengal, studying cholera. He held that cholera was a germ that propagated itself as it flew through a muggy atmosphere; and stuck in the branches of trees like a wool-flake. The germ could be rendered sterile, he said, by "Mellish's Own Invincible Fumigatory"—a heavy violet-black powder—"the result of fifteen years' scientific investigation, Sir!"

Inventors seem very much alike as a caste. They talk loudly, especially about "conspiracies of monopolists"; they beat upon the table with their fists; and they secrete fragments of their inventions about their persons.

Mellish said that there was a Medical "Ring" at Simla, headed by the Surgeon-General, who was in league, apparently, with all the Hospital Assistants in the Empire. I forget exactly how he proved it, but it had something to do with "skulking up to the Hills"; and what Mellish wanted was the independent evidence of the Viceroy—"Steward of our Most Gracious Majesty the Queen, Sir." So Mellish went up to Simla, with eighty-four pounds of Fumigatory in his trunk, to speak to the Viceroy and to show him the merits of the invention.

But it is easier to see a Viceroy than to talk to him, unless you chance to be as important as Mellishe of Madras. He was a six-thousand-rupee man, so great that his daughters never "married." They "contracted alliances." He himself was not paid. He "received emoluments," and his journeys about the country were "tours of observation." His business was to stir up the people in Madras with a long pole—as you stir up tench in a pond—and the people had to come up out of their comfortable old ways and gasp—"This is Enlightenment and Progress. Isn't it fine!" Then they gave Mellishe statues and jasmine garlands, in the hope of getting rid of him.

Mellishe came up to Simla "to confer with the Viceroy." That was one of his perquisites. The Viceroy knew nothing of Mellishe except that he was "one of those middle-class deities who seem necessary to the spiritual comfort of this Paradise of the Middle-classes," and that, in all probability, he had "suggested, designed, founded, and endowed all the public institutions in Madras." Which proves that His Excellency, though dreamy, had experience of the ways of six-thousand-rupee men.

Mellishe's name was E. Mellishe, and Mellish's was E. S. Mellish, and they were both staying at the same hotel, and the Fate that looks after the Indian Empire ordained that Wonder should blunder and drop the final "*e*"; that the Chaprassi should help him, and that the note which ran—

"DEAR MR. MELLISH—Can you set aside your other engagements, and lunch with us at two to-morrow? His Excellency has an hour at your disposal then,"

should be given to Mellish with the Fumigatory. He nearly wept with pride and delight, and at the appointed hour cantered to Peterhoff, a big paper-bag full of the Fumigatory in his coat-tail pockets. He had his chance, and he meant to make the most of it. Mellishe of Madras had been so portentously solemn about his "conference," that Wonder had arranged for a private tiffin—no A.-D.-C.'s, no Wonder, no one but the Viceroy, who said plaintively that he feared being left alone with unmuzzled autocrats like the great Mellishe of Madras.

But his guest did not bore the Viceroy. On the contrary, he amused him. Mellish was nervously anxious to go straight to his Fumigatory, and talked at random until tiffin was over and His Excellency asked him to smoke. The Viceroy was pleased with Mellish because he did not talk "shop."

As soon as the cheroots were lighted, Mellish spoke like a man; beginning with his cholera-theory, reviewing his fifteen years' "scientific labors," the machinations of the "Simla Ring," and the excellence of his Fumigatory, while the Viceroy watched him between half-shut eyes and thought—"Evidently this is the wrong tiger; but it is an original animal." Mellish's hair was standing on end with excitement, and he stammered. He began groping in his coat-tails and, before the Viceroy knew what was about to happen, he had tipped a bagful of his powder into the big silver ash-tray.

"J-j-judge for yourself, Sir," said Mellish. "Y' Excellency shall judge for yourself! Absolutely infallible, on my honor."

He plunged the lighted end of his cigar into the powder, which began to smoke like a volcano, and send up fat, greasy wreaths of copper-colored smoke. In five seconds the room was filled with a most pungent and sickening stench—a reek that took fierce hold of the trap of your windpipe and shut it. The powder hissed and fizzed, and sent out blue and green sparks, and the smoke rose till you could neither see, nor breathe, nor gasp. Mellish, however, was used to it.

"Nitrate of strontia," he shouted; "baryta, bone-meal, *et cetera!* Thousand cubic feet smoke per cubic inch. Not a germ could live—not a germ, Y' Excellency!"

But His Excellency had fled, and was coughing at the foot of the stairs, while all Peterhoff hummed like a hive. Red Lancers came in, and the head Chaprassi who speaks English came in, and mace-bearers came in, and ladies ran downstairs screaming "Fire"; for the smoke was drifting through the house and oozing out of the windows, and bellying along the verandas, and wreathing and writhing across the gardens. No one could enter the room where Mellish was lecturing on his Fumigatory, till that unspeakable powder had burned itself out.

Then an Aid-de-Camp, who desired the V. C., rushed through the rolling clouds and hauled Mellish into the hall. The Viceroy was prostrate with laughter, and could only waggle his hands feebly at Mellish, who was shaking a fresh bagful of powder at him.

"Glorious! Glorious!" sobbed His Excellency. "Not a germ, as you justly observe, could exist! I can swear it. A magnificent success!"

Then he laughed till the tears came, and Wonder, who had caught the real Mellishe snorting on the Mall, entered and was deeply shocked at the scene. But the Viceroy was delighted, because he saw that Wonder would presently depart. Mellish with the Fumigatory was also pleased, for he felt that he had smashed the Simla Medical "Ring."

. . . .

Few men could tell a story like His Excellency when he took the trouble, and his account of "my dear, good Wonder's friend with the powder" went the round of Simla, and flippant folk made Wonder unhappy by their remarks.

But His Excellency told the tale once too often—for Wonder. As he meant to do. It was at a Seepee Picnic. Wonder was sitting just behind the Viceroy.

"And I really thought for a moment," wound up His Excellency, "that my dear good Wonder had hired an assassin to clear his way to the throne!"

Every one laughed; but there was a delicate sub-tinkle in the Viceroy's tone which Wonder understood. He found that his health was giving way; and the Viceroy allowed him to go, and presented him with a flaming "character" for use at Home among big people.

"My fault entirely," said His Excellency, in after seasons, with a twinkle in his eye. "My inconsistency must always have been distasteful to such a masterly man."

KIDNAPPED

There is a tide in the affairs of men,
Which, taken any way you please, is bad,
And strands them in forsaken guts and creeks
No decent soul would think of visiting.
You cannot stop the tide; but, now and then,
You may arrest some rash adventurer
Who—h'm—will hardly thank you for your pains.
—*Vibart's Moralities*

We are a high-caste and enlightened race, and infant-marriage is very shocking and the consequences are sometimes peculiar; but, nevertheless, the Hindoo notion—which is the Continental notion, which is the aboriginal notion—of arranging marriages irrespective of the personal inclinations of the married, is sound. Think for a minute, and you will see that it must be so; unless, of course, you believe in "affinities." In which case you had better not read this tale. How can a man who has never married; who cannot be trusted to pick up at sight a moderately sound horse; whose head is hot and upset with visions of domestic felicity, go about the choosing of a wife? He cannot see straight or think straight if he tries; and the same disadvantages exist in the case of a girl's fancies. But when mature, married, and discreet people arrange a match between a boy and a girl, they do it sensibly, with a view to the future, and the young couple live happily ever afterward. As everybody knows.

Properly speaking, Government should establish a Matrimonial Department, efficiently officered, with a Jury of Matrons, a Judge of the Chief Court, a Senior Chaplain, and an Awful Warning, in the shape of a love-match that has gone wrong, chained to the trees in the courtyard. All marriages should be made through the Department, which might be subordinate to the Educational Department, under the same penalty as that attaching to the transfer of land without a stamped document. But Government won't take suggestions. It pretends that it is too busy. However, I will put my notion on record, and explain the example that illustrates the theory.

Once upon a time, there was a good young man—a first-class officer in his own Department—a man with a career before him and, possibly, a K.C.I.E. at the end of it. All his superiors spoke well of him, because he knew how to hold his tongue and his pen at the proper times. There are, to-day, only eleven men in India who possess this secret; and they have all, with one exception, attained great honor and enormous incomes.

This good young man was quiet and self-contained—too old for his years by far. Which always carries its own punishment. Had a Subaltern, or a Tea-Planter's Assistant, or anybody who enjoys life and has no care for to-morrow, done what he tried to do, not a soul would have cared. But when Peythroppe—the estimable, virtuous, economical, quiet, hard-working, young Peythroppe—fell, there was a flutter through five Departments.

The manner of his fall was in this way. He met a Miss Castries—d'Castries it was originally, but the family dropped the d' for administrative reasons—and he fell in love with her even more energetically than he worked. Understand clearly that there was not a breath of a word to be said against Miss Castries—not a shadow of a breath. She was good and very lovely—possessed what innocent people at Home call a "Spanish" complexion, with thick blue-black hair growing low down on the forehead, into a "widow's peak," and big violet eyes under eyebrows as black and as straight as the borders of a "Gazette Extraordinary," when a big man dies. But—but—but—Well, she was a *very* sweet girl and very pious, but for many reasons she was "impossible." Quite so. All good Mammas know what "impossible" means. It was obviously absurd that Peythroppe should marry her. The little opal-tinted onyx at the base of her finger-nails said this as plainly as print. Further, marriage with Miss Castries meant marriage with several other Castries — Honorary Lieutenant Castries her Papa, Mrs. Eulalie Castries her Mamma, and all the ramifications of the Castries family, on incomes ranging from Rs.175 to Rs.470 a month, and *their* wives and connections again.

It would have been cheaper for Peythroppe to have assaulted a Commissioner with a dog-whip, or to have burned the records of a Deputy-Commissioner's Office, than to have contracted an alliance with the Castries. It would have weighted his after-career less—even under a Government which never forgets and *never* forgives. Everybody saw this but Peythroppe. He was going to marry Miss Castries, he was—being of age and drawing a good income—and woebetide the house that would not afterward receive Mrs. Virginie Saulez Peythroppe with the deference due to her husband's rank. That was Peythroppe's ultimatum, and any remonstrance drove him frantic.

These sudden madnesses most afflict the sanest men. There was a case once—but I will tell you of that later on. You cannot account for the mania except under a theory directly contradicting the one about the Place wherein marriages are made. Peythroppe was burningly anxious to put a millstone round his neck at the outset of his career; and argument had not the least effect on him. He was going to marry Miss Castries, and the business was his own business. He would thank you to keep your advice to yourself. With a man in this condition, mere words only fix him in his purpose. Of course he cannot see that marriage in India does not concern the individual but the Government he serves.

Do you remember Mrs. Hauksbee—the most wonderful woman in India? She saved Pluffles from Mrs. Reiver, won Tarrion his appointment in the Foreign Office, and was defeated in open field by Mrs. Cusack-Bremmil. She heard of the lamentable condition of Peythroppe, and her brain struck out the plan that saved him. She had the wisdom of the

Serpent, the logical coherence of the Man, the fearlessness of the Child, and the triple intuition of the Woman. Never—no, never—as long as a tonga buckets down the Solon dip, or the couples go a-riding at the back of Summer Hill, will there be such a genius as Mrs. Hauksbee. She attended the consultation of Three Men on Peythroppe's case; and she stood up with the lash of her riding-whip between her lips and spake.

. . . .

Three weeks later, Peythroppe dined with the Three Men, and the "Gazette of India" came in. Peythroppe found to his surprise that he had been gazetted a month's leave. Don't ask me how this was managed. I believe firmly that, if Mrs. Hauksbee gave the order, the whole Great Indian Administration would stand on its head. The Three Men had also a month's leave each. Peythroppe put the "Gazette" down and said bad words. Then there came from the compound the soft "pad-pad" of camels—"thieves' camels," the Bikaneer breed that don't bubble and howl when they sit down and get up.

After that, I don't know what happened. This much is certain. Peythroppe disappeared—vanished like smoke—and the long foot-rest chair in the house of the Three Men was broken to splinters. Also a bedstead departed from one of the bedrooms.

Mrs. Hauksbee said that Mr. Peythroppe was shooting in Rajputana with the Three Men; so we were compelled to believe her.

At the end of the month, Peythroppe was gazetted twenty days' extension of leave; but there was wrath and lamentation in the house of Castries. The marriage-day had been fixed, but the bridegroom never came: and the D'Silvas, Pereiras, and Ducketts lifted their voices and mocked Honorary Lieutenant Castries as one who had been basely imposed upon. Mrs. Hauksbee went to the wedding, and was much astonished when Peythroppe did not appear. After seven weeks, Peythroppe and the Three Men returned from

Rajputana. Peythroppe was in hard tough condition, rather white, and more self-contained than ever.

One of the Three Men had a cut on his nose, caused by the kick of a gun. Twelve-bores kick rather curiously.

Then came Honorary Lieutenant Castries, seeking for the blood of his perfidious son-in-law to be. He said things—vulgar and "impossible" things which showed the raw rough "ranker" below the "Honorary," and I fancy Peythroppe's eyes were opened. Anyhow, he held his peace till the end; when he spoke briefly. Honorary Lieutenant Castries asked for a "peg" before he went away to die or bring a suit for breach of promise.

Miss Castries was a *very* good girl. She said that she would have no breach of promise suits. She said that, if she was not a lady, she was refined enough to know that ladies kept their broken hearts to themselves; and, as she ruled her parents, nothing happened. Later on, she married a most respectable and gentlemanly person. He traveled for an enterprising firm in Calcutta, and was all that a good husband should be.

So Peythroppe came to his right mind again, and did much good work, and was honored by all who knew him. One of these days he will marry; but he will marry a sweet pink-and-white maiden, on the Government House List, with a little money and some influential connections, as every wise man should. And he will never, all his life, tell her what happened during the seven weeks of his shooting-tour in Rajputana.

But just think how much trouble and expense—for camel-hire is not cheap, and those Bikaneer brutes had to be fed like humans—might have been saved by a properly conducted Matrimonial Department, under the control of the Director-General of Education, but corresponding direct with the Viceroy.

THE ARREST OF LIEUTENANT GOLIGHTLY

"I've forgotten the countersign," sez 'e.

"Oh! You 'ave, 'ave you?" sez I.

"But I'm the Colonel," sez 'e.

"Oh! You are, are you?" sez I. "Colonel nor no Colonel, you waits 'ere till I'm relieved, an' the Sargint reports on your ugly old mug. *Choop!*" sez I.

. . . .

An' s'elp me soul, 'twas the Colonel after all! But I was a recruity then.—*The Unedited Autobiography of Private Ortheris*

If there was one thing on which Golightly prided himself more than another, it was looking like "an Officer and a Gentleman." He said it was for the honor of the Service that he attired himself so elaborately; but those who knew him best said that it was just personal vanity. There was no harm about Golightly—not an ounce. He recognized a horse when he saw one, and could do more than fill a cantle. He played a very fair game at billiards, and was a sound man at the whist-table. Every one liked him; and nobody ever dreamed of seeing him handcuffed on a station platform as a deserter. But this sad thing happened.

He was going down from Dalhousie, at the end of his leave—riding down. He had run his leave as fine as he dared, and wanted to come down in a hurry.

It was fairly warm at Dalhousie, and, knowing what to expect below, he descended in a new *khaki* suit—tight fitting—of a delicate olive-green; a peacock-blue tie, white collar, and a snowy white *solah* helmet. He prided himself on looking neat even when he was riding post. He did look neat, and he was so deeply concerned about his appearance before he started that he quite forgot to take anything but some small change with him. He left all his notes at the hotel. His servants had gone down the road before him, to be ready in waiting at Pathankote with a change of gear. That was what he called traveling in "light marching-order." He was proud of his faculty of organization—what we call *bundobust*.

Twenty-two miles out of Dalhousie it began to rain—not a mere hill-shower, but a good, tepid, monsoonish downpour. Golightly bustled on, wishing that he had brought an umbrella. The dust on the roads turned into mud, and the pony mired a good deal. So did Golightly's *khaki* gaiters. But he kept on steadily and tried to think how pleasant the coolth was.

His next pony was rather a brute at starting, and, Golightly's hands being slippery with the rain, contrived to get rid of Golightly at a corner. He chased the animal, caught it, and went ahead briskly. The spill had not improved his clothes or his temper, and he had lost one spur. He kept the other one employed. By the time that stage was ended, the pony had had as much exercise as he wanted, and, in spite of the rain, Golightly was sweating freely. At the end of another miserable half hour Golightly found the world disappear before his eyes in clammy pulp. The rain had turned the pith of his huge and snowy *solah-topee* into an evil-smelling dough, and it had closed on his head like a half-opened mushroom. Also the green lining was beginning to run.

Golightly did not say anything worth recording here. He tore off and squeezed up as much of the brim as was in his eyes and plowed on. The back of the helmet was flapping on his neck and the sides stuck to his ears, but the leather band and green lining kept things roughly together, so that the hat did not actually melt away where it flapped.

Presently, the pulp and the green stuff made a sort of slimy mildew which ran over Golightly in several directions—down his back and bosom for choice. The *khaki* color ran too—it was really shockingly bad dye—and sections of Golightly were brown, and patches were violet, and contours were ocher, and streaks were ruddy-red, and blotches were nearly white, according to the nature and peculiarities of the dye. When he took out his handkerchief to wipe his face, and the green of the hat-lining and the purple stuff that had soaked through on to his neck from the tie became thoroughly mixed, the effect was amazing.

Near Dhar the rain stopped and the evening sun came out and dried him up slightly. It fixed the colors, too. Three miles from Pathankote the last pony fell dead lame, and Golightly was forced to walk. He pushed on into Pathankote to find his servants. He did not know then that his *khitmatgar* had stopped by the roadside to get drunk, and would come on the next day saying that he had sprained his ankle. When he got into Pathankote he couldn't find his servants, his boots were stiff and ropy with mud, and there were large quantities of dust about his body. The blue tie had run as much as the *khaki*. So he took it off with the collar and threw it away. Then he said something about servants generally and tried to get a peg. He paid eight annas for the drink, and this revealed to him that he had only six annas more in his pocket—or in the world as he stood at that hour.

He went to the Station-Master to negotiate for a first-class ticket to Khasa, where he was stationed. The booking-clerk said something to the Station-Master, the Station-Master said something to the Telegraph Clerk, and the three looked at him with curiosity. They asked him to wait for half an hour, while they telegraphed to Umritsar for authority. So he waited and four constables came and grouped themselves picturesquely round him. Just as he was preparing to ask them to go away, the Station-Master said that he would give the *Sahib* a ticket to Umritsar, if the *Sahib* would kindly come inside the booking-office. Golightly stepped inside, and the next thing he knew was that a constable was attached to each of his legs and arms, while the Station-Master was trying to cram a mail-bag over his head.

There was a very fair scuffle all round the booking-office,

and Golightly took a nasty cut over his eye through falling against a table. But the constables were too much for him, and they and the Station-Master handcuffed him securely. As soon as the mail-bag was slipped, he began expressing his opinions, and the head constable said, "Without doubt this is the soldier-Englishman we required. Listen to the abuse!" Then Golightly asked the Station-Master what the this and the that the proceedings meant. The Station-Master told him he was "Private John Binkle of the —— Regiment, 5 ft. 9 in., fair hair, gray eyes, and a dissipated appearance, no marks on the body," who had deserted a fortnight ago. Golightly began explaining at great length; and the more he explained the less the Station-Master believed him. He said that no Lieutenant could look such a ruffian as did Golightly, and that his instructions were to send his capture under proper escort to Umritsar. Golightly was feeling very damp and uncomfortable and the language he used was not fit for publication, even in an expurgated form. The four constables saw him safe to Umritsar in an "intermediate" compartment, and he spent the four-hour journey in abusing them as fluently as his knowledge of the vernaculars allowed.

At Umritsar he was bundled out on the platform into the arms of a Corporal and two men of the —— Regiment. Golightly drew himself up and tried to carry off matters jauntily. He did not feel too jaunty in handcuffs, with four constables behind him, and the blood from the cut on his forehead stiffening on his left cheek. The Corporal was not jocular either. Golightly got as far as—"This is a very absurd mistake, my men," when the Corporal told him to "stow his lip" and come along. Golightly did not want to come along. He desired to stop and explain. He explained very well indeed, until the Corporal cut in with—"*You* a orficer! It's the like o' *you* as brings disgrace on the likes of *us*. Bloomin' fine orficer you are! I know your regiment. The Rogue's March is the quickstep where you come from. You're a black shame to the Service."

Golightly kept his temper, and began explaining all over

again from the beginning. Then he was marched out of the rain into the refreshment-room and told not to make a qualified fool of himself. The men were going to run him up to Fort Govindghar. And "running up" is a performance almost as undignified as the Frog March.

Golightly was nearly hysterical with rage and the chill and the mistake and the handcuffs and the headache that the cut on his forehead had given him. He really laid himself out to express what was in his mind. When he had quite finished and his throat was feeling dry, one of the men said, "I've 'eard a few beggars in the clink blind, stiff and crack on a bit; but I've never 'eard any one to touch this ere 'orficer.'" They were not angry with him. They rather admired him. They had some beer at the refreshment-room, and offered Golightly some too, because he had "swore won'erful." They asked him to tell them all about the adventures of Private John Binkle while he was loose on the country-side; and that made Golightly wilder than ever. If he had kept his wits about him he would have been quiet until an officer came; but he attempted to run.

Now the butt of a Martini in the small of your back hurts a great deal, and rotten, rain-soaked *khaki* tears easily when two men are jerking at your collar.

Golightly rose from the floor feeling very sick and giddy, with his shirt ripped open all down his breast and nearly all down his back. He yielded to his luck, and at that point the down-train from Lahore came in, carrying one of Golightly's Majors.

This is the Major's evidence in full—

"There was the sound of a scuffle in the second-class refreshment-room, so I went in and saw the most villainous loafer that I ever set eyes on. His boots and breeches were plastered with mud and beer-stains. He wore a muddy-white dunghill sort of thing on his head, and it hung down in slips on his shoulders which were a good deal scratched. He was half in and half out of a shirt as nearly in two pieces as it could be, and he was begging the guard to look at the name on the tail of it. As he had rucked the shirt all over his head, I couldn't at first see who he was, but I fancied that he was a man in the first stage of D. T. from the way he swore while he wrestled with his rags. When he turned round, and I had made allowances for a lump as big as a pork-pie over one eye, and some green war-paint on the face, and some violet stripes round the neck, I saw that it was Golightly. He was very glad to see me,' said the Major, "and he hoped I would not tell the Mess about it. *I* didn't, but you can, if you like, now that Golightly has gone Home."

Golightly spent the greater part of that summer in trying to get the Corporal and the two soldiers tried by Court-Martial for arresting an "officer and a gentleman." They were, of course, very sorry for their error. But the tale leaked into the regimental canteen, and thence ran about the Province.

IN THE HOUSE OF SUDDHOO

A stone's throw out on either hand
From that well-ordered road we tread,
And all the world is wild and strange:
Churel and ghoul and *Djinn* and sprite
Shall bear us company to-night,
For we have reached the Oldest Land
Wherein the Powers of Darkness range.

—*From the Dusk to the Dawn*

THE house of Suddhoo, near the Taksali Gate, is two-storied, with four carved windows of old brown wood, and a flat roof. You may recognize it by five red hand-prints arranged like the Five of Diamonds on the whitewash between the upper windows. Bhagwan Dass the grocer and a man who says he gets his living by seal-cutting live in the lower story with a troop of wives, servants, friends, and retainers. The two upper rooms used to be occupied by Janoo and Azizun and a little black-and-tan terrier that was stolen from an Englishman's house and given to Janoo by a soldier. To-day, only Janoo lives in the upper rooms. Suddhoo sleeps on the roof generally, except when he sleeps in the street. He used to go to Peshawar in the cold weather to visit his son, who sells curiosities near the Edwardes' Gate, and then he slept under a real mud roof. Suddhoo is a great friend of mine, because his cousin had a son who secured, thanks to my recommendation, the post of head-messenger to a big firm in the Station. Suddhoo says that God will make me a Lieutenant-Governor one of these days. I daresay his prophecy will come true. He is very, very old, with white hair and no teeth worth showing, and he has outlived his wits—outlived nearly everything except his fondness for his son at Peshawar. Janoo and Azizun are Kashmiris, Ladies of the City, and theirs was an ancient and more or less honorable profession; but Azizun has since married a medical student from the North-West and has settled down to a most respectable life somewhere near Bareilly. Bhagwan Dass is an extortionate and an adulterator. He is very rich. The man who is supposed to get his living by seal-cutting pretends to be very poor. This lets you know as much as is necessary of the four principal tenants in the house of Suddhoo. Then there is Me of course; but I am only the chorus that comes in at the end to explain things. So I do not count.

Suddhoo was not clever. The man who pretended to cut seals was the cleverest of them all—Bhagwan Dass only knew how to lie—except Janoo. She was also beautiful, but that was her own affair.

Suddhoo's son at Peshawar was attacked by pleurisy, and old Suddhoo was troubled. The seal-cutter man heard of Suddhoo's anxiety and made capital out of it. He was abreast of the times. He got a friend in Peshawar to telegraph daily accounts of the son's health. And here the story begins.

Suddhoo's cousin's son told me, one evening, that Suddhoo wanted to see me; that he was too old and feeble to come personally, and that I should be conferring an everlasting honor on the House of Suddhoo if I went to him. I went; but I think, seeing how well off Suddhoo was then, that he might have sent something better than an *ekka*, which jolted fearfully, to haul out a future Lieutenant-Governor to the City on a muggy April evening. The *ekka* did not run quickly. It was full dark when we pulled up opposite the door of Ranjit Singh's Tomb near the main gate of the Fort. Here was Suddhoo, and he said that, by reason of my condescension, it was absolutely certain that I should become a Lieutenant-Governor while my hair was yet black. Then we talked about the weather and the state of my health, and the wheat crops, for fifteen minutes, in the Huzuri Bagh, under the stars.

Suddhoo came to the point at last. He said that Janoo had told him that there was an order of the *Sirkar* against magic, because it was feared that magic might one day kill the Empress of India. I didn't know anything about the state of the law; but I fancied that something interesting was going to happen. I said that so far from magic being discouraged by the Government it was highly commended. The greatest officials of the State practiced it themselves. (If the Financial Statement isn't magic, I don't know what is.) Then, to encourage him further, I said that, if there was any *jadoo* afoot, I had not the least objection to giving it my countenance and sanction, and to seeing that it was clean *jadoo*—white magic, as distinguished from the unclean *jadoo* which kills folk. It took a long time before Suddhoo admitted that this was just what he had asked me to come for. Then he told me, in jerks and quavers, that the man who said he cut seals was a sorcerer of the cleanest kind; that every day he gave Suddhoo news of the sick son in Peshawar more quickly than the lightning could fly, and that this news was always corroborated by the letters. Further, that he had told Suddhoo how a great danger was threatening his son, which could be removed by clean *jadoo;* and, of course, heavy payment. I began to see exactly how the land lay, and told Suddhoo that I also understood a little *jadoo* in the

Western line, and would go to his house to see that everything was done decently and in order. We set off together; and on the way Suddhoo told me that he had paid the seal-cutter between one hundred and two hundred rupees already; and the *jadoo* of that night would cost two hundred more. Which was cheap, he said, considering the greatness of his son's danger; but I do not think he meant it.

The lights were all cloaked in the front of the house when we arrived. I could hear awful noises from behind the seal-cutter's shop-front, as if some one were groaning his soul out. Suddhoo shook all over, and while we groped our way upstairs told me that the *jadoo* had begun. Janoo and Azizun met us at the stair-head, and told us that the *jadoo*-work was coming off in their rooms, because there was more space there. Janoo is a lady of a freethinking turn of mind. She whispered that the *jadoo* was an invention to get money out of Suddhoo, and that the seal-cutter would go to a hot place when he died. Suddhoo was nearly crying with fear and old age. He kept walking up and down the room in the half-light, repeating his son's name over and over again, and asking Azizun if the seal-cutter ought not to make a reduction in the case of his own landlord. Janoo pulled me over to the shadow in the recess of the carved bow-windows. The boards were up, and the rooms were only lit by one tiny oil-lamp. There was no chance of my being seen if I stayed still.

Presently, the groans below ceased, and we heard steps on the staircase. That was the seal-cutter. He stopped outside the door as the terrier barked and Azizun fumbled at the chain, and he told Suddhoo to blow out the lamp. This left the place in jet darkness, except for the red glow from the two *huqas* that belonged to Janoo and Azizun. The seal-cutter came in, and I heard Suddhoo throw himself down on the floor and groan. Azizun caught her breath, and Janoo backed on to one of the beds with a shudder. There was a clink of something metallic, and then shot up a pale blue-green flame near the ground. The light was just enough to show Azizun, pressed against one corner of the room with the terrier between her knees; Janoo, with her hands clasped, leaning forward as she sat on the bed; Suddhoo, face down, quivering, and the seal-cutter.

I hope I may never see another man like that seal-cutter. He was stripped to the waist, with a wreath of white jasmine as thick as my wrist round his forehead, a salmon colored loin-cloth round his middle, and a steel bangle on each ankle. This was not awe-inspiring. It was the face of the man that turned me cold. It was blue-gray in the first place. In the second, the eyes were rolled back till you could only see the whites of them; and, in the third, the face was the face of a demon—a ghoul—anything you please except of the sleek, oily old ruffian who sat in the daytime over his turning-lathe downstairs. He was lying on his stomach with his arms turned and crossed behind him, as if he had been thrown down pinioned. His head and neck were the only parts of him off the floor. They were nearly at right angles to the body, like the head of a cobra at spring. It was ghastly. In the center of the room, on the bare earth floor, stood a big, deep, brass basin, with a pale blue-green light floating in the center like a night-light. Round that basin the man on the floor wriggled himself three times. How he did it I do not know. I could see the muscles ripple along his spine and fall smooth again; but I could not see any other motion. The head seemed the only thing alive about him, except that slow curl and uncurl of the laboring back-muscles. Janoo from the bed was breathing seventy to the minute; Azizun held her hands before her eyes; and old Suddhoo, fingering at the dirt that had got into his white beard, was crying to himself. The horror of it was that the creeping, crawly thing made no sound—only crawled! And, remember, this lasted for ten minutes, while the terrier whined, and Azizun shuddered, and Janoo gasped, and Suddhoo cried.

I felt the hair lift at the back of my head, and my heart thump like a thermantidote paddle. Luckily, the seal-cutter betrayed himself by his most impressive trick and made me calm again. After he had finished that unspeakable triple-crawl, he stretched his head away from the floor as high as he could, and sent out a jet of fire from his nostrils. Now I knew how fire-spouting is done—I can do it myself—so I felt at ease. The business was a fraud. If he had only kept to that crawl without trying to raise the effect, goodness knows what I might not have thought. Both the girls shrieked at the jet of fire and the head dropped, chin-down on the floor, with a thud; the whole body lying then like a corpse with its arms trussed. There was a pause of five full minutes after this, and the blue-green flame died down. Janoo stooped to settle one of her anklets, while Azizun turned her face to the wall and took the terrier in her arms. Suddhoo put out an arm mechanically to Janoo's *huqa*, and she slid it across the floor with her foot. Directly above the body and on the wall, were a couple of flaming portraits, in stamped-paper frames, of the Queen and the Prince of Wales. They looked down on the performance, and, to my thinking, seemed to heighten the grotesqueness of it all.

Just when the silence was getting unendurable, the body turned over and rolled away from the basin to the side of the room, where it lay stomach-up. There was a faint "plop" from the basin—exactly like the noise a fish makes when it takes a fly—and the green light in the center revived.

I looked at the basin, and saw, bobbing in the water, the dried, shriveled, black head of a native baby—open eyes, open mouth, and shaved scalp. It was worse, being so very sudden, than the crawling exhibition. We had no time to say anything before it began to speak.

Read Poe's account of the voice that came from the mesmerized dying man, and you will realize less than one half of the horror of that head's voice.

There was an interval of a second or two between each word, and a sort of "ring, ring, ring," in the note of the voice, like the timbre of a bell. It pealed slowly, as if talking to itself, for several minutes before I got rid of my cold sweat. Then the blessed solution struck me. I looked at the body lying near the doorway, and saw, just where the hollow of the throat joins on the shoulders, a muscle that had nothing to do with any man's regular breathing twitching away steadily. The whole thing was a careful reproduction of the Egyptian teraphin that one reads about sometimes; and the voice was as clever and as appalling a piece of ventriloquism as one could wish to hear. All this time the head was "lip-lip-lapping" against the side of the basin, and speaking. It told Suddhoo, on his face again whining, of his son's illness and of the state of the illness up to the evening of that very night. I always shall respect the seal-cutter for keeping so faithfully to the time of the Peshawar telegrams. It went on to say that skilled doctors were night and day watching over the man's life; and that he would eventually recover if the fee to the potent sorcerer, whose servant was the head in the basin, were doubled.

Here the mistake from the artistic point of view came in. To ask for twice your stipulated fee in a voice that Lazarus might have used when he rose from the dead, is absurd. Janoo, who is really a woman of masculine intellect, saw this as quickly as I did. I heard her say, "Asli nahin! Fareib!" scornfully under her breath; and just as she said so, the light in the basin died out, the head stopped talking, and we heard the room door creak on its hinges. Then Janoo struck a match, lighted the lamp, and we saw that head, basin, and seal-cutter were gone. Suddhoo was wringing his hands and explaining to any one who cared to listen, that, if his chances of eternal salvation depended on it, he could not raise another two hundred rupees. Azizun was nearly in hysterics in the corner; while Janoo sat down composedly on one of the beds to discuss the probabilities of the whole thing being a *bunao*, or "make-up."

I explained as much as I knew of the seal-cutter's way of *jadoo;* but her argument was much more simple—"The magic that is always demanding gifts is no true magic," said she. "My mother told me that the only potent love-spells are those which are told you for love. This seal-cutter man is a liar and a devil. I dare not tell, do anything, or get anything done, because I am in debt to Bhagwan Dass the bunnia for two gold rings and a heavy anklet. I must get my food from his shop. The seal-cutter is the friend of Bhagwan Dass, and he would poison my food. A fool's *jadoo* has been going on for ten days, and has cost Suddhoo many rupees each night. The seal-cutter used black hens and lemons and *mantras* before. He never showed us anything like this till to-night. Azizun is a fool, and will be a *purdahnashin* soon. Suddhoo has lost his strength and his wits. See now! I had hoped to get from Suddhoo many rupees while he lived, and many more after his death; and behold, he is spending everything on that offspring of a devil and a she-ass, the seal-cutter!"

Here I said, "But what induced Suddhoo to drag me into the business? Of course I can speak to the seal-cutter, and he shall refund. The whole thing is child's talk—shame—and senseless."

"Suddhoo *is* an old child," said Janoo. "He has lived on the roofs these seventy years and is as senseless as a milch-goat. He brought you here to assure himself that he was not breaking any law of the *Sirkar*, whose salt he ate many years ago. He worships the dust off the feet of the seal-cutter, and that cow-devourer has forbidden him to go and see his son. What does Suddhoo know of your laws or the lightning-post? I have to watch his money going day by day to that lying beast below."

Janoo stamped her foot on the floor and nearly cried with vexation; while Suddhoo was whimpering under a banket in the corner, and Azizun was trying to guide the pipe-stem to his foolish old mouth.

. . . .

Now, the case stands thus. Unthinkingly, I have laid myself open to the charge of aiding and abetting the seal-cutter in obtaining money under false pretenses, which is forbidden by Section 420 of the Indian Penal Code. I am helpless in the matter for these reasons. I cannot inform the Police. What witnesses would support my statements? Janoo refuses flatly, and Azizun is a veiled woman somewhere near Bareilly—lost in this big India of ours. I dare not again take the law into my own hands, and speak to the seal-cutter; for certain am I that, not only would Suddhoo disbelieve me, but this step would end in the poisoning of Janoo, who is bound hand and foot by her debt to the *bunnia*. Suddhoo is an old dotard; and whenever we meet mumbles my idiotic joke that the *Sirkar* rather patronizes the Black Art than otherwise. His son is well now; but Suddhoo is completely under the influence of the seal-cutter, by whose advice he regulates the affairs of his life. Janoo watches daily the money that she hoped to wheedle out of Suddhoo taken by the seal-cutter, and becomes daily more furious and sullen.

She will never tell, because she dare not; but, unless something happens to prevent her, I am afraid that the seal-cutter will die of cholera—the white arsenic kind—about the middle of May. And thus I shall be privy to a murder in the House of Suddhoo.

HIS WEDDED WIFE

Cry "Murder!" in the market-place, and each
Will turn upon his neighbor anxious eyes
That ask—"Art thou the man?" We hunted Cain,
Some centuries ago, across the world.
That bred the fear our own misdeeds maintain
To-day.—*Vibart's Moralities*

SHAKESPEARE says something about worms, or it may be giants or beetles, turning if you tread on them too severely. The safest plan is never to tread on a worm—not even on the last new subaltern from Home, with his buttons hardly out of their tissue-paper, and the red of sappy English beef in his cheeks. This is a story of the worm that turned. For the sake of brevity, we will call Henry Augustus Ramsay Faizanne, "The Worm," though he really was an exceedingly pretty boy, without a hair on his face, and with a waist like a girl's, when he came out to the Second "Shikarris" and was made unhappy in several ways. The "Shikarris" are a high-caste regiment, and you must be able to do things well—play a banjo, or ride more than little, or sing, or act—to get on with them.

The Worm did nothing except fall off his pony, and knock chips out of gate-posts with his trap. Even that became monotonous after a time. He objected to whist, cut the cloth at billiards, sang out of tune, kept very much to himself, and wrote to his Mamma and sisters at Home. Four of these five things were vices which the "Shikarris" objected to and set themselves to eradicate. Every one knows how subalterns are, by brother subalterns, softened and not permitted to be ferocious. It is good and wholesome, and does no one any harm, unless tempers are lost; and then there is trouble. There was a man once—

The "Shikarris" *shikarred* The Worm very much, and he bore everything without winking. He was so good and so anxious to learn, and flushed so pink, that his education was cut short, and he was left to his own devices by every one except the Senior Subaltern, who continued to make life a burden to The Worm. The Senior Subaltern meant no harm; but his chaff was coarse and he didn't quite understand where to stop. He had been waiting too long for his Company; and that always sours a man. Also he was in love, which made him worse.

One day, after he had borrowed The Worm's trap for a lady who never existed, had used it himself all the afternoon, had sent a note to The Worm, purporting to come from the lady, and was telling the Mess all about it, The Worm rose in his place and said, in his quiet, lady-like voice —"That was a very pretty sell; but I'll lay you a month's pay to a month's pay when you get your step, that I work a sell on you that you'll remember for the rest of your days, and the Regiment after you when you're dead or broke." The Worm wasn't angry in the least, and the rest of the Mess shouted. Then the Senior Subaltern looked at The Worm from the boots upward, and down again, and said—"Done, Baby." The Worm held the rest of the Mess to witness that the bet had been taken, and retired into a book with a sweet smile.

Two months passed, and the Senior Subaltern still educated The Worm, who began to move about a little more as the hot weather came on. I have said that the Senior Subaltern was in love. The curious thing is that a girl was in love with the Senior Subaltern. Though the Colonel said awful things, and the Majors snorted and the married Captains looked unutterable wisdom, and the juniors scoffed, those two were engaged.

The Senior Subaltern was so pleased with getting his Company and his acceptance at the same time that he forgot to bother the Worm. The girl was a pretty girl, and had money of her own. She does not come into this story at all.

One night, at the beginning of the hot weather, all the Mess, except The Worm, who had gone to his own room to write Home letters, were sitting on the platform outside the Mess House. The Band had finished playing, but no one wanted to go in. And the Captains' wives were there also. The folly of a man in love is unlimited. The Senior Subaltern had been holding forth on the merits of the girl he was engaged to, and the ladies were purring approval while the men yawned, when there was a rustle of skirts in the dark, and a tired, faint voice lifted itself.

"Where's my husband?"

I do not wish in the least to reflect on the morality of the "Shikarris"; but it is on record that four men jumped up as if they had been shot. Three of them were married men. Perhaps they were afraid that their wives had come from Home unbeknownst. The fourth said that he had acted on the impulse of the moment. He explained this afterward.

Then the voice cried, "Oh, Lionel!" Lionel was the Senior Subaltern's name. A woman came into the little circle of light by the candles on the peg-tables, stretching out her hands to the dark where the Senior Subaltern was, and sobbing. We rose to our feet, feeling that things were going to happen and ready to believe the worst. In this bad, small world of ours, one knows so little of the life of the next man—which, after all, is entirely his own concern—that one is not surprised when a crash comes. Anything might turn up any day for any one. Perhaps the Senior Subaltern had been trapped in his youth. Men are crippled that way occasionally. We didn't know; we wanted to hear; and the Captains' wives were as anxious as we. If he had been trapped, he was to be excused; for the woman from nowhere, in the dusty shoes and gray traveling-dress, was very lovely, with black hair and great eyes full of tears. She was tall, with a fine figure, and her voice had a running sob in it pitiful to hear. As soon as the Senior Subaltern stood up, she threw her arms round his neck, and called him "my darling," and said she could not bear waiting alone in England, and his letters were so short and cold, and she was his to the end of the world, and would he forgive her? This did not sound quite like a lady's way of speaking. It was too demonstrative.

Things seemed black indeed, and the Captains' wives peered under their eyebrows at the Senior Subaltern, and the Colonel's face set like the Day of Judgment framed in gray bristles, and no one spoke for a while.

Next the Colonel said, very shortly, "Well, Sir?" and the woman sobbed afresh. The Senior Subaltern was half choked with the arms round his neck, but he gasped out—"It's a damned lie! I never had a wife in my life!"—"Don't swear," said the Colonel. "Come into the Mess. We must sift this clear somehow," and he sighed to himself, for he believed in his "Shikarris," did the Colonel.

We trooped into the ante-room, under the full lights, and there we saw how beautiful the woman was. She stood up in the middle of us all, sometimes choking with crying, then hard and proud, and then holding out her arms to the Senior Subaltern. It was like the fourth act of a tragedy. She told us how the Senior Subaltern had married her when he was Home on leave eighteen months before; and she seemed to know all that we knew, and more too, of his people and his past life. He was white and ashy-gray, trying now and again to break into the torrent of her words; and we, noting how lovely she was and what a criminal he looked, esteemed him a beast of the worst kind. We felt sorry for him, though.

I shall never forget the indictment of the Senior Subaltern by his wife. Nor will he. It was so sudden, rushing out of the dark, unannounced, into our dull lives. The Captains' wives stood back; but their eyes were alight, and you could see that they had already convicted and sentenced the Senior Subaltern. The Colonel seemed five years older. One Major was shading his eyes with his hand and watching the woman from underneath it. Another was chewing his mustache and smiling quietly as if he were witnessing a play. Full in the open space in the center, by the whist-tables, the Senior Subaltern's terrier was hunting for fleas. I remember all this as clearly as though a photograph were in my hand. I remember the look of horror on the Senior Subaltern's face. It was rather like seeing a man hanged; but much more interesting. Finally, the woman wound up by saying that the Senior Subaltern carried a double F. M. in tattoo on his left shoulder. We all knew that, and to our innocent minds it seemed to clinch the matter. But one of the bachelor Majors said very politely, "I presume that your marriage-certificate would be more to the purpose?"

That roused the woman. She stood up and sneered at the Senior Subaltern for a cur, and abused the Major and the Colonel and all the rest. Then she wept, and then she pulled a paper from her breast, saying imperially, "Take that! And let my husband—my lawfully wedded husband —read it aloud—if he dare!"

There was a hush, and the men looked into each other's

eyes as the Senior Subaltern came forward in a dazed and dizzy way, and took the paper. We were wondering, as we stared, whether there was anything against any one of us that might turn up later on. The Senior Subaltern's throat was dry; but, as he ran his eye over the paper, he broke out into a hoarse cackle of relief, and said to the woman, "You young blackguard!" But the woman had fled through a door, and on the paper was written, "This is to certify that I, The Worm, have paid in full my debts to the Senior Subaltern, and, further, that the Senior Subaltern is my debtor, by agreement on the 23d of February, as by the Mess attested, to the extent of one month's Captain's pay, in the lawful currency of the Indian Empire."

Then a deputation set off for The Worm's quarters and found him, betwixt and between, unlacing his stays, with the hat, wig, and serge dress, on the bed. He came over as he was, and the "Shikarris" shouted till the Gunners' Mess sent over to know if they might have a share of the fun. I think we were all, except the Colonel and the Senior Subaltern, a little disappointed that the scandal had come to nothing. But that is human nature. There could be no two words about The Worm's acting. It leaned as near to a nasty tragedy as anything this side of a joke can. When most of the Subalterns sat upon him with sofa-cushions to find out why he had not said that acting was his strong point, he answered very quietly, "I don't think you ever asked me. I used to act at Home with my sisters." But no acting with girls could account for The Worm's display that night. Personally, I think it was in bad taste. Besides being dangerous. There is no sort of use in playing with fire, even for fun.

The "Shikarris" made him President of the Regimental Dramatic Club; and, when the Senior Subaltern paid up his debt, which he did at once, The Worm sank the money in scenery and dresses. He was a good Worm; and the "Shikarris" are proud of him. The only drawback is that he has been christened "Mrs. Senior Subaltern"; and, as there are now two Mrs. Senior Subalterns in the Station, this is sometimes confusing to strangers.

Later on, I will tell you of a case something like this, but with all the jest left out and nothing in it but real trouble.

THE BROKEN-LINK HANDICAP

While the snaffle holds, or the long-neck stings,
While the big beam tilts, or the last bell rings,
While horses are horses to train and to race,
Then women and wine take a second place
For me—for me—
While a short "ten-three"
Has a field to squander or fence to face!

—Song of the G. R.

THERE are more ways of running a horse to suit your book than pulling his head off in the straight. Some men forget this. Understand clearly that all racing is rotten—as everything connected with losing money must be. In India, in addition to its inherent rottenness, it has the merit of being two-thirds sham; looking pretty on paper only. Every one knows every one else far too well for business purposes. How on earth can you rack and harry and post a man for his losings, when you are fond of his wife, and live in the same Station with him? He says, "On the Monday following," "I can't settle just yet." You say, "All right, old man," and think yourself lucky if you pull off nine hundred out of a two-thousand-rupee debt. Any way you look at it, Indian racing is immoral, and expensively immoral. Which is much worse. If a man wants your money, he ought to ask for it, or send round a subscription-list, instead of juggling about the country, with an Australian larrikin; a "brumby," with as much breed as the boy; a brace of *chumars* in gold-laced caps; three or four *ekka*-ponies with hogged manes, and a switch-tailed demirep of a mare called Arab because she has a kink in her flag. Racing leads to the *shroff* quicker than anything else. But if you have no conscience and no sentiments, and good hands, and some knowledge of pace, and ten years' experience of horses, and several thousand rupees a month, I believe that you can occasionally contrive to pay your shoeing-bills.

Did you ever know Shackles—b. w. g., 15. 1⅜—coarse, loose, mule-like ears—barrel as long as a gate-post—tough as a telegraph-wire—and the queerest brute that ever looked through a bridle? He was of no brand, being one of an ear-nicked mob taken into the *Bucephalus* at £4:10s. a head to make up freight, and sold raw and out of condition at Calcutta for Rs.275. People who lost money on him called him a "brumby"; but if ever any horse had Harpoon's shoulders and The Gin's temper, Shackles was that horse. Two miles was his own particular distance. He trained himself, ran himself, and rode himself; and, if his jockey insulted him by giving him hints, he shut up at once and bucked the boy off. He objected to dictation. Two or three of his owners did not understand this, and lost money in consequence. At last he was bought by a man who discovered that, if a race was to be won, Shackles, and Shackles only, would win it in his own way, so long as his jockey sat still. This man had a riding-boy called Brunt—a lad from Perth, West Australia—and he taught Brunt, with a trainer's whip, the hardest thing a jock can learn—to sit still, to sit still, and to keep on sitting still. When Brunt fairly grasped this truth, Shackles devastated the country. No weight could stop him at his own distance; and the fame of Shackles spread from Ajmir in the South, to Chedputter in the North. There was no horse like Shackles, so long as he was allowed to do his work in his own way. But he was beaten in the end; and the story of his fall is enough to make angels weep.

At the lower end of the Chedputter race-course, just before the turn into the straight, the track passes close to a couple of old brick-mounds inclosing a funnel-shaped hollow. The big end of the funnel is not six feet from the railings on the off-side. The astounding peculiarity of the course is that, if you stand at one particular place, about half a mile away, inside the course, and speak at ordinary pitch, your voice just hits the funnel of the brick-mounds and makes a curious whining echo there. A man discovered this one morning by accident while out training with a friend. He marked the place to stand and speak from with a couple of bricks, and he kept his knowledge to himself. *Every* peculiarity of a course is worth remembering in a country where rats play the mischief with the elephant-litter, and Stewards build jumps to suit their own stables. This man ran a very fairish country-bred, a long, racking high mare with the temper of a fiend and the paces of an airy wandering seraph—a drifty, glidy stretch. The mare was, as a delicate tribute to Mrs. Reiver, called "The Lady Regula Baddun"—or for short, Regula Baddun.

Shackles' jockey, Brunt, was a quite well-behaved boy, but his nerve had been shaken. He began his career by riding jump-races in Melbourne, where a few Stewards want lynching, and was one of the jockeys who came through the awful butchery—perhaps you will recollect it—of the Maribyrnong Plate. The walls were colonial ramparts—logs of *jarrah* spiked into masonry—with wings as strong as Church buttresses. Once in his stride, a horse had to jump or fall. He couldn't run out. In the Maribyrnong Plate, twelve horses were jammed at the second wall. Red Hat, leading, fell this side, and threw out The Gled, and the ruck came up behind and the space between wing and wing was one struggling, screaming, kicking shambles. Four jockeys were taken out dead; three were very badly hurt, and Brunt was among the three. He told the story of the Maribyrnong Plate sometimes; and when he described how Whalley on Red Hat, said, as the mare fell under him—"God ha' mercy, I'm done for!" and how, next instant, Sithee There and White Otter had crushed the life out of poor Whalley, and the dust hid a small hell of men and horses, no one marveled that Brunt had dropped jump-races and Australia together. Regula Baddun's owner knew that story by heart. Brunt never varied it in the telling. He had no education.

Shackles came to the Chedputter Autumn races one year, and his owner walked about insulting the sportsmen of Chedputter generally, till they went to the Honorary Secretary in a body and said, "Appoint handicappers, and arrange a race which shall break Shackles and humble the pride of his owner." The Districts rose against Shackles and sent up of their best; Ousel, who was supposed to be able to do his mile in 1-53; Petard, the stud-bred, trained by a cavalry regiment who knew how to train; Gringalet, the ewe-lamb of the 75th; Bobolink, the pride of Peshawar; and many others.

They called that race The Broken-Link Handicap, because it was to smash Shackles; and the Handicappers piled on the weights, and the Fund gave eight hundred rupees, and the distance was "round the course for all horses." Shackles' owner said, "You can arrange the race with regard to Shackles only. So long as you don't bury him under weight-cloths, I don't mind." Regula Baddun's owner said, "I throw in my mare to fret Ousel. Six furlongs is Regula's distance, and she will then lie down and die. So also will Ousel, for his jockey doesn't understand a waiting race." Now, this was a lie, for Regula had been in work for two months at Dehra, and her chances were good, always supposing that Shackles broke a blood-vessel—or Brunt moved on him.

The plunging in the lotteries was fine. They filled eight thousand-rupee lotteries on the Broken-Link Handicap, and the account in the "Pioneer" said that "favoritism was divided." In plain English, the various contingents were wild on their respective horses; for the Handicappers had done their work well. The Honorary Secretary shouted himself hoarse through the din; and the smoke of the cheroots was like the smoke, and the rattling of the dice-boxes like the rattle of small-arm fire.

Ten horses started—very level—and Regula Baddun's

owner cantered out on his hack to a place inside the circle of the course, where two bricks had been thrown. He faced toward the brick-mounds at the lower end of the course and waited.

The story of the running is in the "Pioneer." At the end of the first mile, Shackles crept out of the ruck, well on the outside, ready to get round the turn, lay hold of the bit and spin up the straight before the others knew he had got away. Brunt was sitting still, perfectly happy, listening to the "drum-drum-drum" of the hoofs behind, and knowing that, in about twenty strides, Shackles would draw one deep breath and go up the last half-mile like the "Flying Dutchman." As Shackles went short to take the turn and came abreast of the brick-mound, Brunt heard, above the noise of the wind in his ears, a whining, wailing voice on the offside, saying—"God ha' mercy, I'm done for!" In one stride, Brunt saw the whole seething smash of the Maribyrnong Plate before him, started in his saddle and gave a yell of terror. The start brought the heels into Shackles' side, and the scream hurt Shackles' feelings. He couldn't stop dead; but he put out his feet and slid along for fifty yards, and then, very gravely and judicially, bucked off Brunt—a shaking, terror-stricken lump, while Regula Baddun made a neck-and-neck race with Bobolink up the straight, and won by a short head—Petard a bad third. Shackles' owner, in the Stand, tried to think that his field-glasses had gone wrong. Regula Baddun's owner, waiting by the two bricks, gave one deep sigh of relief, and cantered back to the Stand. He had won, in lotteries and bets, about fifteen thousand.

It was a Broken-link Handicap with a vengeance. It broke nearly all the men concerned, and nearly broke the heart of Shackles' owner. He went down to interview Brunt. The boy lay, livid and gasping with fright, where he had tumbled off. The sin of losing the race never seemed to strike him. All he knew was that Whalley had "called" him, that the "call" was a warning; and, were he cut in two for it, he would never get up again. His nerve had gone altogether, and he only asked his master to give him a good thrashing, and let him go. He was fit for nothing, he said. He got his dismissal, and crept up to the paddock, white as chalk, with blue lips, his knees giving way under him. People said nasty things in the paddock; but Brunt never heeded. He changed into tweeds, took his stick and went down the road, still shaking with fright, and muttering over and over again—"God ha' mercy, I'm done for!" To the best of my knowledge and belief he spoke the truth.

So now you know how the Broken-link Handicap was run and won. Of course you don't believe it. You would credit anything about Russia's designs on India, or the recommendations of the Currency Commission; but a little bit of sober fact is more than you can stand.

BEYOND THE PALE

Love heeds not caste nor sleep a broken bed. I went in search of love and lost myself.—*Hindu Proverb*

A MAN should, whatever happens, keep to his own caste, race and breed. Let the White go to the White and the Black to the Black. Then, whatever trouble falls is in the ordinary course of things—neither sudden, alien, nor unexpected.

This is the story of a man who willfully stepped beyond the safe limits of decent everyday society, and paid for it heavily.

He knew too much in the first instance; and he saw too much in the second. He took too deep an interest in native life; but he will never do so again.

Deep away in the heart of the City, behind Jitha Megji's *bustee*, lies Amir Nath's Gully, which ends in a dead-wall pierced by one grated window. At the head of the Gully is a big cowbyre, and the walls on either side of the Gully are without windows. Neither Suchet Singh nor Gaur Chand approve of their women-folk looking into the world. If Durga Charan had been of their opinion, he would have been a happier man to-day, and little Bisesa would have been able to knead her own bread. Her room looked out through the grated window into the narrow dark Gully where the sun never came and where the buffaloes wallowed in the blue slime. She was a widow, about fifteen years old, and she prayed the Gods, day and night, to send her a lover; for she did not approve of living alone.

One day, the man—Trejago his name was—came into Amir Nath's Gully on an aimless wandering; and, after he had passed the buffaloes, stumbled over a big heap of cattle-food.

Then he saw that the Gully ended in a trap, and heard a little laugh from behind the grated window. It was a pretty little laugh, and Trejago, knowing that, for all practical purposes, the old "Arabian Nights" are good guides, went forward to the window, and whispered that verse of "The Love Song of Har Dyal" which begins:

Can a man stand upright in the face of the naked Sun; or a Lover in the Presence of his Beloved?

If my feet fail me, O Heart of my Heart, am I to blame, being blinded by the glimpse of your beauty?

There came the faint *tchink* of a woman's bracelets from behind the grating, and a little voice went on with the song at the fifth verse:

Alas! alas! Can the Moon tell the Lotus of her love when the Gate of Heaven is shut and the clouds gather for the rains?

They have taken my Beloved, and driven her with the pack-horses to the North.

There are iron chains on the feet that were set on my heart.

Call to the bowmen to make ready—

The voice stopped suddenly, and Trejago walked out of Amir Nath's Gully, wondering who in the world could have capped "The Love Song of Har Dyal" so neatly.

Next morning, as he was driving to office, an old woman threw a packet into his dogcart. In the packet was the half of a broken glass-bangle, one flower of the blood-red *dhak*, a pinch of *bhusa* or cattle-food, and eleven cardamoms. That packet was a letter—not a clumsy compromising letter, but an innocent unintelligible lover's epistle.

Trejago knew far too much about these things, as I have said. No Englishman should be able to translate object-letters. But Trejago spread all the trifles on the lid of his office-box and began to puzzle them out.

A broken glass-bangle stands for a Hindu widow all India over; because, when her husband dies, a woman's bracelets are broken on her wrists. Trejago saw the meaning of the little bit of the glass. The flower of the *dhak* means diversely "desire," "come," "write," or "danger," according to the other things with it. One cardamom means "jealousy"; but when any article is duplicated in an object-letter, it loses its symbolic meaning and stands merely for one of a number indicating time, or, if incense, curds, or saffron be sent also, place. The message ran then—"A widow—*dhak* flower and *bhusa*—at eleven o'clock." The pinch of *bhusa* enlightened Trejago. He saw—this kind of letter leaves much to instinctive knowledge—that the *bhusa* referred to the big heap of cattle-food over which he had fallen in Amir Nath's Gully, and that the message must come from the person behind the grating; she being a widow. So the message ran then—"A widow, in the Gully in which is the heap of *bhusa*, desires you to come at eleven o'clock."

Trejago threw all the rubbish into the fireplace and laughed. He knew that men in the East do not make love under windows at eleven in the forenoon, nor do women fix appointments a week in advance. So he went, that very night at eleven, into Amir Nath's Gully, clad in a *boorka*, which cloaks a man as well as a woman. Directly the gongs of the City made the hour, the little voice behind the grating took up "The Love Song of Har Dyal" at the verse where the Panthan girl calls upon Har Dyal to return. The song is really pretty in the Vernacular. In English you miss the wail of it. It runs something like this:

"Alone upon the housetops, to the North
I turn and watch the lightning in the sky—
The glamour of thy footsteps in the North,
Come back to me, Beloved, or I die!

"Below my feet the still bazaar is laid,
Far, far, below the weary camels lie—
The camels and the captives of thy raid.
Come back to me, Beloved, or I die!

"My father's wife is old and harsh with years,
And drudge of all my father's house am I.—
My bread is sorrow and my drink is tears,
Come back to me, Beloved, or I die!"

As the song stopped, Trejago stepped up under the grating and whispered—"I am here."

Bisesa was good to look upon.

That night was the beginning of many strange things, and of a double life so wild that Trejago to-day sometimes wonders if it were not all a dream. Bisesa, or her old handmaiden who had thrown the object-letter, had detached the heavy grating from the brick-work of the wall; so that the window slid inside, leaving only a square of raw masonry into which an active man might climb.

In the day-time, Trejago drove through his routine of office-work, or put on his calling-clothes and called on the ladies of the Station; wondering how long they would know him if they knew of poor little Bisesa. At night, when all the City was still, came the walk under the evil-smelling *boorka*, the patrol through Jitha Megji's *bustee*, the quick turn into Amir Nath's Gully between the sleeping cattle and the dead walls, and then, last of all, Bisesa, and the deep, even breathing of the old woman who slept outside the door of the bare little room that Durga Charan allotted to his sister's daughter. Who or what Durga Charan was, Trejago never inquired; and why in the world he was not discovered and knifed never occurred to him till his madness was over, and Bisesa . . . But this comes later.

Bisesa was an endless delight to Trejago. She was as ignorant as a bird; and her distorted versions of the rumors from the outside world that had reached her in her room, amused Trejago almost as much as her lisping attempts to pronounce his name—"Christopher." The first syllable was always more than she could manage, and she made funny little gestures with her roseleaf hands, as one throwing the name away, and then, kneeling before Trejago asked him, exactly as an Englishwoman would do, if he were sure he loved her. Trejago swore that he loved her more than any one else in the world. Which was true.

After a month of this folly, the exigencies of his other life compelled Trejago to be especially attentive to a lady of his acquaintance. You may take it for a fact that anything of this kind is not only noticed and discussed by a man's own race but by some hundred and fifty natives as well. Trejago had to walk with this lady and talk to her at the Band-stand, and once or twice to drive with her; never for an instant dreaming that this would affect his dearer, out-of-the way life. But the news flew, in the usual mysterious fashion, from mouth to mouth, till Bisesa's duenna heard of it and told Bisesa. The child was so troubled that she did the household work evilly, and was beaten by Durga Charan's wife in consequence.

A week later, Bisesa taxed Trejago with the flirtation. She understood no gradations and spoke openly. Trejago laughed and Bisesa stamped her little feet—little feet, light as marigold flowers, that could lie in the palm of a man's one hand.

Much that is written about Oriental passion and impulsiveness is exaggerated and compiled at second-hand, but a little of it is true; and when an Englishman finds that little, it is quite as startling as any passion in his own proper life. Bisesa raged and stormed, and finally threatened to kill herself if Trejago did not at once drop the alien *Memsahib* who had come between them. Trejago tried to explain, and to show her that she did not understand these things from a Western standpoint. Bisesa drew herself up, and said simply—

"I do not. I know only this—it is not good that I should have made you dearer than my own heart to me, *Sahib.* You are an Englishman. I am only a black girl"—she was fairer than bar-gold in the Mint—"and the widow of a black man."

Then she sobbed and said—"But on my soul and my Mother's soul, I love you. There shall no harm come to you, whatever happens to me."

Trejago argued with the child, and tried to soothe her, but she seemed quite unreasonably disturbed. Nothing would satisfy her save that all relations between them should end. He was to go away at once. And he went. As he dropped out of the window, she kissed his forehead twice, and he walked home wondering.

A week, and then three weeks, passed without a sign from Bisesa. Trejago, thinking that the rupture had lasted quite long enough, went down to Amir Nath's Gully for the fifth time in the three weeks, hoping that his rap at the sill of the shifting grating would be answered. He was not disappointed.

There was a young moon, and one stream of light fell down into Amir Nath's Gully, and struck the grating which was drawn away as he knocked. From the black dark, Bisesa held out her arms into the moonlight. Both hands had been cut off at the wrists, and the stumps were nearly healed.

Then, as Bisesa bowed her head between her arms and sobbed, some one in the room grunted like a wild beast, and something sharp—knife, sword, or spear—thrust at Trejago in his *boorka.* The stroke missed his body, but cut into one of the muscles of the groin, and he limped slightly from the wound for the rest of his days.

The grating went into its place. There was no sign whatever from inside the house—nothing but the moonlight strip on the high wall, and the blackness of Amir Nath's Gully behind.

The next thing Trejago remembers, after raging and shouting like a madman between those pitiless walls, is that he found himself near the river as the dawn was breaking, threw away his *boorka* and went home bareheaded.

. . . .

What was the tragedy—whether Bisesa had, in a fit of causeless despair, told everything, or the intrigue had been discovered and she tortured to tell; whether Durga Charan knew his name and what became of Bisesa—Trejago does not know to this day. Something horrible had happened, and the thought of what it must have been, comes upon Trejago in the night now and again, and keeps him company till the morning. One special feature of the case is that he does not know where lies the front of Durga Charan's house. It may open on to a courtyard common to two or more houses, or it may lie behind any one of the gates of Jitha Megji's *bustee*. Trejago cannot tell. He cannot get Bisesa—poor little Bisesa—back again. He has lost her in the City where each man's house is as guarded and as unknowable as the grave; and the grating that opens into Amir Nath's Gully has been walled up.

But Trejago pays his calls regularly, and is reckoned a very decent sort of man.

There is nothing peculiar about him, except a slight stiffness, caused by a riding-strain, in the right leg.

IN ERROR

They burned a corpse upon the sand—
The light shone out afar;
It guided home the plunging boats
That beat from Zanzibar.
Spirit of Fire, where'er Thy altars rise,
Thou art Light of Guidance to our eyes!
—*Salsette Boat-Song*

THERE is hope for a man who gets publicly and riotously drunk more often than he ought to do; but there is no hope for the man who drinks secretly and alone in his own house—the man who is never seen to drink.

This is a rule; so there must be an exception to prove it. Moriarty's case was that exception.

He was a Civil Engineer, and the Government, very kindly, put him quite by himself in an out-district, with nobody but natives to talk to and a great deal of work to do. He did his work well in the four years he was utterly alone; but he picked up the vice of secret and solitary drinking, and came up out of the wilderness more old and worn and haggard than the dead-alive life had any right to make him. You know the saying that a man who has been alone in the jungle for more than a year is never quite sane all his life after. People credited Moriarty's queerness of manner and moody ways to the solitude, and said that it showed how Government spoiled the futures of its best men. Moriarty had built himself the plinth of a very good reputation in the bridge-dam-girder line. But he knew, every night of the week, that he was taking steps to undermine that reputation with L. L. L. and Christopher and little nips of liqueurs, and filth of that kind. He had a sound constitution and a great brain, or else he would have broken down and died like a sick camel in the district. As better men have done before him.

Government ordered him to Simla after he had come out of the desert; and he went up meaning to try for a post then vacant. That season, Mrs. Reiver—perhaps you will remember her—was in the height of her power, and many men lay under her yoke. Everything bad that could be said has already been said about Mrs. Reiver, in another tale. Moriarty was heavily-built and handsome, very quiet and nervously anxious to please his neighbors when he wasn't sunk in a brown study. He started a good deal at sudden noises or if spoken to without warning; and, when you watched him drinking his glass of water at dinner, you could see the hand shake a little. But all this was put down to nervousness, and the quiet, steady, sip-sip-sip, fill and sip-sip-sip again that went on in his own room when he was by himself, was never known. Which was miraculous, seeing how everything in a man's private life is public property in India.

Moriarty was drawn, not into Mrs. Reiver's set, because they were not his sort, but into the power of Mrs. Reiver, and he fell down in front of her and made a goddess of her. This was due to his coming fresh out of the jungle to a big town. He could not scale things properly or see who was what.

Because Mrs. Reiver was cold and hard, he said she was stately and dignified. Because she had no brains, and could not talk cleverly, he said she was reserved and shy. Mrs. Reiver shy! Because she was unworthy of honor or reverence from any one, he reverenced her from a distance and dowed her with all the virtues in the Bible and most of those in Shakespeare.

This big, dark, abstracted man, who was so nervous when a pony cantered behind him, used to moon in the train of Mrs. Reiver, blushing with pleasure when she threw a word or two his way. His admiration was strictly platonic; even other women saw and admitted this. He did not move out in Simla, so he heard nothing against his idol: which was satisfactory. Mrs. Reiver took no special notice of him, beyond seeing that he was added to her list of admirers, and going for a walk with him now and then, just to show that he was her property, claimable as such. Moriarty must have done most of the talking, for Mrs. Reiver couldn't talk much to a man of his stamp; and the little she said could not have been profitable. What Moriarty believed in, as he had good reason to, was Mrs. Reiver's influence over him, and, in that belief, set himself seriously to try to do away with the vice that only he himself knew of.

His experiences while he was fighting with it must have been peculiar, but he never described them. Sometimes he would hold off from everything except water for a week. Then, on a rainy night, when no one had asked him out to dinner, and there was a big fire in his room, and everything comfortable, he would sit down and make a big night of it by adding little nip to little nip, planning big schemes of reformation meanwhile, until he threw himself on his bed hopelessly drunk. He suffered next morning.

One night the big crash came. He was troubled in his own mind over his attempts to make himself "worthy of the friendship" of Mrs. Reiver. The past ten days had been very bad ones, and the end of it all was that he received the arrears of two and three-quarter years of sipping in one attack of delirium tremens of the subdued kind; beginning with suicidal depression, going on to fits and starts and hysteria, and ending with downright raving. As he sat in a chair in front of the fire, or walked up and down the room picking a handkerchief to pieces, you heard what poor Moriarty really thought of Mrs. Reiver, for he raved about her and his own fall for the most part; though he raveled some P. W. D. accounts into the same skein of thought. He talked and talked, and talked in a low dry whisper to himself, and there was no stopping him. He seemed to know that there was something wrong, and twice tried to pull himself together and confer rationally with the Doctor; but his mind ran out of control at once, and he fell back to a whisper and the story of his troubles. It is terrible to hear a big man babbling like a child of all that a man usually locks up, and puts away in the deep of his heart. Moriarty read out his very soul for the benefit of any one who was in the room between ten-thirty that night and two-forty-five next morning.

From what he said, one gathered how immense an influence Mrs. Reiver held over him, and how thoroughly he felt for his own lapse. His whisperings cannot, of course, be put down here; but they were very instructive—as showing the errors of his estimates.

. . . .

When the trouble was over, and his few acquaintances were pitying him for the bad attack of jungle-fever that had so pulled him down, Moriarty swore a big oath to himself and went abroad again with Mrs. Reiver till the end of the season, adoring her in a quiet and deferential way as an angel from heaven. Later on, he took to riding—not hacking, but honest riding—which was good proof that he was improving, and you could slam doors behind him without his jumping to his feet with a gasp. That, again, was hopeful.

How he kept his oath and what it cost him in the beginning nobody knows. He certainly managed to compass the hardest thing that a man who has drunk heavily can do. He took his peg and wine at dinner; but he never drank alone, and never let what he drank have the least hold on him.

Once he told a bosom-friend the story of his great trouble, and how the "influence of a pure honest woman, and an angel as well" had saved him. When the man—startled at anything good being laid to Mrs. Reiver's door—laughed, it cost him Moriarty's friendship. Moriarty, who is married now to a woman ten thousand times better than Mrs. Reiver—a woman who believes that there is no man on earth as good and clever as her husband—will go down to his grave vowing and protesting that Mrs. Reiver saved him from ruin in both worlds.

That she knew anything of Moriarty's weakness nobody believed for a moment. That she would have cut him dead, thrown him over, and acquainted all her friends with her discovery, if she had known of it, nobody who knew her doubted for an instant.

Moriarty thought her something she never was, and in that belief saved himself. Which was just as good as though she had been everything that he had imagined.

But the question is, What claim will Mrs. Reiver have to the credit of Moriarty's salvation, when her day of reckoning comes?

A BANK FRAUD

He drank strong waters and his speech was coarse;
He purchased raiment and forbore to pay;
He stuck a trusting junior with a horse,
And won Gymkhanas in a doubtful way.
Then, 'twixt a vice and folly, turned aside
To do good deeds, and straight to cloak them, lied.
—*The Mess Room*

IF Reggie Burke were in India now, he would resent this tale being told; but as he is in Hongkong and won't see it, the telling is safe. He was the man who worked the big fraud on the Sind and Sialkote Bank. He was manager of an up-country Branch, and a sound practical man with a large experience of native loan and insurance work. He could combine the frivolities of ordinary life with his work, and yet do well. Reggie Burke rode anything that would let him get up, danced as neatly as he rode, and was wanted for every sort of amusement in the Station.

As he said himself, and as many men found out rather to their surprise, there were two Burkes, both very much at your service. "Reggie Burke," between four and ten, ready for anything from a hot-weather gymkhana to a riding-picnic, and, between ten and four, "Mr. Reginald Burke, Manager of the Sind and Sialkote Branch Bank." You might play polo with him one afternoon and hear him express his opinions when a man crossed; and you might call on him next morning to raise a two-thousand rupee loan on a five hundred pound insurance policy, eighty pounds paid in premiums. He would recognize you, but you would have some trouble in recognizing him.

The Directors of the Bank—it had its headquarters in Calcutta and its General Manager's word carried weight with the Government—picked their men well. They had tested Reggie up to a fairly severe breaking-strain. They trusted him just as much as Directors ever trust Managers. You must see for yourself whether their trust was misplaced.

Reggie's Branch was in a big Station, and worked with the usual staff—one Manager, one Accountant, both English, a Cashier, and a horde of native clerks; besides the Police patrol at nights outside. The bulk of its work, for it was in a thriving district, was *hoondi* and accommodation of all kinds. A fool has no grip of this sort of business; and a clever man who does not go about among his clients, and know more than a little of their affairs, is worse than a fool. Reggie was young-looking, clean-shaved, with a twinkle in his eye, and a head that nothing short of a gallon of the Gunners' Madeira could make any impression on.

One day, at a big dinner, he announced casually that the Directors had shifted on to him a Natural Curiosity, from England, in the Accountant line. He was perfectly correct. Mr. Silas Riley, Accountant, was a most curious animal—a long, gawky, rawboned Yorkshireman, full of the savage self-conceit that blossoms only in the best county in England. Arrogance was a mild word for the mental attitude of Mr. S. Riley. He had worked himself up, after seven years, to a Cashier's position in a Huddersfield Bank; and all his experience lay among the factories of the North. Perhaps he would have done better on the Bombay side, where they are happy with one-half per cent profits, and money is cheap.

He was useless for Upper India and a wheat Province, where a man wants a large head and a touch of imagination if he is to turn out a satisfactory balance-sheet.

He was wonderfully narrow-minded in business, and, being new to the country, had no notion that Indian banking is totally distinct from Home work. Like most clever self-made men, he had much simplicity in his nature; and, somehow or other, had construed the ordinarily polite terms of his letter of engagement into a belief that the Directors had chosen him on account of his special and brilliant talents, and that they set great store by him. This notion grew and crystallized; thus adding to his natural North-country conceit. Further, he was delicate, suffered from some trouble in his chest, and was short in his temper.

You will admit that Reggie had reason to call his new Accountant a Natural Curiosity. The two men failed to hit it off at all. Riley considered Reggie a wild, feather-headed idiot, given to Heaven only knew what dissipation in low places called "Messes," and totally unfit for the serious and solemn vocation of banking. He could never get over Reggie's look of youth and "you-be-damned" air; and he couldn't understand Reggie's friends—clean-built, careless men in the Army—who rode over to big Sunday breakfasts at the Bank, and told sultry stories till Riley got up and left the room. Riley was always showing Reggie how the business ought to be conducted, and Reggie had more than once to remind him that seven years' limited experience between Huddersfield and Beverley did not qualify a man to steer a big up-country business. Then Riley sulked, and referred to himself as a pillar of the Bank and a cherished friend of the Directors, and Reggie tore his hair. If a man's English subordinates fail him in India, he comes to a hard time indeed, for native help has strict limitations. In the winter Riley went sick for weeks at a time with his lung complaint, and this threw more work on Reggie. But he preferred it to the everlasting friction when Riley was well.

One of the Traveling Inspectors of the Bank discovered

these collapses and reported them to the Directors. Now Riley had been foisted on the Bank by an M.P., who wanted the support of Riley's father, who, again, was anxious to get his son out to a warmer climate because of those lungs. The M.P. had interest in the Bank; but one of the Directors wanted to advance a nominee of his own; and, after Riley's father had died, he made the rest of the Board see that an Accountant who was sick for half the year had better give place to a healthy man. If Riley had known the real story of his appointment, he might have behaved better; but, knowing nothing, his stretches of sickness alternated with restless, persistent, meddling irritation of Reggie, and all the hundred ways in which conceit in a subordinate situation can find play. Reggie used to call him striking and hair curling names behind his back as a relief to his own feelings; but he never abused him to his face, because he said, "Riley is such a frail beast that half of his loathsome conceit is due to pains in the chest."

Late one April, Riley went very sick indeed. The Doctor punched him and thumped him, and told him he would be better before long. Then the Doctor went to Reggie and said —"Do you know how sick your Accountant is?"—"No!" said Reggie. "The worse the better, confound him! He's a clacking nuisance when he's well. I'll let you take away the Bank Safe if you can drug him silent for this hot weather."

But the Doctor did not laugh—"Man, I'm not joking," he said. "I'll give him another three months in his bed and a week or so more to die in. On my honor and reputation that's all the grace he has in this world. Consumption has hold of him to the marrow."

Reggie's face changed at once into the face of "Mr. Reginald Burke," and he answered, "What can I do?"— "Nothing," said the Doctor. "For all practical purposes the man is dead already. Keep him quiet and cheerful, and tell him he's going to recover. That's all. I'll look after him to the end, of course."

The Doctor went away, and Reggie sat down to open the evening mail. His first letter was one from the Directors, intimating for his information that Mr. Riley was to resign, under a month's notice, by the terms of his agreement, telling Reggie that their letter to Riley would follow, and advising Reggie of the coming of a new Accountant, a man whom Regie knew and liked.

Reggie lighted a cheroot, and, before he had finished smoking, he had sketched the outline of a fraud. He put away —burked—the Directors' letter, and went in to talk to Riley, who was as ungracious as usual, and fretting himself over the way the Bank would run during his illness. He never thought of the extra work on Reggie's shoulders, but solely of the damage to his own prospects of advancement. Then Reggie assured him that everything would be well, and that he, Reggie, would confer with Riley daily on the management of the Bank. Riley was a little soothed, but he hinted in as many words that he did not think much of Reggie's business capacity. Reggie was humble. And he had letters in his desk from the Directors that a Gilbarte or a Hardie might have been proud of!

The days passed in the big darkened house, and the Directors' letter of dismissal to Riley came and was put away by Reggie, who, every evening, brought the books to Riley's room, and showed him what had been going forward, while Riley snarled. Reggie did his best to make statements pleasing to Riley, but the Accountant was sure that the Bank was going to rack and ruin without him. In June, as the lying in bed told on his spirit, he asked whether his absence had been noted by the Directors, and Reggie said that they had written most sympathetic letters, hoping that he would be able to resume his valuable services before long. He showed Riley the letters; and Riley said that the Directors ought to have written to him direct. A few days later, Reggie opened Riley's mail in the half-light of the room, and gave him the sheet—not the envelope—of a letter to Riley from the Directors. Riley said he would thank Reggie not to interfere with his private papers, specially as Reggie knew he was too weak to open his own letters. Reggie apologized.

Then Riley's mood changed, and he lectured Reggie on his evil ways: his horses and his bad friends. "Of course lying here, on my back, Mr. Burke, I can't keep you straight; but when I'm well, I *do* hope you'll pay some heed to my words." Reggie, who had dropped polo, and dinners, and tennis and all, to attend to Riley, said that he was penitent and settled Riley's head on the pillow and heard him fret and contradict in hard, dry, hacking whispers, without a sign of impatience. This, at the end of a heavy day's office work, doing double duty, in the latter half of June.

When the new Accountant came, Reggie told him the facts of the case, and announced to Riley that he had a guest staying with him. Riley said that he might have had more consideration than to entertain his "doubtful friends" at such a time. Reggie made Carron, the new Accountant, sleep at the Club in consequence. Carron's arrival took some of the heavy work off his shoulders, and he had time to attend to Riley's exactions—to explain, soothe, invent, and settle and re-settle the poor wretch in bed, and to forge complimentary letters from Calcutta. At the end of the first month Riley wished to send some money home to his mother. Reggie sent the draft. At the end of the second month Riley's salary came in just the same. Reggie paid it out of his own pocket, and, with it, wrote Riley a beautiful letter from the Directors.

Riley was very ill indeed, but the flame of his life burned unsteadily. Now and then he would be cheerful and confident about the future, sketching plans for going Home and seeing his mother. Reggie listened patiently when the office-work was over, and encouraged him.

At other times Riley insisted on Reggie reading the Bible and grim "Methody" tracts to him. Out of these tracts he pointed morals directed at his Manager. But he always found time to worry Reggie about the working of the Bank, and to show him where the weak points lay.

This indoor, sickroom life and constant strains wore Reggie down a good deal, and shook his nerves, and lowered his billiard play by forty points. But the business of the Bank, and the business of the sickroom, had to go on, though the glass was 116° in the shade.

At the end of the third month Riley was sinking fast, and had begun to realize that he was very sick. But the conceit that made him worry Reggie kept him from believing the worst. "He wants some sort of mental stimulant if he is to drag on," said the Doctor. "Keep him interested in life if you care about his living." So Riley, contrary to all the laws of business and the finance, received a 25-per-cent rise of salary from the Directors. The "mental stimulant" succeeded beautifully. Riley was happy and cheerful, and, as is often the case in consumption, healthiest in mind when the body was weakest. He lingered for a full month, snarling and fretting about the Bank, talking of the future, hearing the Bible read, lecturing Reggie on sin, and wondering when he would be able to move abroad.

But at the end of September, one mercilessly hot evening, he rose up in his bed with a little gasp, and said quickly to Reggie—"Mr. Burke, I am going to die. I know it in myself. My chest is all hollow inside, and there's nothing to breathe with. To the best of my knowledge I have done nowt"—he was returning to the talk of his boyhood—"to lie heavy on my conscience. God be thanked, I have been preserved from the grosser forms of sin; and I counsel *you*, Mr. Burke . . ."

Here his voice died down, and Reggie stooped over him.

"Send my salary for September to my Mother . . . done great things with the Bank if I had been spared . . . mistaken policy . . . no fault of mine . . ."

Then he turned his face to the wall and died.

Reggie drew the sheet over Its face, and went out into the veranda, with his last "mental stimulant"—a letter of condolence and sympathy from the Directors—unused in his pocket.

"If I'd been only ten minutes earlier," thought Reggie, "I might have heartened him up to pull through another day."

TODS' AMENDMENT

The World hath set its heavy yoke
Upon the old white-bearded folk
Who strive to please the King.
God's mercy is upon the young,
God's wisdom in the baby tongue
That fears not anything.

—*The Parable of Chajju Bhaga*

Now Tods' Mamma was a singularly charming woman, and every one in Simla knew Tods. Most men had saved him from death on occasions. He was beyond his *ayah's* control altogether, and periled his life daily to find out what would happen if you pulled a Mountain Battery mule's tail. He was an utterly fearless young Pagan, about six years old, and the only baby who ever broke the holy calm of the Supreme Legislative Council.

It happened this way: Tods' pet kid got loose, and fled up the hill, off the Boileaugunge Road, Tods after it, until it burst in to the Viceregal Lodge lawn, then attached to "Peterhoff." The Council were sitting at the time, and the windows were open because it was warm. The Red Lancer in the porch told Tods to go away; but Tods knew the Red Lancer and most of the Members of Council personally. Moreover, he had firm hold of the kid's collar, and was being dragged all across the flower-beds. "Give my *salaam* to the long Councilor *Sahib*, and ask him to help me take *Moti* back!" gasped Tods. The Council heard the noise through the open windows; and, after an interval, was seen the shocking spectacle of a Legal Member and a Lieutenant-Governor helping, under the direct patronage of a Commander-in-Chief and a Viceroy, one small and very dirty boy in a sailor's suit and a tangle of brown hair, to coerce a lively and rebellious kid. They headed it off down the path to the Mall, and

Tods went home in triumph and told his Mamma that *all* the Councilor *Sahibs* had been helping him to catch *Moti*. Whereat his Mamma smacked Tods for interfering with the administration of the Empire; but Tods met the Legal Member the next day, and told him in confidence that if the Legal Member ever wanted to catch a goat, he, Tods, would give him all the help in his power. "Thank you, Tods," said the Legal Member.

Tods was the idol of some eighty *jhampanis*, and half as many *saises*. He saluted them all as "O Brother." It never entered his head that any living human being could disobey his orders; and he was the buffer between the servants and his Mamma's wrath. The working of that household turned on Tods, who was adored by every one from the *dhoby* to the dog boy. Even Futteh Khan, the villainous loafer *khit* from Mussoorie, shirked risking Tods' displeasure for fear his co-mates should look down on him.

So Tods had honor in the land from Boileaugunge to Chota Simla, and ruled justly according to his lights. Of course, he spoke Urdu, but he had also mastered many queer side-speeches like the *chotee bolee* of the women, and held grave converse with shopkeepers and Hill-coolies alike. He was precocious for his age, and his mixing with natives had taught him some of the more bitter truths of life: the meanness and the sordidness of it. He used, over his bread and milk, to deliver solemn and serious aphorisms, translated from the vernacular into the English, that made his Mamma jump and vow that Tods *must* go Home next hot weather.

Just when Tods was in the bloom of his power, the Supreme Legislature were hacking out a Bill for the Sub-Montane Tracts, a revision of the then Act, smaller than the Punjab Land Bill, but affecting a few hundred thousand people none the less. The Legal Member had built, and bolstered, and embroidered, and amended that Bill, till it looked beautiful on paper. Then the Council began to settle what they called the "minor details." As if any Englishman legislating for natives knows enough to know which are the minor and which are the major points, from the native point of view, of any measure! That Bill was a triumph of "safeguarding the interests of the tenant." One clause provided that land should not be leased on longer terms than five years at a stretch; because, if the landlord had a tenant bound down for, say, twenty years, he would squeeze the very life out of him. The notion was to keep up a stream of independent cultivators in the Sub-Montane Tracts; and ethnologically and politically the notion was correct. The only drawback was that it was altogether wrong. A native's life in India implies the life of his son. Wherefore, you cannot legislate for one generation at a time. You must consider the next from the native point of view. Curiously enough, the native now and then, and in Northern India more particularly, hates being overprotected against himself. There was a Naga village once, where they lived on dead *and* buried Commissariat mules. . . . But that is another story.

For many reasons, to be explained later, the people concerned objected to the Bill. The Native Member in Council knew as much about Punjabis as he knew about Charing Cross. He had said in Calcutta that "the Bill was entirely in accord with the desires of that large and important class, the cultivators"; and so on, and so on. The Legal Member's knowledge of natives was limited to English-speaking Durbaris, and his own red *chaprassis*, the Sub-Montane Tracts concerned no one in particular, the Deputy Commissioners were a good deal too driven to make representations, and the measure was one which dealt with small land-holders only. Nevertheless, the Legal Member prayed that it might be correct, for he was a nervously conscientious man. He did not know that no man can tell what natives think unless he mixes with them with the varnish off. And not always then. But he did the best he knew. And the measure came up to the Supreme Council for the final touches, while Tods patroled the Burra Simla Bazaar in his morning rides, and played with the monkey belonging to Ditta Mull, the *bunnia*, and listened, as a child listens, to all the stray talk about this new freak of the *Lord Sahib's*.

One day there was a dinner-party, at the house of Tods' Mamma, and the Legal Member came. Tods was in bed, but he kept awake till he heard the bursts of laughter from the men over the coffee. Then he paddled out in his little red flannel dressing-gown and his night-suit and took refuge by the side of his father, knowing that he would not be sent back. "See the miseries of having a family!" said Tods' father, giving Tods three prunes, some water in a glass that had been used for claret, and telling him to sit still. Tods sucked the prunes slowly, knowing that he would have to go when they were finished, and sipped the pink water like a man of the world, as he listened to the conversation. Presently, the Legal Member, talking "shop" to the Head of a Department, mentioned his Bill by its full name—"The Sub-Montane Tracts *Ryotwary* Revised Enactment." Tods caught the one native word and lifting up his small voice said—

"Oh, I know *all* about that! Has it been *murramutted* yet, Councilor *Sahib?*"

"How much?" said the Legal Member.

"*Murramutted*—mended.—Put *theek*, you know—made nice to please Ditta Mull!"

The Legal Member left his place and moved up next to Tods. "What do you know about *ryotwari*, little man?" he said.

"I'm not a little man, I'm Tods, and I know *all* about it. Ditta Mull, and Choga Lall, and Amir Nath, and—oh, *lakhs* of my friends tell me about it in the bazaars when I talk to them."

"Oh, they do—do they? What do they say, Tods?"

Tods tucked his feet under his red flannel dressing-gown and said—"I must *fink*."

The Legal Member waited patiently. Then Tods with infinite compassion—

"You don't speak my talk, do you, Councilor *Sahib?*"

"No; I am sorry to say I do not," said the Legal Member.

"Very well," said Tods, "I must *fink* in English."

He spent a minute putting his ideas in order, and began very slowly, translating in his mind from the vernacular to English, as many Anglo-Indian children do. You must remember that the Legal Member helped him on by questions when he halted, for Tods was not equal to the sustained flight of oratory that follows.

"Ditta Mull says, 'This thing is the talk of a child, and was made up by fools.' But *I* don't think you are a fool, Councilor *Sahib*," said Tods hastily. "You caught my goat. This is what Ditta Mull says—'I am not a fool, and why should the Sirkar say I am a child? I can see if the land is good and if the landlord is good. If I am a fool, the sin is upon my own head. For five years I take my ground for which I have saved money, and a wife I take too, and a little son is born.' Ditta Mull has one daughter now, but he *says* he will have a son, soon. And he says, 'At the end of five years, by this new *bundobust*, I must go. If I do not go, I must get fresh seals and *takkus*-stamps on the papers, perhaps in the middle of the harvest, and to go to the law-courts once is wisdom, but to go twice is *Jehannum.*' That is *quite* true," explained Tods gravely. "All my friends say so. And Ditta Mull says, 'Always fresh *takkus* and paying money to *vakils* and *chaprassis* and law-courts every five years, or else the landlord makes me go. Why do I want to go? Am I a fool? If I am a fool and do not know, after forty years, good land when I see it, let me die! But if the new *bundobust* says for *fifteen* years, that it is good and wise. My little son is a man, and I am burned, and he takes the ground or another ground, paying only once for the *takkus*-stamps on the papers, and his little son is born, and at the end of fifteen years is a man too. But what profit is there in five years and fresh papers? Nothing but *dikh*, trouble, *dikh*. We are not young men who take these lands, but old ones—not farmers, but tradesmen with a little money —and for fifteen years we shall have peace. Nor are we children that the Sirkar should treat us so.' "

Here Tods stopped short, for the whole table were listening. The Legal Member said to Tods, "Is that all?"

"All I can remember," said Tods. "But you should see Ditta Mull's big monkey. It's just like a Councilor *Sahib.*"

"Tods! Go to bed," said his father.

Tods gathered up his dressing-gown tail and departed.

The Legal Member brought his hand down on the table with a crash—"By Jove!" said the Legal Member, "I believe the boy is right. The short tenure *is* the weak point."

He left early, thinking over what Tods had said. Now, it was obviously impossible for the Legal Member to play with a *bunnia's* monkey, by way of getting understanding; but he did better. He made inquiries, always bearing in mind the fact that the real native—not the hybrid, University-trained mule—is as timid as a colt, and, little by little, he coaxed some of the men whom the measure concerned most intimately to give in their views, which squared very closely with Tods' evidence.

So the Bill was amended in that clause; and the Legal Member was filled with an uneasy suspicion that Native Members represent very little except the Orders they carry on their bosoms. But he put the thought from him as illiberal. He was a most Liberal man.

After a time, the news spread through the bazaars that Tods had got the Bill recast in the tenure-clause, and if Tods' Mamma had not interfered, Tods would have made himself sick on the baskets of fruit and pistachio nuts and Cabuli grapes and almonds that crowded the veranda. Till he went Home, Tods ranked some few degrees before the Viceroy in popular estimation. But for the little life of him Tods could not understand why.

In the Legal Member's private paper-box still lies the rough draft of the Sub-Montane Tracts *Ryotwary* Revised Enactment; and, opposite the twenty-second clause, penciled in blue chalk, and signed by the Legal Member, are the words, "*Tods' Amendment.*"

THE DAUGHTER OF THE REGIMENT

Jain 'Ardin' was a Sarjint's wife,
  A Sarjint's wife wus she.
She married of 'im in Orldershort
  An' comed acrost the sea.
(*Chorus*) 'Ave you never 'eard tell o' Jain 'Ardin'?
  Jain 'Ardin'?
  Jain 'Ardin'?
'Ave you never 'eard tell o' Jain 'Ardin'?
The pride o' the Companee?

—*Old Barrack-Room Ballad*

"A GENTLEMAN who doesn't know the Circasian Circle ought not to stand up for it—puttin' everybody out." That was what Miss McKenna said, and the Sergeant who was my *vis-à-vis* looked the same thing. I was afraid of Miss McKenna. She was six feet high, all yellow freckles and red hair, and was simply clad in white satin shoes, a pink muslin dress, an apple-green stuff sash, and black silk gloves, with yellow roses in her hair. Wherefore I fled from Miss McKenna and sought my friend Private Mulvaney, who was at the cant—refreshment-table.

"So you've been dancin' with little Jhansi McKenna, Sorr—she that's goin' to marry Corp'ril Slane? Whin you next conversh wid your lorruds an' your ladies, tell thim you've danced wid little Jhansi. 'Tis a thing to be proud av."

But I wasn't proud. I was humble. I saw a story in Private Mulvaney's eye; and besides, if he stayed too long at the bar, he would, I knew, qualify for more pack-drill. Now to meet an esteemed friend doing pack drill outside the guard-room is embarrassing, especially if you happen to be walking with his Commanding Officer.

"Come on to the parade-ground, Mulvaney, it's cooler there, and tell me about Miss McKenna. What is she, and who is she, and why is she called 'Jhansi'?"

"D'ye mane to say you've niver heard av Ould Pummeloe's daughter? An' you thinkin' you know things! I'm wid ye in a minut' whin me poipe's lit."

We came out under the stars. Mulvaney sat down on one of the artillery bridges, and began in the usual way: his pipe between his teeth, his big hands clasped and dropped between his knees, and his cap well on the back of his head—

"Whin Mrs. Mulvaney, that is, was Miss Shad that was, you were a dale younger than you are now, an' the Army was dif'rint in sev'ril e-senshuls. Bhoys have no call for to marry nowadays, an' that's why the Army has so few rale, good, honust, swearin', strapagin', tinder-hearted, heavy-futted wives as ut used to have whin I was a Corp'ril. I was rejuced aftherward—but no matther—I was a Corp'ril wanst. In thim times, a man lived *an'* died wid his regiment; an' by natur', he married whin he was a *man*. Whin I was Corp'ril—Mother av Hivin, how the rigimint has died an' been borrun since that day!—my Color-Sar'jint was Ould McKenna, an' a married man tu. An' his woife—his first woife, for he married three times did McKenna—was Bridget McKenna, from Portarlington, like mesilf. I've misremembered fwhat her first name was; but in B Comp'ny we called her 'Ould Pummeloe,' by reason av her figure, which was entirely cir-cum-fe-renshill. Like the big dhrum! Now that woman—God rock her sowl to rest in glory!—was for everlastin' havin' childher; an' McKenna, whin the fifth or sixth come squallin' on to the musther-roll, swore he wud number thim off in future. But Ould Pummeloe she prayed av him to christen them after the names av the stations they was borrun in. So there was Colaba McKenna, an' Muttra McKenna, an 'a whole Presidincy av other McKennas, an' little Jhansi, dancin' over yonder. Whin the childher wasn't bornin', they was dying; for, av our childher die like sheep in these days, they died like flies thin. I lost me own little Shad—but no matther. 'Tis long ago, and Mrs. Mulvaney niver had another.

"I'm digresshin. Wan divil's hot summer, there come

an order from some mad ijjit, whose name I misremember, for the rigimint to go up-country. Maybe they wanted to know how the new rail carried throops. They knew! On me sowl, they knew before they was done! Old Pummeloe had just buried Muttra McKenna; an', the season bein' onwholesim, only little Jhansi McKenna, who was four year ould thin, was left on hand.

"Five children gone in fourteen months. 'Twas harrd, wasn't ut?

"So we wint up to our new station in that blazin' heat—may the curse av Saint Lawrence conshume the man who gave the ordher! Will I iver forget that move? They gave us two wake thrains to the rigimint; an' we was eight hundher' and sivinty strong. There was A, B, C, an' D Companies in the secon' thrain, wid twelve women, no orficers' ladies, an' thirteen childher. We was to go six hundher' miles, an' railways was new in thim days. Whin we had been a night in the belly av the thrain—the men ragin' in their shirts an' dhrinkin' anything they cud find, an' eatin' bad fruit-stuff whin they cud, for we cudn't stop 'em—I was a Corp'ril thin—the cholera bruk out wid the dawnin' av the day.

"Pray to the Saints, you may niver see cholera in a throop-thrain! 'Tis like the judgmint av God hittin' down from the nakid sky! We run into a rest-camp—as ut might have been Ludianny, but not by any means so comfortable. The Orficer Commandin' sent a telegrapt up the line, three hundher' mile up, askin' for help. Faith, we wanted ut, for ivry sowl av the followers ran for the dear life as soon as the thrain stopped; an' by the time that telegrapt was writ, there wasn't a naygur in the station exceptin' the telegrapt-clerk—an' he only bekase he was held down to his chair by the scruff av his sneakin' black neck. Thin the day began wid the noise in the carr'ges, an' the rattle av the men on the platform fallin' over, arms an' all, as they stud for to answer the Comp'ny muster-roll before goin' over to the camp. 'Tisn't for me to say what like the cholera was like. May be the

Doctor cud ha' tould, av he hadn't dropped on to the platform from the door av a carriage where we was takin' out the dead. He died wid the rest. Some bhoys had died in the night. We tuk out siven, and twenty more was sickenin' as we tuk thim. The women was huddled up anyways, screamin' wid fear.

"Sez the Commandin' Orficer whose name I misremember, 'Take the women over to that tope av trees yonder. Get thim out av the camp. 'Tis no place for thim.'

"Ould Pummeloe was sittin' on her beddin'-rowl, thryin' to kape little Jhansi quiet. 'Go off to that tope!' sez the Orficer. 'Go out av the men's way!'

" 'Be damned av I do!' sez Ould Pummeloe, an' little Jhansi, squattin' by her mother's side, squeaks out, 'Be damned av I do,' tu. Thin Ould Pummeloe turns to the women an' she sez, 'Are ye goin' to let the bhoys die while you're picnickin', ye sluts?' sez she. ''Tis wather they want. Come on an' help.'

"Wid that, she turns up her sleeves an' steps out for a well behind the rest-camp—little Jhansi trottin' behind with a *lotah* an' string, an' the other women followin' like lambs, wid horse-buckets and cookin' pots. Whin all the things was full, Ould Pummeloe marches back into camp—'twas like a battlefield wid all the glory missin'—at the hid av the rigimint av women.

" 'McKenna, me man!' she sez, wid a voice on her like grand-roun's challenge, 'tell the bhoys to be quiet. Ould Pummeloe's comin' to look afther thim—wid free dhrinks.'

"Thin we cheered, an' the cheerin' in the lines was louder than the noise av the poor divils wid the sickness on thim. But not much.

"You see, we was a new an' raw rigimint in those days, an' we cud make neither head nor tail av the sickness; an' so we was useless. The men was goin' roun' an' about like dumb sheep, waitin' for the nex' man to fall over, an' sayin' undher their spache, 'Fwhat is ut? In the name av God, *fwhat* is ut?' 'Twas horrible. But through ut all, up an' down, an' down an' up, wint Ould Pummeloe an' little Jhansi—all we cud see av the baby, undher a dead man's helmut wid the chin-strap swingin' about her little stummick—up an' down wid the wather an' fwhat brandy there was.

"Now an' thin Ould Pummeloe, the tears runnin' down her fat, red face, sez, 'Me bhoys, me poor, dead, darlin' bhoys!' But, for the most, she was thryin' to put heart into the men an' kape thim stiddy; and little Jhansi was tellin' thim all they wud be 'betther in the mornin'.' 'Twas a thrick she'd picked up from hearin' Ould Pummeloe whin Muttra was burnin' out wid fever. In the mornin'! 'Twas the iverlastin' mornin' at St. Pether's Gate was the mornin' for seven-an'-twenty good men; and twenty more was sick to the death in that bitter, burnin' sun. But the women worked like angils as I've said, an' the men like divils, till two doctors come down from above, and we was rescued.

"But, just before that, Ould Pummeloe, on her knees over a bhoy in my squad—right-cot man to me he was in the barrick—tellin' him the worrud av the Church that niver failed a man yet, sez, 'Hould me up, bhoys! I'm feelin' bloody sick!' 'Twas the sun, not the cholera, did ut. She misremembered she was only wearin' her ould black bonnet, an' she died wid 'McKenna, me man,' houldin' her up, an' the bhoys howled whin they buried her.

"That night, a big wind blew, an' blew, an' blew, an' blew the tents flat. But it blew the cholera away an' niver another case there was all the while we was waitin'—ten days in quarintin'. Av you will belave me, the thrack av the sickness in the camp was for all the wurruld the thrack av a man walkin' four times in a figur-av-eight through the tents. They say 'tis the Wandherin' Jew takes the cholera wid him. I believe ut.

"An' *that*," said Mulvaney illogically, "is the cause why little Jhansi McKenna is fwhat she is. She was brought up by the Quartermaster Sergeant's wife whin McKenna died, but she b'longs to B Comp'ny; and this tale I'm tellin' you—*wid* a proper appreciashin av Jhansi McKenna—I've belted into ivry recruity av the Comp'ny as he was drafted. 'Faith, 'twas me belted Corp'ril Slane into askin' the girl!"

"Not really?"

"Man, I did! She's no beauty to look at, but she's Ould Pummeloe's daughter, an' 'tis my juty to provide for her. Jut before Slane got his promotion I sez to him, 'Slane,' sez I, 'to-morrow 'twill be insubordinashin av me to chastise you; but, by the sowl av Ould Pummeloe, who is now in glory, av you don't give me your wurrud to ask Jhansi McKenna at wanst, I'll peel the flesh off your bones wid a brass huk to-night. 'Tis a dishgrace to B Comp'ny she's been single so long!' sez I. Was I goin' to let a three-year-ould preshume to discoorse wid me—my will bein' set? No! Slane wint an' asked her. He's a good bhoy is Slane. Wan av these days he'll get into the Com'ssariat an' dhrive a buggy wid his—savin's. So I provided for Ould Pummeloe's daughter; an' now you go along an' dance agin wid her."

And I did.

I felt a respect for Miss Jhansi McKenna; and I went to her wedding later on.

Perhaps I will tell you about that one of these days.

IN THE PRIDE OF HIS YOUTH

"Stopped in the straight when the race was his own!
Look at him cutting it—cur to the bone!"
"Ask, ere the youngster be rated and chidden,
What did he carry and how was he ridden?
Maybe they used him too much at the start;
Maybe Fate's weight-cloths are breaking his heart."

—*Life's Handicap*

When I was telling you of the joke that The Worm played off on the Senior Subaltern, I promised a somewhat similar tale, but with all the jest left out. This is that tale.

Dicky Hatt was kidnapped in his early, early youth—neither by landlady's daughter, housemaid, barmaid, nor cook, but by a girl so nearly of his own caste that only a woman could have said she was just the least little bit in the world below it. This happened a month before he came out to India, and five days after his one-and-twentieth birthday. The girl was nineteen—six years older than Dicky in the things of this world, that is to say—and, for the time, twice as foolish as he.

Excepting, always, falling off a horse, there is nothing more fatally easy than marriage before the Registrar. The ceremony costs less than fifty shillings, and is remarkably like walking into a pawn-shop. After the declarations of residence have been put in, four minutes will cover the rest of the proceedings—fees, attestation, and all. Then the Registrar slides the blotting-pad over the names, and says grimly with his pen between his teeth, "Now you're man and wife"; and the couple walk out into the street feeling as if something were horribly illegal somewhere.

But that ceremony holds and can drag a man to his undoing just as thoroughly as the "long as ye both shall live" curse from the altar-rails, with the bridesmaids giggling behind, and "The Voice that breathed o'er Eden" lifting the roof off. In this manner was Dicky Hatt kidnapped, and he considered it vastly fine, for he had received an appointment in India which carried a magnificent salary from the Home point of view. The marriage was to be kept secret for a year. Then Mrs. Dicky Hatt was to come out, and the rest of life was to be a glorious golden mist. That was how they sketched it under the Addison Road Station lamps; and, after one short month, came Gravesend and Dicky steaming out to his new life, and the girl crying in a thirty-shillings a week bed-and-living-room, in a back-street off Montpelier Square near the Knightsbridge Barracks.

But the country that Dicky came to was a hard land where men of twenty-one were reckoned very small boys indeed, and life was expensive. The salary that loomed so large six thousand miles away did not go far. Particularly when Dicky divided it by two, and remitted more than the fair half, at 1-6$\frac{7}{8}$, to Montpelier Square. One hundred and thirty-five rupees out of three hundred and thirty is not much to live on; but it was absurd to suppose that Mrs. Hatt could exist forever on the £20 held back by Dicky from his outfit allowance. Dicky saw this and remitted at once; always remembering that Rs.700 were to be paid, twelve months later, for a first-class passage out for a lady. When you add to these trifling details the natural instincts of a boy beginning a new life in a new country and longing to go about and enjoy himself, and the necessity for grappling with strange work—which, properly speaking, should take up a boy's undivided attention—you will see that Dicky started handicapped. He saw it himself for a breath or two; but he did not guess the full beauty of his future.

As the hot weather began, the shackles settled on him and ate into his flesh. First would come letters—big, crossed, seven-sheet letters—from his wife, telling him how she longed to see him, and what a Heaven upon earth would be their property when they met. Then some boy of the chummery wherein Dicky lodged would pound on the door of his bare little room, and tell him to come out to look at a pony—the very thing to suit him. Dicky could not afford ponies. He had to explain this. Dicky could not afford living in the chummery, modest as it was. He had to explain this before he moved to a single room next the office where he worked all day. He kept house on a green oil-cloth table-cover, one chair, one bedstead, one photograph, one tooth-glass very strong and thick, a seven-rupee eight-anna filter, and messing by contract at thirty-seven rupees a month. Which last item was extortion. He had no punkah, for a punkah costs fifteen rupees a month; but he slept on the roof of the office with all his wife's letters under his pillow. Now and again he was asked out to dinner, where he got both a punkah and an iced drink. But this was seldom, for people objected to recognizing a boy who had evidently the instincts of a Scotch tallow-chandler, and who lived in such a nasty fashion. Dicky could not subscribe to any amusement, so he found no amusement except the pleasure of turning over his Bank-book and reading what it said about "loans on approved security." That cost nothing. He remitted through a Bombay Bank, by the way, and the Station knew nothing of his private affairs.

Every month he sent Home all he could possibly spare for his wife and for another reason which was expected to explain itself shortly, and would require more money.

About this time Dicky was overtaken with the nervous, haunting fear that besets married men when they are out of sorts. He had no pension to look to. What if he should die suddenly, and leave his wife unprovided for? The thought used to lay hold of him in the still, hot nights on the roof, till the shaking of his heart made him think that he was going to die then and there of heart-disease. Now this is a frame of mind which no boy has a right to know. It is a strong man's trouble; but, coming when it did, it nearly drove poor punkah-less, perspiring Dicky Hatt mad. He could tell no one about it.

A certain amount of "screw" is as necessary for a man as for a billiard-ball. It makes them both do wonderful things. Dicky needed money badly, and he worked for it like a horse. But, naturally, the men who owned him knew that a boy can live very comfortably on a certain income—pay in India is a matter of age not merit, you see, and, if their particular boy wished to work like two boys, Business forbid that they should stop him. But Business forbid that they should give him an increase of pay at his present ridiculously immature age. So Dicky won certain rises of salary—ample for a boy—not enough for a wife and a child—certainly too little for the seven-hundred-rupee passage that he and Mrs. Hatt had discussed so lightly once upon a time. And with this he was forced to be content.

Somehow, all his money seemed to fade away in Home drafts and the crushing Exchange, and the tone of the Home letters changed and grew querulous. "Why wouldn't Dicky have his wife and the baby out? Surely he had a salary—a fine salary—and it was too bad of him to enjoy himself in India. But would he—could he—make the next draft a little more elastic?" Here followed a list of baby's kit, as long as a Parsee's bill. Then Dicky, whose heart yearned to his wife and the little son he had never seen—which, again, is a feeling no boy is entitled to—enlarged the draft and wrote queer half-boy, half-man letters, saying that life was not so enjoyable after all and would the little wife wait yet a little longer? But the little wife, however much she approved of money, objected to waiting, and there was a strange, hard sort of ring in her letters that Dicky didn't understand. How could he, poor boy?

Later on still—just as Dicky had been told—ápropos of another youngster who had "made a fool of himself," as the saying is—that matrimony would not only ruin his further chances of advancement, but would lose him his present appointment—came the news that the baby, his own little, little son, had died, and, behind this, forty lines of an angry woman's scrawl, saying the death might have been averted if certain things, all costing money, had been done, or if the mother and the baby had been with Dicky. The letter struck at Dicky's naked heart; but, not being officially entitled to a baby, he could show no sign of trouble.

How Dicky won through the next four months, and what hope he kept alight to force him into his work, no one dare say. He pounded on, the seven-hundred-rupee passage as far away as ever, and his style of living unchanged, except when he launched into a new filter. There was the strain of his office-work, and the strain of his remittances, and the knowledge of his boy's death, which touched the boy more, perhaps, than it would have touched a man; and, beyond all, the enduring strain of his daily life. Gray-headed seniors who approved of his thrift and his fashion of denying himself everything pleasant, reminded him of the old saw that says—

"If a youth would be distinguished in his
art, art, art,
He must keep the girls away from his
heart, heart, heart."

And Dicky, who fancied he had been through every trouble that a man is permitted to know, had to laugh and agree; with the last line of his balanced Bank-book jingling in his head day and night.

But he had one more sorrow to digest before the end. There arrived a letter from the little wife—the natural sequence of the others if Dicky had only known it—and the burden of that letter was "gone with a handsomer man than you." It was a rather curious production, without stops, something like this—"She was not going to wait forever and the baby was dead and Dicky was only a boy and he would never set eyes on her again and why hadn't he waved his handkerchief to her when he left Gravesend and God was her judge she was a wicked woman but Dicky was worse enjoying himself in India and this other man loved the ground she trod on and would Dicky ever forgive her for she would never forgive Dicky; and there was no address to write to."

Instead of thanking his stars that he was free, Dicky discovered exactly how an injured husband feels—again, not at all the knowledge to which a boy is entitled—for his mind went back to his wife as he remembered her in the thirty-shilling "suite" in Montpelier Square, when the dawn of his last morning in England was breaking, and she was crying in the bed. Whereat he rolled about on his bed and bit his fingers. He never stopped to think whether, if he had met Mrs. Hatt after those two years, he would have discovered that he and she had grown quite different and new persons. This, theoretically, he ought to have done. He spent the night after the English Mail came in rather severe pain.

Next morning, Dicky Hatt felt disinclined to work. He argued that he had missed the pleasure of youth. He was tired, and he had tasted all the sorrow in life before three-and-twenty. His Honor was gone—that was the man; and now he, too, would go to the Devil—that was the boy in him. So he put his head down on the green oil-cloth table-cover, and wept before resigning his post, and all it offered.

But the reward of his services came. He was given three days to reconsider himself, and the Head of the establishment, after some telegraphings, said that it was a most unusual step, but, in view of the ability that Mr. Hatt had displayed at such and such a time, at such and such junctures, he was in a position to offer him an infinitely superior post—first on probation and later, in the natural course of things, on confirmation. "And how much does the post carry?" said Dicky. "Six hundred and fifty rupees," said the Head slowly, expecting to see the young man sink with gratitude and joy.

And it came then! The seven-hundred-rupee-passage, and enough to have saved the wife, and the little son, and to have allowed of assured and open marriage, came then. Dicky burst into a roar of laughter—laughter he could not check—nasty, jangling merriment that seemed as if it would go on forever. When he had recovered himself he said, quite seriously, "I'm tired of work. I'm an old man now. It's about time I retired. And I will."

"The boy's mad!" said the Head.

I think he was right; but Dicky Hatt never reappeared to settle the question.

PIG

Go, stalk the red deer o'er the heather,
  Ride, follow the fox if you can!
But, for pleasure and profit together,
  Allow me the hunting of Man—
The chase of the Human, the search for the Soul
  To its ruin—the hunting of Man.

—*The Old Shikarri*

I BELIEVE the difference began in the matter of a horse, with a twist in his temper, whom Pinecoffin sold to Nafferton and by whom Nafferton was nearly slain. There may have been other causes of offense; the horse was the official stalking-horse. Nafferton was very angry; but Pinecoffin laughed, and said that he had never guaranteed the beast's manners. Nafferton laughed too, though he vowed that he would write off his fall against Pinecoffin if he waited five years. Now, a Dalesman from beyond Skipton will forgive an injury when the Strid lets a man live; but a South Devon man is as soft as a Dartmoor bog. You can see from their names that Nafferton had the race-advantage of Pinecoffin. He was a peculiar man, and his notions of humor were cruel. He taught me a new and fascinating form of *shikar*. He hounded Pinecoffin from Mithankot to Jagadri, and from Gurgaon to Abbottabad—up and across the Punjab, a large Province, and in places remarkably dry. He said that he had no intention of allowing Assistant Commissioners to "sell him pups," in the shape of ramping, screaming countrybreds, without making their lives a burden to them.

Most Assistant Commissioners develop a bent for some special work after their first hot weather in the country. The boys with digestions hope to write their names large on the Frontier, and struggle for dreary places like Bannu and

Kohat. The bilious ones climb into the Secretariat. Which is very bad for the liver. Others are bitten with a mania for District work, Ghuznivide coins or Persian poetry; while some, who come of farmers' stock, find that the smell of the Earth after the Rains gets into their blood, and calls them to "develop the resources of the Province." These men are enthusiasts. Pinecoffin belonged to their class. He knew a great many facts bearing on the cost of bullocks and temporary wells, and opium-scrapers, and what happens if you burn too much rubbish on a field in the hope of enriching used-up soil. All the Pinecoffins come of a land-holding breed, and so the land only took back her own again. Unfortunately—most unfortunately for Pinecoffin—he was a Civilian, as well as a farmer. Nafferton watched him, and thought about the horse. Nafferton said, "See me chase that boy till he drops!" I said, "You can't get your knife into an Assistant Commissioner." Nafferton told me that I did not understand the administration of the Province.

Our Government is rather peculiar. It gushes on the agricultural and general information side, and will supply a moderately respectable man with all sorts of "economic statistics," if he speaks to it prettily. For instance, you are interested in gold-washing in the sands of the Sutlej. You pull the string, and find that it wakes up half a dozen Departments, and finally communicates, say, with a friend of yours in the Telegraph, who once wrote some notes on the customs of the gold-washers when he was on construction-work in their part of the Empire. He may or may not be pleased at being ordered to write out everything he knows for your benefit. This depends on his temperament. The bigger man you are, the more information and the greater trouble can you raise.

Nafferton was not a big man; but he had the reputation of being very "earnest." An "earnest" man can do much with a Government. There was an earnest man once who nearly wrecked . . . but all India knows *that* story. I am not sure what real "earnestness" is. A very fair imitation can be manufactured by neglecting to dress decently, by mooning about in a dreamy, misty sort of way, by taking office-work home, after staying in office till seven, and by receiving crowds of native gentlemen on Sundays. That is one sort of "earnestness."

Nafferton cast about for a peg whereon to hang his earnestness, and for a string that would communicate with Pinecoffin. He found both. They were Pig. Nafferton became an earnest inquirer after Pig. He informed the Government that he had a scheme whereby a very large percentage of the British Army in India could be fed, at a very large saving, on Pig. Then he hinted that Pinecoffin might supply him with the "varied information necessary to the proper inception of the scheme." So the Government wrote on the back of the letter, "Instruct Mr. Pinecoffin to furnish Mr. Nafferton with any information in his power. Government is very prone to writing things on the backs of letters which, later, lead to trouble and confusion.

Nafferton had not the faintest interest in Pig, but he knew that Pinecoffin would flounce into the trap. Pinecoffin was delighted at being consulted about Pig. The Indian Pig is not exactly an important factor in agricultural life; but Nafferton explained to Pinecoffin that there was room for improvement, and corresponded direct with that young man.

You may think that there is not much to be evolved from Pig. It all depends how you set to work. Pinecoffin being a Civilian and wishing to do things thoroughly, began with an essay on the Primitive Pig, the Mythology of the Pig, and the Dravidian Pig. Nafferton filed that information—twenty-seven fools-cap sheets—and wanted to know about the distribution of the Pig in the Punjab, and how it stood the Plains in the hot weather. From this point onward, remember that I am giving you only the barest outlines of the affair—the guy-ropes, as it were, of the web that Nafferton spun round Pinecoffin.

Pinecoffin made a colored Pig-population map, and collected observations on the comparative longevity of Pig (*a*) in the sub-montane tracts of the Himalayas, and (*b*) in the Rechna Doab. Nafferton filed that, and asked what sort of people looked after Pig. This started an ethnological excursus on swineherds, and drew from Pinecoffin long tables showing the proportion per thousand of the caste in the Derajat. Nafferton filed that bundle, and explained that the figures which he wanted referred to the Cis-Sutlej states, where he understood that Pigs were very fine and large, and where he proposed to start a Piggery. By this time, Government had quite forgotten their instructions to Mr. Pinecoffin. They were like the gentlemen, in Keats' poem, who turned well-oiled wheels to skin other people. But Pinecoffin was just entering into the spirit of the Pig-hunt, as Nafferton well knew he would do. He had a fair amount of work of his own to clear away; but he sat up of nights reducing Pig to five places of decimals for the honor of his Service. He was not going to appear ignorant of so easy a subject as Pig.

Then Government sent him on special duty to Kohat, to "inquire into" the big, seven-foot, iron-shod spades of that District. People had been killing each other with those peaceful tools; and Government wished to know "whether a modified form of agricultural implement could not, tentatively and as a temporary measure, be introduced among the agricultural population without needlessly or unduly exacerbating the existing religious sentiments of the peasantry."

Between those spades and Nafferton's Pig, Pinecoffin was rather heavily burdened.

Nafferton now began to take up "(*a*) The food-supply of the indigenous Pig, with a view to the improvement of its capacities as a flesh-former. (*b*) The acclimatization of the exotic Pig, maintaining its distinctive peculiarities." Pinecoffin replied exhaustively that the exotic Pig would become merged in the indigenous type; and quoted horse-breeding statistics to prove this. The side-issue was debated at great length on Pinecoffin's side, till Nafferton owned that he had been in the wrong, and moved the previous question. When Pinecoffin had quite written himself out about flesh-formers, and fibrins, and glucose and the nitrogenous constituents of maize and lucerne, Nafferton raised the question of expense. By this time Pinecoffin, who had been transferred from Kohat, had developed a Pig theory of his own, which he stated in thirty-three folio pages—all carefully filed by Nafferton. Who asked for more.

These things took ten months, and Pinecoffin's interest in the potential Piggery seemed to die down after he had stated his own views. But Nafferton bombarded him with letters on "the Imperial aspect of the scheme, as tending to officialize the sale of pork, and thereby calculated to give offense to the Mohammedan population of Upper India." He guessed that Pinecoffin would want some broad, free-hand work after his niggling, stippling, decimal details. Pinecoffin handled the latest development of the case in masterly style, and proved that no "popular ebullition of excitement was to be apprehended." Nafferton said that there was nothing like Civilian insight in matters of this kind, and lured him up a by-path—"the possible profits to accrue to the Government from the sale of hog-bristles." There is an extensive literature of hog-bristles, and the shoe, brush, and color-man's trades recognize more varieties of bristles than you would think possible. After Pinecoffin had wondered a little at Nafferton's rage for information, he sent back a monograph, fifty-one pages, on "Products of the Pig." This led him, under Nafferton's tender handling, straight to the Cawnpore factories, the trade in hog-skin for saddles—and thence to the tanners. Pinecoffin wrote that pomegranate-seed was the best cure for hog skin, and suggested—for the past fourteen months had wearied him—that Nafferton should "raise his pigs before he tanned them."

Nafferton went back to the second section of his fifth question. How could the exotic Pig be brought to give as much pork as it did in the West and yet "assume the essentially hirsute characteristics of its oriental congener"? Pinecoffin felt dazed, for he had forgotten what he had written sixteen months before, and fancied that he was about to reopen the entire question. He was too far involved in the hideous tangle to retreat, and, in a weak moment, he wrote, "Consult my first letter." Which related to the Dravidian Pig. As a matter of fact, Pinecoffin had still to reach the acclimatization stage; having gone off on a side-issue on the merging of types.

Then Nafferton really unmasked his batteries! He complained to the Government, in stately language, of "the paucity of help accorded to me in my earnest attempts to start a potentially remunerative industry, and the flippancy with which my requests for information are treated by a gentleman whose pseudo-scholarly attainments should at least have taught him the primary differences between the Dravidian and the Berkshire variety of the genus *Sus.* If I am to understand that the letter to which he refers me, contains his serious views on the acclimatization of a valuable, though possibly uncleanly, animal, I am reluctantly compelled to believe," etc., etc.

There was a new man at the head of the Department of Castigation. The wretched Pinecoffin was told that the Service was made for the Country, and not the Country for the Service, and that he had better begin to supply information about Pigs.

Pinecoffin answered insanely that he had written everything that could be written about Pig, and that some furlough was due to him.

Nafferton got a copy of that letter, and sent it, with the essay on the Dravidian Pig, to a down-country paper which printed both in full. The essay was rather high-flown; but if the Editor had seen the stacks of paper, in Pinecoffin's handwriting, on Nafferton's table, he would not have been so sarcastic about the "nebulous discursiveness and blatant self-sufficiency of the modern Competition-*wallah*, and his utter inability to grasp the practical issues of a practical question." Many friends cut out these remarks and sent them to Pinecoffin.

I have already stated that Pinecoffin came of a soft stock.

This last stroke frightened and shook him. He could not understand it; but he felt that he had been, somehow, shamelessly betrayed by Nafferton. He realized that he had wrapped himself up in the Pigskin without need, and that he could not well set himself right with his Government. All his acquaintances asked after his "nebulous discursiveness" or his "blatant self-sufficiency," and this made him miserable.

He took a train and went to Nafferton, whom he had not seen since the Pig business began. He also took the cutting from the paper, and blustered feebly and called Nafferton names, and then died down to a watery, weak protest of the "I-say-it's-too-bad-you-know" order.

Nafferton was very sympathetic.

"I'm afraid I've given you a good deal of trouble, haven't I?" said he.

"Trouble!" whimpered Pinecoffin; "I don't mind the trouble so much, though that was bad enough; but what I resent is this showing up in print. It will stick to me like a burr all through my service. And I *did* do my best for your interminable swine. It's too bad of you—on my soul it is!"

"I don't know," said Nafferton. "Have you ever been stuck with a horse? It isn't the money I mind, though that is bad enough; but what I resent is the chaff that follows, especially from the boy who stuck me. But I think we'll cry quits now."

Pinecoffin found nothing to say save bad words; and Nafferton smiled ever so sweetly, and asked him to dinner.

THE ROUT OF THE WHITE HUSSARS

It was not in the open fight
  We threw away the sword,
But in the lonely watching
  In the darkness by the ford.
The waters lapped, the night-wind blew,
Full-armed the Fear was born and grew,
And we were flying ere we knew
  From panic in the night.—*Beoni Bar*

SOME people hold that an English Cavalry regiment cannot run. This is a mistake. I have seen four hundred and thirty-seven sabers flying over the face of the country in abject terror—have seen the best Regiment that ever drew bridle wiped off the Army List for the space of two hours. If you repeat this tale to the White Hussars they will, in all probability, treat you severely. They are not proud of the incident.

You may know the White Hussars by their "side," which is greater than that of all the Cavalry Regiments on the roster. If this is not a sufficient mark, you may know them by their old brandy. It has been sixty years in the Mess and is worth going far to taste. Ask for the "McGaire" old brandy, and see that you get it. If the Mess Sergeant thinks that you are uneducated, and that the genuine article will be lost on you, he will treat you accordingly. He is a good man. But, when you are at Mess, you must never talk to your hosts about forced marches or long-distance rides. The Mess are very sensitive; and, if they think that you are laughing at them, will tell you so.

As the White Hussars say, it was all the Colonel's fault. He was a new man, and he ought never to have taken the Command. He said that the Regiment was not smart enough. This to the White Hussars, who knew that they could walk round any Horse and through any Guns, and over any Foot on the face of the earth! That insult was the first cause of offense.

Then the Colonel cast the Drum-Horse—the Drum-Horse of the White Hussars! Perhaps you do not see what an unspeakable crime he had committed. I will try to make it clear. The soul of the Regiment lives in the Drum-Horse who carries the silver kettle-drums. He is nearly always a big piebald Waler. That is a point of honor; and a Regiment will spend anything you please on a piebald. He is beyond the ordinary laws of casting. His work is very light, and he only maneuvers at a footpace. Wherefore, so long as he can step out and look handsome, his well-being is assured. He knows more about the Regiment than the Adjutant, and could not make a mistake if he tried.

The Drum-Horse of the White Hussars was only eighteen years old, and perfectly equal to his duties. He had at least six years' more work in him, and carried himself with all the pomp and dignity of a Drum-Major of the Guards. The Regiment had paid Rs.1,200 for him.

But the Colonel said that he must go, and he was cast in due form and replaced by a washy, bay beast, as ugly as a mule, with a ewe-neck, rat-tail, and cow-hocks. The Drummer detested that animal, and the best of the Band-horses put back their ears and showed the whites of their eyes at the very sight of him. They knew him for an upstart and no gentleman. I fancy that the Colonel's ideas of smartness extended to the Band, and that he wanted to make it take part in the regular parade movements. A Cavalry Band is a sacred thing. It only turns out for Commanding Officers' parades, and the Band Master is one degree more important than the Colonel. He is a High Priest and the "Keel Row" is his holy song. The "Keel Row" is the Cavalry Trot; and the man who has never heard that tune rising, high and shrill, above the rattle of the Regiment going past the saluting-base, has something yet to hear and understand.

When the Colonel cast the Drum-Horse of the White Hussars, there was nearly a mutiny.

The officers were angry, the Regiment were furious, and the Bandsmen swore—like troopers. The Drum-Horse was going to be put up to auction—public auction—to be bought, perhaps, by a Parsee and put into a cart! It was worse than exposing the inner life of the Regiment to the whole world, or selling the Mess Plate to a Jew—a Black Jew.

The Colonel was a mean man and a bully. He knew what the Regiment thought about his action; and, when the troopers offered to buy the Drum-Horse, he said that their offer was mutinous and forbidden by the Regulations.

But one of the Subalterns—Hogan-Yale, an Irishman—bought the Drum-Horse for Rs.160 at the sale; and the Colonel was wroth. Yale professed repentance—he was unnaturally submissive—and said that, as he had only made the purchase to save the horse from possible ill-treatment and starvation, he would now shoot him and end the business. This appeared to soothe the Colonel, for he wanted the Drum-Horse disposed of. He felt that he had made a mistake, and could not of course acknowledge it. Meantime, the presence of the Drum-Horse was an annoyance to him.

Yale took to himself a glass of the old brandy, three cheroots, and his friend Martyn; and they all left the Mess together. Yale and Martyn conferred for two hours in Yale's quarters; but only the bull-terrier who keeps watch over Yale's boot-trees knows what they said. A horse, hooded and sheeted to his ears, left Yale's stables and was taken, very unwillingly, into the Civil Lines. Yale's groom went with him. Two men broke into the Regimental Theater and took several paint-pots and some large scenery-brushes. Then night fell over the Cantonments, and there was a noise as of a horse kicking his loose-box to pieces in Yale's stables. Yale had a big, old, white Waler trap-horse.

The next day was a Thursday, and the men, hearing that Yale was going to shoot the Drum-Horse in the evening, determined to give the beast a regular regimental funeral—a finer one than they would have given the Colonel had he died just then. They got a bullock-cart and some sacking, and mounds and mounds of roses, and the body, under sacking, was carried out to the place where the anthrax cases were cremated; two-thirds of the Regiment following. There was no Band, but they all sang "The Place where the old Horse died" as something respectful and appropriate to the occasion. When the corpse was dumped into the grave, and the men began throwing down armfuls of roses to cover it, the Farrier-Sergeant ripped out an oath and said aloud, "Why, it ain't the Drum-Horse any more than it's me!" The Troop-Sergeant-Majors asked him whether he had left his head in the Canteen. The Farrier-Sergeant said that he knew the Drum-Horse's feet as well as he knew his own; but he was silenced when he saw the regimental number burned in on the poor stiff, upturned near-fore.

Thus was the Drum-Horse of the White Hussars buried; the Farrier-Sergeant grumbling. The sacking that covered the corpse was smeared in places with black paint; and the Farrier-Sergeant drew attention to this fact. But the Troop-Sergeant-Major of E Troop kicked him severely on the shin, and told him that he was undoubtedly drunk.

On the Monday following the burial, the Colonel sought revenge on the White Hussars. Unfortunately, being at that time temporarily in Command of the Station, he ordered a Brigade field-day. He said that he wished to make the Regiment "sweat for their damned insolence," and he carried out his notion thoroughly. That Monday was one of the hardest days in the memory of the White Hussars. They were thrown against a skeleton-enemy, and pushed forward, and withdrawn, and dismounted, and "scientifically handled" in every possible fashion over dusty country, till they sweated profusely. Their only amusement came late in the day when they fell upon the battery of Horse Artillery and chased it for two miles. This was a personal question, and most of the troopers had money on the event; the Gunners saying openly that they had the legs of the White Hussars. They were wrong. A march-past concluded the campaign, and when the Regiment got back to their Lines, the men were coated with dirt from spur to chin-strap.

The White Hussars have one great and peculiar privilege. They won it at Fontenoy, I think.

Many Regiments possess special rights such as wearing collars with undress uniform, or a bow of ribbon between the shoulders, or red and white roses in their helmets on certain days of the year. Some rights are connected with regimental saints, and some with regimental successes. All are valued highly; but none so highly as the right of the White Hussars to have the Band playing when their horses are being watered in the Lines. Only one tune is played, and that tune never varies. I don't know its real name, but the White Hussars call it, "Take me to London again." It sounds very pretty. The Regiment would sooner be struck off the roster than forego their distinction.

After the "dismiss" was sounded, the officers rode off home to prepare for stables; and the men filed into the lines riding easy. That is to say, they opened their tight buttons, shifted their helmets, and began to joke or to swear as the humor took them; the more careful slipping off and easing girths and curbs. A good trooper values his mount exactly as much as he values himself, and believes, or should believe, that the two together are irresistible where women or men, girls or guns, are concerned.

Then the Orderly-Officer gave the order, "Water horses," and the Regiment loafed off to the squadron-troughs which were in rear of the stables and between these and the barracks. There were four huge troughs, one for each squadron, arranged *en échelon*, so that the whole Regiment could water in ten minutes if it liked. But it lingered for seventeen as a rule, while the Band played.

The Band struck up as the squadrons filed off to the troughs, and the men slipped their feet out of the stirrups and chaffed each other. The sun was just setting in a big, hot bed of red cloud, and the road to the Civil Lines seemed to run straight into the sun's eye. There was a little dot on the road. It grew and grew till it showed as a horse, with a sort of gridiron-thing on his back. The red cloud glared through the bars of the gridiron. Some of the troopers shaded their eyes with their hands and said—"What the mischief 'as that there 'orse got on 'im?"

In another minute they heard a neigh that every soul—horse and man—in the Regiment knew, and saw, heading straight toward the Band, the dead Drum-Horse of the White Hussars!

On his withers banged and bumped the kettle-drums draped in crape, and on his back, very stiff and soldierly, sat a bareheaded skeleton.

The Band stopped playing, and, for a moment, there was a hush.

Then some one in E Troop—men said it was the Troop-Sergeant-Major—swung his horse round and yelled. No one can account exactly for what happened afterward; but it seems that, at least, one man in each troop set an example of panic, and the rest followed like sheep. The horses that had barely put their muzzles into the troughs reared and capered; but as soon as the Band broke, which it did when the ghost of the Drum-Horse was about a furlong distant, all hoofs followed suit, and the clatter of the stampede—quite different from the orderly throb and roar of a movement on parade, or the rough horse-play of watering in camp—made them only more terrified. They felt that the men on their backs were afraid of something. When horses once know that, all is over except the butchery.

Troop after troop turned from the troughs and ran—anywhere and everywhere—like spilled quicksilver. It was a most extraordinary spectacle, for men and horses were in all stages of easiness, and the carbine-buckets flopping against their sides urged the horses on. Men were shouting and cursing, and trying to pull clear of the Band, which was being chased by the Drum-Horse whose rider had fallen forward and seemed to be spurring for a wager.

The Colonel had gone over to the Mess for a drink. Most of the officers were with him, and the Subaltern of the Day was preparing to go down to the lines, and receive the watering reports from the Troop-Sergeant-Majors. When "Take me to London again" stopped, after twenty bars, every one in the Mess said, "What on earth has happened?" A minute later, they heard unmilitary noises, and saw, far across the plain, the White Hussars scattered, and broken, and flying.

The Colonel was speechless with rage, for he thought that the Regiment had risen against him or was unanimously drunk. The Band, a disorganized mob, tore past, and at its heels labored the Drum-Horse—the dead and buried Drum-Horse—with the jolting, clattering skeleton. Hogan-Yale whispered softly to Martyn—"No wire will stand that treatment," and the Band, which had doubled like a hare, came back again. But the rest of the Regiment was gone, was rioting all over the Province, for the dusk had shut in and each man was howling to his neighbor that the Drum-Horse was on his flank. Troop-horses are far too tenderly treated as a rule. They can, on emergencies, do a great deal, even with seventeen stone on their backs. As the troopers found out.

How long this panic lasted I cannot say. I believe that when the moon rose the men saw they had nothing to fear, and, by twos and threes and half-troops, crept back into Cantonments very much ashamed of themselves. Meantime, the Drum-Horse, disgusted at his treatment by old friends, pulled up, wheeled round, and trotted up to the Mess veranda-steps for bread. No one liked to run; but no one cared to go forward till the Colonel made a movement and laid hold of the skeleton's foot. The Band had halted some distance away, and now came back slowly. The Colonel called it, individually and collectively, every evil name that occurred to him at the time; for he had set his hand on the bosom of the Drum Horse and found flesh and blood. Then he beat the kettle-drums with his clinched fist, and discovered that they were but made of silvered paper and bamboo. Next, still swearing, he tried to drag the skeleton out of the saddle, but found that it had been wired into the cantle. The sight of the Colonel, with his arms round the skeleton's pelvis and his knee in the old Drum-Horse's stomach, was striking. Not to say amusing. He worried the thing off in a minute or two, and threw it down on the ground, saying to the Band—"Here, you curs, that's what you're afraid of." The skeleton did not look pretty in the twilight. The Band-Sergeant seemed to recognize it, for he began to chuckle and choke. "Shall I take it away, sir?" said the Band-Sergeant. "Yes," said the Colonel, "take it to Hell, and ride there yourselves!"

The Band-Sergeant saluted, hoisted the skeleton across his saddle-bow, and led off to the stables. Then the Colonel began to make inquiries for the rest of the Regiment, and the language he used was wonderful. He would disband the Regiment—he would court-martial every soul in it—he would not command such a set of rabble, and so on, and so on. As the men dropped in, his language grew wilder, until at last it exceeded the utmost limits of free speech allowed even to a Colonel of Horse.

Martyn took Hogan-Yale aside and suggested compulsory retirement from the Service as a necessity when all was discovered. Martyn was the weaker man of the two. Hogan-Yale put up his eyebrows and remarked, first, that he was the son of a Lord, and, secondly, that he was as innocent as the babe unborn of the theatrical resurrection of the Drum-Horse.

"My instructions," said Yale, with a singularly sweet smile, "were that the Drum-Horse should be sent back as impressively as possible. I ask you, *am* I responsible if a mule-headed friend sends him back in such a manner as to disturb the peace of mind of a regiment of Her Majesty's Cavalry?"

Martyn said, "You are a great man, and will in time become a General; but I'd give my chance of a troop to be safe out of this affair."

Providence saved Martyn and Hogan-Yale. The Second-in-Command led the Colonel away to the little curtained alcove wherein the Subalterns of the White Hussars were accustomed to play poker of nights; and there, after many oaths on the Colonel's part, they talked together in low tones. I fancy that the Second-in-Command must have represented the scare as the work of some trooper whom it would be hopeless to detect; and I know that he dwelt upon the sin and the shame of making a public laughing-stock of the scare.

"They will call us," said the Second-in-Command, who had really a fine imagination—"they will call us the 'Fly-by-Nights'; they will call us the 'Ghost Hunters'; they will nickname us from one end of the Army List to the other. All the explanation in the world won't make outsiders understand that the officers were away when the panic began. For the honor of the Regiment and for your own sake keep this thing quiet."

The Colonel was so exhausted with anger that soothing him down was not so difficult as might be imagined. He was made to see, gently and by degrees, that it was obviously impossible to court-martial the whole Regiment and equally impossible to proceed against any subaltern who, in his belief, had any concern in the hoax.

"But the beast's alive! He's never been shot at all!" shouted the Colonel. "It's flat flagrant disobedience! I've known a man broke for less—damn sight less. They're mocking me, I tell you, Mutman! They're mocking me!"

Once more, the Second-in-Command set himself to soothe the Colonel, and wrestled with him for half an hour. At the end of that time, the Regimental Sergeant-Major reported himself. The situation was rather novel to him; but he was not a man to be put out by circumstances. He saluted and said, "Regiment all come back, Sir." Then, to propitiate the Colonel—"An' none of the 'orses any the worse, Sir."

The Colonel only snorted and answered—"You'd better tuck the men into their cots, then, and see that they don't wake up and cry in the night." The Sergeant withdrew.

His little stroke of humor pleased the Colonel, and, further, he felt slightly ashamed of the language he had been using. The Second-in-Command worried him again, and the two sat talking far into the night.

Next day but one, there was a Commanding Officer's parade, and the Colonel harangued the White Hussars vigorously. The pith of his speech was that, since the Drum-Horse in his old age had proved himself capable of cutting up the whole Regiment, he should return to his post of pride at the head of the Band, *but* the Regiment were a set of ruffians with bad consciences.

The White Hussars shouted, and threw everything movable about them into the air, and when the parade was over, they cheered the Colonel till they couldn't speak. No cheers were put up for Lieutenant Hogan-Yale, who smiled very sweetly in the background.

Said the Second-in-Command to the Colonel, unofficially—

"These little things insure popularity, and do not the least affect discipline."

"But I went back on my word," said the Colonel.

"Never mind," said the Second-in-Command. "The White Hussars will follow you anywhere from to-day. Regiments are just like women. They will do anything for trinketry."

A week later, Hogan-Yale received an extraordinary letter from some one who signed himself "Secretary, *Charity and Zeal*, 3709, E.C.," and asked for "the return of our skeleton which we have reason to believe is in your possession."

"Who the deuce is this lunatic who trades in bones?" said Hogan-Yale.

"Beg you pardon, Sir," said the Band-Sergeant, "but the skeleton is with me, an' I'll return it if you'll pay the carriage into the Civil Lines. There's a coffin with it, Sir."

Hogan-Yale smiled and handed two rupees to the Band-Sergeant, saying, "Write the date on the skull, will you?"

If you doubt this story, and know where to go, you can

see the date on the skeleton. But don't mention the matter to the White Hussars.

I happen to know something about it, because I prepared the Drum-Horse for his resurrection. He did not take kindly to the skeleton at all.

THE BRONCKHORST DIVORCE-CASE

In the daytime, when she moved about me,
  In the night, when she was sleeping at my side—
I was wearied, I was wearied of her presence,
Day by day and night by night I grew to hate her—
  Would God that she or I had died!—*Confessions*

THERE was a man called Bronckhorst—a three-cornered, middle-aged man in the Army—gray as a badger, and, some people said, with a touch of country-blood in him. That, however, cannot be proved. Mrs. Bronckhorst was not exactly young, though fifteen years younger than her husband. She was a large, pale, quiet woman, with heavy eyelids over weak eyes, and hair that turned red or yellow as the lights fell on it.

Bronckhorst was not nice in any way. He had no respect for the pretty public and private lies that make life a little less nasty than it is. His manner toward his wife was coarse. There are many things—including actual assault with the clinched fist—that a wife will endure; but seldom a wife can bear—as Mrs. Bronckhorst bore—with a long course of brutal, hard chaff, making light of her weaknesses, her headaches, her small fits of gayety, her dresses, her queer little attempts to make herself attractive to her husband when she knows that she is not what she has been, and—worst of all—the love that she spends on her children. That particular sort of heavy-handed jest was specially dear to Bronckhorst. I suppose that he had first slipped into it, meaning no harm, in the honeymoon, when folk find their ordinary stock of endearments run short, and so go to the other extreme to express their feelings. A similar impulse makes a man say, "Hutt, you old beast!" when a favorite horse nuzzles his coat-front. Unluckily, when the reaction of marriage sets in, the form of speech remains, and, the tenderness having died out, hurts the wife more than she cares to say. But Mrs. Bronckhorst was devoted to her "Teddy" as she called him. Perhaps that was why he objected to her. Perhaps—this is only a theory to account for his infamous behavior later on—he gave way to the queer, savage feeling that sometimes takes by the throat a husband twenty years married, when he sees, across the table, the same same face of his wedded wife, and knows that, as he has sat facing it, so must he continue to sit until the day of its death or his own. Most men and all women know the spasm. It only lasts for three breaths as a rule, must be a "throw-back" to times when men and women were rather worse than they are now, and is too unpleasant to be discussed.

Dinner at the Bronckhorsts' was an infliction few men cared to undergo. Bronckhorst took a pleasure in saying things that made his wife wince. When their little boy came in at dessert, Bronckhorst used to give him half a glass of wine, and naturally enough, the poor little mite got first riotous, next miserable, and was removed screaming. Bronckhorst asked if that was the way Teddy usually behaved, and whether Mrs. Bronckhorst could not spare some of her time "to teach the little beggar decency." Mrs. Bronckhorst, who loved the boy more than her own life, tried not to cry—her spirit seemed to have been broken by her marriage. Lastly, Bronckhorst used to say, "There! That'll do, that'll do. For God's sake try to behave like a rational woman. Go into the drawing-room." Mrs. Bronckhorst would go, trying to carry it all off with a smile; and the guest of the evening would feel angry and uncomfortable.

After three years of this cheerful life—for Mrs. Bronckhorst had no women-friends to talk to—the Station was startled by the news that Bronckhorst had instituted proceedings *on the criminal count*, against a man called Biel, who certainly had been rather attentive to Mrs. Bronckhorst whenever she had appeared in public. The utter want of reserve with which Bronckhorst treated his own dishonor helped us to know that the evidence against Biel would be entirely circumstantial and native. There were no letters; but Bronckhorst said openly that he would rack Heaven and Earth until he saw Biel superintending the manufacture of carpets in the Central Jail. Mrs. Bronckhorst kept entirely to her house, and let charitable folks say what they pleased. Opinions were divided. Some two-thirds of the Station jumped at once to the conclusion that Biel was guilty; but a dozen men who knew and liked him held by him. Biel was furious and surprised. He denied the whole thing, and vowed that he would thrash Bronckhorst within an inch of his life. No jury, we knew, would convict a man on the criminal count on native evidence in a land where you can buy a murder-charge, including the corpse, all complete for fifty-four rupees; but Biel did not care to scrape through by the benefit of a doubt. He wanted the whole thing cleared; but, as he said one night—"He can prove anything with servants' evidence, and I've only my bare word." This was almost a month before the case came on; and beyond agreeing with Biel, we could do little. All that we could be sure of was that the native evidence would be bad enough to blast Biel's character for the rest of his service; for when a native begins perjury he perjures himself thoroughly. He does not boggle over details.

Some genius at the end of the table whereat the affair was being talked over, said, "Look here! I don't believe lawyers are any good. Get a man to wire to Strickland, and beg him to come down and pull us through."

Strickland was about a hundred and eighty miles up the line. He had not long been married to Miss Youghal, but he scented in the telegram a chance of return to the old detective work that his soul lusted after, and next night he came in and heard our story. He finished his pipe and said oracularly, "We must get at the evidence. *Oorya* bearer, Mussulman *khit* and sweeper *ayah*, I suppose, are the pillars of the charge. I am on in this piece; but I'm afraid I'm getting rusty in my talk."

He rose and went into Biel's bedroom, where his trunk had been put, and shut the door. An hour later, we heard him say, "I hadn't the heart to part with my old make-ups when I married. Will this do?" There was a loathly *faquir* salaaming in the doorway.

"Now lend me fifty rupees," said Strickland, "and give me your Words of Honor that you won't tell my wife."

He got all that he asked for, and left the house while the table drank his health. What he did only he himself knows. A *faquir* hung about Bronckhorst's compound for twelve days. Then a sweeper appeared, and when Biel heard of *him*, he said that Strickland was an angel full-fledged. Whether the sweeper made love to Janki, Mrs. Bronckhorst's *ayah*, is a question which concerns Strickland exclusively.

He came back at the end of three weeks, and said quietly, "You spoke the truth, Biel. The whole business is put up from beginning to end. 'Jove! It almost astonishes *me!* That Bronckhorst-beast isn't fit to live."

There was uproar and shouting, and Biel said, "How are you going to prove it? You can't say that you've been trespassing on Bronckhorst's compound in disguise!"

"No," said Strickland. "Tell your lawyer-fool, whoever he is, to get up something strong about 'inherent improbabilities' and 'discrepancies of evidence.' He won't have to speak, but it will make him happy. *I'm* going to run this business."

Biel held his tongue, and the other men waited to see what would happen. They trusted Strickland as men trust quiet men. When the case came off the Court was crowded. Strickland hung about in the veranda of the Court, till he met the Mohammedan *khitmatgar*. Then he murmured a *faquir's* blessing in his ear, and asked him how his second wife did. The man spun round, and, as he looked into the eyes of "Estreeken *Sahib*," his jaw dropped. You must remember that before Strickland was married, he was, as I have told you already, a power among natives. Strickland whispered a rather coarse vernacular proverb to the effect that he was abreast of all that was going on and went into the Court armed with a gut trainer's-whip.

The Mohammedan was the first witness and Strickland beamed upon him from the back of the Court. The man moistened his lips with his tongue and, in his abject fear of "Estreeken *Sahib*," the *faquir*, went back on every detail of his evidence—said he was a poor man and God was his witness that he had forgotten everything that Bronckhorst *Sahib* had told him to say. Between his terror of Strickland, the Judge, and Bronckhorst he collapsed weeping.

Then began the panic among the witnesses. Janki, the *ayah*, leering chastely behind her veil, turned gray, and the bearer left the Court. He said that his Mamma was dying and that it was not wholesome for any man to lie unthriftily in the presence of "Estreeken *Sahib*."

Biel said politely to Bronckhorst, "Your witnesses don't seem to work. Haven't you any forged letters to produce?" But Bronckhorst was swaying to and fro in his chair, and there was a dead pause after Biel had been called to order.

Bronckhorst's Counsel saw the look on his client's face, and without more ado, pitched his papers on the little green baize table, and mumbled something about having been misinformed. The whole court applauded wildly, like soldiers at a theater, and the Judge began to say what he thought.

. . . .

Biel came out of the court, and Strickland dropped a gut trainer's-whip in the veranda. Ten minutes later, Biel was cutting Bronckhorst into ribbons behind the old Court cells, quietly and without scandal. What was left of Bronckhorst was sent home in a carriage; and his wife wept over it and nursed it into a man again.

Later on, after Biel had managed to hush up the countercharge against Bronckhorst of fabricating false evidence,

Mrs. Bronckhorst, with her faint watery smile, said that there had been a mistake, but it wasn't her Teddy's fault altogether. She would wait till her Teddy came back to her. Perhaps he had grown tired of her, or she had tried his patience, and perhaps we wouldn't cut her any more, and perhaps the mothers would let their children play with "little Teddy" again. He was so lonely. Then the Station invited Mrs. Bronckhorst everywhere, until Bronckhorst was fit to appear in public, when he went Home and took his wife with him. According to latest advices, her Teddy did come back to her, and they are moderately happy. Though, of course, he can never forgive her the thrashing that she was the indirect means of getting for him.

. . . .

What Biel wants to know is, "Why didn't I press home the charge against the Bronckhorst-brute, and have him run in?"

What Mrs. Strickland wants to know is, "How *did* my husband bring such a lovely, lovely Waler from your Station? I know *all* his money-affairs; and I'm *certain* he didn't *buy* it."

What I want to know is, "How do women like Mrs. Bronckhorst come to marry men like Bronckhorst?"

And my conundrum is the most unanswerable of the three.

VENUS ANNODOMINI

And the years went on, as the years must do;
But our great Diana was always new--
Fresh, and blooming, and blonde, and fair,
With azure eyes and with aureate hair;
And all the folk, as they came or went,
Offered her praise to her heart's content.

—*Diana of Ephesus*

SHE had nothing to do with Number Eighteen in the Braccio Nuovo of the Vatican, between Visconti's Ceres and the God of the Nile. She was purely an Indian deity—an Anglo-Indian deity, that is to say—and we called her *the* Venus Annodomini, to distinguish her from other Annodominis of the same everlasting order. There was a legend among the Hills that she had once been young; but no living man was prepared to come forward and say boldly that the legend was true. Men rode up to Simla, and stayed, and went away and made their name and did their life's work, and returned again to find the Venus Annodomini exactly as they had left her. She was as immutable as the Hills. But not quite so green. All that a girl of eighteen could do in the way of riding, walking, dancing, picnicking and over-exertion generally, the Venus Annodomini did, and showed no sign of fatigue or trace of weariness. Besides perpetual youth, she had discovered, men said, the secret of perpetual health; and her fame spread about the land. From a mere woman, she grew to be an Institution, insomuch that no young man could be said to be properly formed, who had not, at some time or another, worshiped at the shrine of the Venus Annodomini. There was no one like her, though there were many imitations. Six years in her eyes were no more than six months to ordinary women; and ten made less visible impression on her than does a week's fever on an ordinary woman. Every one adored her, and in return she was pleasant and courteous to nearly every one. Youth had been a habit of hers for so long, that she could not part with it—never realized, in fact, the necessity of parting with it—and took for her more chosen associates young people.

Among the worshipers of the Venus Annodomini was young Gayerson. "Very Young Gayerson" he was called to distinguish him from his father, "Young" Gayerson, a Bengal Civilian, who affected the customs—as he had the heart—of youth. "Very Young" Gayerson was not content to worship placidly and for form's sake, as the other young men did, or to accept a ride or a dance, or a talk from the Venus Annodomini in a properly humble and thankful spirit. He was exacting, and, therefore, the Venus Annodomini repressed him. He worried himself nearly sick in a futile sort of way over her; and his devotion and earnestness made him appear either shy or boisterous or rude, as his mood might vary, by the side of the older men who, with him, bowed before the Venus Annodomini. She was sorry for him. He reminded her of a lad who, three-and-twenty years ago, had professed a boundless devotion for her, and for whom in return she had felt something more than a week's weakness. But that lad had fallen away and married another woman less than a year after he had worshiped her; and the Venus Annodomini had almost—not quite—forgotten his name. "Very Young" Gayerson had the same big blue eyes and the same way of pouting his underlip when he was excited or troubled. But the Venus Annodomini checked him sternly none the less. Too much zeal was a thing that she did not approve of; preferring, instead, a tempered and sober tenderness.

"Very Young" Gayerson was miserable, and took no trouble to conceal his wretchedness. He was in the Army —a Line regiment, I think, but am not certain—and, since his face was a looking-glass and his forehead an open book, by reason of his innocence, his brothers-in-arms made his life a burden to him and imbittered his naturally sweet disposition. No one except "Very Young" Gayerson, and he never told his views, knew how old "Very Young" Gayerson believed the Venus Annodomini to be. Perhaps he thought her five-and-twenty, or perhaps she told him that she was this age. "Very Young" Gayerson would have forded the Indus in flood to carry her lightest word, and had implicit faith in her. Every one liked him and every one was sorry when they saw him so bound a slave of the Venus Annodomini. Every one, too, admitted that it was not her fault; for the Venus Annodomini differed from Mrs. Hauksbee and Mrs. Reiver in this particular—she never moved a finger to attract any one; but, like Ninon de L'Enclos, all men were attracted to her. One could admire and respect Mrs. Hauksbee, despise and avoid Mrs. Reiver, but one was forced to adore the Venus Annodomini.

"Very Young" Gayerson's papa held a Division or a Collectorate or something administrative in a particularly unpleasant part of Bengal—full of Babus who edited newspapers proving that "Young" Gayerson was a "Nero" and a "Scylla" and a "Charybdis"; and, in addition to the Babus, there was a good deal of dysentery and cholera abroad for nine months of the year. "Young" Gayerson—he was about five-and-forty—rather liked Babus, they amused him, but he objected to dysentery, and when he could get away, went to Darjiling for the most part. This particular season he fancied that he would come up to Simla and see his boy. The boy was not altogether pleased. He told the Venus Annodomini that his father was coming up, and she flushed a little and said that she should be delighted to make his acquaintance. Then she looked long and thoughtfully at "Very Young" Gayerson, because she was very, very sorry for him, and he was a very, very big idiot.

"My daughter is coming out in a fortnight, Mr. Gayerson," she said.

"Your *what?*" said he.

"Daughter," said the Venus Annodomini. "She's been out for a year at Home already, and I want her to see a little of India. She is nineteen and a very sensible, nice girl, I believe."

"Very Young" Gayerson, who was a short twenty-two years old, nearly fell out of his chair with astonishment; for he had persisted in believing, against all belief, in the youth of the Venus Annodomini. She, with her back to the curtained window, watched the effect of her sentences and smiled.

"Very Young" Gayerson's papa came up twelve days later, and had not been in Simla four-and-twenty hours, before two men, old acquaintances of his, had told him how "Very Young" Gayerson had been conducting himself.

"Young" Gayerson laughed a good deal, and inquired who the Venus Annodomini might be. Which proves that he had been living in Bengal where nobody knows anything except the rate of Exchange. Then he said boys will be boys, and spoke to his son about the matter. "Very Young" Gayerson said that he felt wretched and unhappy; and "Young" Gayerson said that he repented of having helped to bring a fool into the world. He suggested that his son had better cut his leave short and go down to his duties. This led to an unfilial answer, and relations were strained, until "Young" Gayerson demanded that they should call on the Venus Annodomini. "Very Young" Gayerson went with his papa, feeling, somehow, uncomfortable and small.

The Venus Annodomini received them graciously, and "Young" Gayerson said, "By Jove! It's Kitty!" "Very Young" Gayerson would have listened for an explanation, if his time had not been taken up with trying to talk to a large, handsome, quiet, well-dressed girl—introduced to him by the Venus Annodomini as her daughter. She was far older in manner, style, and repose than "Very Young" Gayerson; and, as he realized this thing, he felt sick.

Presently, he heard the Venus Annodomini saying, "Do you know that your son is one of my most devoted admirers?"

"I don't wonder," said "Young" Gayerson. Here he raised his voice, "He follows his father's footsteps. Didn't I worship the ground you trod on, ever so long ago, Kitty—and you haven't changed since then. How strange it all seems!"

"Very Young" Gayerson said nothing. His conversation with the daughter of the Venus Annodomini was, through the rest of the call, fragmentary and disjointed.

. . . .

"At five to-morrow then," said the Venus Annodomini. "And mind you are punctual."

"At five punctually," said "Young" Gayerson. "You can lend your old father a horse I daresay, youngster, can't you? I'm going for a ride to-morrow afternoon."

"Certainly," said "Very Young" Gayerson. "I am going down to-morrow morning. My ponies are at your service, Sir."

The Venus Annodomini looked at him across the half-light of the room, and her big gray eyes filled with moisture. She rose and shook hands with him.

"Good-by, Tom," whispered the Venus Annodomini.

THE BISARA OF POOREE

Little Blind Fish, thou art marvelous wise,
Little Blind Fish, who put out thy eyes?
Open thy ears while I whisper my wish—
Bring me a lover, thou little Blind Fish.
—*The Charm of the Bisara*

SOME natives say that it came from the other side of Kulu, where the eleven-inch Temple Sapphire is. Others that it was made at the Devil-Shrine of Ao-Chung in Thibet, was stolen by a Kafir, from him by a Gurkha, from him again by a Lahouli, from him by a *khitmatgar*, and by this latter sold to an Englishman, so all its virtue was lost; because, to work properly, the Bisara of Pooree must be stolen—with bloodshed if possible, but, at any rate, stolen.

These stories of the coming into India are all false. It was made at Pooree ages since—the manner of its making would fill a small book—was stolen by one of the Temple dancing-girls there, for her own purposes, and then passed on from hand to hand, steadily northward, till it reached Hanlê: always bearing the same name—the Bisara of Pooree. In shape it is a tiny square box of silver, studded outside with eight small balas-rubies. Inside the box, which opens with a spring, is a little eyeless fish, carved from some sort of dark, shiny nut and wrapped in a shred of faded gold-cloth. That is the Bisara of Pooree, and it were better for a man to take a king-cobra in his hand than to touch the Bisara of Pooree.

All kinds of magic are out of date, and done away with except in India where nothing changes in spite of the shiny, top-scum stuff that people call "civilization." Any man who knows about the Bisara of Pooree will tell you what its powers are—always supposing that it has been honestly stolen. It is the only regularly working, trustworthy love-charm in the country, with one exception. [The other charm is in the hands of a trooper of the Nizam's Horse, at a place called Tuprani, due north of Hyderabad.] This can be depended upon for a fact. Some one else may explain it.

If the Bisara be not stolen, but given or bought or found, it turns against its owner in three years, and leads to ruin or death. This is another fact which you may explain when you have time. Meanwhile, you can laugh at it. At present, the Bisara is safe on a hack-pony's neck, inside the blue bead-necklace that keeps off the Evil-Eye. If the pony-driver ever finds it, and wears it, or gives it to his wife, I am sorry for him.

A very dirty hill-coolie woman, with goitre, owned it at Theog in 1884. It came into Simla from the north before Churton's *khitmatgar* bought it, and sold it, for three times its silver-value, to Churton, who collected curiosities. The servant knew no more what he had bought than the master; but a man looking over Churton's collection of curiosities—Churton was an Assistant Commissioner, by the way—saw and held his tongue. He was an Englishman; but knew how to believe. Which shows that he was different from most Englishmen. He knew that it was dangerous to have any share in the little box when working or dormant; for Love unsought is a terrible gift.

Pack—"Grubby" Pack, as we used to call him—was, in every way, a nasty little man, who must have crawled into the Army by mistake. He was three inches taller than his sword, but not half so strong. And the sword was a fifty-shilling, tailor-made one. Nobody liked him, and, I suppose, it was his wizenedness and worthlessness that made him fall so hopelessly in love with Miss Hollis, who was good and sweet, and five-foot-seven in her tennis-shoes. He was not content with falling in love quietly, but brought all the strength of his miserable little nature into the business.

If he had not been so objectionable, one might have pitied him. He vapored, and fretted, and fumed, and trotted up and down, and tried to make himself pleasing in Miss Hollis' big, quiet, gray eyes, and failed. It was one of the cases that you sometimes meet, even in our country where we marry by Code, of a really blind attachment all on one side, without the faintest possibility of return. Miss Hollis looked on Pack as some sort of vermin running about the road. He had no prospects beyond Captain's pay, and no wits to help that out by one penny. In a large-sized man, love like his would have been touching. In a good man it would have been grand. He being what he was, it was only a nuisance.

You will believe this much. What you will not believe is what follows: Churton, and The Man who Knew what the Bisara was, were lunching at the Simla Club together. Churton was complaining of life in general. His best mare had rolled out of stable down the cliff and had broken her back; his decisions were being reversed by the upper Courts more than an Assistant Commissioner of eight years' standing has a right to expect; he knew liver and fever, and, for weeks past, had felt out of sorts. Altogether, he was disgusted and disheartened.

Simla Club dining-room is built, as all the world knows, in two sections, with an arch-arrangement dividing them. Come in, turn to your own left, take the table under the window, and you cannot see any one who has come in, turned to the right, and taken a table on the right side of the arch. Curiously enough, every word that you say can be heard, not only by the other diner, but by the servants beyond the screen through which they bring dinner. This is worth knowing; an echoing-room is a trap to be forewarned against.

Half in fun, and half hoping to be believed, The Man who Knew told Churton the story of the Bisara of Pooree at rather greater length than I have told it to you in this place; winding up with a suggestion that Churton might as well throw the little box down the hill and see whether all his troubles would go with it. In ordinary ears, English ears, the tale was only an interesting bit of folklore. Churton laughed, said that he felt better for his tiffin, and went out. Pack had been tiffining by himself to the right of the arch, and had heard everything. He was nearly mad with his absurd infatuation for Miss Hollis, that all Simla had been laughing about.

It is a curious thing that, when a man hates or loves beyond reason, he is ready to go beyond reason to gratify his feelings. Which he would not do for money or power merely. Depend upon it, Solomon would never have built altars to Ashtaroth and all those ladies with queer names, if there had not been trouble of some kind in his *zenana*, and nowhere else. But this is beside the story. The facts of the case are these: Pack called on Churton next day when Churton was out, left his card, and stole the Bisara of Pooree from its place under the clock on the mantel-piece! Stole it like the thief he was by nature. Three days later all Simla was electrified by the news that Miss Hollis had accepted Pack—the shriveled rat, Pack! Do you desire clearer evidence than this? The Bisara of Pooree had been stolen, and it worked as it had always done when won by foul means.

There are three or four times in a man's life when he is justified in meddling with other people's affairs to play Providence.

The Man who Knew felt that he was justified; but believing and acting on a belief are quite different things. The insolent satisfaction of Pack as he ambled by the side of Miss Hollis, and Churton's striking release from liver, as soon as the Bisara of Pooree had gone, decided The Man. He explained to Churton, and Churton laughed, because he was not brought up to believe that men on the Government House List steal—at least little things. But the miraculous acceptance by Miss Hollis of that tailor, Pack, decided him to take steps on suspicion. He vowed that he only wanted to find out where his ruby-studded silver box had vanished to. You cannot accuse a man on the Government House List of stealing. And if you rifle his room, you are a thief yourself.

Churton, prompted by The Man who Knew, decided on burglary. If he found nothing in Pack's room . . . but it is not nice to think of what would have happened in that case.

Pack went to a dance at Benmore—Benmore was Benmore in those days, and not an office—and danced fifteen waltzes out of twenty-two with Miss Hollis. Churton and The Man took all the keys that they could lay hands on, and went to Pack's room in the hotel, certain that his servants would be away. Pack was a cheap soul. He had not purchased a decent cash-box to keep his papers in, but one of those native imitations that you buy for ten rupees. It opened to any sort of key, and there at the bottom, under Pack's Insurance Policy, lay the Bisara of Pooree!

Churton called Pack names, put the Bisara of Pooree in his pocket, and went to the dance with The Man. At least, he came in time for supper, and saw the beginning of the end in Miss Hollis' eyes. She was hysterical after supper, and was taken away by her Mamma.

At the dance, with the abominable Bisara in his pocket, Churton twisted his foot on one of the steps leading down to the old Rink, and had to be sent home in a 'rickshaw, grumbling. He did not believe in the Bisara of Pooree any the more for this manifestation, but he sought out Pack and called him some ugly names; and "thief" was the mildest of them. Pack took the names with the nervous smile of a little man who wants both soul and body to resent an insult, and went his way. There was no public scandal.

A week later, Pack got his definite dismissal from Miss Hollis. There had been a mistake in the placing of her affections, she said. So he went away to Madras, where he can do no great harm even if he lives to be a Colonel.

Churton insisted upon The Man who Knew taking the Bisara of Pooree as a gift. The Man took it, went down to the Cart-Road at once, found a cart-pony with a blue bead-necklace, fastened the Bisara of Pooree inside the necklace with a piece of shoe-string, and thanked Heaven that he was rid of a danger. Remember, in case you ever find it, that you must not destroy the Bisara of Pooree. I have not time to explain why just now, but the power lies in the little wooden fish. Mister Gubernatis or Max Müller could tell you more about it than I.

You will say that all this story is made up. Very well. If ever you come across a little, silver, ruby-studded box, seven-eighths of an inch long by three-quarters wide, with a dark brown wooden fish, wrapped in gold cloth, inside it, keep it. Keep it for three years, and then you will discover for yourself whether my story is true or false.

Better still, steal it as Pack did, and you will be sorry that you had not killed yourself in the beginning.

A FRIEND'S FRIEND

Wherefore slew you the stranger? He brought me dishonor.
I saddled my mare Bijli. I set him upon her.
I gave him rice and goat's flesh. He bared me to laughter;
When he was gone from my tent, swift I followed after,
Taking a sword in my hand. The hot wine had filled him:
Under the stars he mocked me. Therefore I killed him.

—*Hadramauti*

THIS tale must be told in the first person for many reasons. The man whom I want to expose is Tranter of the Bombay side. I want Tranter black-balled at his Club, divorced from his wife, turned out of Service, and cast into prison, until I get an apology from him in writing. I wish to warn the world against Tranter of the Bombay side.

You know the casual way in which men pass on acquaintances in India? It is a great convenience, because you can get rid of a man you don't like by writing a letter of introduction and putting him, with it, into the train. T. G.'s are best treated thus. If you keep them moving, they have no time to say insulting and offensive things about "Anglo-Indian Society."

One day, late in the cold weather, I got a letter of preparation from Tranter of the Bombay side, advising me of the advent of a T. G., a man called Jevon; and saying, as usual, that any kindness shown to Jevon would be a kindness to Tranter. Every one knows the regular form of these communications.

Two days afterward, Jevon turned up with his letter of introduction, and I did what I could for him. He was lint-haired, fresh-colored, and very English. But he held no views about the Government of India. Nor did he insist on shooting tigers on the Station Mall, as some T. G.'s do. Nor did he call us "colonists," and dine in a flannel-shirt and tweeds, under that delusion as other T. G.'s do. He was well behaved and very grateful for the little I won for him—most grateful of all when I secured him an invitation for the Afghan Ball, and introduced him to a Mrs. Deemes, a lady for whom I had a great respect and admiration, who danced like the shadow of a leaf in a light wind. I set great store by the friendship of Mrs. Deemes; but, had I known what was coming, I would have broken Jevon's neck with a curtain-pole before getting him that invitation.

But I did not know, and he dined, at the Club, I think, on the night of the ball. I dined at home. When I went to the dance, the first man I met asked me whether I had seen Jevon. "No," said I. "He's at the Club. Hasn't he come?"—"Come!" said the man. "Yes, he's very much come. You'd better look at him."

I sought for Jevon. I found him sitting on a bench and smiling to himself and a programme. Half a look was enough for me. On that one night, of all others, he had begun a long and thirsty evening, by taking too much! He was breathing heavily through his nose, his eyes were rather red, and he appeared very satisfied with all the earth. I put up a little prayer that the waltzing would work off the wine, and went about programme-filling, feeling uncomfortable. But I saw Jevon walk up to Mrs. Deemes for the first dance, and I knew that all the waltzing on the card was not enough to keep Jevon's rebellious legs steady. That couple went round six times. I counted. Mrs. Deemes dropped Jevon's arm and came across to me.

I am not going to repeat what Mrs. Deemes said to me; because she was very angry indeed. I am not going to write what I said to Mrs. Deemes, because I didn't say anything. I only wished that I had killed Jevon first and been hanged for it. Mrs. Deemes drew her pencil through all the dances that I had booked with her, and went away, leaving me to remember that what I ought to have said was that Mrs. Deemes had asked to be introduced to Jevon because he danced well; and that I really had not carefully worked out a plot to get her insulted. But I felt that argument was no good, and that I had better try to stop Jevon from waltzing me into more trouble. He, however, was gone, and about every third dance I set off to hunt for him. This ruined what little pleasure I expected from the entertainment.

Just before supper I caught Jevon, at the buffet with his legs wide apart, talking to a very fat and indignant chaperone. "If this person is a friend of yours, as I understand he is, I would recommend you to take him home," said she. "He is unfit for decent society." Then I knew that goodness only knew what Jevon had been doing, and I tried to get him away.

But Jevon wasn't going; not he. He knew what was good for him, he did; and he wasn't going to be dictated to by any loconial nigger-driver, he wasn't; and I was the friend who had formed his infant mind and brought him up to buy Benares brassware and fear God, so I was; and we would have many more blazing good drunks together, so we would; and all the she-camels in black silk in the world shouldn't make him withdraw his opinion that there was nothing better than Benedictine to give one an appetite. And then . . . but he was my guest.

I set him in a quiet corner of the supper-room, and went to find a wall-prop that I could trust. There was a good and kindly Subaltern—may Heaven bless that Subaltern, and make him a Commander-in-Chief!—who heard of my trouble. He was not dancing himself, and he owned a head like five-year-old teak-balks. He said that he would look after Jevon till the end of the ball.

" 'Don't suppose you much mind what I do with him?" said he.

"Mind!" said I. "No! You can murder the beast if you like."

But the Subaltern did not murder him. He trotted off to the supper-room, and sat down by Jevon, drinking peg for peg with him. I saw the two fairly established, and went away, feeling more easy.

When "The Roast Beef of Old England" sounded, I heard of Jevon's performances between the first dance and my meeting with him at the buffet. After Mrs. Deemes had cast him off, it seems that he had found his way into the gallery, and offered to conduct the Band or to play any instrument in it just as the Bandmaster pleased.

When the Bandmaster refused, Jevon said that he wasn't appreciated, and he yearned for sympathy. So he trundled downstairs and sat out four dances with four girls, and proposed to three of them. One of the girls was a married woman, by the way. Then he went into the whist-room, and fell face down and wept on the hearth-rug in front of the fire, because he had fallen into a den of card-sharpers, and his Mamma had always warned him against bad company. He had done a lot of other things, too, and had taken about three quarts of mixed liquors. Besides, speaking of me in the most scandalous fashion!

All the women wanted him turned out, and all the men wanted him kicked. The worst of it was, that every one said it was my fault. Now, I put it to you how on earth could I have known that this innocent, fluffy T. G. would break out in this disgusting manner? You see he had gone round the world nearly, and his vocabulary of abuse was cosmopolitan, though mainly Japanese, which he had picked up in a low tea-house at Hakodate. It sounded like whistling.

While I was listening to first one man and then another telling me of Jevon's shameless behavior and asking me for his blood, I wondered where he was. I was prepared to sacrifice him to Society on the spot.

But Jevon was gone, and, far away in the corner of the supper-room, sat my dear, good Subaltern, a little flushed, eating salad. I went over and said, "Where's Jevon?"—"In the cloakroom," said the Subaltern. "He'll keep till the women have gone. Don't you interfere with my prisoner." I didn't want to interfere, but I peeped into the cloakroom, and found my guest put to bed on some rolled-up carpets, all comfy, his collar free, and a wet swab on his head.

The rest of the evening I spent in making timid attempts to explain things to Mrs. Deemes and three or four other ladies, and trying to clear my character—for I am a respectable man—from the shameful slurs that my guest had cast upon it. Libel was no word for what he had said.

When I wasn't trying to explain, I was running off to the cloakroom to see that Jevon wasn't dead of apoplexy. I didn't want him to die on my hands. He had eaten my salt.

At last that ghastly ball ended, though I was not in the least restored to Mrs. Deemes' favor. When the ladies had gone, and some one was calling for songs at the second supper, that angelic Subaltern told the servants to bring in the Sahib who was in the cloakroom, and clear away one end of the supper-table. While this was being done, we formed ourselves into a Board of Punishment with the Doctor for President.

Jevon came in on four men's shoulders, and was put down on the table like a corpse in a dissecting-room, while the Doctor lectured on the evils of intemperance and Jevon snored. Then we set to work.

We corked the whole of his face. We filled his hair with meringue-cream till it looked like a white wig. To protect everything till it dried, a man in the Ordnance Department, who understood the work, luted a big blue paper cap from a cracker, with meringue-cream, low down on Jevon's forehead. This was punishment, not play, remember. We took gelatine off crackers, and stuck blue gelatine on his nose, and yellow gelatine on his chin, and green and red gelatine on his cheeks, pressing each dab down till it held as firm as goldbeaters' skin.

We put a ham-frill round his neck, and tied it in a bow in front. He nodded like a mandarin.

We fixed gelatine on the back of his hands, and burned-corked them inside, and put small cutlet-frills round his wrists, and tied both wrists together with string. We waxed up the ends of his mustache with isinglass. He looked very martial.

We turned him over, pinned up his coat-tails between his shoulders, and put a rosette of cutlet-frills there. We took up the red cloth from the ball-room to the supper-room, and wound him up in it. There were sixty feet of red cloth, six feet broad; and he rolled up into a big fat bundle, with only that amazing head sticking out.

Lastly, we tied up the surplus of the cloth beyond his feet with cocoanut-fiber string as tightly as we knew how. We were so angry that we hardly laughed at all.

Just as we finished, we heard the rumble of bullock-carts taking away some chairs and things that the General's wife had lent for the ball. So we hoisted Jevon, like a roll of carpets, into one of the carts, and the carts went away.

Now the most extraordinary part of this tale is that never again did I see or hear anything of Jevon, T. G. He vanished utterly. He was not delivered at the General's house with the carpets. He just went into the black darkness of the end of the night, and was swallowed up. Perhaps he died and was thrown into the river.

But, alive or dead, I have often wondered how he got rid of the red cloth and the meringue-cream. I wonder still whether Mrs. Deemes will ever take any notice of me again, and whether I shall live down the infamous stories that Jevon set afloat about my manners and customs between the first and the ninth waltz of the Afghan Ball. They stick closer than cream.

Wherefore, I want Tranter of the Bombay side, dead or alive. But dead for preference.

THE GATE OF THE HUNDRED SORROWS

If I can attain Heaven for a pice, why should you be envious?
—*Opium Smoker's Proverb*

THIS is no work of mine. My friend, Gabral Misquitta, the half-caste, spoke it all, between moonset and morning, six weeks before he died; and I took it down from his mouth as he answered my questions. So:

It lies between the Coppersmith's Gully and the pipe-stem sellers' quarter, within a hundred yards, too, as the crow flies, of the Mosque of Wazir Khan. I don't mind telling any one this much, but I defy him to find the Gate, however well he may think he knows the City. You might even go through the very gully it stands in a hundred times, and be none the wiser. We used to call the gully, "The Gully of the Black Smoke," but its native name is altogether different of course. A loaded donkey couldn't pass between the walls; and, at one point, just before you reach the Gate, a bulged house-front makes people go along all sidewise.

It isn't really a gate though. It's a house. Old Fung-Tching had it first five years ago. He was a boot-maker in Calcutta. They say that he murdered his wife there when he was drunk. That was why he dropped bazaar-rum and took to the Black Smoke instead. Later on, he came up north and opened the Gate as a house where you could get your smoke in peace and quiet. Mind you, it was a *pukka*, respectable opium-house, and not one of those stifling, sweltering *chandoo-khanas*, that you can find all over the City. No; the old man knew his business thoroughly, and he was most clean for a Chinaman. He was a one-eyed little chap, not much more than five feet high, and both his middle fingers were gone. All the same, he was the handiest man at rolling black pills I have ever seen. Never seemed to be touched by the Smoke, either; and what he took day and night, night and day, was a caution. I've been at it five years, and I can do my fair share of the Smoke with any one; but I was a child to Fung-Tching that way. All the same, the old man was keen on his money: very keen; and that's what I can't understand. I heard he saved a good deal before he died, but his nephew has got all that now; and the old man's gone back to China to be buried.

He kept the big upper room, where his best customers gathered, as neat as a new pin. In one corner used to stand Fung-Tching's Joss—almost as ugly as Fung-Tching—and there were always sticks burning under his nose; but you never smelled 'em when the pipes were going thick. Opposite the Joss was Fung-Tching's coffin. He had spent a good deal of his savings on that, and whenever a new man came to the Gate he was always introduced to it. It was lacquered black, with red and gold writings on it, and I've heard that Fung-Tching brought it out all the way from China. I don't know whether that's true or not, but I know that, if I came first in the evening, I used to spread my mat just at the foot of it. It was a quiet corner, you see, and a sort of breeze from the gully came in at the window now and then. Besides the mats, there was no other furniture in the room—only the coffin, and the old Joss all green and blue and purple with age and polish.

Fung-Tching never told us why he called the place "The Gate of the Hundred Sorrows." (He was the only Chinaman I know who used bad-sounding fancy names. Most of them are flowery. As you'll see in Calcutta.) We used to find that out for ourselves. Nothing grows on you so much, if you're white, as the Black Smoke. A yellow man is made different. Opium doesn't tell on him scarcely at all; but white and black suffer a good deal. Of course, there are some people that the Smoke doesn't touch any more than tobacco would at first. They just doze a bit, as one would fall asleep naturally, and next morning they are almost fit for work. Now, I was one of that sort when I began, but I've been at it for five years pretty steadily, and it's different now. There was an old aunt of mine, down Agra way, and she left me a little at her death. About sixty rupees a month secured. Sixty isn't much. I can recollect a time, 'seems hundreds and hundreds of years ago, that I was getting my three hundred a month, and pickings, when I was working on a big timber-contract in Calcutta.

I didn't stick to that work for long. The Black Smoke does not allow of much other business; and even though I am very little affected by it, as men go, I couldn't do a day's work now to save my life. After all, sixty rupees is what I want. When old Fung-Tching was alive he used to draw the money for me, give me about half of it to live on (I eat very little), and the rest he kept himself. I was free of the Gate at any time of the day and night, and could smoke and sleep there when I liked, so I didn't care. I know the old man made a good thing out of it; but that's no matter. Nothing matters much to me; and besides, the money always came fresh and fresh each month.

There was ten of us met at the Gate when the place was first opened. Me, and two Baboos from a Government Office somewhere in Anarkulli, but they got the sack and couldn't pay (no man who has to work in the daylight can do the Black Smoke for any length of time straight on); a Chinaman that was Fung-Tching's nephew; a bazaar-woman that had got a lot of money somehow; an English loafer—Mac-Somebody I think, but I have forgotten—that smoked heaps, but never seemed to pay anything (they said he had saved Fung-Tching's life at some trial in Calcutta when he was a barrister); another Eurasian, like myself, from Madras; a half-caste woman, and a couple of men who said they had come from the North. I think they must have been Persians or Afghans or something. There are not more than five of us living now, but we come regular. I don't know what happened to the Baboos; but the bazaar-woman she died after six months of the Gate, and I think Fung-Tching took her bangles and nose-ring for himself. But I'm not certain. The Englishman, he drank as well as smoked, and he dropped off. One of the Persians got killed in a row at night by the big well near the mosque a long time ago, and the Police shut up the well, because they said it was full of foul air. They found him dead at the bottom of it. So you see, there is only me, the Chinaman, the half-caste woman that we call the *Memsahib* (she used to live with Fung-Tching), the other Eurasian, and one of the Persians. The *Memsahib* looks very old now. I think she was a young woman when the Gate was opened; but we are all old for the matter of that. Hundreds and hundreds of years old. It is very hard to keep count of time in the Gate, and, besides, time doesn't matter to me. I draw my sixty rupees fresh and fresh every month. A very, very long while ago, when I used to be getting three hundred and fifty rupees a month, and pickings, on a big timber-contract at Calcutta, I had a wife of sorts. But she's dead now. People said that I killed her by taking to the Black Smoke. Perhaps I did, but it's so long since that it doesn't matter. Sometimes when I first came to the Gate, I used to feel sorry for it; but that's all over and done with long ago, and I draw my sixty rupees fresh and fresh every month, and am quite happy. Not *drunk* happy, you know, but always quiet and soothed and contented.

How did I take to it? It began at Calcutta. I used to try it in my own house, just to see what it was like. I never went very far, but I think my wife must have died then. Anyhow, I found myself here, and got to know Fung-Tching. I don't remember rightly how that came about; but he told me of the Gate and I used to go there, and, somehow, I have never got away from it since. Mind you, though, the Gate was a respectable place in Fung-Tching's time where you could be comfortable, and not at all like the *chandoo-khanas* where the niggers go. No; it was clean and quiet, and not crowded. Of course, there were others besides us ten and the man; but we always had a mat apiece, with a wadded woolen headpiece, all covered with black and red dragons and things; just like the coffin in the corner.

At the end of one's third pipe the dragons used to move about and fight. I've watched 'em many and many a night through. I used to regulate my Smoke that way, and now it takes a dozen pipes to make 'em stir. Besides, they are all torn and dirty, like the mats, and old Fung-Tching is dead. He died a couple of years ago, and gave me the pipe I always use now—a silver one, with queer beasts crawling up and down the receiver-bottle below the cup. Before that, I think, I used a big bamboo stem with a copper cup, a very small one, and a green jade mouthpiece. It was a little thicker than a walking-stick stem, and smoked sweet, very sweet. The bamboo seemed to suck up the smoke. Silver doesn't, and I've got to clean it out now and then, that's a great deal of trouble, but I smoke it for the old man's sake. He must have made a good thing out of me, but he always gave me clean mats and pillows, and the best stuff you could get anywhere.

When he died, his nephew Tsin-ling took up the Gate, and he called it the "Temple of the Three Possessions"; but we old ones speak of it as the "Hundred Sorrows," all the same. The nephew does things very shabbily, and I think the *Memsahib* must help him. She lives with him; same as she used to do with the old man. The two let in all sorts of low people, niggers and all, and the Black Smoke isn't as good as it used to be. I've found burned brand in my pipe over and over again. The old man would have died if that had happened in his time. Besides, the room is never cleaned, and all the mats are torn and cut at the edges. The coffin is gone —gone to China again—with the old man and two ounces of Smoke inside it, in case he should want 'em on the way.

The Joss doesn't get so many sticks burned under his nose as he used to; that's a sign of ill-luck, as sure as Death. He's all brown, too, and no one ever attends to him. That's the *Memsahib's* work, I know; because, when Tsin-ling tried to burn gilt paper before him, she said it was a waste of money, and, if he kept a stick burning very slowly, the Joss wouldn't know the difference. So now we've got the sticks mixed with a lot of glue, and they take half an hour longer to burn, and smell stinky. Let alone the smell of the room by itself. No business can get on if they try that sort of thing. The Joss doesn't like it. I can see that. Late at night, sometimes, he turns all sorts of queer colors—blue and green and red—just as he used to do when old Fung-Tching was alive; and he rolls his eyes and stamps his feet like a devil. I don't know why I don't leave the place and smoke quietly in a little room of my own in the bazaar. Most like, Tsin-ling would kill me if I went away—he draws my sixty rupees now—and besides, it's so much trouble, and I've grown to be very fond of the Gate. It's not much to look at. Not what it was in the old man's time, but I couldn't leave it. I've seen so many come in and out. And I've seen so many die here on the mats that I should be afraid of dying in the open now. I've seen some things that people would call strange enough; but nothing is strange when you're on the Black Smoke, except the Black Smoke. And if it was, it wouldn't matter. Fung-Tching used to be very particular about his pepole, and never got in any one who'd give trouble by dying messy and such. But the nephew isn't half so careful. He tells everywhere that he keeps a "first-chop" house. Never tries to get men in quietly, and make them comfortable like Fung-Tching did. That's why the Gate is getting a little bit more known than it used to be. Among the niggers, of course. The nephew daren't get a white, or, for matter of that, a mixed skin into the place. He has to keep us three, of course—me and the *Memsahib* and the other Eurasian. We're fixtures. But he wouldn't give us credit for a pipeful—not for anything.

One of these days, I hope, I shall die in the Gate. The Persian and the Madras man are terribly shaky now. They've got a boy to light their pipes for them. I always do that myself. Most like, I shall see them carried out before me. I don't think I shall ever outlive the *Memsahib* or Tsin-ling. Women last longer than men at the Black Smoke, and Tsin-ling has a deal of the old man's blood in him, though he does smoke cheap stuff. The bazaar-woman knew when she was going two days before her time; and she died on a clean mat with a nicely wadded pillow, and the old man hung up her pipe just above the Joss. He was always fond of her, I fancy. But he took her bangles just the same.

I should like to die like the bazaar-woman—on a clean, cool mat with a pipe of good stuff between my lips. When I feel I'm going, I shall ask Tsin-ling for them, and he can draw my sixty rupees a month, fresh and fresh, as long as he pleases. Then I shall lie back, quiet and comfortable, and watch the black and red dragons have their last big fight together; and then . . .

Well, it doesn't matter. Nothing matters much to me—only I wish Tsin-ling wouldn't put bran into the Black Smoke.

THE MADNESS OF PRIVATE ORTHERIS

Oh! Where would I be when my froat was dry?
Oh! Where would I be when the bullets fly?
Oh! Where would I be when I come to die?
Why,
Somewheres anigh my chum.
If 'e's liquor 'e'll give me some,
If I'm dyin' 'e'll 'old my 'ead,
An' 'e'll write 'em 'Ome when I'm dead.—
Gawd send us a trusty chum!
—*Barrack-Room Ballad*

My friends Mulvaney and Ortheris had gone on a shooting-expedition for one day. Learoyd was still in hospital, recovering from fever picked up in Burma. They sent me an invitation to join them, and were genuinely pained when I brought beer—almost enough beer to satisfy two Privates of the Line . . . and Me.

" 'Twasn't for that we bid you welkim, Sorr," said Mulvaney sulkily. " 'Twas for the pleasure av your comp'ny."

Ortheris came to the rescue with—"Well, 'e won't be none the worse for bringin' liquor with 'im. We ain't a file o' Dooks. We're bloomin' Tommies, ye cantankris Hirishman; an' 'ere's your very good 'ealth!"

We shot all the forenoon, and killed two pariah-dogs, four green parrots, sitting, one kite by the burning-ghaut, one snake flying, one mud-turtle, and eight crows. Game was plentiful. Then we sat down to tiffin—"bull-mate an' bran-bread," Mulvaney called it—by the side of the river, and took pot shots at the crocodiles in the intervals of cutting up the food with our only pocket-knife. Then we drank up all the beer, and threw the bottles into the water and fired at them. After that, we eased belts and stretched ourselves on the warm sand and smoked. We were too lazy to continue shooting.

Ortheris heaved a big sigh, as he lay on his stomach with his head between his fists. Then he swore quietly into the blue sky.

"Fwhat's that for?" said Mulvaney. "Have ye not drunk enough?"

"Tott'nim Court Road, an' a gal I fancied there. Wot's the good of sodgerin'?"

"Orth'ris, me son," said Mulvaney hastily, " 'tis more than likely you've got throuble in your inside wid the beer. I feel that way mesilf whin my liver gets rusty."

Ortheris went on slowly, not heeding the interruption—

"I'm a Tommy—a bloomin', eight-anna, dog-stealin' Tommy, with a number instead of a decent name. Wot's the good o' me? If I 'ad a stayed at 'Ome, I might a married that gal and a kep' a little shorp in the 'Ammersmith 'Igh.—'S. Orth'ris, Prac-ti-cal Taxi-der-mist.' With a stuff' fox, like they 'as in the Haylesbury Dairies, in the winder, an' a little case of blue and yaller glass-heyes, an' a little wife to call 'shorp!' 'shorp!' when the door-bell rung. As it *his*, I'm on'y a Tommy—a Bloomin', Gawd-forsaken, Beer-swillin' Tommy. 'Rest on your harms—'*versed.* Stan' at—*hease; 'Shun.* 'Verse—*harms*—Right an' lef'—*tarrn.* Slow—*march.* 'Alt—*front.* Rest on your harms—'*versed.* With blank-cartridge—*load.*' An' that's the end o' me." He was quoting fragments from Funeral Parties' Orders.

"Stop ut!" shouted Mulvaney. "Whin you've fired into nothin' as often as me, over a better man than yoursilf, you will not make a mock av thim orders. 'Tis worse than whislin' the 'Dead March' in barricks. An' you full as a tick, an' the sun cool, an' all an' all! I take shame for you. You're no better than a Pagin—you an' your firin'-parties an' your glass-eyes. Won't *you* stop ut, Sorr?"

What could I do? Could I tell Ortheris anything that he did not know of the pleasures of his life? I was not a Chaplain nor a Subaltern, and Ortheris had a right to speak as he thought fit.

"Let him run, Mulvaney," I said. "It's the beer."

"No! 'Tisn't the beer," said Mulvaney. "I know fwhat's comin'. He's tuk this way now an' agin, an' it's bad—it's bad—for I'm fond av the bhoy."

Indeed, Mulvaney seemed needlessly anxious; but I knew that he looked after Ortheris in a fatherly way.

"Let me talk, let me talk," said Ortheris dreamily. "D'you stop your parrit screamin' of a 'ot day, when the cage is a-cookin' 'is pore little pink toes orf, Mulvaney?"

"Pink toes! D'ye mane to say you've pink toes undher your bullswools, ye blandanderin' "—Mulvaney gathered himself together for a terrific denunciation—"school-misthress! Pink toes! How much Bass wid the label did that ravin' child dhrink?"

" 'Tain't Bass," said Ortheris. "It's a bitterer beer nor that. It's 'ome-sickness!"

"Hark to him! An' he goin' Home in the 'Sherapis' in the inside av four months!"

"I don't care. It's all one to me. 'Ow d'you know I ain't 'fraid o' dyin' 'fore I gets my discharge paipers?" He recommenced, in a sing-song voice, the "Orders."

I had never seen this side of Ortheris' character before, but evidently Mulvaney had, and attached serious importance to it. While Ortheris babbled, with his head on his arms, Mulvaney whispered to me—

"He's always tuk this way whin he's been checked overmuch by the childher they make Sarjints nowadays. That an' havin' nothin' to do. I can't make ut out anyways."

"Well, what does it matter? Let him talk himself through."

Ortheris began singing a parody of "The Ramrod Corps," full of cheerful allusions to battle, murder, and sudden death. He looked out across the river as he sang; and his face was quite strange to me. Mulvaney caught me by the elbow to insure attention.

"Matther! It matthers everything! 'Tis some sort av fit that's on him. I've seen ut. 'Twill hould him all this night, an' in the middle av it he'll get out av his cot an' go rakin' in the rack for his 'coutermints. Thin he'll come over to me an' say, 'I'm goin' to Bombay. Answer for me in the mornin'.' Thin me an' him will fight as we've done before—him to go an' me to hould him—an' so we'll both come on the books for disturbin' in barricks. I've belted him, an' I've bruk his head, an' I've talked to him, but 'tis no manner av use whin the fit's on him. He's as good a bhoy as ever stepped whin his mind's clear. I know fwhat's comin', though, this night in barricks. Lord send he doesn't loose on me whin I rise to knock him down. 'Tis that that's in my mind day an' night."

This put the case in a much less pleasant light, and fully accounted for Mulvaney's anxiety. He seemed to be trying to coax Ortheris out of the fit; for he shouted down the bank where the boy was lying—

"Listen now, you wid the 'pore pink toes' an' the glass eyes! Did you shwim the Irriwaddy at night, behin' me, as a bhoy shud; or were you hidin' under a bed, as you was at Ahmid Kheyl?"

This was at once a gross insult and a direct lie, and Mulvaney meant it to bring on a fight. But Ortheris seemed shut up in some sort of trance. He answered slowly, without a sign of irritation, in the same cadenced voice as he had used for his firing-party orders—

"*Hi* swum the Irriwaddy in the night, as you know, for to take the town of Lungtungpen, nakid an' without fear.

Hand where I was at Ahmed Kheyl, you know, and four bloomin' Pathans know too. But that was summat to do, an' I didn't think o' dyin'. Now I'm sick to go 'Ome—go 'Ome—go 'Ome! No, I ain't mammysick, because my uncle brung me up, but I'm sick for London again; sick for the sounds of 'er, an' the sights of 'er, and the stinks of 'er; orange-peel and hasphalt an' gas comin' in over Vaux'all Bridge. Sick for the rail goin' down to Box 'Ill, with your gal on your knee an' a new clay pipe in your face. That, an' the Stran' lights where you knows ev'ry one, an' the Copper that takes you up is a old friend that tuk you up before, when you was a little smitchy boy lying loose 'tween the Temple an' the Dark Harches. No bloomin' guard-mountin', no bloomin' rotten-stone, nor khaki, an' yourself your own master with a gal to take an' see the Humaners practicin' a-hookin' dead corpses out of the Serpentine o' Sundays. An' I lef' all that for to serve the Widder beyond the seas, where there ain't no women and there ain't no liquor worth 'avin', and there ain't nothin' to see, nor do, nor say, nor feel, nor think. Lord love you, Stanley Orth'ris, but you're a bigger bloomin' fool than the rest o' the reg'ment and Mulvaney wired together! There's the Widder sittin' at 'Ome with a gold crownd on 'er 'ead; and 'ere am Hi, Stanley Orth'ris, the Widder's property, a rottin' FOOL!"

His voice rose at the end of the sentence, and he wound up with a six-shot Anglo-Vernacular oath. Mulvaney said nothing, but looked at me as if he expected that I could bring peace to poor Ortheris' troubled brain.

I remembered once at Rawal Pindi having seen a man, nearly mad with drink, sobered by being made a fool of. Some regiments may know what I mean. I hoped that we might slake off Ortheris in the same way, though he was perfectly sober. So I said—"What's the use of grousing there, and speaking against The Widow?"

"I didn't!" said Ortheris. "S'elp me, Gawd, I never said a word agin 'er, an' I wouldn't—not if I was to desert this minute!"

Here was my opening. "Well, you meant to, anyhow. What's the use of cracking-on for nothing? Would you slip it now if you got the chance?"

"On'y try me!" said Ortheris, jumping to his feet as if he had been stung.

Mulvaney jumped too. "Fwhat are you going to do?" said he.

"Help Ortheris down to Bombay or Karachi, which ever he likes. You can report that he separated from you before tiffin, and left his gun on the bank here!"

"I'm to report that—am I?" said Mulvaney slowly. "Very well. If Orth'ris manes to desert now, and will desert now, an' you, Sorr, who have been a frind to me an' to him, will help him to ut, I, Terence Mulvaney, on my oath which I've never bruk yet, will report as you say. But"—here he stepped up to Ortheris, and shook the stock of the fowling-piece in his face—"your fistes help you, Stanley Orth'ris, if ever I come across you agin!"

"I don't care!" said Ortheris. "I'm sick o' this dorg's life. Give me a chanst. Don't play with me. Le' me go!"

"Strip," said I, "and change with me, and then I'll tell you what to do."

I hoped that the absurdity of this would check Ortheris; but he had kicked off his ammunition-boots and got rid of his tunic almost before I had loosed my shirt-collar. Mulvaney gripped me by the arm—

"The fit's on him: the fit's workin' on him still! By my Honor and Sowl, we shall be accessiry to a desartion yet. Only twenty-eight days, as you say, Sorr, or fifty-six, but think o' the shame—the black shame to him an' me!" I had never seen Mulvaney so excited.

But Ortheris was quite calm, and, as soon as he had exchanged clothes with me, and I stood up a Private of the Line, he said shortly, "Now! Come on. What nex'? D'ye mean fair. What must I do to get out o' this 'ere a-Hell?"

I told him that, if he would wait for two or three hours near the river, I would ride into the Station and come back with one hundred rupees. He would, with that money in his pocket, walk to the nearest side-station on the line, about five miles away, and would there take a first-class ticket for Karachi. Knowing that he had no money on him when he went out shooting, his regiment would not immediately wire to the seaports, but would hunt for him in the native villages near the river. Further, no one would think of seeking a deserter in a first-class carriage. At Karachi, he was to buy white clothes and ship, if he could, on a cargo-steamer.

Here he broke in. If I helped him to Karachi, he would arrange all the rest. Then I ordered him to wait where he was until it was dark enough for me to ride into the station without my dress being noticed. Now God in His wisdom has made the heart of the British Soldier, who is very often an unlicked ruffian, as soft as the heart of a little child, in order that he may believe in and follow his officers into tight and nasty places. He does not so readily come to believe in a "civilian," but, when he does, he believes implicitly and like a dog. I had had the honor of the friendship of Private Ortheris, at intervals, for more than three years, and we had dealt with each other as man by man. Consequently, he considered that all my words were true, and not spoken lightly.

Mulvaney and I left him in the high grass near the river-bank, and went away, still keeping to the high grass, toward my horse. The shirt scratched me horribly.

We waited nearly two hours for the dusk to fall and allow me to ride off. We spoke of Ortheris in whispers, and strained our ears to catch any sound from the spot where we had left him. But we heard nothing except the wind in the plume-grass.

"I've bruk his head," said Mulvaney earnestly, "time an' agin. I've nearly kilt him wid the belt, an' *yet* I can't knock thim fits out av his soft head. No! An' he's not soft, for he's reasonable an' likely by natur'. Fwhat is ut? Is ut his breedin' which is nothin', or his edukashin which he niver got? You that think ye know things, answer me that."

But I found no answer. I was wondering how long Ortheris, in the bank of the river, would hold out, and whether

I should be forced to help him to desert, as I had given my word.

Just as the dusk shut down and, with a very heavy heart, I was beginning to saddle up my horse, we heard wild shouts from the river.

The devils had departed from Private Stanley Ortheris, No. 22,639, B Company. The loneliness, the dusk, and the waiting had driven them out as I had hoped. We set off at the double and found him plunging about wildly through the grass, with his coat off—my coat off, I mean. He was calling for us like a madman.

When we reached him he was dripping with perspiration, and trembling like a startled horse. We had great difficulty in soothing him. He complained that he was in civilian kit, and wanted to tear my clothes off his body. I ordered him to strip, and we made a second exchange as quickly as possible.

The rasp of his own "grayback" shirt and the squeak of his boots seemed to bring him to himself. He put his hands before his eyes and said:

"Wot was it? I ain't mad, I ain't sunstrook, an' I've bin an' gone an' said, an' bin an' gone an' done . . . *Wot* 'ave I bin an' done!"

"Fwhat have you done?" said Mulvaney. "You've dishgraced yourself—though that's no matter. You've dishgraced B Comp'ny, an' worst av all, you've dishgraced *Me!* Me that taught you how for to walk abroad like a man—whin you was a dhirty little, fish-backed little, whimperin' little recruity. As you are now, Stanley Orth'ris!"

Ortheris said nothing for a while. Then he unslung his belt, heavy with the badges of half a dozen regiments that his own had lain with, and handed it over to Mulvaney.

"I'm too little for to mill you, Mulvaney," said he, "an' you've strook me before; but you can take an' cut me in two with this 'ere if you like."

Mulvaney turned to me.

"Lave me to talk to him, Sorr," said Mulvaney.

I left, and on my way home thought a good deal over

Ortheris in particular, and my friend Private Thomas Atkins whom I love, in general. But I could not come to any conclusion of any kind whatever.

THE STORY OF MUHAMMAD DIN

Who is the happy man? He that sees in his own house at home, little children crowned with dust, leaping and falling and crying.—*Munichandra*, translated by Professor Peterson

THE polo-ball was an old one, scarred, chipped, and dinted. It stood on the mantel-piece among the pipe-stems which Imam Din, *khitmatgar*, was cleaning for me.

"Does the Heaven-born want this ball?" said Imam Din deferentially.

The Heaven-born set no particular store by it; but of what use was a polo-ball to a *khitmatgar?*

"By Your Honor's favor, I have a little son. He has seen this ball, and desires it to play with. I do not want it for myself."

No one would for an instant accuse portly old Imam Din of wanting to play with polo-balls. He carried out the battered thing into the veranda; and there followed a hurricane of joyful squeaks, a patter of small feet, and the *thud-thud-thud* of the ball rolling along the ground. Evidently the little son had been waiting outside the door to secure his treasure. But how had he managed to see that polo-ball?

Next day, coming back from office half an hour earlier than usual, I was aware of a small figure in the dining-room —a tiny, plump figure in a ridiculously inadequate shirt which came, perhaps, half-way down the tubby stomach. It wandered round the room, thumb in mouth, crooning to itself as it took stock of the pictures. Undoubtedly this was the "little son."

He had no business in my room, of course; but was so deeply absorbed in his discoveries that he never noticed me in the doorway. I stepped into the room and startled him nearly into a fit. He sat down on the ground with a gasp.

His eyes opened, and his mouth followed suit. I knew what was coming, and fled, followed by a long, dry howl which reached the servants' quarters far more quickly than any command of mine had ever done. In ten seconds Imam Din was in the dining-room. Then despairing sobs arose, and I returned to find Imam Din admonishing the small sinner who was using most of his shirt as a handkerchief.

"This boy," said Imam Din judicially, "is a *budmash*—a big *budmash*. He will, without doubt, go to the *jail-khana* for his behavior." Renewed yells from the penitent, and an elaborate apology to myself from Imam Din.

"Tell the baby," said I, "that the *Sahib* is not angry, and take him away." Imam Din conveyed my forgiveness to the offender, who had now gathered all his shirt round his neck, stringwise, and the yell subsided into a sob. The two set off for the door. "His name," said Imam Din, as though the name were part of the crime, "is Muhammad Din, and he is a *budmash*." Freed from present danger, Muhammad Din turned round in his father's arms, and said gravely, "It is true that my name is Muhammad Din, *Tahib*, but I am not a *budmash*. I am a *man!*"

From that day dated my acquaintance with Muhammad Din. Never again did he come into my dining-room, but on the neutral ground of the garden we greeted each other with much state, though our conversation was confined to "*Talaam, Tahib*" from his side, and "*Salaam, Muhammad Din*" from mine. Daily on my return from office, the little white shirt, and the fat little body used to rise from the shade of the creeper-covered trellis where they had been hid; and daily I checked my horse here, that my salutation might not be slurred over or given unseemly.

Muhammad Din never had any companions. He used to trot about the compound, in and out of the castor-oil bushes, on mysterious errands of his own. One day I stumbled upon some of his handiwork far down the grounds. He had half buried the polo-ball in dust, and stuck six shriveled old marigold flowers in a circle round it. Outside that circle again was a rude square, traced out in bits of red brick alternating with fragments of broken china; the whole bounded by a little bank of dust. The water-man from the well-curb put in a plea for the small architect, saying that it was only the play of a baby and did not much disfigure my garden.

Heaven knows that I had no intention of touching the child's work then or later; but, that evening, a stroll through the garden brought me unawares full on it; so that I trampled, before I knew, marigold-heads, dust-bank, and fragments of broken soap-dish into confusion past all hope of mending. Next morning, I came upon Muhammad Din crying softly to himself over the ruin I had wrought. Some one had cruelly told him that the *Sahib* was very angry with him for spoiling the garden, and had scattered his rubbish, using bad language the while. Muhammad Din labored for an hour at effacing every trace of the dust-bank and pottery fragments, and it was with a tearful and apologetic face that he said, "*Talaam, Tahib,*" when I came home from office. A hasty inquiry resulted in Imam Din informing Muhammad Din that, by my singular favor, he was permitted to disport himself as he pleased. Whereat the child took heart and fell to tracing the ground-plan of an edifice which was to eclipse the marigold polo-ball creation.

For some months, the chubby little eccentricity revolved in his humble orbit among the castor-oil bushes and in the dust; always fashioning magnificent palaces from stale flowers thrown away by the bearer, smooth water-worn pebbles, bits of broken glass, and feathers pulled, I fancy, from my fowls—always alone, and always crooning to himself.

A gayly-spotted sea-shell was dropped one day close to the last of his little buildings; and I looked that Muhammad Din should build something more than ordinarily splendid on the strength of it. Nor was I disappointed. He meditated for the better part of an hour, and his crooning rose to a jubilant song. Then he began tracing in the dust. It would certainly be a wondrous palace, this one, for it was two yards long and a yard broad in ground-plan. But the palace was never completed.

Next day there was no Muhammad Din at the head of the carriage-drive, and no "*Talaam, Tahib*" to welcome my return. I had grown accustomed to the greeting, and its omission troubled me. Next day Imam Din told me that the child was suffering slightly from fever and needed quinine. He got the medicine, and an English Doctor.

"They have no stamina, these brats," said the Doctor, as he left Imam Din's quarters.

A week later, though I would have given much to have avoided it, I met on the road to the Mussulman burying-ground Imam Din, accompanied by one other friend, carrying in his arms, wrapped in a white cloth, all that was left of little Muhammad Din.

ON THE STRENGTH OF A LIKENESS

If your mirror be broken, look into still water; but have a care that you do not fall in.—*Hindu Proverb*

NEXT to a requited attachment, one of the most convenient things that a young man can carry about with him at the beginning of his career is an unrequited attachment. It makes him feel important and business-like, and *blasé*, and cynical; and whenever he has a touch of liver, or suffers from want of exercise, he can mourn over his lost love, and be very happy in a tender, twilight fashion.

Hannasyde's affair of the heart had been a godsend to him. It was four years old, and the girl had long since given up thinking of it. She had married and had many cares of her own. In the beginning, she had told Hannasyde that, "while she could never be anything more than a sister to him, she would always take the deepest interest in his welfare." This startlingly new and original remark gave Hannasyde something to think over for two years; and his own vanity filled in the other twenty-four months. Hannasyde was quite different from Phil Garron, but, none the less, had several points in common with that far too lucky man.

He kept his unrequited attachment by him as men keep a well-smoked pipe—for comfort's sake, and because it had grown dear in the using. It brought him happily through one Simla season. Hannasyde was not lovely. There was a crudity in his manners, and a roughness in the way in which he helped a lady on to her horse, that did not attract the other sex to him. Even if he had cast about for their favor, which he did not. He kept his wounded heart all to himself for a while.

Then trouble came to him. All who go to Simla know the slope from the Telegraph to the Public Works Office. Hannasyde was loafing up the hill, one September morning between calling hours, when a 'rickshaw came down in a hurry, and in the 'rickshaw sat the living, breathing image of the girl who had made him so happily unhappy. Hannasyde leaned against the railings and gasped. He wanted to run downhill after the 'rickshaw, but that was impossible; so he went forward with most of his blood in his temples. It was impossible, for many reasons, that the woman in the 'rickshaw could be the girl he had known. She was, he discovered later, the wife of a man from Dindigul, or Coimbatore, or some out-of-the-way place, and she had come up to Simla early in the season for the good of her health. She was going back to Dindigul, or wherever it was, at the end of the season; and in all likelihood would never return to Simla again; her proper Hill-station being Ootacamund. That night Hannasyde, raw and savage from the raking up of all old feelings, took counsel with himself for one measured hour. What he decided upon was this; and you must decide for yourself how much genuine affection for the old Love, and how much a very natural inclination to go abroad and enjoy himself, affected the decision. Mrs. Landys-Haggert would never in all human likelihood cross his path again. So whatever he did didn't much matter. She was marvelously like the girl who "took a deep interest" and the rest of the formula. All things considered, it would be pleasant to make the acquaintance of Mrs. Landys-Haggert, and for a little time—only a very little time—to make believe that he was with Alice Chisane again. Every one is more or less mad on one point. Hannasyde's particular monomania was his old love, Alice Chisane.

He made it his business to get introduced to Mrs. Haggert, and the introduction prospered. He also made it his business to see as much as he could of that lady. When a man is in earnest as to interviews, the facilities which Simla offers are startling. There are garden-parties, and tennis-parties, and picnics, and luncheons at Annandale, and rifle-matches, and dinners and balls; besides rides and walks, which are matters of private arrangement. Hannasyde had started with the intention of seeing a likeness, and he ended by doing much more. He wanted to be deceived, he meant to be deceived, and he deceived himself very thoroughly. Not only were the face and figure the face and figure of Alice Chisane, but the voice and lower tones were exactly the same, and so were the turns of speech; and the little mannerisms, that every woman has, of gait and gesticulation, were absolutely and identically the same. The turn of the head was the same; the tired look in the eyes at the end of a long walk was the same; the stoop-and-wrench over the saddle to hold in a pulling horse was the same; and once, most marvelous of all, Mrs. Landys-Haggert singing to herself in the next room, while Hannasyde was waiting to take her for a ride, hummed, note for note, with a throaty quiver of the voice in the second line, "Poor Wandering One!" exactly as Alice Chisane had hummed it for Hannasyde in the dusk of an English drawing-room. In the actual woman herself—in the soul of her—there was not the least likeness; she and Alice Chisane being cast in different molds. But all that Hannasyde wanted to know and see and think about, was this maddening and perplexing likeness of face and voice and manner. He was bent on making a fool of himself that way; and he was in no sort disappointed.

Open and obvious devotion from any sort of man is always pleasant to any sort of woman; but Mrs. Landys-Haggert, being a woman of the world, could make nothing of Hannasyde's admiration.

He would take any amount of trouble—he was a selfish man habitually—to meet and forestall, if possible, her wishes. Anything she told him to do was law; and he was, there could be no doubting it, fond of her company so long as she talked to him, and kept on talking about trivialities. But when she launched into expression of her personal views and her wrongs, those small social differences that make the spice of Simla life, Hannasyde was neither pleased nor interested. He didn't want to know anything about Mrs. Landys-Haggert, or her experiences in the past—she had traveled nearly all over the world, and could talk cleverly—he wanted the likeness of Alice Chisane before his eyes and her voice in his ears. Anything outside that, reminding him of another personality, jarred, and he showed that it did.

Under the new Post Office, one evening, Mrs. Landys-Haggert turned on him, and spoke her mind shortly and without warning. "Mr. Hannasyde," said she, "will you be good enough to explain why you have appointed yourself my special *cavalier servente?* I don't understand it. But I am perfectly certain, somehow or other, that you don't care the least little bit in the world for *me*." This seems to support, by the way, the theory that no man can act or tell lies to a woman without being found out. Hannasyde was taken off his guard. His defense never was a strong one, because he was always thinking of himself, and he blurted out, before he knew what he was saying, this inexpedient answer, "No more I do."

The queerness of the situation and the reply, made Mrs. Landys-Haggert laugh. Then it all came out; and at the end of Hannasyde's lucid explanation Mrs. Haggert said, with the least little touch of scorn in her voice, "So I'm to act as the lay-figure for you to hang the rags of your tattered affections on, am I?"

Hannasyde didn't see what answer was required, and he devoted himself generally and vaguely to the praise of Alice Chisane, which was unsatisfactory. Now it is to be thoroughly made clear that Mrs. Haggert had not the shadow of a ghost of an interest in Hannasdye. Only . . . only no woman likes being made love through instead of to—specially on behalf of a musty divinity of four years' standing.

Hannasyde did not see that he had made any very particular exhibition of himself. He was glad to find a sympathetic soul in the arid wastes of Simla.

When the season ended, Hannasyde went down to his own place and Mrs. Haggert to hers. "It was like making love to a ghost," said Hannasyde to himself, "and it doesn't matter; and now I'll get to my work." But he found himself thinking steadily of the Haggert-Chisane ghost; and he could not be certain whether it was Haggert or Chisane that made up the greater part of the pretty phantom.

. . . .

He got understanding a month later.

A peculiar point of this peculiar country is the way in which a heartless Government transfers men from one end of the Empire to the other. You can never be sure of getting rid of a friend or an enemy till he or she dies. There was a case once—but that's another story.

Haggert's Department ordered him up from Dindigul to the Frontier at two days' notice, and he went through, losing money at every step, from Dindigul to his station. He dropped Mrs. Haggert at Lucknow, to stay with some friends there, to take part in a big ball at the Chutter Munzil, and to come on when he had made the new home a little comfortable. Lucknow was Hannasyde's station, and Mrs. Haggert stayed a week there. Hannasyde went to meet her. As the train came in, he discovered what he had been thinking of for the past month. The unwisdom of his conduct also struck him. The Lucknow week, with two dances, and an unlimited quantity of rides together, clinched matters; and Hannasyde found himself pacing this circle of thought: He adored Alice Chisane, at least he *had* adored her. *And* he admired Mrs. Landys-Haggert because she was like Alice Chisane. *But* Mrs. Landys-Haggert was not in the least like Alice Chisane, being a thousand times more adorable. *Now* Alice Chisane was "the bride of another," and so was Mrs. Landys-Haggert, and a good and honest wife too. *Therefore* he, Hannasyde, was . . . here he called himself several hard names, and wished that he had been wise in the beginning.

Whether Mrs. Landys-Haggert saw what was going on in his mind, she alone knows. He seemed to take an unqualified interest in everything connected with herself, as distinguished from the Alice-Chisane likeness, and he said one or two things which, if Alice Chisane had been still betrothed to him, could scarcely have been excused, even on the grounds of the likeness. But Mrs. Haggert turned the remarks aside, and spent a long time in making Hannasyde see what a comfort and a pleasure she had been to him because of her strange resemblance to his old love. Hannasyde groaned in his saddle and said, "Yes, indeed," and busied himself with preparations for her departure to the Frontier, feeling very small and miserable.

The last day of her stay at Lucknow came, and Hannasyde saw her off at the Railway Station. She was very grateful for his kindness and the trouble he had taken, and smiled pleasantly and sympathetically as one who knew the Alice-Chisane reason of that kindness. And Hannasyde abused the coolies with the luggage, and hustled the people on the platform, and prayed that the roof might fall in and slay him.

As the train went out slowly, Mrs. Landys-Haggert leaned out of the window to say good-by—"On second thoughts *au revoir*, Mr. Hannasyde. I go Home in the Spring, and perhaps I may meet you in Town."

Hannasyde shook hands, and said very earnestly and adoringly—"I hope to Heaven I shall never see your face again!"

And Mrs. Haggert understood.

WRESSLEY OF THE FOREIGN OFFICE

I closed and drew for my Love's sake,
  That now is false to me,
And I slew the Riever of Tarrant Moss,
  And set Dumeny free.

And ever they give me praise and gold,
  And ever I moan my loss;
For I struck the blow for my false Love's sake,
  And not for the men of the Moss!

—*Tarrant Moss*

One of the many curses of our life in India is the want of atmosphere in the painter's sense. There are no half-tints worth noticing. Men stand out all crude and raw, with nothing to tone them down, and nothing to scale them against. They do their work, and grow to think that there is nothing but their work, and nothing like their work, and that they are the real pivots on which the Administration turns. Here is an instance of this feeling. A half-caste clerk was ruling forms in a Pay office. He said to me, "Do you know what would happen if I added or took away one single line on this sheet?" Then, with the air of a conspirator, "It would disorganize the whole of the Treasury payments throughout the whole of the Presidency Circle! Think of that!"

If men had not this delusion as to the ultra-importance of their own particular employments, I suppose that they would sit down and kill themselves. But their weakness is wearisome, particularly when the listener knows that he himself commits exactly the same sin.

Even the Secretariat believes that it does good when it asks an over-driven Executive Officer to take a census of wheat-weevils through a district of five thousand square miles.

There was a man once in the Foreign Office—a man who had grown middle-aged in the Department, and was commonly said, by irreverent juniors, to be able to repeat Aitchison's "Treaties and Sunnuds" backward in his sleep. What he did with his stored knowledge only the Secretary knew; and he, naturally, would not publish the news abroad. This man's name was Wressley, and it was the Shibboleth, in those days, to say—"Wressley knows more about the Central Indian States than any living man." If you did not say this, you were considered one of mean understanding.

Nowadays, the man who says that he knows the ravel of the inter-tribal complications across the Border is of more use; but, in Wressley's time, much attention was paid to the Central Indian States. They were called "foci" and "factors," and all manner of imposing names.

And here the curse of Anglo-Indian life fell heavily. When Wressley lifted up his voice, and spoke about such-and-such a succession to such-and-such a throne, the Foreign Office were silent, and Heads of Departments repeated the last two or three words of Wressley's sentences, and tacked "yes, yes," on to them, and knew that they were assisting the Empire to grapple with serious political contingencies. In most big undertakings, one or two men do the work while the rest sit near and talk till the ripe decorations begin to fall.

Wressley was the working-member of the Foreign Office firm, and, to keep him up to his duties when he showed signs of flagging, he was made much of by his superiors and told what a fine fellow he was. He did not require coaxing, because he was of tough build, but what he received confirmed him in the belief that there was no one quite so absolutely and imperatively necessary to the stability of India as Wressley of the Foregin Office. There might be other good men, but the known, honored and trusted man among men was Wressley of the Foreign Office. We had a Viceroy in those days who knew exactly when to "gentle" a fractious big man, and to hearten-up a collar-galled little one, and so keep all his team level. He conveyed to Wressley the impression which I have just set down; and even tough men are apt to be disorganized by a Viceroy's praise. There was a case once—but that is another story.

All India knew Wressley's name and office—it was in Thacker and Spink's Directory—but who he was personally, or what he did, or what his special merits were, not fifty men knew or cared. His work filled all his time, and he found no leisure to cultivate acquaintances beyond those of dead Rajput chiefs with *Ahir* blots in their scutcheons. Wressley would have made a very good Clerk in the Herald's College had he not been a Bengal Civilian.

Upon a day, between office and office, great trouble came to Wressley—overwhelmed him, knocked him down, and left him gasping as though he had been a little schoolboy. Without reason, against prudence, and at a moment's notice, he fell in love with a frivolous, golden-haired girl who used to tear about Simla Mall on a high, rough waler, with a blue velvet jockey-cap crammed over her eyes. Her name was Venner—Tillie Venner—and she was delightful. She took Wressley's heart at a hand-gallop, and Wressley found that it was not good for man to live alone; even with half the Foreign Office Records in his presses.

Then Simla laughed, for Wressley in love was slightly ridiculous. He did his best to interest the girl in himself—that is to say, his work—and she, after the manner of women, did her best to appear interested in what, behind his back, she called "Mr. W'essley's Wajahs"; for she lisped very prettily. She did not understand one little thing about them, but she acted as if she did. Men have married on that sort of error before now.

Providence, however, had care of Wressley. He was immensely struck with Miss Venner's intelligence. He would have been more impressed had he heard her private and confidential accounts of his calls. He held peculiar notions as to the wooing of girls. He said that the best work of a man's career should be laid reverently at their feet. Ruskin writes something like this somewhere, I think; but in ordinary life a few kisses are better and save time.

About a month after he had lost his heart to Miss Venner, and had been doing his work vilely in consequence, the first idea of his "Native Rule in Central India" struck Wressley and filled him with joy. It was, as he sketched it, a great thing—the work of his life—a really comprehensive survey of a most fascinating subject—to be written with all the special and laboriously acquired knowledge of Wressley of the Foreign Office—a gift fit for an Empress.

He told Miss Venner that he was going to take leave, and hoped, on his return, to bring her a present worthy of her acceptance. Would she wait? Certainly she would. Wressley drew seventeen hundred rupees a month. She would wait a year for that. Her Mamma would help her to wait.

So Wressley took one year's leave and all the available documents, about a truck-load, that he could lay hands on, and went down to Central India with his notion hot in his head. He began his book in the land he was writing of. Too much official correspondence had made him a frigid workman, and he must have guessed that he needed the white light of local color on his palette. This is a dangerous paint for amateurs to play with.

Heavens, how that man worked! He caught his Rajahs, analyzed his Rajahs, and traced them up into the mists of Time and beyond, with their queens and their concubines. He dated and cross-dated, pedigreed and triple-pedigreed, compared, noted, connoted, wove, strung, sorted, selected, inferred, calendared and counter-calendared for ten hours a day. And, because this sudden and new light of Love was upon him, he turned those dry bones of history and dirty records of misdeeds into things to weep or to laugh over as he pleased. His heart and soul were at the end of his pen, and they got into the ink. He was dowered with sympathy, insight, humor, and style for two hundred and thirty days and nights; and his book was a Book. He had his vast special knowledge with him, so to speak; but the spirit, the woven-in human Touch, the poetry and the power of the output, were beyond all special knowledge. But I doubt whether he knew the gift that was in him then, and thus he may have lost some happiness. He was toiling for Tillie Venner, not for himself. Men often do their best work blind, for some one else's sake.

Also, though this has nothing to do with the story, in India where every one knows every one else, you can watch men being driven, by the women who govern them, out of the rank-and-file and sent to take up points alone. A good man, once started, goes forward; but an average man, so soon as the woman loses interest in his success as a tribute to her power, comes back to the battalion and is no more heard of.

Wressley bore the first copy of his book to Simla, and, blushing and stammering, presented it to Miss Venner. She read a little of it. I give her review *verbatim*—"Oh, your book? It's all about those howwid Wajahs. I didn't understand it."

. . . .

Wressley of the Foreign Office was broken, smashed—I am not exaggerating—by this one frivolous little girl. All that he could say feebly was—"But—but it's my *magnum opus!* The work of my life." Miss Venner did not know what *magnum opus* meant; but she knew that Captain Kerrington had won three races at the last Gymkhana. Wressley didn't press her to wait for him any longer. He had sense enough for that.

Then came the reaction after the year's strain, and Wressley went back to the Foreign Office and his "Wajahs," a compiling, gazetteering, report-writing hack, who would have been dear at three hundred rupees a month. He abided by Miss Venner's review. Which proves that the inspiration in the book was purely temporary and unconnected with himself. Nevertheless, he had no right to sink, in a hill-tarn, five packing-cases, brought up at enormous expense from Bombay, of the best book of Indian history ever written.

When he sold off before retiring, some years later, I was turning over his shelves, and came across the only existing copy of "Native Rule in Central India"—the copy that Miss Venner could not understand. I read it, sitting on his mule-trunks, as long as the light lasted, and offered him his own price for it. He looked over my shoulder for a few pages and said to himself drearily: "Now, how in the world did I come to write such damned good stuff as that?"

Then to me—"Take it and keep it. Write one of your penny-farthing yarns about its birth. Perhaps—perhaps—the whole business may have been ordained to that end."

Which, knowing what Wressley of the Foreign Office was once, struck me as about the bitterest thing that I had ever heard a man say of his own work.

BY WORD OF MOUTH

Not though you die to-night, O Sweet, and wail,
A specter at my door,
Shall mortal Fear make Love immortal fail—
I shall but love you more,
Who, from Death's house returning, give me still
One moment's comfort in my matchless ill.
—*Shadow Houses*

THIS tale may be explained by those who know how souls are made, and where the bounds of the Possible are put down. I have lived long enough in this India to know that it is best to know nothing, and can only write the story as it happened.

Dumoise was our Civil Surgeon at Meridki, and we called him "Dormouse," because he was a round little, sleepy little man. He was a good Doctor and never quarreled with any one, not even with our Deputy Commissioner who had the manners of a bargee and the tact of a horse. He married a girl as round and as sleepy-looking as himself. She was a Miss Hillardyce, daughter of "Squash" Hillardyce of the Berars, who married his Chief's daughter by mistake. But that is another story.

A honeymoon in India is seldom more than a week long;

but there is nothing to hinder a couple from extending it over two or three years. India is a delightful country for married folk who are wrapped up in one another. They can live absolutely alone and without interruption—just as the Dormice did. Those two little people retired from the world after their marriage, and were very happy. They were forced, of course, to give occasional dinners, but they made no friends thereby, and the Station went its own way and forgot them; only saying, occasionally, that Dormouse was the best of good fellows though dull. A Civil Surgeon who never quarrels is a rarity, appreciated as such.

Few people can afford to play Robinson Crusoe anywhere—least of all in India, where we are few in the land and very much dependent on each other's kind offices. Dumoise was wrong in shutting himself from the world for a year, and he discovered his mistake when an epidemic of typhoid broke out in the Station in the heart of the cold weather, and his wife went down. He was a shy little man, and five days were wasted before he realized that Mrs. Dumoise was burning with something worse than simple fever, and three days more passed before he ventured to call on Mrs. Shute, the Engineer's wife, and timidly speak about his trouble. Nearly every household in India knows that Doctors are very helpless in typhoid. The battle must be fought out between Death and the Nurses minute by minute and degree by degree. Mrs. Shute almost boxed Dumoise's ears for what she called his "criminal delay," and went off at once to look after the poor girl. We had seven cases of typhoid in the Station that winter and, as the average of death is about one in every five cases, we felt certain that we should have to lose somebody. But all did their best. The women sat up nursing the women, and the men turned to and tended the bachelors who were down, and we wrestled with those typhoid cases for fifty-six days, and brought them through the Valley of the Shadow in triumph. But, just when we thought all was over, and were going to give a dance to celebrate the victory, little Mrs. Dumoise got a relapse and died in a week and the Station went to the funeral. Dumoise broke down utterly at the brink of the grave, and had to be taken away.

After the death, Dumoise crept into his own house and refused to be comforted. He did his duties perfectly, but we all felt that he should go on leave, and the other men of his own Service told him so. Dumoise was very thankful for the suggestion—he was thankful for anything in those days—and went to Chini on a walking-tour. Chini is some twenty marches from Simla, in the heart of the Hills, and the scenery is good if you are in trouble. You pass through big, still deodar-forests, and under big, still cliffs, and over big, still grass-downs swelling like a woman's breasts; and the wind across the grass, and the rain among the deodars says—"Hush—hush—hush." So little Dumoise was packed off to Chini, to wear down his grief with a full-plate camera and a rifle. He took also a useless bearer, because the man had been his wife's favorite servant. He was idle and a thief, but Dumoise trusted everything to him.

On his way back from Chini, Dumoise turned aside to Bagi, through the Forest Reserve which is on the spur of Mount Huttoo. Some men who have traveled more than a little say that the march from Kotegarh to Bagi is one of the finest in creation. It runs through dark wet forest, and ends suddenly in bleak, nipped hillside and black rocks. Bagi dâk-bungalow is open to all the winds and is bitterly cold. Few people go to Bagi. Perhaps that was the reason why Dumoise went there. He halted at seven in the evening, and his bearer went down the hillside to the village to engage coolies for the next day's march. The sun had set, and the night-winds were beginning to croon among the rocks. Dumoise leaned on the railing of the veranda, waiting for his bearer to return. The man came back almost immediately after he had disappeared, and at such a rate that Dumoise fancied he must have crossed a bear. He was running as hard as he could up the face of the hill.

But there was no bear to account for his terror. He raced to the veranda and fell down, the blood spurting from his nose and his face iron-gray. Then he gurgled—"I have seen the *Memsahib!* I have seen the *Memsahib!*"

"Where?" said Dumoise.

"Down there, walking on the road to the village. She was in a blue dress, and she lifted the veil of her bonnet and said—'Ram Dass, give my *salaams* to the *Sahib*, and tell him that I shall meet him next month at Nuddea.' Then I ran away, because I was afraid."

What Dumoise said or did I do not know. Ram Dass declares that he said nothing, but walked up and down the veranda all the cold night, waiting for the *Memsahib* to come up the hill and stretching out his arms into the dark like a madman. But no *Memsahib* came, and, next day, he went on to Simla cross-questioning the bearer every hour.

Ram Dass could only say that he had met Mrs. Dumoise and that she had lifted up her veil and given him the message which he had faithfully repeated to Dumoise. To this statement Ram Dass adhered. He did not know where Nuddea was, had no friends at Nuddea, and would most certainly never go to Nuddea; even though his pay were doubled.

Nuddea is in Bengal and has nothing whatever to do with a Doctor serving in the Punjab. It must be more than twelve hundred miles south of Meridki.

Dumoise went through Simla without halting, and returned to Meridki, there to take over charge from the man who had been officiating for him during his tour. There were some Dispensary accounts to be explained, and some recent orders of the Surgeon-General to be noted, and, altogether, the taking-over was a full day's work. In the evening, Dumoise told his *locum tenens*, who was an old friend of his bachelor days, what had happened at Bagi; and the man said that Ram Dass might as well have chosen Tuticorin while he was about it.

At that moment, a telegraph-peon came in with a telegram from Simla, ordering Dumoise not to take over charge at Meridki, but to go at once to Nuddea on special duty.

There was a nasty outbreak of cholera at Nuddea, and the Bengal Government, being short-handed, as usual, had borrowed a Surgeon from the Punjab.

Dumoise threw the telegram across the table and said—"Well?"

The other Doctor said nothing. It was all that he could say.

Then he remembered that Dumoise had passed through Simla on his way from Bagi; and thus might, possibly, have heard first news of the impending transfer.

He tried to put the question, and the implied suspicion into words, but Dumoise stopped him with—"If I had desired *that*, I should never have come back from Chini. I was shooting there. I wish to live, for I have things to do . . . but I shall not be sorry."

The other man bowed his head, and helped, in the twilight, to pack up Dumoise's just opened trunks. Ram Dass entered with the lamps.

"Where is the Sahib going?" he asked.

"To Nuddea," said Dumoise softly.

Ram Dass clawed Dumoise's knees and boots and begged him not to go. Ram Dass wept and howled till he was turned out of the room. Then he wrapped up all his belongings and came back to ask for a character. He was not going to Nuddea to see his Sahib die and, perhaps, to die himself.

So Dumoise gave the man his wages and went down to Nuddea alone; the other Doctor bidding him good-by as one under sentence of death.

Eleven days later he had joined his Memsahib; and the Bengal Government had to borrow a fresh Doctor to cope with that epidemic at Nuddea. The first importation lay dead in Chooadanga Dâk-Bungalow.

TO BE FILED FOR REFERENCE

By the hoof of the Wild Goat up-tossed
From the Cliff where She lay in the Sun,
Fell the Stone
To the Tarn where the daylight is lost;
So She fell from the light of the Sun,
And alone.

Now the fall was ordained from the first,
With the Goat and the Cliff and the Tarn,
But the Stone
Knows only Her life is accursed,
As She sinks in the depths of the Tarn,
And alone.

Oh, Thou who hast builded the world!
Oh, Thou who hast lighted the Sun!
Oh, Thou who hast darkened the Tarn!
Judge Thou
The sin of the Stone that was hurled
By the Goat from the light of the Sun,
As She sinks in the mire of the Tarn,
Even now—even now—even now!

—From the Unpublished Papers of McIntosh Jellaludin

"SAY is it dawn, is it dusk in thy Bower,
Thou whom I long for, who longest for me?
Oh, be it night—be it—"

Here he fell over a little camel-colt that was sleeping in the Serai where the horse-traders and the best of the blackguards from Central Asia live; and, because he was very drunk indeed and the night was dark, he could not rise again till I helped him. That was the beginning of my acquaintance with McIntosh Jellaludin. When a loafer, and drunk, sings "The Song of the Bower," he must be worth cultivating. He got off the camel's back and said, rather thickly, "I—I—I'm a bit screwed, but a dip in Loggerhead will put me right again; and, I say, have you spoken to Symonds about the mare's knees?"

Now Loggerhead was six thousand weary miles away from us, close to Mesopotamia, where you mustn't fish and poaching is impossible, and Charley Symonds' stable a half mile further across the paddocks. It was strange to hear all the old names, on a May night, among the horses and camels of the Sultan Caravanserai. Then the man seemed to remember himself and sober down at the same time. He leaned against the camel and pointed to a corner of the Serai where a lamp was burning.

"I live there," said he, "and I should be extremely obliged if you would be good enough to help my mutinous feet thither; for I am more than usually drunk—most—most phenomenally tight. But not in respect to my head. 'My brain cries out against'—how does it go? But my head rides on the—rolls on the dunghill, I should have said, and controls the qualm."

I helped him through the gangs of tethered horses and he collapsed on the edge of the veranda in front of the line of native quarters.

"Thanks—a thousand thanks! Oh, Moon and little, little Stars! To think that a man should so shamelessly . . . Infamous liquor too. Ovid in exile drank no worse. Better. It was frozen. Alas! I had no ice. Good-night. I would introduce you to my wife were I sober—or she civilized."

A native woman came out of the darkness of the room, and began calling the man names; so I went away. He was the most interesting loafer that I had had the pleasure of knowing for a long time; and later on, he became a friend of mine. He was a tall, well-built, fair man, fearfully shaken with drink, and he looked nearer fifty than the thirty-five which, he said, was his real age. When a man begins to sink in India, and is not sent Home by his friends as soon as may be, he falls very low from a respectable point of view. By the time that he changes his creed, as did McIntosh, he is past redemption.

In most big cities, natives will tell you of two or three

Sahibs, generally low-caste, who have turned Hindu or Mussulman, and who live more or less as such. But it is not often that you can get to know them. As McIntosh himself used to say, "If I change my religion for my stomach's sake, I do not seek to become a martyr to missionaries, nor am I anxious for notoriety."

At the outset of acquaintance McIntosh warned me. "Remember this. I am not an object for charity. I require neither your money, your food, nor your cast-off raiment. I am that rare animal, a self-supporting drunkard. If you choose, I will smoke with you, for the tobacco of the bazaars does not, I admit, suit my palate; and I will borrow any books which you may not specially value. It is more than likely that I shall sell them for bottles of excessively filthy country-liquors. In return, you shall share such hospitality as my house affords. Here is a charpoy on which two can sit, and it is possible that there may, from time to time, be food in that platter. Drink, unfortunately, you will find on the premises at any hour: and thus I make you welcome to all my poor establishment."

I was admitted to the McIntosh household—I and my good tobacco. But nothing else. Unluckily, one cannot visit a loafer in the Serai by day. Friends buying horses would not understand it. Consequently, I was obliged to see McIntosh after dark. He laughed at this, and said simply, "You are perfectly right. When I enjoyed a position in society, rather higher than yours, I should have done exactly the same thing. Good Heavens! I was once"—he spoke as though he had fallen from the Command of a Regiment—"an Oxford Man!" This accounted for the reference to Charley Symonds' stable.

"You," said McIntosh slowly, "have not had that advantage; but, to outward appearance, you do not seem possessed of a craving for strong drinks. On the whole, I fancy that you are the luckier of the two. Yet I am not certain. You are—forgive my saying so even while I am smoking your excellent tobacco—painfully ignorant of many things."

We were sitting together on the edge of his bedstead, for he owned no chairs, watching the horses being watered for the night, while the native woman was preparing dinner. I did not like being patronized by a loafer, but I was his guest for the time being, though he owned only one very torn alpaca-coat and a pair of trousers made out of gunny-bags. He took the pipe out of his mouth, and went on judicially, "All things considered, I doubt whether you are the luckier. I do not refer to your extremely limited classical attainments, or your excruciating quantities, but to your gross ignorance of matters more immediately under your notice. That, for instance," he pointed to a woman cleaning a samovar near the well in the center of the Serai. She was flicking the water out of the spout in regular cadenced jerks.

"There are ways and ways of cleaning samovars. If you knew why she was doing her work in that particular fashion, you would know what the Spanish Monk meant when he said:

" 'I the Trinity illustrate,
Drinking watered orange-pulp—
In three sips the Arian frustrate,
While he drains his at one gulp—'

and many other things which now are hidden from your eyes. However, Mrs. McIntosh has prepared dinner. Let us come and eat after the fashion of the people of the country—of whom, by the way, you know nothing."

The native woman dipped her hand in the dish with us. This was wrong. The wife should always wait until the husband has eaten. McIntosh Jellaludin apologized, saying—

"It is an English prejudice which I have not been able to overcome; and she loves me. Why, I have never been able to understand. I foregathered with her at Jullundur, three years ago, and she has remained with me ever since. I believe her to be moral, and know her to be skilled in cookery."

He patted the woman's head as he spoke, and she cooed softly. She was not pretty to look at.

McIntosh never told me what position he had held before his fall. He was, when sober, a scholar and a gentleman.

When drunk, he was rather more of the first than the second. He used to get drunk about once a week for two days. On those occasions the native woman tended him while he raved in all tongues except his own. One day, indeed, he began reciting "Atalanta in Calydon," and went through it to the end, beating time to the swing of the verse with a bedstead-leg. But he did most of his ravings in Greek or German. The man's mind was a perfect rag-bag of useless things. Once, when he was beginning to get sober, he told me that I was the only rational being in the Inferno into which he had descended—a Virgil in the Shades, he said—and that, in return for my tobacco, he would, before he died, give me the materials of a new Inferno that should make me greater than Dante. Then he fell asleep on a horse-blanket and woke up quite calm.

"Man," said he, "when you have reached the uttermost depths of degradation, little incidents which would vex a higher life are to you of no consequence. Last night, my soul was among the Gods; but I make no doubt that my bestial body was writhing down here in the garbage."

"You were abominably drunk, if that's what you mean," I said.

"I *was* drunk—filthily drunk. I who am the son of a man with whom you have no concern—I who was once Fellow of a College whose buttery-hatch you have not seen. I was loathsomely drunk. But consider how lightly I am touched. It is nothing to me. Less than nothing; for I do not even feel the headache which should be my portion. Now, in a higher life, how ghastly would have been my punishment, how bitter my repentance! Believe me, my friend with the neglected education, the highest is as the lowest—always supposing each degree extreme."

He turned round on the blanket, put his head between his fists and continued—"On the Soul which I have lost and on the Conscience which I have killed, I tell you that I cannot feel! I am as the Gods, knowing good and evil, but untouched by either. Is this enviable or is it not?"

...hen a man has lost the warning of "next morning's ...d," he must be in a bad state. I answered, looking at ...McIntosh on the blanket, with his hair over his eyes and his lips blue-white, that I did not think the insensibility good enough.

"For pity's sake, don't say that! I tell you, it *is* good and most enviable. Think of my consolations!"

"Have you so many, then, McIntosh?"

"Certainly; your attempts at sarcasm which is essentially the weapon of a cultured man, are crude. First, my attainments, my classical and literary knowledge, blurred, perhaps, by immoderate drinking—which reminds me that before my soul went to the Gods last night, I sold the Pickering Horace you so kindly lent me. Ditta Mull the clothesman has it. It fetched ten annas, and may be redeemed for a rupee—but still infinitely superior to yours. Secondly, the abiding affection of Mrs. McIntosh, best of wives. Thirdly, a monument, more enduring than brass, which I have built up in the seven years of my degradation."

He stopped here, and crawled across the room for a drink of water. He was very shaky and sick.

He referred several times to his "treasure"—some great possession that he owned—but I held this to be the raving of drink. He was as poor and as proud as he could be. His manner was not pleasant, but he knew enough about the natives, among whom seven years of his life had been spent, to make his acquaintance worth having. He used actually to laugh at Strickland as an ignorant man—"ignorant West and East," he said. His boast was, first, that he was an Oxford Man of rare and shining parts, which may or may not have been true—I did not know enough to check his statements—and, secondly, that he "had his hand on the pulse of native life"—which was a fact. As an Oxford man, he struck me as a prig: he was always throwing his education about. As a Mohammedan *faquir*—as McIntosh Jellaludin—he was all that I wanted for my own ends. He smoked several pounds of my tobacco, and taught me several ounces of things worth knowing; but he would never accept any gifts, not even when the cold weather came, and gripped the poor thin chest under the poor thin alpaca-coat. He grew very angry, and said that I had insulted him, and that he was not going into hospital. He had lived like a beast and he would die rationally, like a man.

As a matter of fact, he died of pneumonia; and on the

night of his death sent over a grubby note asking me to come and help him to die.

The native woman was weeping by the side of the bed. McIntosh, wrapped in a cotton cloth, was too weak to resent a fur coat being thrown over him. He was very active as far as his mind was concerned, and his eyes were blazing. When he had abused the Doctor who came with me, so foully that the indignant old fellow left, he cursed me for a few minutes and calmed down.

Then he told his wife to fetch out "The Book" from a hole in the wall. She brought out a big bundle, wrapped in the tail of a petticoat, of old sheets of miscellaneous note-paper, all numbered and covered with fine cramped writing. McIntosh plowed his hand through the rubbish and stirred it up lovingly.

"This," he said, "is my work—the Book of McIntosh Jellaludin, showing what he saw and how he lived, and what befell him and others; being also an account of the life and sins and death of Mother Maturin. What Mirza Murad Ali Beg's book is to all other books on native life, will my work be to Mirza Murad Ali Beg's!"

This, as will be conceded by any one who knows Mirza Murad Ali Beg's book, was a sweeping statement. The papers did not look specially valuable; but McIntosh handled them as if they were currency-notes. Then said he slowly:

"In despite the many weaknesses of your education, you have been good to me. I will speak of your tobacco when I reach the Gods. I owe you much thanks for many kindnesses. But I abominate indebtedness. For this reason, I bequeath to you now the monument more enduring than brass—my one book—rude and imperfect in parts, but oh how rare in others! I wonder if you will understand it. It is a gift more honorable than . . . Bah! where is my brain rambling to? You will mutilate it horribly. You will knock out the gems you call Latin quotations, you Philistine, and you will butcher the style to carve into your own jerky jargon; but you cannot destroy the whole of it. I bequeath it to you. Ethel . . . My brain again! . . . Mrs. McIntosh, bear witness that I give the *Sahib* all these papers. They would be of no use to you, Heart of my Heart; and I lay it upon you," he turned to me here, "that you do not let my book die in its present form. It is yours unconditionally —the story of McIntosh Jellaludin, which is *not* the story of McIntosh Jellaludin, but of a greater man than he, and of a far greater woman. Listen now! I am neither mad nor drunk! That book will make you famous."

I said, "Thank you," as the native woman put the bundle into my arms.

"My only baby!" said McIntosh, with a smile. He was sinking fast, but he continued to talk as long as breath remained. I waited for the end; knowing that, in six cases out of ten, a dying man calls for his mother. He turned on his side and said:

"Say how it came into your possession. No one will believe you, but my name, at least, will live. You will treat it brutally, I know you will. Some of it must go; the public are fools and prudish fools. I was their servant once. But do your mangling gently—very gently. It is a great work, and I have paid for it in seven years' damnation."

His voice stopped for ten or twelve breaths, and then he began mumbling a prayer of some kind in Greek. The native woman cried very bitterly. Lastly, he rose in bed and said, as loudly as slowly—"Not guilty, my Lord!"

Then he fell back, and the stupor held him till he died. The native woman ran into the Serai among the horses, and screamed and beat her breasts; for she had loved him.

Perhaps his last sentence in life told what McIntosh had once gone through; but, saving the big bundle of old sheets in the cloth, there was nothing in his room to say who or what he had been.

The papers were in a hopeless muddle.

Strickland helped me to sort them, and he said that the writer was either an extreme liar or a most wonderful person. He thought the former. One of these days, you may be able to judge for yourselves. The bundle needed much expurgation and was full of Greek nonsense, at the head of the chapters, which has all been cut out.

If the thing is ever published, some one may perhaps remember this story, now printed as a safeguard to prove that McIntosh Jellaludin and not I myself wrote the Book of Mother Maturin.

I don't want the "Giant's Robe" to come true in my case.

END OF VOLUME TWO